Praise 1
Falling Angels Saga:

"*Boyfriend from Hell* is a fun, somewhat-tongue-in-cheek story that starts with a laugh and keeps them coming throughout the entire book."

—Penelope Adams, *Paranormal Romance Guild*

"A thrilling suspense / mystery / fantasy book mixed with reality and some romance scenes that will get you hooked up till the end."

—Lalaine Faye, *Lalaine's Fiction Book Reviews*

"*Boyfriend from Hell* was a great surprise. I didn't know what to expect before reading it but it was a fast and fun read that made me laugh more than once. What made *Boyfriend from Hell* unique to me was the sometimes tongue-in-cheek tone it had. It's a great YA that's also poking fun at some of the predictable Young Adult clichés. If you like paranormal YA but sometimes find yourself rolling your eyes at the way the characters are acting, you'll love this book too."

—-Lisa Choboter, *Cold Moon Violet Books*

"E. Van Lowe's fluid and masterful writing made this book one that I needed to finish."

—Elizabeth Talbott, *Fishmuffins of Doom*

"E. Van Lowe does a great job of capturing teenage angst, dating woes, and parental issues without over-doing it. *Earth Angel* was just as fun to read as *Boyfriend from Hell*."

—Nicole Etolen, *Pretty Opinionated*

"I just finished the last sentence and I'm left stung that I have to wait for the final book to come out. I can't wait! I loved the first book, and was so excited by a story of a girl battling Satan. I mean, how cool is that?"

—Freda Mans, *Freda's Voice*

Other Books by E. Van Lowe:

THE SECRETS OF LOVE AND DEATH

E. VAN LOWE
AND SAL CONTE

White Whisker Books
Los Angeles

To my brother, Leonard,
who was a good friend, a great advisor,
and the most annoying pain in the butt growing up.

Print version ISBN:978-0-9863265-1-6
Library of Congress Control Number: 2015909161

Editor, Christopher Meeks
Book design, Deborah Daly

Published by White Whisker Books, Los Angeles, 2015

Prologue

S p r i n g   1 9 8 4

I don't wanna go out!"Marty McKenzie was scrunching up his face, looking very much like that prune-faced old guy in the Six Flags commercials. He'd been lying on the floor playing with his Legos, which were splayed out before him like the ruins of an ancient city.

"See, that's the thing," said Marty's older sister, Allison. She pushed her glasses up onto her nose. "You're not goin' with me."

Marty's expression shifted, morphing from one of protest to one of concern—dire concern. He stopped playing and sat up. They weren't real Legos. His father had bought the blocks for Marty's fifth birthday when he visited almost a year ago. He told Marty they were Legos, but Marty new better. He didn't say anything. He didn't want his father feeling bad about being gypped at the Lego store. The Legos were one of the few gifts Marty's father had ever bought for him. He treasured them.

"You can't leave me," he said, his voice going high and whiny, like a baby's. Even he heard it.

"I'm not leaving you. I'm treating you like a grownup for once in your life. You don't want me treatin' you like a little baby anymore, right?" Allison knew full well no little kid wants to be treated like a baby, especially one as close to being a baby as Marty was.

"But Mommy says I'm not to be left home alone," Marty replied, his voice going even higher. He tried keeping it level. *Put some base into yer voice, I say!* Yet the babiness crept back in.

"That's because Mom thinks you're a little baby," Allison said, laying on the word—*baaaby*—extra heavy. "But I know better." She winked at him. "We both do, don't we?" she said, playing her six-year-old brother like a well-worn instrument.

Marty nodded. He was ascared of being left in the apartment all by himself. But he knew if he told Allison about the monster that lived in the closet, or the one that hung out under his bed, she'd laugh and call him a scaredy-cat, or worse, a *baaaby*.

Even at his age, Marty was wise enough to know that at twelve, Allison was too old to understand there really were monsters out there, monsters that had their eyes on tasty little kids.

A few years ago she would have sympathized with him. A few years ago they'd both hidden under the covers, quaking in the darkness and talking in loud voices until the monsters went away. But somewhere between the sixth and seventh grades the monsters stopped being real for Allison, around the same time she started writing boys' names on the inside cover of her notebook.

"Where're ya goin'?" Marty asked, trying to add some grownup to his voice and failing miserably at it.

"To the mall, with some friends. We're shopping for something fun to wear to a party next weekend."

"Can I—"

"No!" the word exploded from her lips. "You can't go to the mall with me, and you *definitely* can't go to the party. It's at night, anyway."

"Who has a party at night time? That's dumb," Marty said, although the idea of a night time party sounded pretty cool, as long as there were lots of lights burning. It was darkness that was scary.

"You are not to answer the door while I'm gone. Do I make myself clear?" she said in a tone very much like one their mother might have used.

Marty nodded again. He was happy for Allison. She'd made some friends. Allison had had a hard time making friends during the past two years as the family bounced from shelter to shelter. Marty knew from first-hand experience that Allison made a wonderful friend. She was kind and caring. Unfortunately, those qualities hadn't been recognized in Allison's last school. In her last school, all they saw was the homeless girl.

"What am I supposed to do the whole time you're gone?" Marty asked.

"The same thing you always do—play. And this time you'll have our bedroom all to yourself. How cool is that?"

Marty looked toward the bedroom he shared with his sister, the only bedroom in the apartment. Their mother slept on the pullout in the living room where he was now playing. His thoughts again turned to the monster that lived in the closet, and his pal lurking under Marty's bed, and Marty could practically see the two of them licking their chops at the thought of having him all to themselves.

"Think I'll play out here while you're gone," he told her with a resigned sigh.

"Suit yourself."

From the look on Allison's face, it hadn't dawned on her that he'd be afraid. To ease her guilt, she built the neatest pillow fort and stocked it with enough books, coloring books, toys and puzzles to keep Marty busy until she got back. She even brought the Captain Crunch cereal box from the kitchen and told him he could snack from it right there in the living room—just like a grownup.

"These are your rations," she said, handing it to him. He smiled at that one, and it eased some of the guilt that had been gripping her heart.

"Thanks."

Allison deposited Marty in the center of the fort, gave him a big hug, and reminded him not to open the door for *anyone*.

"This is just between you and me," she said, her voice lowering dramatically. "I don't want you blabbin' my business to Mom when she gets home from work. Got it?"

Marty nodded. His tongue was desert dry.

"I'll bring you some ice cream, you little con man," she said, rubbing her hand across the top of his head.

"That'd be nice," he replied with the shadow of a smile. "Chocolate."

It would be the last thing they'd ever say to each other.

The sound of Allison moving away from the door, her footsteps retreating down the stairs—*away, away, away*—died in Marty's ears. "Good riddance to bad rubbish," he called. Of course, she couldn't hear him. He laughed high and loud. It was a fake laugh and when it died, Marty realized he was alone.

The first thing he noticed about being alone was how quiet the apartment was without Allison or his mother there. No chattering voices of the two of them going at it again, no music from the radio filling up the empty spaces. Phoebe kept the radio on whenever she was home.

"Dance to the music!" Sometimes she'd sing along with a song on the radio, grab Marty and dance him around the apartment. "You're my new leading man," she'd say, twirling him.

"Stop, Mom!" he'd cry out, but he enjoyed dancing with her. He especially enjoyed that she was happy again.

With both Phoebe and Allison gone, the apartment was nighttime quiet, even though Marty could see the bright Spring sun streaming in through the living room blinds, casting long shadows on the faded carpet.

He looked down at the treasure Allison had dumped in his fort before she left. *Think I'll read. I'm a big boy now, and that's what big boys do. We don't play; we read.*

Marty picked up his favorite book, *Tall Timber Tales,* about Paul Bunyan and Babe the Blue Ox. He decided to read the part about where Babe drank the entire Grand Coulee River. He wasn't sure how big the Grand Coulee was, but he knew it was a lot of water.

He'd gotten the book when he was small, picked it out himself off a table at The Salvation Army. Allison used to read it to him at night back at the shelter, back when all he could do was look at the pictures. But now that he was a big boy, he could read it all by himself—sort of. He opened to the section with the picture of Babe drinking the river and pretended to read… *What was that?*

A sound. A soft, sliding sound had come from Marty and Allison's bedroom. It sounded to Marty as though someone or…*something* had slid out from underneath his bed.

"Hello." No answer. Of course there wasn't an answer. There's nothing there. *It's just my magination.* Allison complained about his overactive magination all the time.

"I know there's no monster there," Marty called out. "So you may as well get back under the bed." Nothing.

Marty glanced down at the book in his lap. He folded it back to the picture of Paul and Babe on the cover. He enjoyed staring at the picture on the cover because when he did, he could magine himself hangin' out with old Paul and Babe. He could magine so good that sometimes it was as if he was right there with them.

Skreek!

Marty's attention was again drawn to the bedroom. He peered wide-eyed around the arm of the old couch because this time he was certain he'd heard the closet door opening, certain he now heard whispering—monster voices.

I gotta get outta here. The thought drifted in like an early season snow, yet stuck like the first big fall of the year. *If I don't leave now, all they'll find of me are bones and clothes.* Monsters only eat the good stuff. Then, another thought drifted in. *Scaredy-cat.*

That's what Allison would call him for being so afraid. *And I thought you were a big boy… I AM A BIG BOY!*

Marty began to rationalize: *I'm a big kid. Big kids can go out all by themselves—just like Allison did.* The idea of him being a big boy was a lot more palatable than thinking he was afraid. Marty clung to it like a lifeline. He wasn't leaving the apartment 'cause he was scared, he was leaving because he wanted to go to the mall, *too*. He wanted to hang out with *his* friends. Shoot.

Marty gingerly got up off the floor and measured his footsteps to the front door. He could hear the monsters gathering in the bedroom, their excited chatter no longer whispered. *Why whisper? He's all alone.* He knew if he tried to run they'd get him. Monsters loved grabbing little boys as they ran. He needed to move toward the door as if he wasn't afraid.

The shelter they'd lived in on Saul Road was a scary place, especially at night. Allison had told him to count to ten whenever he needed to walk down the long hallway all by himself. She told him whenever he was afraid to take a deep breath, count to ten and let it out slowly. "Just keep telling yourself there's nothing there, and pretty soon you'll be down the hall."

Marty had used the trick several hair-raising times at the shelter, and it seemed to have worked, so he gently placed the Paul Bunyan book on top of a pillow and sucked in a lung full of air. *One.* He took a furtive step over the pillowed wall, one foot now resting just outside the fort, the other still in. *Two.* Now the other leg came over, *easy, easy.* He let out a little bit of the air as both feet rested outside the fort.

Gotta get to the door. Gotta move to the door like I'm not afraid. If I'm afraid, they'll get me.

Three.

Marty took a jangly step toward the door, then—*four, five, six, seven, eight, nine, ten.* He bolted across the room. Arriving at the door, he flung it open and let out the deep breath in a big *whoosh!* The monsters had quieted down. They only bothered little kids, and he'd proven he was a big boy now.

Kathunk!

This new sound came just as Marty was thinking he was safe. It caught him off guard, and he nearly leapt out of his skin like a snake in shed-mode. He charged out the front door, fleeing into the corridor of the apartment building.

It was the sound of Marty's book falling from the pillow and hitting the floor that had alarmed him, but to Marty's imaginative ears, it was the sound of a monster exiting the bedroom, looking for a little boy to eat.

Marty looked back at the apartment door hanging open, and decided to leave it open. He surmised that if the door was wide open maybe the monsters'd leave while he's gone and never come back. He was too young to realize that leaving the front door open in a neighborhood as iffy as theirs was an invitation for the McKenzie's precious possessions to walk away along with the monsters.

He moved downstairs and out into the crowded street. It was broad daylight, and the sun beat down on the top of Marty's head feeling good. The street was teeming with people, and Marty was no longer afraid. The people were passing by as if he belonged there. Not one person said: "Hey little boy, where's your mother?"

Allison is going to crap a brick when she sees me at the mall, Marty thought with a grin. "What are you doing here?" "Oh, just came to hang out with some of my boys. You know, Paul, Babe, the crew." *Hahaaa!*

Yet as Marty continued walking, it started getting scary out on the street all by himself. Everyone looked as if they knew where they were going. *But so do I. I'm going to the mall.*

As he neared the Canal Street alley, his footsteps slowed. The Canal Street alley wasn't actually an alley. It was a narrow pedestrian walkway between two tall buildings that connected Main Street with Fair Oaks. On any given Saturday the alley was heavily trafficked. Call it a fluke, call it a moment in time, call it a curveball, but when Marty arrived at the alley on Saturday June fifteenth nineteen eighty-four, it was ominously vacant of foot traffic.

He thought he remembered the alley being the shortcut to the mall. He remembered going through the alley with Allison and his mother to go shopping. Or was that his magination? No. He was sure.

He stopped at the alley entrance. His first inclination was to wait for other pedestrians to pass through and then mosey through along with them. With the buildings being so close together, the alley was heavily shadowed; the shadows were really scary.

But Marty also remembered he was a big boy now. He waited another few minutes, and when no one came along, he breathed in deeply and entered the ally all by himself. *One.* The cobblestones of the alley felt odd and slick beneath his feet. It was then he realized he was still in his footsie PJs. He didn't have on any shoes. *Dumb! Allison is gonna crap a brick when she sees me out here without my sneaks on.* But it was too late to turn back. He was closer to the mall than he was to the apartment. Who needs shoes anyway? *Two.* There were several scary looking doorways lining the alley, and a big marquee near the end that read Bijou Theater.

Three. Marty moved past the first of the ominous doorways and, as he did, he let out a little bit of the air. *Not much further.*

That's when he heard a door scraping open up ahead. It startled him, the scraping sound in the quiet alley, like something out of a horror movie. His eyes grew wide as something emerged from the doorway, stepping into the alley. At first he thought it was a clown, but clowns are freakin' scary and this thing wasn't. This thing seemed warm, and cuddly, and friendly. Out of the doorway, down the alley, stepped a life-size blue teddy bear.

Marty knew it wasn't a real bear. It couldn't be. Right? It was a person in a bear costume, just like at the amusement park. Wasn't it?

The giant teddy bear looked at Marty. It stopped moving, eyeing him cautiously, like a deer in the woods seeing a hunter for the first time.

Is it trembling?

At that moment the teddy bear seemed real. The teddy bear also seemed to be afraid of him. Marty started to call out *It's okay, don't run, I'm not gonna hurt you.* But before he could speak, the teddy bear began to dance. It was a silly teddy bear dance and Marty was happy to see that the teddy bear had overcome his fear.

The teddy bear was a lot like Marty. Hadn't Marty been afraid not too long ago? Now they were both in the alley, unafraid. The kindred bear danced his silly dance up the alley toward Marty, and for the first time since Allison had left him in the apartment all alone, Marty smiled.

book one

Four years later...

CHAPTER ONE

Marty was gone now. That's what his friend called it. Not here, not there, just gone. Like a shoe box full of yesterdays that had been tightly sealed with a neat red ribbon—gone. *The Other Place*, that's what his friend called where they were now. Marty didn't like The Other Place, but there was nothing he could do about it. His friend promised him that soon there'd be others, that The Other Place could be a happy place. Marty liked that. It would be better when there were more of them.

Turtle

Ambushed!

When Turtle Dawson turned the corner he was surprised, no make that stunned, to discover Ansley Meade and the other Meade boys coming toward him up the block. He froze for a nanosecond. It was too late to duck back around the corner and head the other way. Turtle could see they'd already spotted him. In fact, from the satisfied smirk on Ansley's lips, they'd been expecting him to come spinning around the corner. *Damn!*

Turtle stood his ground. Even though his legs were wobbly like Jello and the thought of peeing his pants tap danced at the outskirts of his consciousness, he stood his ground. He had to. He couldn't out run them. Heck, Turtle couldn't outrun anyone, not with the girth he was carrying.

Turtle was a fat boy with brown skin the color of milk chocolate that grew darker when he was angry or embarrassed. Right now, he was frightened. Turtle weighed in at one hundred seventy-five (*hefty*—that's what his mother called him) pounds. That was an easy forty pounds heavier than any kid in his class with the exception of Ross Rainey, who tipped the scales at two hundred.

"Well, lookie, lookie. Isn't that Lard Ass down there?" Ansley asked at the top of his lungs, his voice trilling joy.

"Yup. That's the fat little creep," one of Ansley's older brothers replied. He was maybe fourteen, a redhead with the beginnings of a mustache dusting his upper lip and freckles on his cheeks. Turtle didn't know his name. He didn't know either of the older brother's names. What he knew was that when Ansley called, his older brothers came, and when they came, it usually meant an ass-whuppin' for the poor kid Ansley had in his sights. This time the poor kid was him.

"You been avoidin' me," Ansley said in a playful sing-song as he stopped a few feet in front of Turtle. He was at least a full inch shorter than Turtle, with dark, unruly hair and beady-mean eyes. He was built like a fire plug. Turtle had to outweigh him by twenty or thirty pounds easy, yet Ansley's diminutive stature seemed to make him all the more intimidating.

One of the older Meade boys silently circled around behind Turtle. He was now surrounded.

"Nuh-uh," Turtle replied, his tongue feeling as if it was swathed in cotton.

"I told you to wait outside the school gate for me yesterday, and you weren't there. You weren't there today, either. You're a bad boy, Lard Ass. And you know what happens to bad boys." Ansley began routinely rolling up his sleeves, as if ass-whippin' was an everyday occurrence for him. School, homework, ass-whippin'.

"My Moms called the school," Turtle blurted. "She said I had to get over to Miller's Grocery right after school or I'd be in deep shit. Said she'd be watin' for me there, and I better be on time. That's why I didn't wait for *you*."

Turtle looked past the two boys in front of him toward the mini-mart in the middle of the block. Maybe the threat of his mother stepping out of Miller's front door at any moment to see what was keeping her son would stave off the ass-whuppin'. Perhaps the reminder there were grown-up adults nearby would curb the Meade boys' thirst for his blood.

"Your mom's in Miller's right now?" the oldest of the Meade boys asked. This one had to be sixteen. He didn't seem as smart as the other older brother, which was saying something since it was clear none of the Meade boys were ever going to win a Rhodes scholarship. He was staring at Turtle, caution creeping into his eyes.

"Uh-huh," Turtle replied, again with the cotton mouth.

"Maybe we ought to do this another time," the older boy said, giving Turtle a sniff at freedom.

"Okay, sure," replied Ansley. "Say, you ever meet Mrs. Lard Ass?" he asked the brother standing closest to him. The boy shook his head. "You?" Ansley said to the brother standing behind Turtle, the oldest one.

"No, I haven't."

"Then I think we should go down to Miller's and introduce ourselves."

Turtle could not keep the pained expression from filling up his face. His mother wasn't at Miller's waiting for him. She was at home watching TV. He was sure she hadn't even noticed he was running late. Some days, it seemed, she didn't notice him at all.

"What's the matter, Lard Ass? You don't think we good enough to meet your Moms?" asked Ansley, a teasing grin curling his lips.

"It's just that…she's…busy." Turtle's voice ticked up a few octaves. He could feel himself beginning to whine as all thoughts of freedom fled up Prospect Avenue, past Miller's Grocery and Crone Drugs and out toward Canal. Gone.

"I bet she's not too busy to meet her son's best friend in the whole wide fuckin' world. Right, Bubba?" The redhead nodded, realization creeping onto his slow-witted face. "Right, Butch?"

Ah. Butch and Bubba. So, now he knew.

Butch must have nodded as well because he cuffed Turtle around the collar, practically yanking him out of his imitation Dr. J's, and the three hooligans began dragging/escorting him up the block toward Miller's Grocery Store. As they went, Turtle envisioned himself getting an extra dose of ass-whuppin' once the boys discovered his mother was, in fact, not waiting for him at Miller's Grocery. The thought of peeing his pants was no longer in the distance. It had become very, very real.

"You know what? Now that I think of it, she's always late," Turtle said, scrambling for a save.

"I betcha she's not late today," Ansley responded. His voice lowered conspiratorially. "I betcha Mrs. Lard Ass stopped eatin' her Tastykakes and hustled her fatness out of the house earlier than usual 'cause she didn't want to keep her little Lard Ass waitin'."

The older boys chuckled at their younger brother's cleverness.

"It's just that—" Ansley turned and, without warning, delivered a right hook into Turtle's soft belly. Turtle felt his flesh jiggle from the blow as pain exploded in his stomach, radiating up into his chest and down into his legs. He knees buckled, and his loose books went spilling onto the sidewalk.

"Stand him up, Butch," Ansley commanded his older brother, who did what he was told, hooking his arms around Turtle's, pinning them to his sides. Ansley moved in, getting in his face. "I hate liars."

"I'm not a liar," Turtle protested. "She's in there," he said with as much conviction as he could muster.

Ansley smacked him in the face—not hard, the sting of the blow only lasting a few seconds, but no less humiliating. "You think you're smarter than me," Ansley said, and there was so much contempt on his face that Turtle felt really afraid—not just the fear of getting his ass kicked—which, by now, was a foregone conclusion—but the fear that something worse was going to happen.

What Turtle mistook for contempt on Ansley's face was actually pain. It was old pain, much older than Ansley, pain that had travelled the earth since the beginning of time and had found its way to him years ago when he was just a tyke, and lodged in his heart like a piece of shrapnel that could not be removed. This ancient pain on Ansley's face announced there was more than an ass whuppin' coming Turtle's way. What Ansley wanted was for Turtle to feel *his* pain.

"No, I don't think I'm smarter than you," Turtle whined. *And was that a drop of pee?*

"Why you always raisin' your hand in class, then?"

"I don't raise my hand. Miss Grant calls on me," Turtle protested. He could feel himself losing it and knew it wouldn't be long before the urine began cascading down his leg. *And, oh boy, wouldn't that be a riot.*

"She don't call on *me*," Ansley said, his words coming through the darkness inside. "She never calls on me." This last line whistled through his lips, seething with contempt.

"That's because…" Turtle's reply trailed off as he thought better of it.

"Because what?" Ansley inquired, his nose was now practically against Turtle's. It smelled as though he'd been drinking. He was thirteen, same age as Turtle, had just finished a long day of school, and yet it smelled as though he'd been drinking.

Turtle knew about drunks; he'd heard stories about Uncle Johnny's violent bar fights when he tied one on.

"Get your hands off my boyfriend," an angry voice called from behind. It was a girl's voice.

Turtle thought he recognized the voice, but he didn't have a girlfriend. Heck, he didn't have the ghost of a chance at having a girlfriend, so she must have been talking to someone else.

"Rita?" Ansley drawled, her name coming out slowly. His tone had changed. He sounded puzzled—no, more than puzzled. He sounded as if he were afraid.

Butch released Turtle, and both boys turned around to see who had changed Ansley's temperament so quickly. Standing before them was a girl Turtle knew from school. She was in his class. The new girl, Rita Calderon. She was a tiny thing, a tad over four feet, wearing jeans and a slate gray top over which hung an oversized boy's varsity jacket. The jacket was blue with white sleeves. The new girl, Rita, was staring at Ansley with fire in her eyes.

"This is none of your business, girl," Butch said, in a threatening tone.

"Of course it's my business," Rita replied, dismissively. She wasn't the least bit intimidated by the older, bigger boy. "He's my boyfriend. Everything he does is my business. Including *fighting*," she said, adding some edge to her voice. She walked up to them, and gently shoved Ansley away from Turtle.

"What? You gonna fight his battles for him?" Ansley said, adding a derisive snicker, trying to regain control of the situation.

Rita removed her backpack and placed it on the ground. Her five flavor *Lifesavers* fingernails had a different color painted carefully on each nail: dark red, Kelly green, lavender, a deep purple, and her pinkies were iridescent blue. Anyone who knew Rita also knew the color of her fingernails changed with her moods. Today her mood had been indifferent—until now.

She pulled a rubber band from one of her pockets, gathered the ends of her curly brown hair and pulled it into a tight chignon. She stood up, and without replying to Ansley's question, flexed, like a dancer preparing for her recital.

"Lard Ass is *not* your boyfriend!" Ansley shrieked. He was thrown by how comfortable she was in her own skin, how at ease she was in the midst of the much larger boys.

"Don't call him that!" Rita said, taking a menacing step toward Ansley. She wagged her index finger in his face, the glossy polish glinting, her neck getting as loose as a goose.

"Whose jacket is that?" Ansley said, taking a step back. "That jacket belongs to your boyfriend, right? Your *real* boyfriend."

"It's mine. I got it at my last school," Rita said, and cracked her knuckles. She actually cracked her knuckles like a *boy* might do. "I took it from a bigger boy because I wanted it. And Theo is my *real* boyfriend."

She knew his name. Turtle couldn't believe she actually knew his name.

Ansley looked from the girl to his brothers who no longer appeared to be backing him up on this one. "I…I don't fight girls," Ansley said. It sounded as if he were practically whining.

"Good. I'm glad to hear it. I guess that makes you a gentleman," Rita replied. Her gaze found Turtle. It softened. "Pick up your things, honey. I need you to walk me home now," she said softly, sweetly, and yet there was no denying the command in her voice.

It was then Turtle realized the three boys had all backed away. The circle around him had been broken. He scrambled to gather his books from the ground.

"Well?" Rita demanded.

"Well, what?" asked Turtle, totally baffled by this amazing little girl.

"What about mine?"

"Oh." Turtle bent back down, hauled up her backpack and strapped it onto his shoulders.

"See that, fellas? *That's* a gentleman," Rita said with a smug smile.

"What kind of punk lets a girl fight his—" The look Rita shot Bubba singed the words from his tongue.

Turtle could not believe these boys were actually afraid of her—a girl. And yet the way she commanded the space around her, she was more than a girl, she was a force to be reckoned with.

"We're going now," she said to him, suddenly turning sweet as sugar water. She rolled down her sleeves, snapped off the rubber band allowing her dark hair to fall around her shoulders. She turned and started across the street.

"This ain't over," Ansley whispered loudly as Turtle moved away.

"Yes, it is!" Rita snapped, without turning around. She continued across the street. Her hips had a slight, womanlike grace to them, gently and confidently swaying as she moved. Yet, there was an undeniable danger about her as well, and all of them knew it. Turtle followed, not yet embarrassed that a girl had stuck up for him. That would come later. For now, he wondered if he'd just met his first girlfriend.

They didn't talk much on the way home. Turtle wanted to thank her but thought if he did it would look as though he needed a girl to fight his battles for him. He didn't need a girl fighting his battles for him—not that he could fight them for himself. But the thought of a girl fighting for him was almost as bad as the ass whuppin' he'd narrowly avoided. Who was he kidding, it was worse. If word got out that a girl had stood up for him, Turtle's doddering reputation would be ruined.

He hadn't paid much attention to Rita in school. She wasn't the kind of girl that had boys carrying their books in front of themselves, hiding the bulges in their pants. She wasn't cutesy or flirty like some of the fast girls who knew how to tweak the hormones of the popular boys. Rita was nearly invisible—like him.

As they walked, Turtle decided she was cute. There was a tiny scar on her upper lip that added a sense of mystery to her. One day he'd ask her how it got there.

"Why'd they want to beat you up?" Rita asked after walking in silence for nearly three blocks. He could hear a hint of Spanish accent along with her drawl. He hadn't noticed it before.

"Smart," Turtle mumbled, embarrassed.

"What did you say, honey? Speak up, now."

"I said because I'm smart." He found himself suddenly annoyed with her. "He told me to stop being a showoff and answerin' all of Miss Grant's questions or he was gonna punch me out."

"But you didn't stop," she said, her tone turning querulous.

"I wanted to, but Miss Grant called on me."

Rita allowed a silence to engulf them as she mulled over what he'd just revealed. "You didn't have to answer," she said softly. "You could've said you didn't know."

"But I *knew* the answer," Turtle replied adamantly, as if lying, even to save his own ass, was out of the question.

She was silent for a moment. "I like smart boys," she said after a while, and smiled at him.

Turtle again wondered if this girl, Rita, was his girlfriend. Of course, how could she be? He didn't even know her. She had light colored eyes. He wasn't sure what color they were. He hadn't noticed her eyes either until just then and didn't want to stare. "How old are you, anyway?" he asked, making an excuse to look into them.

Rita stopped walking and faced him. They were green. "A lady never tells her age. And a gentleman never asks," she replied, her face lighting up. There was a teasing quality to her voice. She was comfortable talking to boys. "We're here," she said, gesturing toward the building they were standing in front of. It was a dingy apartment building on a street lined with more dingy apartment buildings. The street had always reminded Turtle of old black and white movies where gangsters pushed dead bodies out of cars.

"Okay," he said. He again thought of thanking her but let it go. He removed her backpack from his shoulders and handed it back to her. Then he stood staring at her for several minutes, not sure if he'd been dismissed.

"What the hell's the matter with you?" she asked, the sweetness in her face dissolving like Alka Seltzer.

"Nothin'."

"Then why the hell are you lookin' at me like you're a pervert or somethin'?"

"Umm, I'm not a pervert," he said, fumbling to get the words out of his mouth. "See you tomorrow...I guess." he added, averting his gaze.

"Not if I see you first."

He raised his eyes to find Rita grinning at him. "Gotcha! See you tomorrow, *boyfriend*," she called sweetly, her tongue contouring the word *boyfriend* as if she were from the Deep South. She shot him a smile, bright as a rainbow, that made his heart thump and his thing harden against his pants. Then, she turned and ran into the building.

CHAPTER TWO

"Why were you in your brother's room?"

Mabry Dawson had been lying in wait for her son when he arrived home from school. If she'd been more alert she might have noticed he'd come in half an hour later than usual, or that his smooth coppery skin was now glowing with perspiration. She noticed neither of these things.

On a normal day, Mabry wouldn't have been waiting for him. On a normal day, she'd have been hunkered down in front of the TV getting her fill of Luke and Laura on *General Hospital*. That's where she was every other day when Turtle arrived home from school. Today she had other fish to fry.

"I wasn't," Turtle responded, surprised that his mother was waiting for him, just like he'd told Ansley Meade she'd be.

"Oh, no? His door was wide open," she said, her eyes narrowing, her gaze turning accusatory. She was a thin woman (not at all how Ansley had envisioned her), with a long face and tight features that could turn witch-like at the drop of a hat. "Bedroom doors don't just open by themselves, do they?" Turtle could practically hear the cackle at the end of her question. *Hahahahahaaa!*

He shook his head back and forth. "I didn't open it," he blurted, feeling the full impact of his mother's accusation. He avoided her eyes. He knew if he looked into them he'd see the hatred looming there. The word *unwanted* whispered in the back of his mind.

"Then I guess they do open by themselves." Her voice lowered. "When I went in, I noticed his things was all moved around. I suppose that happened all by itself, too?" She glared at Turtle, her brown skin glowing, waiting for the boy to spill his ample guts. He continued avoiding her gaze.

Turtle knew Mabry insisted on keeping A.D.'s room a certain way, like a museum almost. "I didn't open it," he said again, his voice quavering. "Maybe Dad went in there for somethin'."

Mabry's eyes squeezed shut, her witchy eyebrows pinching tight. "You know how I feel about you going into your brother's room." she said, her voice dipping even lower.

"Why don't you like me?" he asked. He hadn't planned on asking the question. He'd thought about his mother's feelings for him—or lack of feelings—more times than he could count, but he never thought he'd put voice to it, mostly because he was afraid of what she might say.

"Don't say that," Mabry said, her eyes springing open like a window shade with a busted spring. Her voice had turned small as her expression shifted to one of surprise. He was looking into her eyes. She was finding it hard to match his gaze.

She took a short step back, almost as if she'd been pushed. "That's a horrible thing to say to your own *mother*." Yet, it was true. They both knew it, the truth shining in her eyes like a new penny.

"You wish it was me instead of him, don't you?"

Now that the truth was out, Turtle could feel the tears coming. He willed them away, biting down on his lower lip until the metallic taste of blood trickled across his tongue. *Unwanted*. He didn't want to give her the satisfaction of seeing him cry.

Mabry's eyes turned glassy as well. "Don't say that," she repeated. "You know that's not true," the words coming in a short, breathy sigh. "I love you, baby. You know that, don't you?" Her shoulders sagged forward. Turtle nodded. He'd said enough.

"Maybe it *was* your father," she said, her voice coming from that distant place that manufactures shame. Mabry forced a smile filled with sadness onto her face. "I'll ask him when he gets in from work. You fix yourself a snack now, ya hear?"

"Right."

Mabry turned and headed back up the corridor where she'd lose herself in reruns of *What's Happening?* until it was time to prepare supper.

Turtle continued to his room where he dropped his books on the floor. Then he plopped down on the bed that had developed a pronounced sag in the middle, reached into his stash box, and rummaged around under the comic books for a *Chocodile*. Hiding snacks was a trick he'd learned from A.D. *If we stash stuff in our room, we can have desert whenever we want to.* Back when A.D. was still alive, their parents had a rule: *no eating allowed in the bedroom.* These days, nobody cared enough to enforce it.

Turtle peeled back the cellophane wrapper and bit into the chocolaty snack.

Unwanted. She don't love me no more. Maybe she never did.

His thoughts didn't linger on the encounter with his mother. Any other day they would have. Any other day his eyes would've filled with despair and he'd have downed two or three *Chocodiles*, beating himself up over his role in losing his parents' love. But this day wasn't like any other.

Turtle's thoughts moved quickly from the encounter with his mother, past the close call he'd had with Ansley and the Meade boys, all the way to the girl. *Why'd she do it?* he wondered.

During their walk home he'd waited for the new girl to spring a *gotcha* on him. Maybe when they turned the corner to her house he'd find Ansley and his brothers waiting with shit-eating grins all over their faces, laughin' themselves into a conniption fit. But when they turned the corner, no gotcha came.

They'd walked mostly in silence, and by the time they'd reached the front of Rita's building, Turtle had developed an ease with her—a girl. He again secretly delighted in the thought that he'd found himself a girlfriend. He tried to dismiss the silly notion, but he couldn't. It made him feel too good.

He didn't realize it, but that was the moment he decided not to finish the *Chocodile*.

He dragged his tongue across his fingertips, devouring the remnants of luscious chocolate that clung to them. He rewrapped the rest of the snack and stashed it back beneath the comics.

It was then he noticed somebody had been in his room as well. Somebody had taken the box containing the scale model of the Millennium Falcon from the back shelf in A.D.'s closet and placed it right on top of his desk. If he hadn't been so preoccupied with Rita he'd've noticed it sooner.

A chill bolted down both Turtle's arms. No one had to tell him the kind of trouble he'd be in if his parents found the Millennium Falcon in his room. The model spaceship was off limits—way, way off limits, which raised the question, if he didn't put it there, who did?

Unwanted.

He didn't want to think it. It pained him to consider it. Moms are supposed to protect their children, yet why else would the Millennium Falcon be in *his* room instead of on the back shelf in A.D.'s closet where it belonged? Dollars to donuts when Turtle's father got home, a little birdy would tell him the Millennium Falcon was sitting on Turtle's desk. Then he'd barge into Turtle's room ready to wail on him. Stan Dawson wasn't the wailing type, but Turtle knew this was a wailing offense.

She ain't gettin' me, Turtle thought. *She may not like me, but she ain't gettin' me. Not today.* When Dad got home and stormed into his room, the Millennium Falcon would not be there. No way Josè.

Turtle picked up the shiny cardboard box and stared at the Star Wars logo on top. Memories of all the fun times they'd had playing Star Wars drifted in, A.D. insisting he was the only one who could play Han Solo because he was the oldest. Sometimes he made Turtle play Chewbacca, the Wookiee.

With the box in his hands, Turtle moved across the room, quietly opening his bedroom door. He could hear Mabry down the hall in the living room chuckling it up at a sitcom rerun.

Gotta put it back, he thought. *Gotta put it back now.* Turtle slid out into the hallway, quiet as a caterpillar, closed his bedroom door, and eased across the hall toward his dead brother's room.

✼ ✼ ✼

A.D.'s bedroom was near spotless, like a museum. In the old days, before the accident, A.D.'s room always looked as though a tornado had passed through. *Clean up in here,* Moms used to say with an exasperated smile. *This room looks like it's been hit by a human tornado. Okay,* they'd call back, and go right on playing. A.D.'s room was never neat. This new, meticulous look came after the accident.

A.D. would hate it in here, Turtle thought, gazing around. *He'd say it looks like a girl's room.* A smile appeared on his lips as he thought of how much his big brother liked messy things; they both did. How many times had Dad stepped on one of their army men buried in the carpet, hopping around as if he'd stepped on a bed of hot coals?

Not funny! he'd holler. They'd laugh, and eventually he'd join them. That was the thing Turtle missed most about A.D.—the laughter, not just the laughter he and his brother shared, but the laughter they all shared, a cornucopia whose riches once spilled over their home.

When A.D. was still alive, the posters that hung on his walls listed this way and that like the leaning posters of Pisa. A.D. always hung them hastily with snatches of Scotch tape when he brought a new poster home, always in too big of a hurry to get the new poster up so he could admire it. They fell off the walls with regularity. Now, the posters hung neatly, lined up in a row like wooden soldiers, supported by some form of invisible tape that kept them from falling down—ever. Even *The Goonies* poster, A.D.'s prized possession, with its dog-eared corners, hung neatly above his bed.

They'd never seen the movie, yet they enjoyed acting out what they thought the movie was about from the trailers. Not seeing it made it more fun. They were *The Goonies,* starring in their own adventure movie.

Now look at this place. The board games on the book shelf: Monopoly, Sorry, Stratego and Mousetrap were stacked neatly, instead of in the helter-skelter stack threatening to topple over they'd once been in. The room had been made perfect, as if A.D. had gone off to summer camp, or had run away from home and could return any moment. They wanted it to be just right for him when he got back. Only thing was, A.D. wasn't away at summer camp, and he hadn't run away. A.D. was dead. He would not be coming home ever again.

As Turtle started across the room toward the closet, he noticed something. *Different.* He couldn't see it as much as he could feel it. He noticed how unnaturally cold the room had become. The window was shut tight. He could see the late afternoon sun beating against the glass. It should have warmed the room up and yet it felt as though he'd just stepped into winter. There was something else wrong in the room, something that made his skin crawl. He felt with dead certainty that someone or *something* was watching him.

He turned back to the bedroom door. It remained closed. "Moms?" he whispered loudly, taking a few halting steps toward the door. "I just came in here to…" Just then a loud guffaw erupted from down the hall.

Stop being a wussy, he thought. That's what A.D. would've called him. *Moms is down there watching TV, and Dad's still at work. Just because you go into a dead kid's room doesn't mean there are ghosts in there.*

He tried laughing it off. He turned back to the closet. It was open.

"What the…" He didn't want to think about it. He didn't want to think that the closet door had been closed seconds ago when he came into the room—he was sure of it—and now it was open. He pretended not to notice, which was hard with the cold closing in on him like a fog, and the feeling of being watched by an unknown presence gnawing at his consciousness.

He scolded himself for being afraid. *Don't be such a wussy. This is A.D.'s room,* he told himself. When A.D. had been alive this was their hangout. They played in the room every single day, spent hours lying on the floor planning their next *Goonies* adventure. They had even shared the room when they were younger, before their parents decided to separate them because they wouldn't go to sleep at night, having too much fun.

After A.D.'s death, Turtle would often come into the room just to lie on the floor, read his comic books while inhaling the fragrance of his brother that had been trapped in the carpeting. He felt close to him when he lay there. He loved A.D., and loved coming into A.D.'s room, so why was he so afraid today?

Because there's something wrong in here. He could feel it, and the sooner he got out, the better. The front wheel of A.D.'s bike, Tyrone—a hand-me-down chrome and black Huffy from the 70s that was squeezed between A.D.'s bed and the wall—slowly turned, the ball bearings in the wheel click-clicking loud and ominously, shattering the silence of the room. Turtle didn't want to think about it.

He moved toward the closet, his hands trembling so much the plastic pieces inside the box began to rattle, crackling together, the sound of a hundred puzzle pieces rattling around in a hollow box. He blocked this from his mind as well, focusing on the need to put the model back.

He was so cold now his own teeth were beginning to chatter.

Gotta put it back. Gotta p-p-p-p put it –b-b-b-b back now.

The open closet door looked like a mouth waiting to gobble him up. *Cut it out, Turtle. Just put the damn thing back!* He yanked the chair from A.D.'s desk, dragged it into the closet—he'd never noticed how dark it was in there before—climbed up onto the chair and placed the model way back on the shelf. Then, he climbed down, closed the closet door and got the hell out of there as fast as he could. As he eased shut the bedroom door and headed back across the hall for his own room, he could've sworn he heard A.D.'s closet door creaking back open. He didn't want to think about it.

CHAPTER THREE

When Turtle arrived at school the next morning, he was disappointed that he didn't see Rita milling about in the yard. He arrived early on the off chance that she'd actually be there waiting for him. He knew it was silly to think she'd be, but the way she called him *boyfriend* had given him hope.

He casually glanced around pretending to observe his classmates at play, yet hoping to see her before he had to go inside. When she didn't appear, his mind conjured up all sorts of crazy reasons why she'd helped him the day before, settling on she was dying and needed to do a good deed before she croaked off to heaven. *She saved me from the bullies, then went home to die. That's why she's not here this morning.* As ridiculous as it seemed, it was the only reason that made sense to him.

Turtle walked into homeroom and moved to his assigned seat next to Ross Rainey, dropping his armful of books onto the desk. Ross and Turtle were the class outcasts, *The Fat Boys*, as some kids called them in not so subtle whispers, after the successful overweight rap group of the same name. Ross insisted *his* weight was a glandular problem.

Turtle began shoveling his books inside his desk.

"What happened after school yesterday?" Ross asked, leaning in, anxious to hear about any beat down that didn't include him.

"Nothin'."

"Oh." He seemed disappointed. "Ansley didn't catch you again, huh?"

"No. He caught up with me. Had his brothers with him, too." There wasn't much about the incident he could actually tell Ross without looking like a dweeb, so he remained tight-lipped. *You let a girl stick up for you? Loser!*

"So what happened?" Ross asked, leaning in, his flabby thigh slipping over the side of his seat.

"Nothin', dude! We talked!" Turtle snapped, getting annoyed with the questioning. His gaze moved across the room to where Ansley was seated. At the moment, Ansley was busy teasing Nancy Richmond about the color of her hair—red—with a new rap he'd made up on the spot.

Look out for the red
on Nancy Richmond's head
hair so damn red
just like a clown named Fred

Turtle thought Ansley noticed him sneaking a peek in his direction, but if he did, he didn't so much as give Turtle a second glance. It seemed Ansley had moved on from his desire to hand Turtle an ass whuppin'. *Good.*

"Call me Jabba," Ross said, dragging Turtle's attention back.

"What?"

"You called me *dude*. The name's Jabba!" Ross insisted.

Aside from being one of *The Fat Boys*, Ross had inherited another nickname, Jabba, after Jabba the Hut, the gelatinous mass of a character from *Star Wars*. It was an obvious insult—*here comes ole Jabba the Hut*, yet Ross delighted in it. He encouraged the nickname, insisting it gave him a certain cachè with the honeys.

"I'm not callin' you that," Turtle responded, annoyed that Ross couldn't see the obvious—that the joke was on him.

"Ansley whupped your ass yesterday, didn't he? Lemme see the pee stains in your underwear." Ross giggled and grabbed for Turtle's waistband.

"Cut it out, Ross," Turtle said, pushing him away.

"Jabba!"

"For your information, he didn't lay a finger on me...*Jabba*," Turtle replied, still annoyed.

Just then, Rita strode nimbly through the front door, beating the late bell by seconds. Turtle's heart sped up the moment she entered the room. She looked radiant. That was the only word he could think of to describe her. Her skin had a sheen to it he hadn't noticed before, as did her hair, and those green eyes were like beacons. It was almost as if she were glowing, lighting up the room as if the Virgin Mary herself had just entered, her halo gleaming.

Rita struggled with her backpack, throwing it from her shoulders. It sounded extra heavy when it hit the floor. Turtle didn't move to help her with the load. She glanced around the room, and finding Turtle's eyes on her, she smiled. Her smile created a warmth in Turtle that set his heart to jitterbugging so violently in his chest he was certain Ross—er, Jabba—

could hear it. He looked away, for fear of exposing himself to Ross and his other classmates.

When Turtle made no attempt to help, Rita released an audible sigh, then hauled up her backpack and moved to her seat. "Good morning, *gentlemen*," she said as she passed his desk. Turtle made it his business not to look at her.

"I knew it," whispered Ross.

"You knew what?" asked Turtle, the beginnings of a cold sweat dusting along his flabby sides.

"The senorita's got the hots for me. She wants a little Jabba juice on her rice and beans," Ross replied, and he began gyrating his hips in his seat, looking like Tweedle Dee twirling a hula hoop. The classmates around him began laughing and hooting—*Go Jabba, go Jabba, go Jabba*—which prompted him to gyrate even more.

"That'll be enough, Mr. Rainey," Mr. Monicker, the home room teacher, called from the front of the room. Michael Monicker was a ten-year vet of the Middle School Wars. He'd seen it all. He began roll call.

Rita didn't look at Turtle again throughout homeroom. In fact, she didn't seem to notice him all morning.

By lunch, Turtle finally accepted he didn't have a girlfriend. He told Ross he wasn't hungry, even though he was, and strolled from the cafeteria out onto the quad in search of her. It wasn't an obvious search. He feigned interest in some boys playing kick ball and another group playing hacky sack, pretending to enjoy the games along with the spring air. Midway through lunch period, he gave up his search and went back inside. What would he say to her, anyway? His heart was feeling like a rock in his chest.

Why'd she do it? He asked himself again. He'd spent the morning dreaming up hundreds of reasons, none of which made sense, although a radio contest giving a million dollars to the person who did the most good deeds in one day had worked its way to the top of the list.

The next time he saw her was in American history, taught by Miss Grant. This was the class that had caused all his troubles. Rita moved to her seat where she continued not to notice him. By then, he was overcome by a sense of desperation. *Why won't she look at me?* He coughed loudly, sneezed, cleared his throat, promising himself that if she so much as glanced in his direction he wouldn't look away. No way Josè. He'd smile, not caring who noticed, hoping to restore the radiance he'd seen on her face that morning. She didn't look his way. She acted as if he wasn't there, driving a spike deep into his already hurting heart.

Near the end of the period, Miss Grant called on him. He'd been so busy despairing over Rita, he hadn't been paying attention.

"My hand wasn't up," he replied.

"I know. But I bet you know about the Emancipation Proclamation, don't you, Theodore?" she said with a smile that was quiet and confident.

"I have no *idea* what you're talking about, Miss Grant," he replied. A burst of laughter erupted from the class. He was certain Ansley was laughing the loudest.

Miss Grant shot him the oddest look before continuing with the lesson, because, of course, he'd answered questions about the Emancipation Proclamation the day before.

Turtle didn't care how she was looking at him. So what if he'd let her down. He was in a dark place. He chastised himself for not helping Rita with her backpack that morning. He wondered if things might have turned out differently if he had. He craved a *Chocodile.*

⁂

"Wait up!"

Turtle had just stepped from the school yard, his stomach complaining loudly about skipping lunch. The pain in his heart was surpassing the one in his stomach, when he heard the call. Ross had been avoiding him after school the past few days. He didn't want to get swept up in the wave of Ansley's ass whippin', but now that Ansley had moved on—he'd barely glanced at Turtle all day—Ross wanted to resume walking home with him.

Turtle stopped and waited for his classmate in silence. His mind was riddled with too much despair to reply.

Ross meandered up. It was a laborious process. "Wanna go by Miller's? I have a few dollars. Anything you want, my friend. My treat. Today is a day of celebration. The liberation of *The Fat Boys*." Ross began making beat box sounds.

Turtle marveled at how easily Ross latched onto the insulting nick names. Of course, *his* nick name wasn't *Lard Ass*. "Sure," he replied, making one last scan of the school grounds for Rita.

They crossed the street and started up toward Prospect Avenue.

"That was pretty cool what you said to Miss Grant this afternoon," Ross said. "Fuck off, bitch!" He exploded with laughter.

"I didn't say that."

"Yeah, yeah, but that's what you meant, and that's how she took it. Is that the deal you made with Ansley Meade?"

"What?"

"To tell her off in front of the whole class?"

"No. I didn't make any deal with Ansley." Turtle was suddenly annoyed that the ass whuppin' had somehow again become the topic of discussion. The ass whuppin' made him think of Rita, and when he thought of Rita, he felt empty inside.

They'd only walked half a block, yet Ross's breathing became wheezy. "Hey, man, slow down. Where are we runnin' off to, anyway?"

"I need to get home, Ross," Turtle lied.

"Jabba!"

They continued around the corner where, to Turtle's delight and amazement, he saw Rita walking a half block ahead of them, the oversized varsity jacket sliding down her shoulders with the weight of the heavy backpack. Turtle couldn't believe his eyes. If Mary, mother of God, appeared before him just then, it would seem less a miracle than this.

As soon as he saw her, Turtle's heart sped up.

"I gotta go, Jabba," his said, picking up the pace even more. He couldn't let her get away.

"I'm not gonna buy you anything if you don't wait up for me," Ross called, his breath whistling.

"That's cool," Turtle said. He began to trot away.

"It's Ansley, isn't it?" Ross called out. Turtle stopped and turned around. "He's comin' for you, isn't he?" Ross said, cautious eyes scanning the neighborhood around him. He leaned over, peering under a parked car. "Where is he?"

"This has got nothing to do with Ansley, *Jabba*," Turtle called back. Then, he was running up the block toward her. He shot one last glance at Ross who'd finally accepted he wasn't about to be attacked. Ross was staring at him in amazement.

"Hey, Rita, slow down," Turtle hollered.

Up ahead, Rita looked over her shoulder. Seeing it was Turtle, she fired off a dismissive gaze, and continued walking.

By the time Turtle caught up with her, he was out of breath. He couldn't tell if it was from running or being in her presence.

"I didn't get a chance to thank you," he said, slowing to a walk alongside her. He felt a stitch in his ribcage, and realized he hadn't run in a long time.

"For what?" she asked.

"For…umm…You know…Yesterday." He was embarrassed at how wimpy he was sounding. "I didn't thank you for helping me out yesterday." There, he said it, getting it all out in one breath and feeling good, even proud of himself for it.

"Oh? I think you thanked me plenty this morning." Rita shot a sharp gaze in his direction.

She may as well have plunged a dagger in his heart. Any pride he'd been feeling whistled out of him like a slowly deflating balloon. "That was shitty of me," he said.

She stopped walking and looked at him with those big, green eyes. "So, you admit it?"

He wanted to look away, but he didn't, he couldn't. As embarrassed as he was, he was also mesmerized by her. "Those books look awfully heavy," he said, changing the subject. He gestured with his nose toward her backpack.

The glimmer of a smile appeared on her lips. "They are," she replied.

"Umm…. Please let me carry them for you?"

Her smile brightened, and just as quickly, vanished. "Why?"

"Why, what?" Turtle was reaching for the backpack when the question stopped him, his arm snapping back like a bungee cord.

"Why you want to carry my books all of a sudden? I practically had to beg you to carry them yesterday." Rita placed her hands on her hips. She had no intention of making it easy for him.

Turtle hadn't realized until that moment he was sweating. Rivulets of perspiration were rolling down his sides, pooling up in the folds of his flesh. "Because, umm. You know…. They look heavy and…."

"Apology accepted. Here ya go," she said, unloading her backpack from her shoulders. Turtle placed his books on the ground and strapped it on.

When he again looked up, he was pleased to see the radiance he'd witnessed that morning had returned. Rita was looking at him, her green eyes shining, a delightful smile illuminating her face. At that moment Turtle didn't care if she was or wasn't his girlfriend. He was grateful to once again to be able to bask in her glow.

They walked, and this time they talked freely. Rita asked him why he didn't answer Miss Grant's question in class. "I know you knew the answer."

"I didn't," he replied, not letting on why he didn't know.

"You can't let people intimidate you."

"I'm not intimidated!" he said, his words coming in a rush. "If I knew the answer, I'd've told her."

"Good," Rita said, treating him to another glorious smile. "I like smart boys," she said again. He treated her to one of his own.

After talking about favorite subjects (his was science, hers English) foods (they both loved hamburgers and pizza), and favorite TV shows (The A-Team, Full House), Turtle finally got up the nerve to ask the question that had been burning up his brain cells since she'd thwarted the ass whuppin'.

"I thanked you for coming to my rescue yesterday, not that I couldn't've handled it by myself, but I didn't ask you why you did it?" he said softly. "Why did you…rescue me?"

She stopped walking and looked at him. "I don't know," she said, searching for the right words. "It looked like you were in trouble. What was I supposed to do?"

It wasn't the answer he'd been hoping for. He hoped she'd've said she was secretly in love with him, had been infatuated since she first arrived at Charles Drew Middle School and couldn't stand to see anyone harm him. Instead, he found his question turning back on him, being answered with a question.

"I don't know." She was talking again, her voice softening, letting him off the hook. He thought he saw a shadow darkening her eyes and got the feeling there was something more to her answer, something she wasn't ready to reveal. The shadow was gone as quickly as it had arrived.

They reached the front of her building, and he realized with a sinking feeling his time with her was coming to an end. *Too soon*, he thought. "You know, you're not supposed to answer a question with a question," he said, stalling, searching for words that would keep her from going inside.

"Who says?" She was smiling again, although this was more a teasing grin. He enjoyed that she was teasing him. Anything to keep that smile on her face.

"I do," he replied, and smiled back, tickled with himself that he could banter with her—a girl. "You said you liked smart boys. It's time you listened to one." He couldn't believe the words that were coming out of his mouth. He wondered how long he could keep it up.

"Well, look at you," Rita said, her smile twisting to the side. "And I thought you were shy."

"That's an assumption. And everyone knows to assume is to make an ass out of you and me…. Wait, that didn't come out right."

"No, no. I think it did. You're an ass." Rita's eyes crinkled with unadulterated laughter. "Don't fall into any holes, cause then you'd be an…" She doubled over, holding her sides she was laughing so hard.

Normally Turtle would have been embarrassed. He was kind of embarrassed, but her radiant smile was so bright it was blinding him and all he could think is how lucky he was to be standing there at that very moment. He'd been wrong about her. She wasn't *cute* as he'd thought the day before. She was actually beautiful, and she was talking to *him*. Of course, he knew he couldn't tell her that, not now, maybe not ever.

"You got me," he said, emitting a burst of self-deprecating laughter. He set his loose books on the ground and removed her backpack from his shoulders.

Rita's expression shifted dramatically. "I'm not ready to go inside," she said, eyeing her backpack as if he were handing her a bug, or a snake. "Let's go somewhere."

That's when he got the bright idea, the thing that would kick-start their relationship, sending it winging away on its tumultuous path.

❧ ❧ ❧

Ansley Meade had wanted to let it go. His brothers, who drew the line at fighting girls—*chickenshit assholes*—had moved on, and Ansley was wise enough to know he wasn't nearly as tough without them as he was when they were standing shoulder-to-ass-whuppin-shoulder.

He told himself that he *had* let it go. Yet, while he pretended he didn't care, he'd kept a secret eye on both of them all day. And just when he was satisfied that the girl was indeed a liar—*I knew that was your real boyfriend's jacket*—and that he could tell his brothers Lard Ass was the *liar* of liars, and they ought to meet up with him and beat the truth out of his lumpy hide—he saw the two of them walking home together. Turtle and Rita. He followed at a close yet discreet distance, and the more he saw, the more he didn't like. He particularly didn't like the way they were talking and laughing, and Lard Ass was carrying her books, as if he could actually be her *boyfriend*.

"This is bullshit!" Ansley grumbled, peeking out from his hidey-hole across the way. *And I'm going to prove it.*

What the hell can she see in that tub of lard, anyway? Nuthin! Ansley hated Turtle for being fat, he hated him more for being smart, and now he'd hit the trifecta—a reason to hate him even more, because Turtle was stupid enough to believe that a girl, *any girl*, would like his fat ass.

I'll show ya, Ansley thought. An ass whuppin' was too good for Turtle. *You think you're so smart. I'll show you what an idiot you really are.* That was when Ansley began to hatch his plan.

❧ ❧ ❧

What none of them realized was that there was a second observer on that spring day, sitting in an old Volkswagen bus parked down the street. This observer had more on his mind than evening a score. For he was certain his long search was coming to an end. He'd finally found the child he was looking for.

36

The boys in the neighborhood called it The Lots. It was a mile and a half of open space grown over with trees, milkweed, and scrub brush just beyond the foot of Canal Street that ran along the edge of the creek. It was unclaimed land that the Foster City government didn't want, and the commercial developers hadn't realized possessed any value—yet.

To the grownup eye, it was nothing more than an oversized vacant lot, an eyesore that some of the businesses in the area secretly used as a dumping ground. Yet to any Foster City boy with an inch of imagination, The Lots was a little piece of heaven. Turtle and A.D. had yards of imagination that they used on their many excursions there. For them, it was a child-size wilderness that ran alongside the creek, a creek that reminded many a Foster City boy of the old the Mississippi that Huck Finn and Jim had cruised on a raft with a wigwam hut.

One day it would be a baseball field like Camden Yards, where A.D. would throw knuckle balls and Turtle would complain he wasn't letting him hit one, until he did. The next day it would be an African Serengeti where the boys pretended that long tree limbs were elephant guns they'd use to bring down big game. Some days it was a quiet spot where they'd bring their comic books and spend hours reading, not saying a word to one another, allowing their imaginations to run free amidst the rhythmic rumbling of Foster Creek.

Turtle brought Rita to The Lots that afternoon. He wasn't sure why. It was very much a guy place and as tough as Rita might have seemed that first day, she was very much a girl—or a *lady*, as she put it. He brought her there because The Lots was his favorite place, a mysterious land that he was tethered to for the memories it held. And if Rita really was his girlfriend, shouldn't he share his best-kept secrets with her? So he brought her there and hoped she'd see in The Lots what he saw.

They picked their way through the scrub brush and debris to a patch of green grass where they could sit and watch Foster Creek wend its way to the river. They alighted on the banks of Foster Creek and began to talk. Turtle talked about A.D., the conversation spilling out of him as if an oil driller had excavated his voice box and opened a precious vein. *We just hit ourselves a gusher.*

He hadn't realized how much he needed to say these things until he did. He stopped after going on for ten full minutes and looked over to see if she'd been rolling her eyes, waiting for him to shut the hell up. She wasn't. She seemed interested, so he continued talking.

"How long since he's been…you know," Rita said, her words taking on a tenderness he hadn't heard in her before.

"Almost two years now." He smiled into her green eyes, realizing he'd made the right choice in bringing her there. "He was my best friend," he said, the air going out of his lungs in a sadness-filled sigh. His emotions were rising, but he no longer cared if she saw him with glassy eyes.

"How…."

"He was hit by a car," he blurted. He'd been waiting for the question and was dying to tell. "He was on his way back from the model shop on Prospect Avenue. He just bought a scale model of The Millennium Falcon, that big space craft in Star Wars."

"I know what it is." He was impressed that she knew.

"We'd been wanting the Millennium Falcon for a *long* time. We planned to assemble it together." The ghost of the fond memory appeared on his lips as a smile. "It cost almost twenty-five dollars."

"That's a lot of money."

"It's motorized," he said by way of explanation. He laughed, and it was as if someone had opened up a jar full of happiness inside. "It was a lot more than we could ever put together, but A.D. figured out a way for us to get it." He leaned in, the smile on his lips widening, as if he was about to spill a juicy piece of gossip. "Whenever my father came home after a night of drinking, he always took off his pants in the living room, I think because they jingled so much and he didn't want to wake my mother. He'd leave em out there 'til morning, and A.D. would sneak out once we heard him snoring, and cadge a few dollar bills. He told me the secret was in not taking too much. If Dad had five singles in his wallet, A.D. would take just one; if he had seven or eight, A.D. would take two, never more."

Rita smiled, delighted with the story. "That's smart."

"I know. The secret is not to get too greedy." He laughed again, his laughter rising like a free bird into the open air. "It took over a year to piece together enough money for The Falcon, but we did it." He stopped talking, the laughter dying on his lips along with the words. His emotions were rising again because he was getting to the hard part of the story, the part he'd never been able to tell, the part where he let A.D. go to the model shop all by himself.

Rita reached over and touched his hand, her multi-colored nails glistening like a rainbow. "That's a good story," she said, her tone bathed in sweetness, her fingers lingering on the top of his hand.

"Yeah. It is. A real good story," he replied. His eyes had become stormy, staring into the undulating waters of Foster Creek, brimming with memories of the past.

Today is one of those days you never forget.

That's what Turtle was thinking when he dropped Rita at her doorstep. He watched her head into the building, the oversized jacket sliding off her shoulders. There was a smile the size of Cleveland plastered across his face. He hadn't had one of those lately.

He didn't start away until the door was safely shut behind her. *That's what a gentleman does; he waits until his lady is safely inside.* The smile, taking up most of Turtle's face, grew in size. Then, he ran.

Running hadn't been Turtle's thing, not for the past two years, but today he felt the urge to get moving and he had to fulfill it. It took several steps to get his thunder thighs going, the muscles of his legs had been latent for so long they'd gone to flab. He took off slowly, a tortoise who didn't stand a chance against the hare, but once he got up a head of steam, he realized he could run all out.

There was a new energy coursing through him, as if a wild stallion were rearing up in his soul, and he had to set it free. He ran ten blocks, most of the way home, sweating and panting, but never tiring. This was different for him. Normally he'd be toasted after one block; after two he'd be doubled over in the gutter along Trinity Avenue, gasping for air. Not today, however. Today he was invincible. Today he could run forever.

Just when he thought he was destined for a life of misery, a burden to parents who no longer wanted him, Rita had come along, an angel of mercy come to rescue him. He had to be careful with his feelings, though. He was falling big time for the mysterious new girl and wasn't sure how she felt about him. Yeah, he knew she liked him. He could tell the way she laughed at his jokes that her laughter was genuine. He knew the hour or so they'd just spent together at The Lots was time she wanted to spend. And the way she touched him when he talked about his brother. He could feel the connection between them. But so what? Spiders have a connection with their babies and then they eat them. Turtle needed to be careful. They could be friends. He could have a *girl* friend, but that didn't mean she was his *girlfriend*.

He'd waited for her to say the words when they'd parted: *Goodbye, boyfriend.* But what she said was: *See you tomorrow.* So he needed to watch his heart for fear of losing it to her, although, truth be told, deep inside he was pretty damn sure it was already a lost cause. An odd feeling had come onto him—the feeling of emptiness while at the same time being full. Feeling completely satisfied and yet thirsting for much more. *Could it be...love?*

"Women," he uttered softly and burst into laughter as he sprinted up the sidewalk. Never thought he'd utter that phrase. And now that he knew the true meaning of it, he laughed some more, the rosiness staying with him all the way home.

The TV was going when he entered the house—Phil Donahue. Mabry didn't call out to him, didn't ask where he'd been, didn't so much as say hello. That was all right. Today he didn't care about the funk; he knew all the good feelings would hold it at bay.

When he arrived at his room he saw his door partway open. He often left his bedroom door open, but he was sure as eggs he hadn't left it open that morning. He'd purposely closed it. If he could have booby-trapped it so he could catch his mother in one of those big sweeping fish nets like in the cartoons, he would've.

A blast of the funk billowed up into his belly, like a peasouper rolling in on the moors. *She's trying to get me again.* Turtle pushed the door open and entered, fully prepared to see the forbidden Millennium Falcon sitting on his desk.

40

CHAPTER FOUR

He gave the room a quick once over before tumbling his books down onto the bed. Then he gave it a more careful examination, like something Sherlock Holmes might have done. The Falcon wasn't there. He let out a slow breezy sigh as relief overtook him.

He hadn't closed his door when he came in, sidetracked by the thought that his mother had been up to something. If he'd closed it, he wouldn't have heard the sound. He was coming to the end of his examination when he heard it—the soft ticking.

At first, he attributed the sound to voices on the TV down the hall. Yet after a while, he realized it wasn't coming from down the hall, the sound was coming from across the hall, from A.D.'s room. It was a faint sound, coming every few minutes or so. A will-o'-the-wisp. He strained to listen, but couldn't make out exactly what it was. A chill snaked down his back as he remembered the strangeness he'd encountered in A.D.'s room the day before, the feeling of being watched.

Tick, tick, tick.

There it was again, a soft ticking, like dice. No. Like pencils knocking together on his brother's desk. No, that wasn't quite right, either. The sound didn't matter; what mattered was someone was in A.D.'s room.

Dad. Dad's home early, and he's messin' around with somethin' in there.

That was the comforting thought Turtle settled on. It was the only thing that made sense, so he hung onto the notion. He stepped out into the corridor and began moving toward the closed door. With each step he noticed the temperature dropping. It was as if he was approaching an open freezer, its chill radiating into the air.

The idea that what was in his brother's room could be something ghostly flared in his mind. That was the thought he didn't allow yesterday.

Yesterday when he was putting the model back, he held the thought away, yet today, he had no choice. There were too many things pointing in that direction. As much as he wanted it to be Dad in that room, he knew, sure as rain, it wasn't.

The summer that Turtle turned nine, some of the older kids in the neighborhood had started rumoring that the abandoned apartment building on Union Avenue was haunted. The building had been abandoned for less than a year, and few of them said they'd even seen the ghost. A.D. insisted they go down to the vacant building and investigate. He said it would be a fun *Goonies* adventure, but Turtle didn't want to go.

Turtle was afraid of ghosts. He was afraid of most things, but ghosts and monsters and darkened basements were in the top three. A.D. told him there was no such thing as ghosts. He said, if the building was haunted by mean ghosts, they'd've hurt someone already. A.D. assured him the real reason the big kids were saying the building was haunted is they were hiding something in there, and A.D. wanted to know what it was.

Turtle admired his brother's fearlessness, but *he* wasn't made that way. Turtle was a scaredy-cat, a *buc-buc-buc-buuuuc*—chicken. Whenever A.D. brought up the subject of going down Union Avenue and exploring the house, by the time he'd finished his nagging, Turtle was usually near tears. After a few days, A. D. stopped pestering his little brother about going down Union Avenue, and soon after that, the haunted house rumor ran out of steam and died. The boys never found out what, if anything, was really hidden in the abandoned building, although Turtle always believed it was a ghost.

Turtle put his ear as close to A.D.'s bedroom door as safety would allow. *Buc-buc-buuuuc.* The cold was coming off the door in waves. His heart strummed in his chest like a bass fiddle. As his ear drew nearer, the ticking stopped. He remained motionless, holding his breath, waiting for the sound to start up again, yet praying it wouldn't.

Push the door open, go inside, and investigate.

The voice in Turtle's head said something that sounded very much like something A.D. might have said.

Turtle responded to the voice: *I got better things to do, like homework.*

Right.

He began backing away from his brother's bedroom door. His eyes remained on the door until he was back inside his own room with the door shut tight.

❦ ❦ ❦

It was around midnight when the thought came to him. He'd been lying in bed for hours, too restless to sleep. At first he thought he couldn't sleep because of all the strangeness surrounding A.D.'s room.

At dinner he casually dropped the Millennium Falcon into conversation.

"Why are you bringing that up now?" Moms asked, her tone edgy.

"I was thinking about Star Wars this afternoon, and…"

"That's not dinner table talk," Mabry said, cutting him off. She'd been about to scoop mashed potatoes from a bowl to his father's plate, and stopped, the spoon suspended in mid-air. "If you're going to talk like that, you need to eat in your room."

Her response surprised him. "It's a movie, Mom," he said, his voice rising. He didn't mind eating in his room, would have preferred it, but wasn't that against the rules?

"It's not a movie we discuss around here. Ever!" she said clipping the 'r.' The word coming out *evah.* She went back to scooping.

Turtle looked to his father in disbelief. Stan Dawson took a passive role in holding his family together during their grief storm. He was a big, powerful man, with a complexion like dark chocolate and a disposition just as sweet. It was said Turtle inherited his beefy build and sweetness from his father.

Stan's philosophy in this difficult time was to stay out of Mabry's way and allow her to grieve. She'd come out of it in time, and then they could be a family again. If they incurred a casualty or two along the way, like a son destined to spend his entire adult life in therapy, so be it. That was the price you paid. They were two years into Stan's philosophy with no end in sight.

"This kind of talk is upsetting to your mother, Turtle. Star Wars and the Millennium Falcon are off limits. Okay?" Stan Dawson asked without raising his voice.

"Okay," Turtle replied. He should have known he wouldn't get any support from the old man.

That was three hours ago. Now Turtle was lying in bed believing Mabry couldn't have been the one who'd brought the Millennium Falcon into his room. *She didn't even want to talk about it,* he mused. *I bet if she'd've seen it in my room yesterday she'd've freaked.* But if his mother didn't put it there, who did?

Ghost.

This was the kind of thing that could have kept Turtle's mind occupied deep into the night, could have had him quaking beneath the sheets, won-

43

dering about the Millennium Falcon and the strange goings on in A.D.'s room, yet it wasn't the thing keeping Turtle from falling asleep that night.

I don't have her phone number. Girl's give their boyfriends their phone numbers.
Rita was the reason he couldn't sleep.

Turtle had come to the decision he was going to ask Rita for her phone number at school the next day. That was going to be the litmus test. If she gave it to him it would prove that Rita was his girlfriend.

But how does a guy just come out and ask a girl for her phone number? He'd never done anything like it before. He'd observed girls passing boys slips of folded paper with their phone numbers hastily scrawled on them. He'd been a participant in passing these notes around the classroom while his teachers' backs were turned. That was as close to a girl's phone number as Turtle had ever been.

He decided right off he wouldn't pass a note. Asking Rita for her number was nobody's business, and if he passed a note, Ansley would probably get his hands on it, and then the teasing would begin.

Hey, Lard Ass, what do you want to talk to her about, Tastykakes?

No. He'd ask Rita himself, in person, staring into those big green eyes that made his heart ache, but he needed a reason to ask. He didn't want to seem stupid about it. He didn't want to seem like a dweeb, either, and he most definitely didn't want to seem desperate.

Teachers asked students to exchange numbers at the start of the semester in case a student was out sick and needed to call someone for a homework assignment.

"Hey, Rita, can I have your phone number?"
"Why?"
"So if I'm out sick I can call you for the assignment."
"Don't you have Ross's phone number for that?"
"Well…yeah. But suppose we're both out sick?"

Okay, that plan had an obvious hole in it. Besides, giving him her phone number to exchange homework wasn't exactly a ringing endorsement that she was his girlfriend. Turtle needed something that said she was giving him her number because she wanted him to have it.

He lay staring at the cracks road-mapping the ceiling, travelling down scenario after scenario of how to ask Rita for her number without seeming stupid, or desperate or lame, and he kept arriving at a dead end of a reason.

So I can call you and talk.

That was the best he could come up with. It was also the riskiest, because if he so blatantly laid his hand on the table, there he'd be, a sitting duck, waiting for her to blow his stupid, lame, desperate, and fat ass right out of the water.

It also happens to be true. He couldn't think of a better way to spend evenings after supper than spinning the night away with Rita on the phone.

Tick, tick, tick.

The sound he'd heard that afternoon was starting again, interrupting his thoughts. It was louder this time. The ticking was coming through loud and clear even though his door was closed. Turtle got out of bed. He didn't want to. *No way Josè.* His first inclination was to pull the covers up over his head, like he'd done so often as a child, lying there 'til daylight came and chased the boogeymen away.

He got out of bed for Rita. He got out of bed because she deserved a boyfriend who was fearless, like A.D., and not a coward, like him. He moved to the bedroom door. *For Rita.* He opened it. *For Rita.* The corridor was dark and silent, the heavy scent of last night's meat loaf hanging in the air. As for the sound—nothing. Maybe he hadn't heard the ticking sound, maybe it had been his overactive imagination, and he could go back to bed and continue with his plan—

Scrunch, scrunch…

A new sound greeted his ears. It was sounding to Turtle as if someone— or *something*—was crumpling paper behind the closed door of his dead brother's room. Yes, that was it! Someone was on the other side of A.D.'s door crumpling up paper.

His heart became a charging bull galloping in his chest as he stepped out into the corridor. The chill was on him again, radiating off of A.D's bedroom door like a fog so thick he could almost taste it, dense like icy pea soup on his tongue. Yet despite the chill, he was sweating. He took short, halting steps toward the door, pushing into the heavy chill, and with each step he told himself he was putting the strangeness to rest. He'd open the door and discover his mother had left the window open while cleaning, and that it wasn't scrunching paper he'd heard, but curtains flapping against the sides of the windows. He told himself in five minutes he'd be laughing about it as he returned to his own room and thoughts of Rita.

He arrived at the door, gripped the icy doorknob and twisted, the doorknob so cold he had to will himself not to let go. He pushed the door open.

Inside the room, the Millennium Falcon box lay open on the floor, its contents spilled out onto the carpet in a hundred or so tiny plastic pieces. A.D. was sitting on the floor amidst the pieces of the Millennium Falcon. He was wearing his blue Spiderman PJs, the ones he had to order special out of a catalogue because none of the local stores carried Spiderman pajamas that could fit a thirteen-year-old.

It was cold in the room, but A.D. didn't seem to notice. He was busy looking at the instruction page that came with the Millennium Falcon, holding it above his head, unfolded in the air, as if he were a driver stranded on the side of the road reading a roadmap. When the door opened, A.D. lowered the instruction sheet. It made a scrunchy, crinkling sound. He smiled mischievously at his brother, his brown eyes sparkling with zest, as if he'd been waiting for him. He looked exactly as he had on the last day Turtle had seen him alive two years ago.

"Get in here, quick, and close the door!" he called in a loud, conspiratorial whisper.

Turtle closed the door, but he did *not* go into the room. Instead, he retreated back into his own room; his heart beating so rapidly in his chest he thought it might burst. He climbed back in bed and this time he did pull the covers up over his head. He lay there trembling, his teeth chattering like a jackhammer. He thought about Rita, about how she deserved a better boyfriend than him, a boyfriend who wasn't so afraid. He lay quaking beneath the covers until morning.

❧ ❧ ❧

Uncle Johnny was a fun lovin' guy. The entire family adored Uncle Johnny until he got drunk. When Uncle Johnny drank too much the fun whooshed right out of him like air out of a flat tire, which is why after five years of marriage, Aunt Jenny left him. Aunt Jenny loved the fun Uncle Johnny—the Uncle Johnny who brought her flowers for no reason, or got up in the middle of the night and said "let's go on an adventure." Then they'd go crabbing in the shallows of Foster River with homemade crab traps. They'd catch a mess of crabs and Uncle Johnny would take them home and make Aunt Jenny his famous cracked crab soufflé for breakfast. Then they'd move out to the porch where they'd eat cracked crab soufflé and drink champagne as the sun came up.

Once they drove up the coast under the light of a full moon, stopping off at a bed & breakfast Uncle Johnny had secretly picked out for a romantic rendezvous.

Another time they went out to the end of Severn pier on a warm summer's night, engulfed in each other's arms looking for the aurora borealis. They never found it; Foster City wasn't far north enough, but that was all right because it was the romance cloaked in adventure that made the night for them.

The fun Uncle Johnny was a precious jewel. However, the mean Uncle

46

Johnny, the one who baited and insulted Aunt Jenny, who spent up his pay-check buying rounds of drinks before coming home angry and broke, ready to take his troubles out on his wife, was an asshole Aunt Jenny could no longer tolerate.

After five years of marriage, Aunt Jenny left Uncle Johnny and moved to Arizona to be with a man who treated her the way a woman ought to be treated. He even bought her a house with a swimming pool. Uncle Johnny moped around for two years after Aunt Jenny left. He stopped drinking and joined the church where he found religion. He hoped his new-found religion would lure Aunt Jenny back. He was lost without her.

His plan worked. One morning Uncle Johnny woke up and Aunt Jenny was lying next to him in bed as if nothing had ever happened. After Aunt Jenny returned, Uncle Johnny was a changed man. He came straight home from work every day. He spent his evenings at home with Aunt Jenny watching TV. Some nights there'd be no TV; instead, Aunt Jenny would tune in an oldies station on the radio, and they'd dance to The Manhattans and The Chi-Lites well into the night, just like the old days. The family was happy for Uncle Johnny. They knew how lonely the years without Aunt Jenny had been. Everyone was pleased he was getting his life back together.

Then Dad started wondering why Uncle Johnny didn't bring Aunt Jenny around anymore. She didn't show up at church with him on Sunday's either. Dad did some investigating and discovered Aunt Jenny hadn't returned to Uncle Johnny as he'd said. She was still living in Arizona with the man who bought her the house with the swimming pool. Dad decided to go over to Uncle Johnny's and confront him about the lie. Uncle Johnny met Dad at the door, and when Dad told him what he'd discovered, Uncle Johnny laughed and said Dad must be crazy. Aunt Jenny wasn't in Arizona in the house with the pool, she was in the kitchen making tacos. Soon after that, Uncle Johnny went away.

A.D. had said poor Uncle Johnny had taken a one way trip to the Twi-light Zone. He said it making his voice sound exactly like Rod Serling's, stiff and nasally. As morose as it was, Turtle thought it was the funniest thing the way A.D. stiffened his voice to sound like Serling on TV. A.D. could get an easy laugh out of him by saying: *Reason number thirty-six why Uncle Johnny has taken a one way trip to the Twilight Zone.*

Now, Turtle realized what had happened to Uncle Johnny wasn't so funny. Mabry had to call him three times to get ready for school that morning. She finally had to stand outside his bedroom door—*Don't make me come in there*—before he dragged himself from beneath the covers.

Can't she hear him in there?

When Turtle finally came out to use the bathroom he could hear A.D. fast at work behind closed doors putting the Millennium Falcon together. He heard paper rustling (A.D. referring to the instructions) then the sound of plastic pieces being snapped together.

How can she not hear that?

Turtle knew why his mother couldn't hear it, because *she* would not be joining him in the Twilight Zone. No way Josè; this was a solo ride, a one-way trip to the other side. One ticket, one passenger.

Turtle was relieved to leave for school that morning. At school he could think about Rita, and his classes, and even Ansley contemplating another ass whuppin—things that didn't make it seem as though he'd jumped the tracks and was going crazy as a bedbug.

He loved A.D. His older brother had been his best friend. He missed him terribly, they all did. But Turtle was the only one who could hear A.D. in the bedroom putting the Millennium Falcon together. Only he had taken his grief to insanity—to the Twilight Zone. A queasiness erupted in his stomach.

When Rita arrived in homeroom that morning, Turtle leapt from his seat and escorted her to hers, carrying her backpack in his arms as if it were a baby. His eyes scanned the students in the room and found everyone gaping at him with the exception of Ansley Meade, who was busy writing on the palm of his hand with a ballpoint pen.

The murmurs he heard heading back to his seat could have been embarrassing. He knew he was going to be the subject of teasing and playful taunts the next few days. That was the plan, to be so busy dealing with the taunts his classmates would hurl at him like hand grenades, he wouldn't be able to think about anything else—like going crazy, for instance.

"What's that all about?" Ross asked when Turtle returned to his seat. Ross's eyes were in a steady Ping-Pong match pinging from Rita to Turtle and back.

"She looked like she needed help," Turtle said, trying to sound cool.

Ross leaned in, cupped his pudgy hand around his mouth. "Are you hittin' that?" he whispered, a sly grin materializing on his lips.

"Shut up!" Turtle snapped. His anger rose quickly, a flash flood coming on without warning. He narrowed his gaze at Ross.

"I'm just sayin', if you are, you should know the senoritas like muff diving." Ross winked and began making lascivious darting motions with his tongue. This enraged Turtle even more.

He leaned in close to Ross, who smelled of *Doritos*. "Say one more word about her, and I swear I'll beat the meatballs off your fat ass right here in class." *Boom!* Snickers erupted from the students in their immediate vicinity.

Ross's eyes grew wide. "Touchy," he said with a snort. It was the last thing he'd say to Turtle all morning.

The news about Turtle and Rita spread quickly. She did nothing to dispel the gossip which gave Turtle hope. By lunch the news about the fat boy and the new girl was all over the eighth grade. Despite the welcome distraction, the queasiness in his stomach remained.

By the end of the school day, Turtle knew what he had to do. He had to face his fears. *For Rita.* He had to go home, go inside the room and engage with the figment of his imagination. Perhaps if he did that the figment would go away and he could get back to his life, a life made better now because Rita was in it.

He was sulky and silent during the walk home from school.

"Everybody's talking about us," Rita said. She was walking next to him, close enough to hold his hand although she didn't. The polish on her nails was a pastiche of blue, pink, yellow and bright, bright green. Turtle nodded. "Do you mind?" she asked. Turtle shook his head.

Of course he didn't mind. *Turtle has a girlfriend* had a wonderful ring to it. Yet the queasiness fox-trotted in his belly, reminding him that before he could delight in the fact that Rita was in his life, he had to deal with the crazies.

You face your fears, you conquer them, he thought. He also thought that most of his life he'd been a scaredy-cat, but the price of living his life in fear had gotten too high.

"You're awfully quiet today, honey," Rita said. "Is something wrong?"

Yes, there's something wrong. I'm falling in love with you and at the same time I'm going crazy. Crazy in love hahahahahaaaaa!

"Just tired," he replied. "I couldn't get to sleep last night. Say, umm…can I have your phone number?" he asked out of the blue, again shifting the dance.

"Of course," she said, and he could tell from the delight ringing in her voice, she was glad he'd asked.

Instead of feeling his own delight, the sickening feeling in his stomach increased. Bile rose into his throat and he swallowed it back down.

They exchanged numbers in front of her building. Just before they parted, she squeezed his hand. If she noticed it was sweaty, she didn't say anything.

"You get some rest now, honey."

Those words should have made his heart sing, but all he could think was that he was going home, and when he got home he was going into the room. Hopefully, while he was in there he'd find his sanity. If he didn't, he wondered if the bed next to Uncle Johnny's was available.

Turtle arrived home and headed straight for his room. Mabry didn't stir from watching her stories. This time he was grateful for the lack of attention. As he neared his bedroom door he could hear a soft whirring sound. It sounded like a tiny electric motor. *Motorized,* he thought. A.D. had finished putting the Millennium Falcon together and was running it across the floor.

Arriving in his own bedroom, Turtle dumped his books onto the bed. Then he went down the hall to the bathroom where he took a good, long piss. When he emerged from the bathroom, he could hear the small motor starting and stopping in A.D.'s room.

No one can hear it but me.

He came back down and stood in front of A.D.'s door. The air around the door no longer seemed cold. It seemed...normal. For some reason, that made his skin crawl. At that moment, he remembered a scene in *The Shining.* Jack Torrance had gone into a bathroom in the Overlook Hotel and found a beautiful, naked young lady in the bathtub. The beautiful lady got out of the bathtub and walked slowly to him. They started kissing, and while they were kissing, Jack looked in the mirror and saw he wasn't kissing a beautiful naked lady at all. He was kissing a corpse, her misshapen, decaying body covered with festering sores.

Turtle didn't see that part of the movie. Turtle never saw any of the scary parts of the horror movies he and A.D. watched together. Turtle spent the scary parts cowering in his seat, his hands over his eyes.

What's happening now? What's happening now?

A.D. always patiently laid out for him what was happening during the scary parts and told him when it was safe to open his eyes.

Turtle now closed his eyes for a moment and said a prayer: *Dear God, give me the strength to go into A.D.'s room and see the room for what it really is.* He prayed that the room would be as it had been for the past two years—quiet, tidy, and unoccupied.

The motor was starting up again. *Duty calls.* Turtle gripped the doorknob so tightly his fingers ached. He was afraid, but he was going in with his eyes wide open. He turned the knob and entered.

CHAPTER FIVE

A.D. was seated on the floor. The Millennium Falcon, all put together, was in his lap. He was examining the rotating gun turret.

When Turtle entered, A.D. looked up from the Falcon. "What's up, Punkinpuss?" He was no longer wearing the Spiderman PJs. He'd changed into a t-shirt and jeans. He smiled at Turtle with a welcoming warmth that tamped down some of Turtles fear. "Sorry I couldn't wait. I've been waiting two years to put this damn thing together." He went back to rotating the gun turret.

Turtle stepped into the room. "You're not really here," he said, the words struggling from his dry throat.

"What?"

"You're not really here," Turtle said louder. "You're in my head."

A.D. chuckled. It was his *you're behaving like an asshole* laugh. "Yeah, right," he said. He looked at Turtle and rolled his eyes. "This thing didn't come together all by itself. It would have been more fun if you'd have done it with me. I should've waited." His expression turned contrite.

"It's cool," Turtle said. He came further into the room. His confrontation with the figment wasn't going as he'd hoped. At least he was no longer afraid. "You put the Millennium Falcon in my room the other day, didn't you?"

"Yeah. It was my secret signal to you that I was coming back."

"I'm going crazy," Turtle said with a forlorn sigh. "I'm gonna wind up in the sanitarium with Uncle Johnny."

A.D. set the Millennium Falcon on the floor. "No, you're not, Mush-mouse. There's nothing wrong with you. I'm back."

"That's impossible," Turtle screeched.

"I know it is. It's kind of complicated but…" His smile broadened. "I'm back. I'm really back." He snatched the Millennium Falcon off the floor. "Check it out," he said, offering it to Turtle.

Turtle shook his head and took a step back. "I gotta go," he said.

"Okay. I'll be here."

When Turtle got back into his own room he dove into the stash box and with shaky hands unwrapped a *Chocodile.* If he were ten years older he would have poured himself a stiff drink. He bit into the *Chocodile,* savoring the sugary sweetness. It helped clear his head.

"What the fuck!" he cried out. He wanted to call Rita. He wanted to talk this out with somebody, but what would he say to her? Anything he said would sound like crazy talk, and if he made that call he knew he could kiss his quote-unquote *girlfriend* goodbye.

Turtle finished the *Chocodile* and slumped back on the bed, his head resting against the pillow, his thoughts swimming. He had to work through this problem on his own. He was starting to believe A.D. wasn't a figment of his imagination. *A.D. is a ghost,* he mused. Turtle was afraid of ghosts, had always been afraid of ghosts, but he wasn't afraid of this one. How could he be? This ghost was his brother back from the dead (if that's what he really was). What does he want? Does he need help crossing over? Is he confined to the bedroom?

Turtle moved to his desk and began making a list of the questions he wanted answered. When the list was complete, he went back across the hall to get some answers from the thing he believed to be his dead brother's ghost.

Rita

On July fifteenth nineteen eighty-one, a man walked into a bodega in Patterson New Jersey and shot Rita Calderon's father in the face. The man didn't know Rita Calderon's father. Josè Calderon was in the bodega buying a pack of Camels. Wrong time, wrong place is how Rita often heard it described. She was five years-old when it happened.

Josè Calderon had seven children with his wife Maria, and two more he didn't talk about. He loved them all, yet the second from the youngest of his legitimate children, Rita, caused a golden glow to appear in his eyes.

"That one is special," he'd tell Maria. "While her brothers and sisters are playing, Marguerita is sitting alone, thinking of ways to help."

It was true. Rita was a helpful child. Rita wanted to help save the whales, the earth, and her mother from the back-breaking labor she endured cleaning white people's homes to help make ends meet.

After Rita's father died of a gunshot wound to the head, Rita's mother found it increasingly difficult to raise the four children that remained at home. Rita and her younger sister, Tora, were sent to live with the eldest of the Calderon children, Sam, and his young wife Elena, in Hasbrouck Heights.

Sam was tall, handsome, and good with his hands. He worked as a mechanic at a local car dealership. He was a customer favorite with his easy-going style and deep knowledge of their cars. He freely gave out advice to help customers keep their cars out of his shop.

Elena was a very pretty girl. She was a natural blonde with Castilian features. Elena, who grew up in the suburbs where she was spoiled by her parents, was what Rita called *a prissy lady*. She didn't like getting her hands dirty. She didn't like doing anything that seemed like work. Elena didn't like Rita, either. She didn't like the way Sam enjoyed talking to his younger sister. She especially didn't like the prideful glow in Sam's eyes when Rita entered a room.

She's not his daughter, she's his sister. Why should he carry on about her so?

Elena had put off having children their first three years of marriage, but when she saw the way Sam looked at his sister, she decided to get pregnant as soon as she could.

"I see the way you look at Rita and Tora. You love children, and I want to share that love with you," Elena said. Sam was delighted. He'd come from a large family and wanted a large family of his own. He'd been wanting to start a family since their wedding night.

On March seventh, nineteen eighty-five, Elena gave birth to fat-cheeked baby boy named Sam Junior. Baby Sam was happy and healthy, with sandy brown hair that they marveled at because he wasn't born bald like most of the boys in the family. His arrival into the Calderon family brought much joy into all of their lives. Elena especially enjoyed the way her husband looked at her when she held their son in her arms.

Life was good, but things changed one day when Elena entered the nursery carrying laundry Tora had done. Eighteen-month-old Sam was standing near the toy box playing with his auntie, Rita. Baby Sam had a sixth sense about his mother. He clearly adored her and always looked up whenever she entered a room, even if no one else knew she was there. When Elena entered the nursery that day, Sam didn't look up. His eyes, filled with a joyful glow, were on Rita.

Elena began to feel threatened. *Who is this child that comes into my life and steals my family's love? I will not have it.* She vowed within herself that Rita must go.

A month after Rita started the eighth grade, the family got word that

Rita's abuela in Foster City, Delaware was having problems. Her memory was starting to fade. Some days she couldn't remember how to get home from the senior center, which was only five blocks from where she lived.

Abuela Maritza was an independent woman. Her sons and grandsons and granddaughters all encouraged her to move to New York or New Jersey where she could be closer to family. Abuela Maritza refused. Foster City was her home.

"I have a wonderful idea," Elena said at dinner one evening. They were having corned beef and cabbage. Elena enjoyed serving foods of other nationalities. She said it gave the family *culture.* "I worry so much for your abuela, Sam. I think since she will not come to her family, one of her family members should go and live with her."

Sam thought it was a splendid idea. "But who?" he asked. "Her brothers, sisters and grandchildren are either too old or have jobs and family responsibilities of their own. I cannot see any of us uprooting ourselves and moving to Foster City."

Elena agreed. "We need to choose a family member who doesn't have any obligations. Rita, for instance."

Rita had known this day was coming. She knew from the looks she received day in and day out that Elena was jealous of her. It pained her that Sam, her own brother, couldn't see the looks or hear the veiled insults tossed at her daily. Sam was blinded by his love for Elena. Rita didn't understand this kind of love between a man and a woman, but she knew her brother had been corrupted by it.

Tora cried and said if Rita left then she wanted to go, too. Sam said he wouldn't hear of either of them leaving. After all, Rita was just a child.

"I want to go," said Rita. "If Abuela Maritza needs help, I want to be there to help her."

"There. You see?" said Elena, jumping at the chance to seal her sister-in-law's fate. "She wants to go. Everyone says how much your sister loves to help. Now's her chance to do some good."

Eight months into the eighth grade, Rita was again uprooted from her home and moved to Foster City. She didn't mind moving so late in the school year. She had always enjoyed visiting her grandparents in Foster City. The small city lifestyle agreed with her. In Foster City it would be easy to keep to herself. She promised herself that she would be happy despite the circumstances surrounding her presence there, happy to help Abuela Maritza, happy to be away from Elena. And one day, she'd send for Tora and her mother.

Rita waited in the vestibule of the apartment building until she was certain Theo had departed. He'd almost spotted her coming back out the day before. It was the day she broke up the fight or ass whuppin' as Theo had called it. She'd pulled open the vestibule door, ready to head home, only to discover Theo was still standing in front of the building, an odd glow in his eyes. She quickly shut the door before he saw her.

Sucking in her breath, Rita now opened the vestibule door and peered out onto the street. She knew if Theo saw her, she'd have to make up a quick excuse as to why she was coming out so soon after going in. He wasn't there. She looked down the block and caught a glimpse of him sprinting away. He looked so silly, the chubby boy running up the street, that a smile appeared on her lips. She liked Theo, and she was glad he'd taken her to his special place, The Lots. He was her first and only friend in her new hometown.

She hadn't planned on making friends with him. She hadn't planned any of it. She was on her way home when she saw the boy who'd teased her by pulling her hair her first day at the new school. The boy was threatening Theo. Two older boys were helping him. Outrage rose in Rita. She realized in that moment that Theo's chubby cheeks reminded her of her nephew, Sam Junior.

"Get your hands off my boyfriend," she called out, knowing full well she had to do something about the injustice that was about to occur. She had to help.

The mean boys were all cowards. She'd suspected as much. She'd heard her father telling her brothers about cowards running in packs, like wolves. Separate the leader and they'll all scatter like the chickens they are. Her father was right, of course. She was glad she'd helped Theo. He was smart and not afraid for others to know it. Theo was brave, although he didn't realize he was just yet. She'd help with that as well.

As Rita journeyed up the dusty road she could hear the calling of the cats, like a siren's song. That meant she was nearing the falling down house she now called home. She could smell the cats as well. It was an obvious odor that saturated the air around the house. Cats weren't dirty animals, but they were hard to clean up after because they buried their feces like precious jewels. Some of them used the litter boxes she was constantly cleaning, but many of Abuela's fifteen cats preferred to go outside where she couldn't find it. *Follow the odor and you'll find the shit.*

Rita arrived on the porch where she removed her jacket and then her top, the afternoon breeze offering refreshment to her skin. She hung them outside as a precaution against picking up any of the cat smell that lingered inside. All of Rita's school clothes were hanging out in the open air, arrayed across the porch like a tapestry of Spanish art.

Two of the cats, George Bailey, a scrawny Siamese mix (who despite Don Juan's posturing was Abuela's favorite), and Desdemona, a skittish gray and black American shorthair, appeared from under the porch. Rita scooped the smallest into her arms. "Hola, George Baily." He sniffed the tips of her fingers and turned his head away, as if Rita had been the one hanging out under the porch all day. With the cat cradled in her arms, she pushed the door open and entered the house she now called home.

"Abuela? Estoy en casa."

CHAPTER SIX

Turtle

They talked.

As the setting sun pushed puppet-like shadows across the carpet, Turtle got comfortable with the notion of chatting with his dead brother's ghost. For the next three days, Turtle spent his afternoons after school, and evenings after supper, in A.D.'s room. Talking. Reminiscing. Horsin' around.

Not long ago, he could think of no better way to spend an evening than chatting with Rita on the phone. Now, he could think of something far better—hanging out with his best friend, big brother.

"Hey, remember Garbage Pail Kids? Remember how all the teachers got together and outlawed them at school, cause they were *dangerous*?" A.D. asked, making the *dangerous* come out in a ridiculous, mocking voice. Both boys got a good sized chuckle out of that one. They'd been lying on the floor, reading comic books, just like the old days. Turtle was catching A.D. up on issues of the X-Men he'd missed. The room was a mess—just the way they liked it.

"Yeah. They called all the parents, and Moms made you throw yours out 'cause they were so *gross*." Turtle made a gaging gesture and both boys nearly busted a gut.

"Not all of them," A.D. said. He sat up with a super-sized shit-eatin' grin on his face.

"You still got Garbage Pail Kids? You been holding out on me, dude?" Turtle put his comic book down.

"The best ones, too. Oozy Suzy, Fryin' Brian, Corroded Carl."

"Bull ticky," Turtle snapped, sounding like an old jazzman.

"I'm tellin' ya, Dude."

"Okay, okay. Here's one you can't possibly have—Adam Bomb."

A.D.'s shit-eatin' grin widened. "The one with a mushroom cloud comin' out of the dude's head?"

"That would be Adam Bomb, Tom."

"Got it," A.D. said and did a little touchdown dance.

"No way Josè! That's a collector's item."

"Got it!" A.D. said again, with authority.

He moved to his closet, pulled out a card box with photos of religious Christmas cards on top, and dumped a pile of *Garbage Pail Kids* trading cards onto the floor. Turtle's mouth dropped open—*shut your trap or you'll catch flies*—dumbfounded. He rifled through the cards. There were cards in A.D.'s collection he didn't know existed.

Turtle couldn't remember the last time he'd laughed so good. Yeah, he knew he was hanging out with a ghost—either ghost or he going crazy, and he was opting for ghost, definitely ghost—but it felt in some ways as though his big brother had truly returned. He knew he missed A.D., but until he was sitting in the room talking to him into the night, he didn't realize his mortal soul had been hollowed out by the loss. But now, the empty spaces were beginning to fill in.

He asked his questions, the ones he'd written down in his notebook, and got very little in the way of answers. After three evenings hanging out with his brother, he no longer cared.

At school he was different. He seemed happier, more confident. Everyone assumed it was because of Rita. Rita did, too. In class, he raised his hand freely and called out his answers in a loud voice, failing to notice that each time he did, Ansley Meade shuddered with rage. He carried Rita's backpack everywhere, making a big fuss over her during the school day. Yet when the school day was over, he always had a reasonable excuse as to why he had to get right home.

Moms was none-the-wiser. She didn't budge from zoning out in front of the TV until it was time to make supper. And the best part was when Turtle got home and hustled down the hall to A.D.'s room, he was always there, waiting with a big conspiratorial grin, as if he'd been dealt a hand with four aces, and the only ones who knew the cards he held were them.

"My friend's Kool," A.D. blurted.

"My friend's Kool *Aid!*" It was a refrain the boys used to do all the time, their take on a popular *Kool-Aid* commercial. Whenever one of the boys blurted *My friend's Kool,* the other had to immediately follow with *My friend's Kool-Aid*. It was a joke that never got old.

"You used to love you some Kool Aid, Mushmouse," A.D. said, the laughter still on his lips.

"I still like Kool-Aid." Turtle hesitated, his voice dropping lower. "Moms doesn't buy it as much as she used to." The funk was swirling in his belly again. *Unwanted.* He pushed it away. *No reason for the funk anymore, not with A.D. sitting right here.*

"You know what I could use right now. A nice *Tahitian Treat,*" A.D. said, rolling onto his side. Turtle's expression turned wary. "What?" asked A.D.

"You...can drink soda?" Turtle asked.

"Will you stop with the spooky talk? I can drink whatever the fuck I wanna drink. How many times I gotta tell you, I'm not a ghost, Punkinpuss. I'm...*back!*"

"I want to believe it, A.D. But it's impossible."

The joy bled from A.D.'s face, leaving him with a frighteningly sullen appearance. "It is impossible. But sometimes the impossible is possible."

"But...you're confined to this room."

A.D. scrambled to his feet, outraged. "Who says? I never said I was confined to this room. Did I ever tell you I was confined to this room?" His voice took on a sharp edge.

How can she not hear that?

"No, but..." Turtle thought about ghosts being confined to certain areas. *I'm not a ghost, Punkinpuss.* "I thought—"

"I didn't leave 'cause I didn't have a reason to. But now I do." A.D. stomped toward the bedroom door. "Let's go."

"W...where?"

"To Miller's Grocery. I'm a hankerin' for a nice, frosty *Tahitian Treat,*" he said, doing his impression of a cowboy. The storm had passed. "You comin' with me, pardner?" The conspiratorial grin inched its way back onto his lips.

⚥ ⚥ ⚥

"Goin' out," Turtle called, wishing his mother would get up off her lazy ass and come ask where he was headed so close to supper.

"Okay," she called back over the sound of *Family Feud.*

I shoulda known. She don't care about me. The funk that normally accompanied such thoughts didn't appear this time, because now Turtle did have someone who cared about him. He wanted his mother to come because he'd been wondering if he was the only one could see the ghost—not that he was crazy or anything. He was certain A.D. had returned, and sharing this with his parents would lift the burden of A.D.'s death.

A pumpkin colored sun was sinking into the cloudless western sky, adding an orange glow to the late afternoon. For the first time in quite a while, Turtle's world was colorful and vivid. From the moment they hit the street, A.D. was full of questions about the changes in the neighborhood.

Who moved into the Johnson house?

The Curries.

They have any kids?

No—they're old. Like fifty.

When they reached the corner of Union Avenue, A.D. stopped. "It's gone," he said. He was staring at the spot where the "haunted" apartment building once stood. His eyelids grew heavy with remorse. "Wow," he said, his voice a whisper.

"Yeah," Turtle replied, wondering what his brother was thinking.

A.D. stared at the modern apartment structure that was now standing where the old abandoned apartment building once stood. "Life goes on," he said, barely audibly. It was a grown up thing for him to say, and Turtle didn't know how to respond. He considered telling his brother he was missed, but passed on the idea because it would make him sound like a wussy.

By the time they arrived on Prospect Avenue, A.D. had turned giddy again. "I can't remember when's I last had a *Tahitian Treat*."

"Me, either." Turtle felt a warmth on his skin, and knew it wasn't from the setting sun. He and A.D. were walking down to Miller's together, just as they'd done a thousand times before.

Visions of when A.D. had to hold his hand to cross the street scrolled before his eyes. They'd venture down to Miller's, broke as a joke, and stand in front of the big glass candy display case that used to run along the back wall of the store, debating the candies they planned to buy when they got their allowance money.

The days of planning made the candy even more delicious. *Charleston Chews, Sweet Tarts, Now and Laters, Pixie Stix, and Twizzlers* were all made sweeter by the wait. The waiting tickled their taste buds, and by the time they'd made their purchases, the candy had taken on an otherworldly deliciousness.

A.D. particularly loved *Milky Way* bars. He'd buy five or six at a time and store them in the stash box to pull out while they lay in bed at night reading their comics with flashlights under the covers. He'd tease Turtle, whose candy was always quickly eaten up, about not sharing the *Milky Ways* with him, yet he always did.

"You know when a *Tahitian Treat* tastes its absolute best?" A. D. asked as they moved past Crone Drugs, nearing Miller's.

"When it's hot out?"

"Nuh-uh. When it's stolen."

"Good one," Turtle said and laughed.

"I'm serious."

The warmth Turtle had been feeling moments earlier, evaporated, his skin prickling with the chill of a boy who'd just plunged into the cold depths of a swimming pool. His brother was smiling, but there was something different about his smile.

"I have the money," Turtle said, patting his pocket.

"It's not about the money. You gotta trust me on this."

Turtle now recognized what was different about A.D.'s smile. It was a challenging smile, the kind boys used on a dare. *I dare you to jump the fence and go into Miss Fowler's garden.*

"But—"

"Look, man. If you don't trust me, it's okay. I been gone a long time. I understand. We don't have to get a *Tahitian Treat.*" A.D. wet his lips and turned, as if to walk away.

"Yes, we do," Turtle blurted, stopping him mid-turn. "I want one, too." At that moment, Turtle's tongue felt as dry as the Sahara in summertime. Nothing better to whet his whistle than a nice, frosty *Tahitian Treat.*

It took all of three minutes for A.D. to explain how to do it. "You go into the back and slide the soda case open real slow like, so old man Miller doesn't hear it slide. Then you just twist off the cap and drink it down, right there on the spot.

"I know you'll be afraid, but that's the reason it tastes so good. Your adrenaline'll be flowing. Adrenaline makes every experience better. You'll see."

A feather of doubt twisted in Turtle's chest. He tried thinking the fear away because if there was one certainty in Turtle's life, it was how much he trusted his big brother. That hadn't changed in the two years since A.D. had been gone. If anything, his trust had grown.

And why shouldn't I trust him? He's never given me a lick of bad advice.

When at eight, Turtle decided to open a lemonade stand, but instead of lemonade, he'd sell his favorite, cherry Kool-Aid, it was A.D. who warned him against it, telling him the big kids would come around and drink up his Kool-Aid without paying the twenty-five cents he was charging. Turtle didn't listen, and when the older kids came around, threatening to drink all his Kool-Aid and trash his stand, it was A.D. who stood up to them, alone, and got them to back down.

When Turtle was nine he discovered he couldn't hit a baseball to save his life. It was A.D. who took the time to teach him not to fear a ball hurtling at him at what felt like a thousand miles an hour. He told him don't worry about it, promised him that by the end of summer, Turtle would be homerin' like Darryl Strawberry.

A.D. took him down to The Lots—those days it was Shea Stadium—and pitched to him every day the first month of summer. He started by standing just ten feet in front of him, lobbing the ball to Turtle underhand, as if he were lobbing eggs he didn't want to break.

He made Turtle swing the heavy bat, the one whose barrel took forever to get moving through the air. By the end of the first week, Turtle had the bat movin' real good, hitting every ball lobbed in his direction. By the end of the month, Turtle was swinging the lighter bat at fast speed pitches from forty-six feet away, connecting with them with Strawberry-like ease, sending the occasional pitch sailing over A.D's head and on into the creek. A.D would holler *Mushmouse done hit himself a homer*, and they'd laugh. He still couldn't hit A.D.'s knuckle ball, but he could knock the stitches off just about anything else.

A.D.'s words of advice had always been nothing but good.

But this is different. This is stealing.

True. But it was A.D., his brother miraculously back from the grave who was telling him...no, not telling, *asking* him to steal. He didn't have to do it. But after all A.D. had done for him, he *wanted* to do it. Didn't he owe him this one thing?

Turtle's guilt over his role in his brother's death pushed its way into his consciousness. It was always lurking in the back somewhere, but he'd built a formidable dam to hold the guilt at bay. Now that his brother was asking him to do such a scary thing, a crack had appeared in the dam, and the guilt came trickling in. No way he could avoid it.

He owed this to A.D. What was the big deal, anyway? It wasn't like he was robbing a bank. It was one little soda. It wouldn't even be missed, and he was thirsty—very, *very* thirsty. *I need a nice, frosty Tahitian Treat. And I need it now*, he thought, bolstering himself. *A.D.'s got my back. He always has.*

A.D. went on to explain that this was something Turtle needed to experience alone. That was a twist he hadn't seen coming. A.D. told him he'd keep old man Miller occupied at the front of the store while Turtle eased into the back to have his special treat.

When Turtle heard the change in the plan, a part of him wanted to call it off. It was starting to sound dangerous. But wasn't danger the point of it? *A.D.'s got my back. He always has.*

Shoulder-to-shoulder, the boys entered the store. The door clattered open, the bell above it sounding their entrance, and gently closed behind them, guided by a whispering hydraulic. It wasn't old man Miller seated behind counter who greeted them, but his wife, Mrs. Miller, who had sweet, doughy features, pudgy arms, and the kindly disposition of a church lady. That was a stroke of luck. Mrs. Miller, who sipped tea from a Styrofoam cup and always had a softback novel open in front of her when she was behind the counter, wasn't as keen on checking the mirrors as her husband.

As the door whispered shut, Turtle realized there'd been another change to the plan. A.D. was no longer with him.

✗ ✗ ✗

Mrs. Miller looked up from her reading: "Hi there, Dawson. Surprised to see you so close to supper time. Your mother send you for something she forgot?" she asked, her voice sounding as sweet as *Pixie Stix*.

"Umm, no. Umm…yeah, I mean…Milk," Turtle rasped, his tongue dry as kindling, lips trembling.

"Get your milk and don't play around. I know your mother likes the family to have supper together. Go on, now."

"Yes, ma'am," Turtle rasped and headed toward the rear of the store on legs feeling very much like angel hair pasta. *That's just my adrenaline flowin'*, he told himself as he wobble-walked to the rear of the store. *Gonna make that Tahitian Treat taste soo good.*

The dairy case, stocked with milk, chocolate milk, yogurt and cottage cheese, ran along the left rear wall. The soda case was around the corner, ducking out of sight against the far wall, toward the store's center aisle. The only way Mrs. Miller could see him back there was if she looked into the surveillance mirrors, which she wasn't inclined to do. As Turtle neared the dairy case, the front door clattered open again. That was another stroke of luck, because the woman who entered and Mrs. Miller seemed as thick as thieves.

"Hey there, Annabelle, I haven't seen you since this morning," called Coralee Calendar, who thought nothing of shooting down to Miller's any time of day in slippers and a hideous floral print housedress, her stretch wig sitting askew atop her head like a bird's nest in a crooked tree

"This morning? You mean since two o'clock, don'tcha?" Laughter.

"You got me. I forgot something else. Girl, my brain is about as good as the Easter Bunny at Christmas dinner."

The two women laughed again, and as they did, Turtle continued past the dairy case, making a right at the *Miller Lite* display with the Bob Uecker

63

standee—*Less filling! Tastes great!*—and on around the corner to the soda case, where he could no longer be seen. As he neared the case, the *Tahitian Treat* bottles called out to him through the thick glass. *Less filling, tastes great,* he thought with a nervous smile. Amidst more laughter, he began sliding the soda case door open. A hatch of butterflies released in his belly. If the door slid along the track too quickly Mrs. Miller would hear it, so Turtle inched the heavy door along, keeping the noise to a minimum.

Beads of sweat appeared on his forehead like the morning dew on his father's Buick. The case was nearly open and the cold was bleeding out, yet sweat began cascading down his forehead, dripping into his eyes, stinging them. The bottles of *Tahitian Treat* on the third row were sweating, too. The moisture on the bottles made his mouth water.

Gonna taste soo good.

The women at the front of the store laughed again as he gripped one of the ice cold bottles. His heart thumped against his chest as he withdrew the drink and guided the chill box door shut. *Easy, easy.*

"I better get what I came for before I forget again," Coralee Calendar chimed, and as they shared another laugh, Turtle felt his window of opportunity rapidly closing.

He twisted the cap. At first he couldn't get a good grip. His hands were slick with sweat and the bottle was slick with dew. So he held his tee shirt over the cap like a glove. *Snap.* The seal broke, carbonated gas whispered out, the hiss of an alley cat, and the cap twisted off with ease.

Turtle was smiling as he brought the mouth of the bottle to his lips. It was a guilty smile. *A.D.'s gonna be so proud of me,* he thought. The soda spilled into his mouth, and A.D. was right. It tasted soo good, better than good. This Tahitian Treat was damn-near the best thing he'd ever tasted. He allowed the cool soda to fill his mouth, the bubbles tickling his tongue, widening his grin as cool liquid slid down his throat. He tipped the bottle more, and the soda overflowed, spilling down the sides of his mouth, dripping onto his chin, and Turtle thought *this is how Conan The Barbarian drinks his sodas.* He slurped his frosty treat like a warrior.

Crash!

As he was nearly finished, a six-foot display of disposable diapers midway up the center aisle tumbled over, the colorful cardboard boxes crashing to the floor. *Plop, plop, plop, plop!*

"Dawson, what are you doing back there?"

Turtle was startled by the crash, and startled even more by Mrs. Miller's call. His jittery hand accidentally dumped soda down the front of his shirt.

"Nothin'," he called back. Depositing the near empty bottle onto a shelf, he hustled for the dairy cooler.

"I told you not to play around," Mrs. Miller called. She sounded annoyed with him.

"I'm comin'!" He snatched up a gallon of milk and high-tailed it for the front of the store.

He tried ignoring the oddball way Mrs. Miller was looking at his sopping brow and drenched t-shirt. She didn't say anything, though. She bagged the milk, told him to say hi to his mama, and he got the hell out of there.

❧ ❧ ❧

A.D. was draped over a litter basket near the corner bustin' a gut when Turtle approached. "I told you it was good, but damn, dude, you didn't have ta take a bath in it," he said, his breath hitching he was laughing so hard. There was meanness in his eyes.

"Not funny," Turtle snarled, his voice thick with anger. "You should have seen the way she was looking at me."

A.D. stopped laughing. "How was she looking at you?"

"Like she knew I was up to something bad back there." His eyes were wet with angry tears.

"You're right, Mushmouse. It was a dirty trick. That's why I couldn't let you go through with it. I'm the one knocked over the *Pull-Ups* display when I saw the lady comin'. Saved your ass again, sucker." A cautious smile pushed onto A.D.'s lips.

"Why didn't you come in with me like you said?" Turtle asked, his eyes stinging with embarrassment.

"I wanted to. But how could I? Mrs. Miller takes a look at me, a boy who's been dead going on two years, and what do I tell her?"

"You tell her the truth. You're back. It's a miracle. Miracles happen all the time," Turtle replied.

"No they don't," A.D. said, his words taking on a sudden, seething tone. "The only thing happens all the time is bad stuff. It's the only thing you can count on, bro. Come on." He started walking.

Turtle watched his brother walking away from him. He'd forgotten about this side of A.D., the sunny sky one moment, giving way to a twisting tornado the next. "It tasted real good," Turtle called. He started up the street after him. "Just like you said."

The storm in A.D.'s eyes passed. He apologized all the way home. Turtle accepted his brother's apology. *No harm, no foul, right?* But he was still shaken by the experience, made worse by the stiffening stickiness of his slowly drying, soda-soaked t-shirt.

To put a smile on his face, A.D. trucked out a golden oldie. "You're not only my brother, you know. You're my best friend, and my friend's Kool."

He waited several moments, checking Turtle's expression, his brown eyes hopeful. Finally the specter of a smile, like a break in the clouds, appeared on Turtle's lips.

"My friends Kool *Aid!*" Turtle said softly. Slow laughter, like ripples in a brook, spilled from both of the boys. The laughter continued to build until they had to stop walking and hold their sides that were now aching with stitches of glorious pain.

The queer looks they received from passers-by made the joke even funnier. They couldn't stop laughing.

By the time they arrived home, they were once again best, best friends.

They started up the walk. "You know I can't come in with you," A.D. said midway up.

Turtle had suspected as much. "I know. When?" he asked.

"Soon."

"They miss you, too," Turtle said, giving birth to an uncomfortable moment of silence. "It's cool," he added. "I'm glad you came back."

"Me, too," A.D. said somberly.

"Where're ya goin' now?"

"The Other Place." Turtle didn't ask about *The Other Place.* Intuition told him *The Other Place* was not to be discussed.

By the time Turtle pushed through the front door, his brother was gone. He didn't walk away. He didn't disappear like ghosts in the movies either, at least not in front of Turtle's eyes. Turtle looked down to pull out his keys. When he raised his eyes again, A.D. was gone.

He entered the house, wondering if his parents had missed him at supper. *Probably not. Probably didn't even notice I wasn't there.*

He was too full of *Tahitian Treat* adventure to eat anyway, so he dropped the milk off in the fridge, and headed for his room, hoping that when he got there, A.D. might be waiting for him. He stopped midway up the hall, surprised to see his father standing outside his bedroom door. Stan Dawson was clutching the fully assembled Millennium Falcon in trembling hands.

❧ ❧ ❧

He'd been observing the boy for several weeks now. It was obvious to anyone who gave a damn about children that the boy was lonely and in pain. The man's heart went out to the boy, but he knew soon enough the boy would be happy, happier than he'd ever been because soon the boy would join the Teddy Bear Club. His mind flashed on the boy's parents, and he felt sick to his stomach. It literally sickened him to think that parents could be so cruel. Why bring a child into the world if you're not going to give him anything but unconditional love? That's what children need, and that's all he ever wanted for any of the children he rescued.

The sick feeling passed as he realized the boy would soon be away from his ungrateful parents, soon on his way to the kind of happiness he deserved.

It was time to purchase a mannequin.

CHAPTER SEVEN

Rita

He was different.

Rita was reading to the cats—*Wifey*, by Judy Blume. Elena would have thrown a tantrum if Rita'd tried reading the book while she lived with them. *Sam, I will not have your sister reading this smut while living under my roof.* Hint, hint. This was Rita's rebellion read. *I'm not under your roof anymore, Elena.* She was finding the book quite enjoyable, and it seemed to be one of the cats' favorites.

Today, however, she was having a hard time concentrating on the words because her mind kept finding its way to Theo. He seemed different lately, and she couldn't put her finger on why. It was as if she were tasting something sweet, yet there was another spice underneath, a flavor she knew but couldn't quite place. She ran her encounters with Theo through her mind, like a football coach reviewing game film.

He was so sweet and shy the afternoon she'd rescued him. *Our first date.* He was even sweeter the following day when he opened up to her about his dead brother at The Lots. And just as sweet the day after that, as well, yet at the same time, he seemed distant. He didn't shun her, not outwardly anyway. *And isn't it just like a boy to ask for your phone number and then never call.*

That was the start of it, the afternoon he'd asked for her phone number. *I couldn't get to sleep last night.* At the time, she'd taken what he'd said at face value. Now, she was having her doubts.

Rita sighed audibly. Boys were so confounding. She liked Theo, though, with his cherubic face, wiry hair, and unsure way of speaking. She found his shyness endearing, and envisioned them spending more time together. She could see herself telling him all about her abuela and the cats during a summer picnic at The Lots. She'd tell him why she lied about where she lived (*I was ashamed*), and they'd laugh (*No need to be*). One day he'd hold her hand and, perhaps, they'd even kiss.

I'm not here for a boyfriend. I'm here to take care of my abuela. The thought rained onto her imaginings, and she scolded herself for being so silly. She tried pushing the Theo questions aside.

Can he smell the cats on me? Try as she might, all roads led back to him.

Don Juan, the big orange tabby, nudged her hand. He wanted her to turn the page. "Sorry. I haven't finished *this* page yet." She moved her hand to her nose and sniffed it.

Don Juan was the ruler of the roost. Abuela said that when Papi Tito died, Don Juan considered himself the man of the house and started acting accordingly. Two nights after papi died, Don Juan came into her bedroom and tried getting into bed with her. As lonely as she felt, Abuela worried that if she let Don Juan into her bed, she'd eventually have a bed filled with cats. When Tito was alive, the bed—at least at night—had always been off limits to the cats. That was his one rule about them.

She attempted to set Don Juan back in his box in the breakfast nook where he usually slept, but he would not have it. Abuela laughed as she told Rita about the battle of wills between her and a cat. No sooner than she'd take Don Juan out of her bed and return him to his box, then he'd return to her room with a soft, chastising mew, and climb back into bed with her.

"Cats are strong-willed animals," Abuela told her. "If your will cannot match theirs, they will dominate you, especially if your cat has a will as strong as Don Juan's. Eventually, I had to allow him to sleep at the foot of the bed, or neither of us would have ever gotten any rest. He accepted the offering as a fair compromise."

"What about the other cats wanting into your bed?" Rita asked.

"Not one of the others ventured past the doorway," Abuela replied with a laugh. "Carlotta and Inigo came separately to my doorway on several nights. Both mewed loudly, asking for permission to enter."

"What happened?"

"Each time they came, Don Juan casually raised his head, gazed at the offender from his perch at the foot of the bed, and twitched his ears." She laughed again. "I've not had a cat in my bed, aside from Don Juan, for seven years."

From the moment Rita arrived, Don Juan had taken to her. As she stood in the doorway that first evening, her luggage on the floor next to her, Don Juan came up and began rubbing against her legs. "He's so friendly," Rita had said, lifting the heavy cat into her arms and nuzzling him.

It was later that Abuela explained Don Juan wasn't entirely being friendly. "When cats do that, they're rubbing their scent on you, claiming you. He was letting the others know you belong to him," she said.

"Shame on you, Don Juan," Rita said, scratching the orange tabby atop his head. "You already have Abuela. Isn't one woman enough?" Don Juan mewed softly and nuzzled her hand.

Abuela insisted his reply was "no."

Rita again scratched Don Juan behind the ears, closed the book and sighed heavily, like an old person. She saw Theo at school every day. She'd just met the boy, and yet she missed him. Rita was annoyed with herself for spending so much time thinking about him. It had to be because she missed her family—Tora, Sam, and Sam junior, whom Theo brought to mind, and, of course, her mother and other brothers and sisters, too.

She was thinking about Theo only because she was lonely. She needed to get him off her mind. There were more important things than a boy to consider.

❊ ❊ ❊

Rita wasn't sure what she'd find on the Saturday afternoon she arrived to stay with Abuela Maritza. The cats were her first surprise. There were so many.

Abuela was a jangly woman with wiry Einstein hair and eyes so green you could literally get lost staring in them. She came to the door regal like a queen, her tiny frame draped in layers of bright silky fabric, three or four of her kitty subjects circling her feet.

When Rita's brother, Sam, had called that first evening to make sure she'd arrived safely, he asked how Abuela was doing.

"She's wonderful," Rita replied. "She's been talking about the family all afternoon."

When Sam asked to speak with Abuela, she told him Abuela was resting. This was partially true.

Abuela did seem fine when Rita first arrived at her door, surveying Rita with a playful scowl. "Who'll be taking care of who?" she'd said with snort. "You see that, Dulcinea? That scrawny thing is your new nanny," she told the underfed gray and black feline weaving between her legs, and then she laughed. It was a playful laugh, not a bit of nastiness to it. This was Abuela's way, playful teasing for those she loved. Yet her teasing could turn venomous for those she did not.

She teased Rita all afternoon about the oversized varsity jacket: "I know that jacket. Does he know you have it?" About boys: "Don't even think about getting pregnant under my roof. There are better ways to ruin your life, like alcohol." And about Elena: "That bwitch is trying to get rid of us both, *no es que ella? Adios, bruja,*" she said, waving her hand dismissively.

Yet Rita also observed signs. The garden she recalled as being a flowering quilt of glorious color was now weeded over, pock marked with ugly brown gopher holes. Not a flower in sight. The house she remembered as being immaculate, was untidy, with dishes in the sink, dirty clothes and dry laundry strewn about like falling leaves.

It took forever for Abuela to prepare supper that first night because she kept losing her way around the kitchen. Eventually, Rita had to take over for her. And she kept forgetting everyone's name, even Rita's. The most disturbing thing happened as suppertime neared. She told Rita they shouldn't eat until Tito got home.

Rita had to remind her that Tito would not be coming home, and when Abuela realized this to be true, an overwhelming sadness appeared in her eyes, as if she was experiencing his death all over again. Later, she reminisced about her days with Tito until Rita put her to bed.

Most of the time, Abuela was fine, fun, and feisty. Her lapses never lasted very long. Yet Rita realized she needed to keep vigilant. Abuela's lapses were like the intermittent beam from a far-off lighthouse. She couldn't predict when Abuela's light would blink out and worried over when the light would go out and stay out forever. Rita understood that she needed to keep Abuela's dimming light a secret. It was a secret she vowed to keep for both their sakes.

In her first days there, Rita went about the task of setting the house right. She washed all the dishes, put away the clean laundry, and washed the dirty. She shampooed the rugs and scrubbed the hard wood floors. She laundered all the curtains and mucked out all the litter boxes, dumping baking soda into the kitty litter, hoping to rid the house of the cat box odor. She left all the windows open all night and placed plug-ins around the house, but she could still smell it. She decided then to air out her school clothes on the porch.

Turtle

There was pain in his father's eyes when Turtle got home that night. On the surface he seemed upset with Turtle. On the surface he looked like any other dad about to punish his kid for doing something he shouldn't have done. For most dads, punishment was part of the fatherhood ritual. *I'm tryin' ta make a man outta that boy.*

Yet Turtle was able to look beyond the surface directly to the pain. It was the pain of loss.

71

"Why did you do this?" Stan asked, looking down at the assembled model in his hands. His words were soft, nearly pleading. "Your mother's in the bedroom right now crying her eyes out. If that's what you were going for, you should be proud of yourself."

Turtle stared at his father, his own eyes blazing. *I didn't do it, you idiot! Wanna know who did? Your other son, the dead one; the son you actually love!*

He knew he couldn't say any of his rampaging thoughts. Blaming his dead brother would sound just as Uncle Johnny must have sounded the evening Dad went over and confronted him about Aunt Jenny. *She's in the kitchen, making tacos.* And would more than likely have the same result.

"I…I…I'm sorry," Turtle stammered instead, the admission of guilt sticking to his tongue like a fly to fly paper.

"You don't need to apologize to me. You need to apologize to your mother."

For what? Turtle's mind raged. *For not bein' the one who got hit by a car?*

"No," Turtle said, the word coming so softly his father almost didn't hear it.

"Excuse me?"

"He was buyin' it for both of us," Turtle said a little louder. Unlike the apology that stuck to his tongue, the truth flowed like river water. "The Millennium Falcon's mine, too."

Stan Dawson stared at his son, his eyes growing twitchy. He reminded Turtle of a rat caught in one of those humane rat traps. "Your mother—"

"He *wanted* to put it together with me. He told me so. It's *ours*, not his, not *hers*."

His father stared harder, as if the sharp gaze could turn Turtle's words into something more tolerable. Then just like a rat caught in a trap, he began looking for a way out of the conversation gone bad.

He shifted his weight from foot to foot. It was obvious to Turtle he wanted to leave, but he couldn't. He was trapped.

"Your mother's down the hall right now, crying her eyes out," Stan said, twitchy eyes searching.

When Stan Dawson realized he couldn't scamper away, he did what any trapped rat would do, he lost it. He threw the Millennium Falcon onto the floor with tremendous force. The tiny spacecraft exploded, pieces of plastic flying every which way as if from a fragment bomb.

Turtle's eyes grew wide as Stan grabbed him around the shoulders, his hands closing on Turtle's fleshy arms like a vise. Turtle cried out. "You're hurting me!"

"I'm your father! You will not talk to me like that," Stan shrieked. He began shaking the boy. It was as if he were shaking a dust mop out the window. The powerful man shook his son violently, and the more he shook, the more trapped he seemed.

"Stop! Dad, stop!" Turtle called, the breath rattling out of him. His father had never laid hands on him before, not like this. He and A.D. had both received the occasional whack on the behind, but those had been calculated and measured. This was out of control. "You're hurting me!"

Turtle's cry snapped Stan back to reality. He released him, and stared down at his hands as if they'd acted on their own. Shame-filled tears bubbled up in his eyes. "Your brother's room is off limits. Do I make myself clear?" he rasped. Without waiting for a response, he said: "If you continue to disobey me, there *will* be consequences." With the threat hanging in the air he careened away, fleeing down the hall to his own bedroom.

❦ ❦ ❦

Turtle was lying in bed in the darkness, having himself a good old-fashioned cry, the kind where your chest heaves uncontrollably and silver strings of snot hang from your nose. He hadn't had one of those since the funeral.

A feeling of desolation swirled in his chest, like a tumbleweed in an old movie where the town was deserted, bouncing along the dusty road. He was feeling as alone and unwanted as a lonely tumbleweed. A miracle had happened. A.D had returned, and while he thought it would fix things, it fixed *nothing*. It didn't matter how A.D. felt about him. *They* hated him. *What's the sense of being alive?* He thought this dark thought and rolled over onto his back.

He tried dredging up thoughts of Rita and his brother returned from the dead—the good things in his life. Yet, at the moment, they were heavily outweighed by the idea he wasn't loved by his own parents—*unloved*—and he never would be. His fingers grazed the spot on his upper forearm where his father had grabbed him. It throbbed to the touch.

"Don't cry." A.D.'s voice came from across the room. "I'm here now." He hadn't heard his brother come in. He should have been embarrassed, A.D. catching him like this, crying like a baby, but he wasn't.

"They don't love me," Turtle blubbered, a spit bubble popping on his lower lip.

"Of course they do. They're just hurtin' is all," came A.D.'s soothing reply.

"They don't!" Turtle cried out. "They love you, and you're dead!"

A.D. didn't respond.

"You've gotta let them know you're back. It's the only way."

"I can't, Punkinpuss. They wouldn't understand."

"*I* don't understand! What did you come back for?"

"For you," A.D. said, and Turtle heard his brother's voice cracking.

He peered through the darkness, looking for him. The moonlight passing through the curtains cast an eerie glow over the room. Turtle glanced around. A.D. wasn't there. That's when he noticed how cold the room had become, and it was getting colder by the moment.

"I have something for you."

Turtle heard A.D.'s voice and sat up in bed. "Where are you?" He squinted into the darkness, and saw a silvery mist hovering near the window. "A.D.?"

"Remember when it was good?" A.D.'s voice asked, the voice coming from the direction of the mist.

"No!" Turtle said, sniffling.

"Sure you do," A.D. insisted.

The mist played against the moonlight like dust motes in the air, yet these motes hung with purpose. The mist drifted toward him, a slow moving cloud. As it neared, the room grew even colder. Turtle hunched the covers up around himself to keep from shivering.

"Close your eyes," the voice in the mist whispered. "Close your eyes and remember the good times."

The chilling mist was hanging just in front of him now. "Okay," Turtle whispered.

A part of him wanted to run. This was ghostly stuff and he was afraid of ghosts. Yet the comforting words of his brother's voice relaxed him.

Turtle closed his eyes and shivered as the mist split into two wishbone-like streams, travelling up his nostrils. He breathed in deeply and, as he inhaled, a wintry chill began to sting the membrane in the back of his nose. It burned, oh, how it burned. It was as if he'd huffed a handful of granulated laundry detergent.

Yet soon the burning subsided, and when it did, long forgotten memories began to play before Turtle's eyes like moving pictures on an old kinescope. He saw his mother, Mabry, swaddling him in his receiving blanket as an infant, days after they'd brought him home from the hospital: *Don't cry, little Mushmouse. Mama's got you,* she said in a voice so filled with love it startled him.

The movie images faded, turning into mist themselves, and suddenly he wasn't watching anymore. He was there.

It was Christmas Eve. A big snow had fallen overnight, and Foster City was about to have a white Christmas. The weatherman said it was their first in over twenty years.

Eleven-year-old A.D. and eight-year-old Turtle buckled on their winter boots, strapped on their parkas, and headed over to The Lots for a Christmas Eve adventure. Instead of an adventure, the boys happened upon a tree. It was a scrawny Charlie Brown Christmas tree that the tree seller must have ditched in The Lots for being too unsightly. Yet when the boys laid their eyes on it they saw a thing of beauty. A.D. got the idea they should take it home and put it up in their room, which they still shared. They would decorate it themselves and have their very own Christmas.

"Maybe Santa will bring us two sets of gifts, one under the family tree and one under ours," Turtle added.

"Maybe," A.D. said and pelted his brother in the arm with a snowball.

They knocked the snow off the tree and carried it home between themselves, Turtle leading the way holding the uppermost branches. Moms got into the act, digging out some unused ornaments. They made more out of old cardboard boxes, cutting shapes with a butter knife and coloring them with Sharpies. Turtle made the angel they placed on the top all by himself, coloring it with red Sharpie because they didn't have silver.

The boys spent the better part of the afternoon decorating the tree— *their* tree. Stan held Turtle as he placed the red angel atop the tree. When he looked at *his* angel on top, it looked so perfect he couldn't stop grinning. A.D. told him what a fine angel it was, and he grinned some more.

At night they turned out the lights and marveled at their handiwork. The moonlight glinting off the shiny ornaments made it seem surreal. The tree didn't have any Christmas tree lights, their dad fearing the scrawny tree might catch fire and burn the whole damn house down, yet it hardly mattered to the boys. Turtle and A.D.'s chests swelled with pride when they looked at their pieced-together work of art. They fell asleep with moonlight in their eyes.

On Christmas morning, the boys awoke to discover they hadn't received two sets of gifts, but the gifts they received had all been placed under *their* tree. Moms and Dad spent the entire morning in the boys' room, playing with them and their toys, helping them into their new socks and sweaters. Moms even brought breakfast in.

"Don't get any ideas. This is the one and only time I'm letting you boys eat in here, so enjoy it," she scolded playfully.

It was the best Christmas ever.

✿ ✿ ✿

Bernadette Pinkstring awoke on Saturday morning with a jolt. She hadn't had one of those in a while. She bolted upright in bed, eyes wide, and realized she was perspiring. At first she thought it was her blood pressure acting up again, but after shuffling off to bathroom where she checked it three times (140/99), she knew it had to be something else. Her pressure was up there, all right, but not in the danger zone. Not for her, at least.

"Oh, Lawdy me," Bernie sighed. The jolt she'd felt meant just one thing; there'd been some powerful spiritual energy nearby.

Any spirit in the area with a bone to pick with a loved one, or affairs they needed settled before they could rest easy, usually found their way to Bernadette Pinkstring. This one hadn't. This one had chosen someone else.

That was all right with Bernie. She'd had her fill of spirits knocking on her door in the middle of the night, disturbing her sleep, or catching up to her on the crosstown bus, making her seem like a crazy person to those seated around her when she asked the spirit quite politely to leave her be.

The question as to why some spirits remained earthbound while others moved on was a puzzling one, and the answer wasn't always clear, even to the spirits themselves. In 1969, Bernie encountered the angry spirit of an attractive twenty year-old woman, Ruby Johnson, while walking home from a parents-teachers night. Ruby's spirit was standing in front of the gate of a lovely cottage on Featherbed Lane looking angry as a polecat. She was wearing a yellow party dress with a pleated skirt. There was blood on the skirt.

The spirit complained to Bernie that she'd been in a fender-bender and was waiting for the tow truck driver to either bring her car back or take her to it. *One or the other, that was it.* The poor thing had no idea she was dead, had been dead for all of five years by the time Bernie happened upon her.

Ruby had been driving home drunk (on Bacardi and coke) from a frat house party at one of the houses on fraternity row, when she lost control of her Ford Falcon, careened into a tree, and wound up on the sidewalk crashed into the gate of the house on Featherbed Lane. Her neck had been snapped like a twig. It took quite a bit of explaining for Bernie to convince Ruby she was dead and needed to get on over to the other side. Eventually, she did.

When Bernie was seven, her grandfather died in his sleep. After the funeral, the family convened at the house for the repast. Bernie had gone into the bedroom to fetch some barrettes from Grandma Ida May's dresser, and there she found her Grandpa, Albert Pinkstring, dressed very nicely in his gray twill suit, straw topper in his hand, seated on the edge of the bed. Grandpa explained to Bernie he had to stay around to look after his wife of forty-three years. He'd always looked after Ida May, and he wasn't going to let death get in the way of duty.

That was the first time for Bernie. That's when she discovered she possessed the gift, the clairvoyance. Bernie's parents didn't believe her at first, but Grandma Ida May did. She sensed Albert's spirit was still in the house. Said Bernie wasn't the first one in the family to have the sight. Her great cousin Oneida (on Albert's side) had it, as did another relative she'd heard about.

It took several trips to Grandma's for a seven-year-old to convince her grandfather he needed to get on over to the other side. When the deed was done and Grandpa Albert had moved on, Grandma Ida May thanked Bernie, baking her her very own peach cobbler for seeing her Albert off safely.

Then there was the time Bernie was contacted by a woman, Debra Mason, who lived in one of the turn-of-the-century apartment houses just off Canal Street. Debra told Bernie the whole thing started when she came in from work one day and found her closet door open. It appeared as though someone had been rummaging through her clothes. She at first assumed it was her fiancé, Donnie, who had a key. But when she asked him about it, he assured her he had no reason to go through her clothes. "I'm not a cross-dresser," he laughingly told her.

Debra was alarmed. Nothing turned up missing, but still, she had all the locks changed and burglar bars put up on all the windows. That put an end to the rummaging for all of two weeks, and then one evening, she and Donnie returned from dinner and found two outfits laid out on the bed. That's when Debra contacted Bernie.

Bernie saw the sprit as soon as she walked in the front door. It was a gorgeous woman, very well-dressed. Turns out the spirit was Debra's mother, Mildred, who'd moved on several years earlier. Mildred explained to Bernie she wasn't going anywhere until she saw her daughter married to that nice, young man.

The outfits Mrs. Mason had laid out were in the colors she wanted Debra to consider as her wedding colors. Debra took her mother's advice— pink and blue. She even pushed up the wedding date three months so her mother could finally find some peace.

The day after the wedding, Bernie entered Debra's bedroom and helped Mrs. Mason get on over to the other side. Bernie said Mildred had tears in her eyes—not for herself. Mildred Mason was happy for her daughter. "What a lovely wedding," she said. "Just lovely."

Then there were the bad ones. Some spirits had evil intentions and only stayed around to make trouble for the living. Those, as fate would have it, were the most powerful spirits—fueled by anger, or meanness, or revenge. Bernie couldn't tell if the nearby spirit she'd sensed that morning had evil intentions or not, but it definitely had ulterior motives. This new spirit was an ornery one. No doubt about it.

Knowing that most of the spirits in Foster City eventually found their way to her, Bernie Pinkstring didn't give this one any more thought. She took an extra dose of her blood pressure medicine and started dressing for her weekly breakfast with the girls—other retired school teachers. She figured she'd find out what this spirit had in mind soon enough, and if she didn't, that was all right, too. She'd had her fill of sprits. She hoped the person dealing with this new spirit could handle its orneriness.

Marty

Marty McKenzie was glad his friend had come along when he did. Marty had been lonely, and scared, and in need of a friend. But now as Marty waited in the darkness, those feelings of loneliness were creeping back. He didn't like it when A.D. left him all alone, and lately he'd been leaving Marty alone for longer and longer periods of time.

A.D. had promised him others would be joining them, but no one else had come.

"Where ya goin?" Marty asked when A.D. was about to take off. It was the same question he'd asked Allison on that last day.

"I found someone who can help us," A.D. said.

"Help us do what?"

"Get revenge," A.D. replied.

CHAPTER EIGHT

Turtle awoke with a Christmas morning glow, vestiges of the memories his brother had aroused in him lingering like the remaining wisps of overnight fog hanging in the air at sunrise. While the memories were already fading, there were things about them that remained.

The image of his mother swaddling him as an infant was one that had remained and was the reason for a good portion of the smile illuminating his face that morning. She had loved him at one time. *Don't cry little Mushmouse. Mama's got you.* Maybe she didn't love him now, but she did once. This long forgotten memory fanned the ashes in his heart, sparking a tiny ember of hope.

The memory conjured other discarded memories, of how when they were small, it was Moms who called him her little Mushmouse and A.D. her little Punkinpuss. Dad had told them she'd gotten the names from an old cartoon she'd watched as a child. Mushmouse—a hillbilly mouse, was sweet, and Punkinpuss—a hillbilly cat and his nemeses, was ornery, just like A.D.. The cartoon characters fought a lot, but they were always together, just like her boys.

Turtle didn't mind the nickname, but soon after A.D. turned eight, he came into the kitchen one Saturday morning while Moms was making pancakes (A.D.'s favorite) and said *I don't want you calling me Punkinpuss anymore.* Turtle saw the darkness in his brother's expression when he'd made the demand. Moms could see it, too. By then the entire family knew about A.D.'s dark side.

Mabry immediately dropped using the nicknames for both of them, yet soon after, A.D. began using the names interchangeably with his younger brother. He was doing it to get under Turtle's skin, but nothing A.D. called Turtle could ever bother him. Turtle idolized his big brother the way so many younger brothers do, and after a while the interchangeable use of names became a personal endearment.

Despite Turtle's delight over A.D.'s return, and the hope-inspiring memories A.D. was able to stir within him, an uneasiness was stirring as well. Maybe A.D. wasn't a ghost, but it was obvious he wasn't exactly human either. No human being could do what he had done.

Sure, A.D. had led them into their share of mischief in the past, like the lifting of the money from Dad's trousers to pay for the Millennium Falcon, or the time A.D. purposely hit their ball over the fence into Miss Fowler's garden, giving them an alibi for pilfering some roses for Mother's Day, but stealing the *Tahitian Treat* was different. Never before had A.D. goaded him into harm's way.

Turtle tried to dismiss the change in his brother. He tried telling himself A.D. had been gone for a long time. *He's adjusting to being back is all. It's the deadness wearing off of him.* He was truly happy for A.D.'s return, and yet, a part of him, perhaps a part that didn't even exist when A.D. was first alive, was observing things from the outside looking in, and that part of him didn't like what he was seeing.

It was Saturday. Normally, Saturday mornings Turtle went down to the living room and watched cartoons, *He-Man And The Masters of the Universe* and *The Smurfs*, while his folks slept in. This Saturday, instead, he went into his brother's room to hang out. They needed to talk, but A.D. wasn't there. Turtle decided to hide out in his own room until his brother, or his parents, came knocking.

Neither happened. Stan and Mabry went about their day as if the Millennium Falcon incident hadn't occurred. Around ten a.m., Turtle heard his mother go into A.D.'s room and begin straightening up the mess they'd created, just as she'd done when A.D. was first alive. Around noon, she knocked on his door, said she was making sandwiches, and headed for the kitchen. Turtle ate his bologna and cheese outside on the front steps. He washed it down with cherry Kool-Aid that Moms had surprised him with. This, too, was a sign of hope for him.

My friend's Kool… My friend's Kool-Aid.

He waited all weekend for his brother to return. Turtle wouldn't see A.D. again until the second week of summer.

☘ ☘ ☘

On Tuesday, after school, Rita told Turtle she needed to tell him something. She ran up on him right after eighth period, before he could scoop

80

up his books and dash off. It was a warm late spring day. By then, Rita had discarded the oversized jacket and was wearing a short sleeved blue shirt that highlighted the green of her eyes. As much as Turtle wanted to get home to see if A.D. had returned, he could tell from her tone that what Rita needed to say was important. Besides, on this day, she was too beautiful to resist.

They went to The Lots. It was Rita's idea. She was monosyllabic during the walk over, and Turtle wondered if she was bringing him to his favorite place in the whole wide world for the break-up talk. If they were breaking up, that meant she really had been his girlfriend. *But not anymore.* There was another *not anymore* just up ahead. If Rita were breaking up with him, the spell The Lots had placed on him so long ago when he was a little boy would be broken, its magic gone forever.

"Nice day," he said as they approached Canal Street. That was stupid. That was something his parents might have said. What he really wanted to say was *Are you breaking up with me?*

"Yes," she replied.

There. That response was suitable for both statements—the one he'd said and the one he'd only thought.

Rita led him to the exact spot where he'd led her when he'd first brought her there. It was impressive that she remembered, but he was too worried to be impressed.

They sat quiet for several minutes, just staring into the creek, watching it do its dance down to the river. Turtle was positive Rita could hear his heart beating over the chattering creek. He decided, it wasn't his heart beating she heard, it was the sound of his heart *breaking.*

He knew in that moment he'd do anything not to lose her—even tell her something that might make him sound like a loony toon. At least it was the truth. The truth had always been his fallback position. The truth had never failed him. Of course, in the past, the truth wasn't also the impossible.

"I need to tell you something," he blurted over the jabbering of the creek.

"Okay," she said, her eyes still fixed on the water. "But me first, okay?"

"Okay," he said, a lump clogging his throat. *Here it comes*, he thought.

"I lied to you," she said. "Well, I didn't actually lie, because I didn't tell you anything, so it wasn't a lie."

"Okay," he said. He had no idea what she was talking about. It wasn't sounding good.

"I don't actually live in the apartment building you walk me home to," she said with a heavy sigh.

He wasn't expecting anything like this. He thought about it for a moment, his emotions pinging. "So I didn't actually walk you home?"

"No," she replied," her voice sounding as sad as he felt. "I'm sorry I misled you."

"Why?" Despite the curveball, the cloud of gloom was actually lifting. She wasn't breaking up with him. It sounded as though she was apologizing.

"I was ashamed."

She told him about Abuela Maritza being a cat lady, and about how she came to be living with her. She told him about the run-down house on Featherbed Lane that had smelled of litter boxes when she first arrived. She talked about the large backyard that had once featured rows of beautiful flowers, with a vegetable garden near the rear wall, but was now overturned by zig-zagging gopher holes. She told him how much she missed her family, and that he reminded her of her nephew, Sam Junior. She told him everything, except about the affliction that was slowly engulfing Abuela like a dark cloud. *That* she could tell no one. By the time she finished talking, they were both laughing about Don Juan Pussycat believing he was the man of the house.

"I thought you stopped walking me home from school because you smelled them on me," she said, her eyes crinkling at the corners with relieved laughter.

"I didn't smell anything. To tell the truth, you smell pretty good…for a girl." They both cracked up at that one. Turtle was relieved as well. He enjoyed the sound of her laughter. It was like a box full of puppies. Pure joy.

"Then why did you stop walking me home from school?" she asked.

Turtle opened his mouth to respond, and a voice spoke up in his mind.

Stop! Things are going pretty good now, m'boy. But you tell her your dead brother has returned from the grave, and I guarantee you things are going to roll downhill so fast you'll have to be Carl Lewis to keep up with them.

"Stuff," he finally said, sounding pathetically vague.

"Oh," she replied, and he could hear her pulling back a little.

"Okay, not stuff. It's personal. I want to tell you, but I can't, not today. But I will. Promise." He lifted his eyes and found hers.

"Of course," she said, and he could feel her coming back to him.

He took her hand in his. "I like you, Rita." He realized his tongue had become dry as stone. *Is this what it feels like to propose?*

"I like you, too." She was looking at him with those green eyes that were too beautiful for words. He could feel his breath abandoning him. He thought he should be getting a hard-on, but his nether regions were numb.

82

"I hope we can…continue to…hang out together," he said, finally fumbling out a sentence.

"Me, too," Rita replied in a raspy whisper.

Turtle placed her hand back in her lap, not because he wanted to, but because his own hand was beginning to sweat, and if she pulled back because of how gunky it felt, he'd die—he'd literally die.

Rita snatched up his hand, leaned in, and kissed him on the lips. It was a quick kiss, a butterfly's touch, her soft lips pressing gently against his. He felt her breath, a subtle blast of sweetness and then, her lips were gone. It happened in an instant, so quick it was almost as if a dream. Yet for Turtle, it was a moment frozen in time. Of all the kisses he would participate in as a teenager, as a young man, and as an adult, he would remember this first kiss as the sweetest.

They spent the rest of the afternoon at The Lots. It was a balmy day with a pre-summer breeze strumming the trees, perfect for talking, laughing. They lay out on the weedy grass and did their homework together. He quizzed her on the solar system. She helped him navigate the conjugating of verbs.

"Why don't you have a backpack?" Rita asked. They had just completed their math homework. Rita was putting her books away; Turtle's were piled up on the weed-covered ground, like oblong boulders.

"I have one," he replied, his eyes turning inward.

Rita waited a few moments. "Oh? Are we playing twenty questions now?"

Turtle smiled. "My brother. He didn't like the idea of carrying his books on his back. Said it made him feel weighted down. He liked to feel free."

"Okay," Rita said, the word coming out slowly. "So that's why your *brother* didn't carry a backpack."

"I like to feel free, too."

Rita didn't say anything more.

Later, as the sun began to set, Rita took Turtle home to meet Abuela. As they walked along to Rita's *real* house, she held his hand. The feelings firing through him like shooting stars spangling the sky were incredible. The touch of her hand on his made his thing harden. It quickly softened out of embarrassment, and then hardened again. This kaleidoscope of hormone-popping emotions felt amazing.

As perfect a day as it had become, thoughts of the secret he promised Rita he would tell began to surface. The thoughts surfaced slowly, like a crocodile in a lazy lagoon stalking prey. He wondered what would happen to their relationship when he told her A.D. was no longer dead.

Rita

She was happy. For the first time since she'd been in Foster City, she was truly happy.

Rita escorted Turtle past her school clothes strung out on the porch like laundry and into the parlor where Abuela sat reading a paperback novel. She was surrounded by her subjects. Two of them, George Bailey and Inigo, were in her lap. Don Juan lay draped along the back of the couch like a large orange shawl.

"Abuela! Quiero presentarte a alguien," Rita called, announcing there was someone she wanted her to meet.

Abuela looked up from her paperback, her green eyes questioning. They came to rest on Turtle, and she smiled. "Un niño," she said, her eyes moving to Rita. There was a playful challenge in them. Rita recalled Abuela's admonition about getting pregnant and blushed.

"This is my friend, Theo," Rita said quickly, trying to will the rouge from her cheeks. "From school," she added. "We do *homework* together."

"Tito?" Abuela's gaze turned quizzical, moving back to Turtle.

"No, Abuela. Theo. Not Tito, *Theo*." Rita held her breath, wondering if Abuela's light had just flickered.

"Oh. It is a pleasure to meet you, Theo. You'll have to excuse my ears. They are not as young as they used to be," Abuela said with a self-deprecating chuckle. Rita exhaled.

"The pleasure's all mine," Turtle replied.

Don Juan hopped down from the couch and approached him.

"That's the man of the house," Rita said with a grin.

"Don Juan," Turtle said knowingly, smiling down at the cat. "I've heard about you."

Upon hearing his name, Don Juan began purring like a motorboat. He glided up to Turtle and leisurely rubbed his back against Turtle's legs. Turtle stooped and hefted the orange cat into his arms. "He likes me," he said, scratching Don Juan behind the ears. The rumble in the cat's chest grew louder, vibrating his fingers.

Rita's eyes found Abuela's, and they both burst into laughter.

"What?" Turtle asked, looking from Rita to Abuela. "Did I say something wrong?"

"No. It's nothing," Rita replied, her eyes crinkling at the corners. "An inside joke." Rita and Abuela continued to laugh.

Before that afternoon, Turtle would have wondered if she were making fun of him, or playing a mean trick. Now, however, he felt a sense of confidence around Rita. By some quirky miracle of fate, he had a girlfriend. Turtle found himself delighting in that truth. Like an elephant basking in a muddy river, he had no desire to move on from there. So he kept his mind still, savoring the idea that *somebody* cared for him, and her name was Rita.

He gazed at Rita and Abuela, taking a moment to enjoy their laughter. "One day, you'll have to let me in on this joke," he said, setting the tabby cat back on the floor.

"One day," Rita replied. Her eyes again found Abuela's, and a new wave of laughter rose into the air.

Mabry

You're not supposed to have favorites. Every mother knows that. *I love them all the same,* that's on page one of the universal mommy/daddy handbook. *But how can your first-born not be your favorite? No shame in it,* Mabry Dawson thought as she set about the task of straightening up the mess Turtle had made of his brother's room. Yet despite the oft-rehearsed justifications she played over in her mind like a song stuck on repeat, she couldn't help but feel shame. Turtle was her baby, her little Mushmouse.

Mabry's clever subconscious concealed her shame, spinning a mummy-suit out of anger and outrage and wrapping her shame in it so neatly, it was practically unrecognizable.

He knew the room was off limits, her conscious mind snarled. *He knew we wanted the model space ship to remain just as we'd found it on the street that day, in the box with a dimple on top.*

She'd heard him all the way down the hall one day earlier, talking, playing, imitating the sound of his brother's laughter. *He's doing it to hurt me,* she thought. *He knows I can hear him down there, and he's doing it to hurt me.* But she never thought he'd do anything like this, take the model space ship from the shelf in A.D.'s closet and assemble it. That was just plain mean. That kind of act of defiance required punishment, *deserved* punishment.

Turtle tried to disarm her by declaring she didn't love him, and it had almost worked. *Of course I love him,* she chimed through the mummy suit, even though she couldn't stand the sight of him. Everything about Turtle—sight, sound, his aged-fruit fragrance—reminded Mabry of her loss. Everything about Turtle reminded Mabry that he was here and A.D. wasn't. How could she ever move past her loss if he was *always* there?

Mabry had stashed a Walkman cassette player in the room that she listened to whenever she came to clean. Sometimes she came to clean when there was nothing to clean. These times she'd sit on the edge of A.D.'s bed listening to the song. She'd recorded just one song on the cassette tape, over and over, Dionne Warwick's *I Say A Little Prayer*.

She was a young girl living in Birmingham when she first heard the song. It was popular, a hit; all of Dionne Warwick's songs were. She liked the song, but it had little effect on her back then before she knew the true meaning of love and prayer.

A week or so after A.D.'s funeral, she'd come into the house from grocery shopping at Miller's. To keep the silence from eating her alive, Mabry turned on the radio, an oldies station, and the song came on. *I Say A Little Prayer*. Never before had a song spoken to Mabry the way that one did. As a thirty-eight-year-old woman, she truly understood what Dionne Warwick was trying to say far better than when she was just a little girl. Listening to the song, it was as if Dionne had recorded it just that day, for her ears only.

That afternoon she went out, bought a Walkman and some recording cassettes. She found the album in a used record bin at Sam Goody's, came home, and recorded the song over and over as Niagara-style tears cascaded down her cheeks. That song spoke the truth. Each morning when she woke up, before she did anything, she said a little prayer. The song mirrored her existence.

Forever and ever he'll stay in my heart.

Now, as Mabry listened to Dionne, cleaning and crying, blotting up tears with a tissue she stuffed in her bosom, a thought came to her out of the clear blue. It occurred just after she'd vacuumed the carpet.

The thought was…

Military school.

That's what parents did in her day with children who were incorrigible and didn't listen—they sent them off to military school.

Mabry found herself tickled by the idea of sending Turtle away to school. She didn't question where the idea had come from or why. She instead focused on the thought that Turtle needed to be taught a lesson. He needed to learn you can't defy your parents and expect there to be no consequences.

It's for his own good. That's what she'd tell Stan, who she knew would raise the rooftops against it. *We can't control him, Stan. That boy needs to be brought down a peg, and this is how we do it.*

Mabry smiled as she ran her spiel through her mind. She moved around the bed and picked up the final pillow from the floor. As she was about to place it back on the bed, she caught a whiff of something—him. The pillow still smelled of A.D. *(how is that possible?),* as if he'd been lying on it hours earlier. Memories came flooding back. She felt the urge to hold the pillow up to her nose and breathe him in, to stand there, allowing herself to drift in memories.

When A.D. lost his first tooth, he put it under his pillow with a note requesting the tooth fairy leave him a one-hundred-dollar bill. So cute.

She should have enjoyed the memory, yet her clever subconscious used this discovery to dredge up a caldron-full of anger.

He needs to be brought down a peg.

Military school will be good for us all, she thought. *We all need a fresh start, him included.* She placed the pillow back on the bed and pulled the Star Trek bedspread up over it, removed her headset and once again wiped away her tears. She called to Turtle that she'd be making lunch soon, then went down the hall to have a chat with Stan. She couldn't help but notice how much better she was feeling.

✼ ✼ ✼

The time was nearly at hand.

The mannequin had been purchased and all preparations had been made. Never before had he seen a child who deserved saving as much as this one. His heart bled for the boy. He wished he could save him today but knew he had to err on the side of caution.

Patience, he told himself. It was patience that had allowed him to do his good work in secrecy for so many years. He wouldn't give in to urges now.

Have patience, young man. I'll be coming for you soon. Summer is upon us, and before summer's end you will be in a much happier place. I promise.

✼ ✼ ✼

Michael Monicker acquired the hat on a trip to New York City. He'd driven there with some of his old college buddies on a bet. They'd been watching old movies on the tube at Michael's place, shooting the shit, drinking beer, and eating pizza they'd picked up from Noe's Pizzeria on Prospect Avenue. Ray Felton, known back then as Radio Ray because of the huge boom box he'd started carrying around, claimed the best pizza in the whole wide-fuckin' world was deep dish from Chicago.

"You want real pizza, and not this sawdust pulp we're shoving down, you go to Gino's on East Superior Street," he said and kissed the tips of his fingers, as if he were Italian.

Rodney Darcy disagreed. "Only an idiot would go to Chicago for pizza. New York is where you go. Ray's. And not one of the two hundred

87

thousand Ray's knock-offs either. The original one, on Eleventh Street in the Village."

With alcohol fueling the fire, the conversation got heated, New York versus Chicago, deep dish versus flat pizza. Not one of them could recall what prompted them to pile into Ray's nineteen sixty-nine Chevy Chevelle, or why they chose to drive all night to New York City, but around two a.m., the idea started floating, and after a while that's what they did.

Rodney Darcy was first behind the wheel because he was from New York, with Radio Ray driving shotgun. Rodney's brother Mike—aka Mike D—Mike Monicker, and a guy they hardly knew named Tony Beal were squeezed into the backseat. The three in the rear were all big men, over two hundred pounds each, but none of them seemed to mind over five hours in cramped quarters to be a part of the Big Pizza Challenge.

By the time they got to New York the next morning, they were tired, hungry, sober, and not one of them was in the mood for pizza. Instead, they stopped at a twenty-four-hour diner on Ninth Avenue where each of them had he-man breakfasts NYC style: pork chops and eggs. Tony Beal, who claimed he was Jewish, chose steak and eggs. They all had home fries and a short stack with tons of coffee.

It was later, while shopping in a vintage clothing store on Sixth Avenue (or Avenue of The America's, if you please) that Mike Monicker first saw the hat. Radio Ray found it on a shelf in the back of the store—a handsome black derby.

Ray placed the hat on his head and said, "Look, Guys, the Kerwood Derby." As it would happen, all five of the guys had been big Rocky and Bullwinkle fans growing up, and each remembered the Kerwood Derby storyline on the old cartoon show. They howled with laughter.

In the old cartoon show, the Kerwood Derby was created by a scientist on the moon to be placed on the head of the moon's idiot prince. The hat made the prince super intelligent. Then the hat was stolen. None of the guys could remember how Rocky and Bullwinkle acquired it, but they all remembered that Boris and Natasha, their Russian nemeses, were hell bent on getting it from them.

As the guys passed the hat from head-to-head, squealing: *I'm smart! I'm smart!* Mike Monicker got what would turn out to be the best idea of his entire adult life.

Mike was a young science teacher in the Foster City school district, just out of college and full of ideas and enthusiasm. Mike made a snap decision to purchase the derby (for a pretty penny, mind you), figuring it would be a wonderful teaching tool in the classroom—a prop to get the kid's attention. He had no idea how successful *his* Kerwood Derby would become.

Once he explained the Kerwood Derby's origins to the kids—*created by a scientist on the moon*—and how he happened to be the proud owner of it—*I would tell you, but then I'd have to kill you*—the popularity of the hat among Mike's students soared.

When a student raised his hand to answer a tough question, sometimes he'd say, *Mr. Monicker, I'm going to need the Kerwood Derby for this one.* Monicker always kept the derby in a place of honor near the front of his classroom where students readily came and propped the adult-size hat on their heads when they needed to answer tough questions.

Students began reserving the Kerwood Derby on test days. It was usually the brightest students, the ones who didn't need a Kerwood Derby's help. Instead, these students enjoyed the idea of adding to the derby's lore.

Pretty soon, teachers of other subjects were borrowing the Kerwood Derby on test days, or for special events. It was such a great motivator. Principal Taft wore the derby to commencement exercises one year. After that, the derby had its own place of honor at each year's commencement exercise.

The derby's reputation grew throughout the school district, as did the reputation of the derby owner, Mike Monicker. He became a regular nominee for state teacher of the year, and while he never won the award, he became highly respected among his peers. By 1988, Mike Monicker was in the midst of a wonderfully rewarding career at Charles Drew Middle School—head of the Science department. He was loved by administrators, teachers, and students alike. Needless to say, it was a shocking surprise when the derby went missing.

CHAPTER NINE

Annabelle Miller was upset. Hell, she was more than upset. She was downright annoyed, and with good reason. After working the store every afternoon that week, putting up with all those snotty-nosed, sugar-craving, after-school knuckleheads four afternoons in a row, here she was on a Thursday night, during prime time TV hours, minding the store again.

She should've been home watching *The Cosby Show* and *Cheers* and *Hill Street Blues*. She'd told George umpteen times they should get a small portable for the store so she wouldn't miss any of her shows on nights like this. The price of portable TVs had come way down, and it'd cost them next to nothing. George's standard response, like a parrot, crowing without thinking, was if she were watching TV instead of the theft mirrors he had installed four years ago, half their inventory would go walking right out the front door along with the Huxtables.

These aren't the old days, Annabelle. The neighborhood has changed.

George was referring to the blacks, Puerto Ricans, and Cubans, who now made up half of their clientele. *Those people have no respect for another man's property,* George constantly reminded her.

Annabelle didn't like when George referred to ethnics as *those people.* Coralee Calendar, Rachel Trueblood, and Mabry Dawson weren't *those people.* They were her friends, had been her friends for a long time.

Annabelle knew she couldn't readily complain about having to be there on a Thursday night no matter how annoyed she was. George was taking care of business at the Rotary, one of several community organizations they belonged to. Those community organizations were the reason their business continued to flourish despite the rise of big box supermarkets, come to squeeze the life out of the mom-and-pops of America. There was no big box supermarket in their community. The local politicians had managed to keep them out—so far, but the local politicians required grease, and the grease was supplied by the community organizations. And so there she sat, while her husband attended to the business of keeping their business from going under.

It was a quiet night. Thursdays often were. *Everyone's at home watching The Cosby Show. I'm not gonna think about it,* Annabelle told herself. *I'm gonna sit here and sip my tea.* Annabelle's "tea" had been replaced in the Styrofoam cup around sundown with rum and coke.

Just after nine p.m. Annabelle's "tea" ran out. A small bottle of Bacardi was stashed in her purse just in case this misfortune occurred. What she needed, however, was another Coke. So Annabelle Miller got off her stool, placed a pencil in her Mary Higgens Clark paperback to hold her place, and ventured down the aisle, headed for the soda case in the back. She was feeling no pain. That's what George used to say when he got liquored up. The "tea" had smoothed away all the edges.

Cheer's is coming on right about now, she thought, smiling as she called up images of Sam and Rebecca, who had replaced Diane when Shelly what's her name went off to become a movie star.

As she moved down the aisle, she could see the top of the *Pull-Ups* display in aisle two. This brought the fat Dawson boy to mind. He'd always been a porker, but since his brother had passed, he'd gained several more unsightly pounds. Annabelle considered the toll Adrian's death had taken on his mother and figured eating everything in sight was how the younger Dawson boy was coping. *They were so close. Poor fat thing's going to eat himself to death. Either that or he's developed a glandular problem like Ross Rainey.* She laughed out loud at that one. *The Fat Boys.* She'd heard the nicknames and secretly thought that one was funny.

She was thinking of the Dawson boy because she knew he'd been up to no good when he was in the store a week ago. She didn't know what, but his mischief had cost her a whole half hour restacking the damn *Pull-Ups* display. She didn't complain to his mother about it. He was a good boy—fat but good—not full of the devil like his brother, rest in peace, and Mabry Dawson didn't need any more grief in her life. The death of her first born had provided more than enough of that.

Annabelle had just passed the dairy case and made the turn when she heard the front door chime. Then it slammed—*hard*—sending shudders through the building as if Foster City had just been struck by its first earthquake. The air pump was there to prevent such slams. A person had to push mightily to make the door slam like that.

"Lawdy, me. You scared the bejesus out of me," Annabelle called. "I'll be right there." She wanted to say *quit slamming the damn door,* but she never sassed a customer.

She checked the mirror in the corner above the dairy case. It was like looking into a fish-eyed lens, but she could see the front of the store quite clearly. The man who'd set the mirrors had done a masterful job.

No one was standing at the front counter.

"Who's there?" she called, her eyes still on the mirror, scanning the entire front of the store. "I'm comin'. I'll be right up."

Just then, the bank of fluorescents overhead began to flicker.

"What the heck is goin' on in here tonight?" she said to no one. No one answered. She chuckled to lighten her mood because, truth be told, things were getting creepy.

The word *robbery* entered her thoughts, and her heart gave a little earthquake shudder of its own. The Miller's had been fortunate when it came to holdups. In the eighteen years they'd owned the store, they'd only been held up five times, twice at gunpoint, and no one had ever been hurt. She'd never been in the store when the robberies occurred. One time it was that nice part-time college student they'd hired for the summer—Jeffrey. The other four times George was behind the counter.

He'd handled the robbers like a pro and told her if anyone ever came in demanding money to give it to them. Life was a whole lot more precious than whatever was in the till.

"Someone there?" she called again.

The overhead lights were flickering rapidly now, setting off a strobe effect, making Annabelle feel as if she were in a big city disco club, not that she'd ever been in one. She thought *this is what it must be like, lights flickering so fast everything seems in some sort of surreal slow motion.* The center bank of overhead fluorescents suddenly began to spark, the sparks raining down on the *Pull-Ups* display in aisle two. Then there was a loud popping sound, and all the overhead lights in the store went out, bathing the store in near darkness.

The soft light emanating from the dairy case cast an eerie yellow glow over the rear of the store. It was then she noticed the encroaching cold. She looked toward the soda case to see if someone had left it open. Nope. The soda case door was closed. Besides, the cold wasn't coming from behind her. It was pushing down on her like a nor'easter from aisle two.

"Hello?" she called. She wasn't expecting an answer, at least not from a human being. The thought that this might be a robbery had fled along with the alcohol haze she'd been feeling when she'd first ventured down the aisle.

Annabelle Miller was now stone sober. She believed in ghosts, believed in the ghost stories she'd heard told over the years by her friend Bernie Pinkstring and others. She also believed she was under attack by one. She didn't know why, and she didn't care. She had to get to the phone at the front of the store where she could call someone, or out into the street, if that was possible. She started up aisle two, venturing into the cold, the flesh on her bare arms chilling to goose flesh as she walked.

The next thing she knew, it was raining *Pull-Ups*. The tops of the *Pull-Ups* boxes high up on the display were torn open as if by magic, and *Pull-Ups* disposable diapers went flying into the air like malformed confetti. One smacked her atop the head. Another hit her in the shoulder as disposable diapers piled up at her feet. Annabelle's heart shuddered again, this time much harder, the air sailing out of her lungs as if she'd been punched in the chest by Leon Spinks.

She stopped walking and leaned heavily against the shelves of aisle two. "What do you want?" she called out. Her legs were growing wobbly. Her voice was weak, and the pain in her chest was getting bad, real bad. It felt as though someone with an iron grip had latched onto her heart and was not intending to let go.

Laughter pierced the silence, coming from behind her, by the soda case. Annabelle Miller squinted into the darkness. "I know that voice," she called, trying to sound intimidating. "If you leave now, I won't tell your mama."

"What did you say to my brother?"

She did know the voice. She couldn't place it just yet, but she knew it. Whoever it was sounded angry.

"Who is your brother, honey?" she asked, attempting to mask her mounting fear with sweetness.

The boy was standing in the shadows. She could see him now, not clearly, but there he was. "No one messes with my brother," he said. He stepped into the aisle.

The hand gripping Annabelle's heart tightened. "Aiii!" The pain was so intense, squeezing her heart, trying to make it pop. She slipped to her knees. "Doctor," she rasped. "Get a doctor." Her eyes grew large and glassy like a cat's eye marble.

The boy started toward her. He moved leisurely, as if he hadn't heard a word she'd said. He was average height, with an athletic build, maybe fourteen or fifteen years–old. *I know this boy.*

"No one messes with my brother." He repeated his deadly sentence as he walked.

"Adrian? Adrian Dawson?" Annabelle was seated on the floor, her head leaning back against the canned green beans. For some reason, in that moment, she thought of a picnic she and George had gone on. It had taken place in Foster City Park back when the park spanned from the center of downtown all the way to the canal. She could see it clear as a sunny day, her first date with George.

He was just back from Vietnam then, thin and wiry, and oh, so ruggedly handsome. She had to keep pinching herself, wondering how it came to be her sitting there with the catch of Foster City and not some other girl.

Annabelle Miller realized her life was flashing before her eyes. The births of her children, Jennifer and Harold, came next, followed by the birth of her granddaughter, Asia. She wasn't fond of the name when she first heard it—*Who names a child after a continent*—but had come to love it as much as she loved the child. She had one regret, that she wouldn't be there for the birth of her second grand, due in three months time.

She looked up and, through rheumy eyes, saw Adrian Dawson standing over her. He looked exactly as he had the last time she'd seen him. Either she was hallucinating, or she was gazing at a ghost, and she was sure as hell she wasn't hallucinating. He knelt beside her.

"I'm having a heart attack," she said. "I'm dying." Her eyes grew hazy. Her hands were scraping at her chest, as if she could peel away the vise that was gripping her heart. "It hurts so bad."

"Don't fight it," he said. "I know about death. It'll be over in no time."

"You're a ghost," she gasped. She wanted to say *I never heard of a ghost killing anyone before*, but his hands were reaching for her throat.

"No ma'am, not a ghost."

Not a ghost? Then, what? she wanted to ask.

She looked up into brown eyes staring back with a frightful rage. "Welcome to the other side," he said.

CHAPTER TEN

It was soon after their first kiss that Turtle and Rita began behaving like a couple. Like husband and wife, they settled into a daily routine. In the mornings, rain or shine, at precisely seven forty-five, Turtle met Rita in front of the wrought iron school gate where he relieved her of the heavy backpack. He carried her backpack everywhere throughout the day, to all her classes, except for their electives. Rita had chorus Wednesday afternoon, and Turtle had taken art. After art class, he would hasten down to the choral room on the first floor, running when he could, walking swiftly when a teacher was in sight. Most days, he arrived before she came out. On those days, he smiled delightedly over the small victory.

Summer was coming, and warm days were in abundance. After school on the warmest days, they went to The Lots where they did their homework and sat by the creek holding hands, the eternal waters of Foster Creek shining in their eyes.

Turtle marveled at how sad his life had been not long ago, with no prospect of hope, only to be transformed into this…wonder. It was a miracle, plain and simple. Even his memory of that special Christmas morning could not compare to the joy he felt sitting on the banks of Foster Creek with Rita at his side.

His existence, once that of a sad, fat, wooly caterpillar, had been transformed by love into a regal, monarch butterfly. Yes, love. The word, though never spoken between them, sang in their tender touches, whispered in the gentle support they offered one another when struggling with a difficult homework problem, and delighted in their kisses.

When the sun dipped into the western part of the sky, Turtle would escort Rita home, never dallying on her porch (the province of love struck teenagers throughout the years). Instead, he'd hasten back to his own home, hoping to find his brother waiting there. The walk back, once a gallows walk, was more enjoyable now. The swirl of funk that had once accompanied him as he walked in the front door—*unwanted*—was no longer there.

There was so much Turtle wanted to tell his brother when he returned, so much joy he wanted to share with him. Yet as the days and then weeks passed with no A.D. in sight, Turtle's haste to get home lessened. It wasn't that he no longer missed his brother. There was something bigger in his life now, something more important.

"I've always wanted to ask you about that scar," Turtle said one afternoon. It was Monday of the last week of school. With no homework to do, Turtle was teaching Rita the fine art of skipping stones.

She blushed when he asked the question, her complexion darkening, and Turtle wondered if he'd gone too far. "It's so ugly," she said dismissively and tossed her stone. *Skip, skip.*

"No, it's not. I like it. It's cool and mysterious." Turtle flung his stone sidearm, the way A.D. had taught him: *skip…skip…skip…skip.*

Rita gazed into his eyes and saw he wasn't lying about the scar. He liked it. She smiled then, and sat down in the soft grass. "If I tell you, all the mystery will be gone," she said, a gentle tease.

Turtle sat down beside her. "It'll still be cool," he said with coaxing grin. "Besides, I'm sure there are more mysteries in your life."

She eyed him thoughtfully. "Someone pushed me as I was walking up a flight of stairs. Actually, not just *someone*, my best friend. She pushed and I tripped and fell into the steel lip of the upper step head first. I needed five stitches." She absently ran the fingers of her left hand along the scar.

"So it was an accident then?"

"No. She was trying to hurt me." Rita stared into the creek. She sighed heavily. "We were in the third grade. Maria Santos had been my best friend since kindergarten. She was a pretty girl, and she knew it, with straight black hair like Morticia Addams." She laughed. "All the boys liked her, but she only had eyes for Hector Avila, with his dark wavy hair and full lips. To us, he looked like a teen idol from *Tiger Beat* or some other heartthrob magazine." She laughed again, yet this laugh seemed darker. "When we played with our dolls, her babies' names were always Hector, her husband's name was Hector. She was infatuated with him." Rita stopped and looked at him. "This is a stupid story."

"No. I want to hear it," Turtle said, his words coming quickly. "It's part of you. I want to know everything about you." She again gazed into his eyes and nodded.

"We were coming back from assembly," she said with a prolonged sigh.

Her eyes were once again on the creek. "We were headed to our classroom on the third floor. The teacher always had us walk in two lines, side-by-side, holding hands. That day, I got paired up with Hector. I couldn't believe my luck. I liked Hector, too," she said, lowering her voice, as if Maria might hear. "But whenever I stood next to Maria Santos, all he, or anyone, could ever see was her."

"Uh-oh," Turtle said, still smiling, although he could feel something chilling was about to occur.

Rita laughed. "Uh-oh is right. Hector had a dog. I don't know what kind of dog it was, but I started asking him about the dog as if I cared. As it turned out, Hector had a lot to say about dogs." She laughed again. It was an easy laugh, and yet there was pain in it. "I don't remember anything he said. I was just happy he was talking to me. *Me.* I felt special. For one moment, I was no longer Maria's shadow. I didn't want him to be my boyfriend or anything. I knew how Maria felt about him. I just wanted a little attention." Her expression darkened. "Then someone pushed me from behind, really hard. My books went flying, I went flying. Blood was every-where."

"Oh, man! Did it hurt?"

"I was too embarrassed to feel any pain. The kids were all laughing at me as little kids do when something like that happens. I looked behind me, and there was Maria, staring at me with eyes of hate."

"I'm sorry," Turtle said, and put his hand on top of hers.

"Later, she called me a backstabber and said she was tired of me. She said she was going to start hanging out with Lucy Sanchez. She told me there were lots of me's in the world but only one her. She told me to keep that in mind the next time I tried to steal somebody's boyfriend. I was nine years old when I discovered how cruel friendship can be."

Turtle didn't know what to say after that. He was sorry he'd asked about the scar, although pleased that Rita had revealed this tiny secret about her-self. He put his arm around her shoulder. "Wanna skip some more stones?" he asked.

"Nah," she replied, her eyes still lost in the waters of the creek.

"Not all friendship is cruel," he said.

She looked into his eyes, but didn't smile. "I know," she replied, her voice a near whisper. "I know." She placed her head on his shoulder, and together they sat silently staring into the creek until the sun went down.

✗ ✗ ✗

Mike Monicker knew how to get the most out of the last days of school. With the lessons all taught, and finals over and done, to keep his students interested, Mike had invented the Kerwood Derby Awards. The awards were given to the top three students in each of his science classes. They were handed out on the next to the last day of school before summer break.

The award itself was a simple pin made out of hatband ribbon, very similar to the ribbon of the Kerwood Derby hatband. While the pin may have been simple, the students deemed the award prestigious. Each year, the winners sported their pins on their prideful chests the last few days of the semester. It was an honor to win the Kerwood Derby Award. No one took it lightly.

Tuesday before summer break, Rita started hinting she thought Turtle might win. "Okay, maybe not first place. Darlene Goldberg may have you there, but definitely second. Second place, easy."

"There are at least ten kids in our class that are good in science, Rita," Turtle protested, although he was pleased she thought he could win.

"Not as good as you. Wear your white shirt on Thursday. And wear a tie."

"A tie!" Turtle practically squealed like a pig.

"You look cute in ties."

"Nobody looks cute in ties. Ties make me look like a dweeb." Although his face was scrunched up, Turtle enjoyed Rita fussing over him as much as he enjoyed fussing over her.

"And get a new pair of slacks. Those are falling off of you." Turtle glanced down at his waistband, which floated dangerously low on his hips. He was losing weight.

He hiked his pants up, his expression turning stiff. There was no way his parents were going to spring for a new pair of slacks for the last two days of school. "I'll wear a tie," he said, "but the new pants is not gonna happen. I'll punch a new hole in my belt instead."

"No. I'll not have my boyfriend looking like a Beverly Hillbilly with his pants cinched around his waist. Bring them over tonight, and I'll take them in."

Turtle was thrilled, although he tried not to show it. And there was that word again—*boyfriend*. He never knew when she was going to spring it on him. She used it sparingly, offering it up like the treat that it was.

"And now *you*," Turtle said with a mischievous grin. "I want all your fingernails to be painted the same color."

"What!" It was Rita's turn to squeal. She was smiling, though.

"I'll not have my girlfriend looking like a package of *Chuckles*," he said, mimicking her tone.

"One color is *boring*," Rita chimed, laying on the *boring* extra hard.

"One color is…" Turtle searched for the right word, "classy," he finally said, adding a satisfied grin.

"Classy's *boring*," Rita groused. She said something more in Spanish that Turtle couldn't understand.

"No fair!" he cried out. "If I can't speak Klingon around you, you can't speak Spanish."

"I *said*, if that's what you want for your special day, that's what you'll have. As you wish," she said, and bowed her head like a fairytale prince.

Later that evening, after dinner, Turtle announced he was going over to Rita's for a little while. His parents were in the living room watching *Three's Company*. They didn't look up. They both grunted at him. *Yes*. They reminded him of horses in a stable, grunting and pawing the earth. Neither asked who she was, where she lived, or when he'd be back.

Unwanted. Unloved. No, he thought. *I **am** wanted.*

Turtle said, "I'll be sure to be back by eleven," and left.

❧ ❧ ❧

He was seated on the old sofa in the living room with a cat on his lap when Rita offered him something to eat. When Turtle said he wasn't hungry, he'd already had dinner, Rita's abuela, who was sitting in the armchair across the room reading a paperback novel, lifted her gaze.

"You have to eat a little something. She's been cooking all afternoon," Abuela said.

"No, I haven't!" Rita screeched, stomping her foot like a petulant child.

"She's been cooking for you," Abuela added, not looking at her granddaughter. "I may be a little forgetful, but I don't ever remember her spending this much time in the kitchen for me," she said with a wry smile.

"Abuela! Me estás avergonzando," Rita barked.

Turtle heard the harshness of her tone, saw the reddening of her complexion. "Umm. I would like a little something. Truth is, I *am* hungry. I just didn't want to admit it."

An ember of a smile appeared on Rita's lips, as her harsh expression softened. "You don't have to," she said with the voice of a little girl.

"I want to," Turtle replied. "Just don't feed me too much, or you won't have to take my pants in."

Rita laughed. Abuela laughed. Turtle laughed, pleased with himself.

The fragrance in the kitchen was heavenly, pungent and new.

"What is it?" Turtle asked as he sat down at the table. A cat weaved between his legs.

"Molcajete. It's like a stew. It's Mexican. I'm not. I found it in a cook book. I'm Puerto Rican." Rita began scooping the stew into a big bowl. "My grandmother lies," she said, lowering her voice. "She enjoys embarrassing me. I make this all the time."

"Still, I'll pretend you made it just for me," Turtle said, prompting Rita to treat him to one of her most glorious smiles.

The molcajete was one of the most delicious meals Turtle had ever eaten, featuring chicken and sausage in a thick, savory broth that tickled as it went down, made even more delectable because it was prepared for him by Rita with her own hands.

"You like Kool Aid?" Rita asked. "I made cherry Kool Aid to wash it down."

Cherry Kool Aid was his favorite. *How could she have known?*

Turtle grinned. "My friend's Kool," he said and chuckled.

"Huh?"

"You don't remember that commercial? It was really popular."

When Rita said she didn't, Turtle told her the commercial and explained the joke shared between him and his brother.

"I don't get it," she said.

"Yeah, I know. Nothing to get. But for some reason, for us, it's funny as hell," he said, his eyes drifting momentarily into the past.

After Rita had taken his pants in, they retired to the back porch where they held hands, listening to the crickets and cats, staring at the garden pockmarked with gopher holes. Turtle knew for certain this had to be the best night of his life. He'd fallen so deeply into glorious love he'd never be able to fall out.

"No sex out there," Abuela called from inside the house.

Rita got up and closed the open door.

ɤ ɤ ɤ

Science was seventh period.

Both Turtle and Rita couldn't help but notice students turning up throughout the day with Kerwood Derby Awards pinned to their chests. Each time Rita saw a student with a pin, she'd point and smile.

"He should have worn a tie," she said of Mark Andruw, a seventh grader who was wearing a pin.

"Don't be so conceited," Turtle said. He was, of course, wearing his white shirt with a blue paisley tie, his once falling down slacks clinging perfectly to his slimmer waist.

Rita stuck her tongue out and waved her camera at him. Her fingernails were all painted the same color—a happy eggshell blue.

When seventh period began, Turtle felt a lump form in his throat. How embarrassing it would be if they had both been wrong. He was obviously dressed up for something special. While no one mentioned it, everyone knew the blue paisley tie was in anticipation of winning a Kerwood Derby Award.

"All right, all right," Mr. Monicker called, quieting the class as he entered the room. "I'm not going to keep you in suspense. I'm sure you've seen students from my earlier classes wearing their Kerwood Derby Awards. Now it's your turn. Are you ready?"

The room fell silent. The lump in Turtle's throat grew larger. He was having trouble breathing around it.

Mr. Monicker did a drumroll with his lips. "And now for the winners of the seventh period Kerwood Derby Awards. Third place goes to Rudolph Simmons. Come on up, Rudy."

There was a smattering of applause as Rudy moved up to the front of the room. Mr. Monicker pinned his award on his blue dress shirt and shook his hand. "Way to go, son."

When Darlene Goldberg was awarded second place, Turtle began recalculating. There were seven other students in their class who had as good a shot as any to win. He was certain the first place winner was not him.

Rita caught his eye and smiled, giving a furtive thumbs up. Turtle smiled back as best he could. He felt sick to his stomach. He knew she'd console him when Lindsay Booker or Jim Mitchell won. The idea of Rita consoling him made him sicker.

"And first place goes to the man in the blue paisley tie—the only one of you who dared dress up for the occasion. Theodore Dawson."

Even though Turtle heard his name, he thought he'd heard someone else's. It was only when Rita started squealing that he knew he'd won.

Turtle practically floated up to the front of the room, grinning like the Cheshire cat as Mr. Monicker pinned on his award. He couldn't believe all the good that had come his way. He had no way of knowing that his tidal wave of good fortune was about to recede.

After Mr. Monicker thanked all the winners and posed for several of Rita's photos, he said he had an important announcement to make. The winners all returned to their seats, and the class quieted.

"During lunch, someone got into our room and made off with the Kerwood Derby." The class let out a collective gasp. "I'm sorry to report this. The derby has meant so much to me and my students over the years. It breaks my heart that someone would stoop so low as to steal something that brings so much pleasure to the students of Charles Drew. I know no one in this class did it, but if any of you should hear anything about the theft, think twice before you conceal it. Remember all the joy the hat has brought and could continue to bring. If you know anything about it, anything at all, I hope you'll be brave enough to report what you know, even if you do it anonymously."

A pall fell over the room. The Kerwood Derby had been a school icon for as far back as any of them could remember.

Ansley Meade's hand rose slowly into the air. Mr. Monicker raised an eyebrow. This was an odd occurrence. In the entire eighteen weeks that Ansley Meade had been in class, not once had he raised his hand.

"Yes, Mr. Meade?"

Ansley stood. "I know who took it, sir," he said, his eyes diving for his shoes as if he were embarrassed to tell.

"Speak up, son. Do you know something about the theft of the Kerwood Derby?"

"I do," he said. "I saw it with my own eyes." He peeked over at Turtle. "It was the new girl who took it, sir. Rita Calderon."

CHAPTER ELEVEN

Mike Monicker

"Liar!" Rita cried out.

Murmurs mushroomed up around the room. This was the kind of drama middle schoolers relished.

"Quiet!" Mr. Monicker called. "Or one of you might be going to the principal's office on the next-to-last-day of the semester."

The murmuring stopped abruptly.

Of all the students in his seventh period class who might have stolen the derby, Mike Monicker would have bet good money on Ansley Meade, and yet here was Ansley pointing the finger at someone else. "And how do you know this?" Mike Monicker asked, attempting to draw the boy out.

"Like I said, I saw it. Saw it with my own eyes," Ansley replied. He shifted his weight from one foot to the other.

Mike knew if he were ever to retrieve the derby from the real thief, he had to carry on as if he was pursuing Ansley's ridiculous lead. "Miss Calderon, what do you have to say for yourself?"

"He's lying," she said. "He's just out to get me is all."

"I don't even know her," Ansley blurted. "I'm sure she's nice *most* of the time. I'm not out to get anyone, sir." His gaze again found Turtle. "I saw her take the derby, and I followed her, you know, like Knight Rider." The class erupted in laughter.

"Silence!" Mike called out. As soon as they were quiet, his eyes were back on Ansley. "And where did your investigation lead, Mr. Meade?" he inquired with soft sarcasm.

"When the sixth period bell rang, she rushed back to homeroom and put it in the back of her cubby."

"So the hat is now in Miss Calderon's cubby?"

"I guess. That's where I saw her put it." Ansley looked over at Rita and affected an apologetic expression. "Sorry, Rita. Normally I wouldn't say anything. I'm not a tattletale. But the Kerwood Derby means too much to too many people. I had to." He cast his eyes downward, an Academy Award winning performance.

"You motherfucker!" Rita exploded.

Ansley cast an appalled eye at Monicker. "Oh, my God! The mouth on her," he said.

"That'll be enough, Miss Calderon. You're in enough trouble as it is," said Mike Monicker. He didn't believe Rita Calderon was in trouble. He believed he was giving Ansley Meade enough rope to hang himself. "Thank you for your honesty, Mr. Meade."

Ansley shrugged. "Sure. You're welcome." He started to sit back down.

"And what were you doing in the corridor at lunchtime?" Mike suddenly asked, freezing Ansley in mid-air.

"Huh?"

"Students aren't allowed to roam the halls between classes. So what were *you* doing in the corridor?"

Ansley gazed at his teacher with an odd expression, as if maybe he was losing control of the situation. "Oh, right," he said, and finished sitting down. "I was having…cramps. I was on my way to the nurse."

Soft titters erupted around him. "You mean like *girls* get?" Craig Piper called out. The laughter began to spread.

"Boys can get em, too! Right, Mr. Monicker?" Ansley cried, his eyes blazing at the students around him.

"Yes, Ansley. It is *possible* for a boy to get a cramp." The load of shit Ansley Meade was dishing up was getting thicker, so thick Mike Monicker thought he might drown in it. "Quiet down, now," he said, again silencing the class.

Turtle

The entire time the farce was going down, Turtle hadn't moved. He'd become Rodin's *The Thinker*, only he wasn't thinking, his mind had become petrified along with his body. His eyes and ears were all that remained operational, and the more he saw and heard, the stiffer he became.

Unwanted.

The thought emerged, floating before his eyes like a balloon with a hideous happy face. If he didn't do something to help Rita, if he wasn't her white knight riding in on a powerful steed, come to save the day, then what good was he to her?

Unwanted.

This attack was aimed at him. This was Ansley's revenge for him getting out of the ass whuppin'. He hadn't moved on as Turtle had thought. He'd been lying in wait, planning to take them both down. It was a masterful plan. *Perfect tens*, Turtle thought.

He recalled the look in Ansley's eyes that afternoon on Prospect Avenue. What was it he'd seen in them? Pain. No, it was more than pain. It was the excruciating pain of Ansley's miserable life, pain he wanted others to feel as well, pain he wanted to share.

Turtle knew he had to do something to save Rita, but he was too stifled by fear, his long-time friend and musical accompanist, to think of what he might do.

"Would you mind showing me where she put my hat?" Mr. Monicker said.

A tight smile creased Ansley's lips. "Sure. No problem," he replied.

Mike Monicker sent a monitor ahead to let Miss Lawrence know they'd be paying a visit to her class. It was the end of the semester. It was certain he wouldn't catch her class in the middle of anything. He gathered his class, told them to remain silent as they walked through the halls, then they walked down to the far end of the building to his homeroom classroom.

Mike Monicker

Two classes were squeezed into room one-oh-three. It was a warm day, and all the bodies heated things up quickly. When everyone was settled, Mike instructed Rita to empty out her cubby in the back of the room.

He saw her shoot Turtle a helpless glance as she moved to her cubby. He didn't know how Ansley had managed it, but he was sure as rain she'd find The Kerwood Derby there.

She removed an old sweater that wasn't hers, some papers that were, and then, in the back she felt it. The hat had been mangled, mashed up and squeezed into a corner. She removed the nearly destroyed hat, and when everyone in the room saw it, they let out gasps of horror. Everyone, that is, except Ansley Meade. He was practically laughing.

When Mike Monicker saw the utter disrespect a student could have for his belongings, he lost it. "How did you get into this room?" he roared, his eyes popping like a madman's. "It was locked. I locked it myself before I went to lunch."

Ansley stood waiting for Rita to respond, until he realized Mr. Monicker was looking at *him*. "Excuse me?" he said, beginning to feel uneasy.

"You know that little girl didn't steal my hat. It was you! Admit it now, and I'll go easy on you."

"I didn't do it!" Ansley cried out. "You think because she's a girl she can't steal? You don't know her. She's not from around here. She's from New Jersey. She's mean!"

"Ansley. We all know it was you. This theft has your fingerprints all over it. *You* just happened to be in the hallway when the thief walked by, *you* followed her, *you* were the only one who saw. I don't have to be Sherlock Holmes to figure this one out, Ansley."

Ansley looked from Mr. Monicker, to Rita, to the faces of his classmates. He couldn't believe how quickly things had turned.

"I saw her, too," a voice called out. The voice belonged to the other fat boy in class, the one who sat next to Turtle in homeroom, Ross Rainey. "I saw her moving through the halls with your hat under her jacket, sir. I saw her come in here." Through his entire speech, Ross was looking at Turtle. "I saw her leave without it."

"I told you! She's mean!" Ansley cried.

This new development threw a wrench into Mike Monicker's plans to bring the Meade boy down. He knew Ross wasn't telling the truth. *Why is he doing this?* They weren't friends. Ansley was always making fun of the fat boys, or threatening to beat them up.

"Mr. Rainey, I want you to think about what you just told me," Mike said, slowly, patiently. "This is a grave accusation. If someone has *threatened* you, forcing you to make it, that person will be facing expulsion. And if you're caught lying, the same will happen to you." He moved closer to the boy. "So I'm going to ask you, did you actually *see* Miss Calderon with the Kerwood Derby?"

"Yes," Ross replied without hesitation. His eyes again found Turtle.

Mike Monicker sighed, as he felt the real culprit slipping through his fingers. "Miss Calderon, do you have anything to say for yourself?"

"I didn't steal the Kerwood Derby," she said, her voice cracking.

Mike was caught between a rock and a hard place. He had no way of proving Ansley Meade had stolen the hat, especially with Ross, an unlikely co-conspirator, backing his story.

"Miss Calderon, get your things. I'm going to have to send you down to the principal's office.

Rita picked up her near empty backpack.

"I helped," Turtle called out. "It was all my idea. I helped Rita steal your hat."

Mike Monicker had no idea what had gotten into these kids, Ross coming to Ansley's rescue, Turtle claiming he helped steal the hat. It was as if the world had turned upside down. Good was bad and bad was good. *What a cluster fuck!*

With a third person corroborating the story that Rita had taken the hat, *and* that he'd helped, Mike had no choice but to follow through with his threat. He stripped Turtle of his Kerwood Derby Award, then, sent both Rita and Turtle down to the office where Principal Taft immediately suspended them for the last day of the semester, pending further investigation in the fall.

✗ ✗ ✗

Turtle and Rita sat in Principal Taft's outer office waiting for Mabry and Rita's grandmother to come pick them up. They sat across from one another in hard chairs. They were forbidden to speak, yet when Miss Miles, the school secretary, took a quick bathroom break, Rita spoke up.

"What the fuck, Theo!" she whispered loudly.

The way she was looking at him made Turtle's heart ache; the cursing made it feel as though it might break. "I couldn't let them railroad you like that. He was trying to get *me*, not *you*," Turtle said, a soft plea.

"And with your help, he got *both* of us. You didn't make things better, Theo. You made them worse."

"Oh? I did," Turtle said, his voice getting small. He leaned back in his chair and let out a heaving sigh. He was dismayed by her response to what he'd done. He was trying to be her white knight. Boyfriends protected girlfriends just as big brothers protected little brothers. From the look of her, she wasn't feeling protected.

Rita saw his pained expression and softened. "Theo, it's—"

"No talking!" Miss Miles hustled back into the room, ending the conversation between them.

Rita shot him a dull, apologetic smile, and Turtle nodded, accepting the unspoken apology.

Rita's grandmother arrived first. She seemed disoriented as she walked into the outer office, although, upon seeing Rita, she offered up the warmest smile. Miss Miles escorted her in to meet with Principal Taft.

"Your grandmother okay? She seems a little out of it," said Turtle when the room was clear.

"Of course she's all right," Rita snapped. "You need to take care of your own situation, *Turtle*," she said, the glow in her eyes turning white hot with fury.

107

She called him Turtle. His father, upon seeing their one-year-old son crawl across the floor while playing with his mother, had declared *doesn't he look like the cutest little turtle?* The nickname had belonged to him for as far back as he could remember, yet when Rita used it, he felt even lower than he'd already been feeling. He liked that she called him Theo. It made him feel special. Rita calling him Turtle made him feel like the bubblegum scum on the soles of his shoes.

Shortly after, Rita's grandmother came out of the office looking none too pleased, and the two of them left. Rita avoided his gaze as they moved away. He was glad she didn't look at him. What he'd seen in her eyes a little while ago was disheartening, and if it were still there he knew his heart would shatter like glass.

Another half hour would pass before Turtle's parents arrived. Just when he thought no one was going to show—*unwanted*—they walked through the door, his father's arm around his mother, as if she were something fragile that might break.

✗ ✗ ✗

Turtle had always been an easy child. They'd never had a peep of trouble out of him until now. It had to be the girl.

When the Dawsons arrived home from school, Stan and Mabry sat Turtle down in the living room and forbade him to ever see the girl again. He complained that his parents hadn't heard the true story, that he and Rita were both innocent. He'd only come to her rescue because *Rita* had been set up by Ansley Meade, and that Ansley Meade had set her up as punishment for *him.*

It was a difficult story for his parents to believe. For them, Turtle was a fossil, frozen in time on the day of the accident. In their eyes, he was still an eleven-year-old, and the concepts of chivalry and revenge were too mature for an eleven-year-old. After hearing Turtle out, Stan Dawson announced that their decision would stand.

They confined him to his room for the rest of the evening. The first thing he thought upon arriving there and throwing himself on the bed was that he needed to call Rita. He needed to fix things between them. That's what was most important. He recalled the sour sound of her voice when she called him *Turtle.*

But how, he wondered, could he accomplish his goal? He couldn't go into the living room or kitchen and just pick up the telephone and call her. Even though his parents didn't care for him, they were on high alert now. It would be an act of insolence to call her. They'd never allow it. Maybe he could sneak out in the morning after his father left for work and find a pay phone. Someway, somehow he had to set things right.

Turtle absentmindedly reached into his stash box for a *Chocodile*. He hadn't replenished his stash in quite some time, and his supply had grown stale. He chose the package with the most give under thumb pressure. Then he lay back, unwrapped the snack, and bit into it. He chewed as he pondered his situation.

There was a time when he ranked *Chocodiles* among his closest friends. Whenever he needed a shoulder to lean on, his *Chocodiles* were always there—comforting, reliable, non-judgmental, consistent. Today the snack seemed foreign and tasteless. He attributed this to staleness, but in truth, it wasn't the snack that had changed. Turtle had wolfed down many a stale *Chocodile* in the past two years with no complaints; rather, it was Turtle who had changed. This was a good thing. He didn't know it at the time, but there were major, life-threatening challenges ahead, challenges where *Chocodiles* would be of no use.

✗ ✗ ✗

He woke up early from a fitful sleep. He'd been dreaming of Rita. They were still in the Principal's outer office in the hard chairs waiting for their parents. The lighting in the office was different, though. It was bright as a summer's day, squinty bright, even though they were indoors. The scowl on Rita's face when she said, *You need to take care of your own situation, Turtle,* made her look as ghastly as the bride of Frankenstein. The searing rage in her eyes, rage aimed at him, had him crying out in his sleep. The crying out had awakened him.

He wanted to fall back to sleep, but how could he sleep with things unresolved as they were? He needed to see her. He needed to know it wasn't over, that this was a mere blip on their life journey together. Most of all, he needed to once again see the glow in her green eyes.

He got out of bed, slipped into a tee shirt and jeans, his thoughts jetting along a mile a minute. Darkness peered in through the window shade. It was three forty-five a.m. First light was at least an hour away, and Turtle didn't see himself walking almost a mile in the darkness to the house on Featherbed Lane. By the time he'd laced up his sneaks, he knew he'd be riding Tyrone over to Rita's.

He grabbed his windbreaker, crept his door open, and ventured into the corridor. A.D.'s door was closed as always. He thought he felt a chill emanating from A.D.'s room, and his heart danced in his chest. What would he say if A.D. was in there? A.D. would tease him about Rita, maybe even call him a doof for getting in trouble the way he did.

You're going over there at four in the morning? Are you in love?

If A.D. asked, he wondered if he'd have the nerve to answer truthfully.

He eased open A.D's bedroom door, grateful to find the room empty as it had been for two years. He eyed Tyrone, sandwiched between the bed and the wall, and pondered how he'd get the bike out without waking his parents.

Turtle reached over the side of the bed and began lifting Tyrone, using just his arms, no legs or back to absorb the weight of the bike. The awkward angle rendered Tyrone both heavy and cumbersome. The front wheel began to turn. Turtle grabbed it in one quick motion, silencing the ball bearings, only now he was supporting Tyrone's entire weight with one hand, his flabby arm muscles screaming in agony. His hand grew slick with greasy sweat. The frame began to slide, and for one horrible moment he thought he was going to drop the bike, waking his parents down the hall with a start. Then he reminded himself of why he was doing this. *For Rita,* he thought, summoning a wellspring of strength he didn't know he had.

By the time he hauled the bike over the side of the bed and onto the floor, he was exhausted and sweating profusely. Still, he found himself chuckling, exhilarated that he'd gotten this far. He slid his windbreaker between the front wheel and frame, tying it off so the wheel wouldn't turn.

He slow-rolled the bike to the door on its creaky hind wheel. Then another thought occurred. Suppose his parents *had* heard him? Suppose they were out there right now? How would he explain himself? He eased open the door, holding his breath against his parents waiting for him on the other side. Upon finding the corridor empty, he let the breath out, even more exhilarated than before. He was going to make it. He could feel his adrenaline flowing as he rolled the bike down the corridor on its hind wheel and out of the house. It was an awesome feeling, a feeling of power. It was as if his lungs were open so wide he could breathe in the entire world. He was taking control of his life.

He walked the bike a few doors down from his own before he removed his windbreaker, freeing the front wheel. Then he mounted Tyrone and pushed off. While the street was still lined with shadows, morning light shone bright in the horizon. He had no fear of the shadows. He felt amazing.

He rode down Trinity, past Prospect Avenue, opting to stay off the main drag for fear of being seen. He moved along the side streets and byways, enjoying the stillness of early morning.

He hadn't been on Tyrone in quite a while, yet the bike pedaled easily as his mind ratcheted from subject to subject, a kind of mindless riding haze. His thoughts settled on how angry A.D. had become when their father first brought the bike home.

"Did you get one for Turtle?" he'd asked, his brow knitted.

"Son, I was lucky to get this one. Mac's son, Gerard, is getting a car now. He won't be riding it anymore, and I remembered how much you boys wanted a bicycle."

"We can't both ride one bike, Dad!" A.D. railed, his very familiar dark side emerging.

"It's okay," Turtle remembered saying, trying to calm his brother down.

"No, it's not okay! He needs to get you one, too. I'm not riding it until he does," A.D. said and stomped off to his room, leaving Stan with a bewildered expression on his face.

"Thanks, Dad," Turtle remembered saying. "He likes it. We both do. He'll come around."

"I'm sorry," his father had said, looking like a man who'd just come in last in the big race. "I can't afford another bike. I can't afford this one."

"It's cool, Dad. He'll come around. You'll see." Turtle began wheeling the bike away.

"You're a good son," Stan called after him.

It was months before A.D. even sat on the bike. It never got much use. There were warm Saturdays when he knew A.D. was just itching to go riding, but because of his sense of loyalty, the bike remained in his room, sandwiched between his bed and the wall. By the end of the year, A.D. was dead.

As Turtle neared the canal, he picked up speed. "Get down, Tyrone!" he cried out into the morning air. He had to laugh at that one.

The first time A.D. had deigned to ride the bike, he pedaled up and down the street calling: "Get down, Tyrone! Get down, Tyrone!" Turtle had no idea where he got the silly cry from, but they laughed and laughed over it, and the name stuck.

The shadows were gone by the time Turtle arrived on Featherbed Lane. He pedaled slowly toward Rita's home, dawn breaking over the canal, the smell of river water in the air. He suddenly realized he hadn't thought beyond arriving there. Now that he was close, he wasn't sure how to proceed.

He couldn't just knock on her front door this early in the morning, especially in light of what had happened at school. He thought about throwing pebbles against her bedroom window, something he'd seen in a movie, but he had no idea which window was hers.

As he neared the house, his heart lurched. Someone was on the porch—a woman, seated on the railing, staring up the road away from him as if in thought, soft plumes of white smoke drifting in the air above her head. As he got closer, he realized it wasn't Grandma, as he had thought, but Rita who was on the porch in a white granny night gown, smoking.

It was an odd sight, the young girl seated on the porch, appearing so grown up. She hadn't yet seen him, and something told him to turn around before she did. She wouldn't want him to see her like this. He thought of the look in her eyes in the principal's outer office. What if those were the eyes that shined upon him as she caught him spying on her in a private moment—angry eyes?

He started to turn back, and the old bike creaked. She turned. "Theo?" she called softly, a sense of disbelief in her voice. "Theo, is that you?"

He couldn't leave now. He had to face the music. Turtle looked up, and, with a withered smile, continued toward her. "Uh-huh," he replied, dry mouthed.

"What are you doing here?" He was still too far away to see her eyes in the low morning light. He was glad of that.

"Umm. I don't know."

As he drew nearer, he was relieved to see a smile on her face. Her brown hair was tucked under a dingy gray cloth that made her looked like a pirate. A very beautiful pirate.

"I can't believe you came all this way." She seemed more than surprised. She seemed delighted.

"You smoke?" he said, stepping onto the lower step of the porch. The old wooden floor boards complained loudly in the quiet morning air.

She immediately put the *Camels* cigarette out. "It's a nasty habit. I don't do it all the time, just when I need to think."

She patted a spot on the rail next to where she was sitting. Turtle left Tyrone at the foot of the steps and joined her on the porch.

"What are you doing here?" she repeated.

"I couldn't sleep."

"Me, either," she said. She remained silent for several minutes, and just when Turtle was about to make up an excuse as to why he couldn't sleep she said: "I'm sorry for the way I spoke to you yesterday. That was totally uncalled for."

"It's okay," he replied, afraid to say more.

"I'm so full of secrets," she said, her voice a desolate whisper. "I wasn't mad at you," she said and squeezed his hand. "I was afraid that you...any-one really, would find out."

"Find out what?"

"My abuela *is* losing it," she said, her voice choked with remorse.

He remembered saying something like: *Your grandmother okay? She seems a little out of it.* He didn't think anything of it at the time.

She told him about the onset of her abuela's Alzheimer's, and that she

112

was happy in Foster City, very happy, but if the wrong people found out how bad things were with her Abuela, she'd be taken away. "That day is coming, Theo. I can tell." She wagged her head slowly back and forth.

Relief washed over Turtle like a drenching summer shower. In some religions, they take the unindoctrinated down to the river to be baptized, holding them under for several minutes, and when the newly baptized emerges, it's as if they're brand new. The relief washing over Turtle made him feel baptized, as it were. This was a new beginning for the both of them. He hadn't lost her. She was still here, still with the glow in her eyes, and because she had shared her most precious secret with him, their relationship was deeper than before.

He tried chastising himself for being filled with joy while she was clearly miserable over her grandmother's condition, but he couldn't help it. He rationalized that the sharing of secrets created a bond that couldn't be broken, although he was moving farther and farther away from ever telling her *his* secret. But he didn't think about that just then; instead, he draped an arm around her shoulder and drew her closer.

"I appreciate you coming to my rescue, Theo. It was a gentlemanly thing to do," Rita said. "Stupid, but gentlemanly."

Turtle laughed, surprising himself at his willingness to be the butt of the joke. "Idiotic is more like it," he said. "I saw them lying about you and my brain froze. I didn't know what do to, but I knew I couldn't let you take the fall by yourself."

"My hero," she said. He wasn't sure if she was being sarcastic, but he knew all had been forgiven.

"I'll get us out of this mess. You'll see." He gave her shoulder a reassuring squeeze.

This was a new role for him—the protector. A.D. had been his protector for as far back as he could remember. His relationship with Rita had started with her protecting him, but now things were balancing out. He was there for her, just as she had been there for him.

"I must look a fright," she said, suddenly feeling self-conscious. She turned away, removed the gray scarf and quickly began taking her hair down.

"You look fine." Turtle had seen his mother with her hair in rollers and face slathered in cream. That was a fright. Rita was far from frightful. With her hair up, the secrets of her face were revealed to him, the indentation around her mouth, the thickness of her eyebrows. She appeared even more beautiful. It was a different type of beauty with her hair hidden under the scarf, fresh-faced and natural.

"You're too kind," Rita replied.

Her hair down, Rita leaned back into his arms, resting her head on his shoulder. They sat engulfed in silence, listening to the day begin. With morning light washing over them, the cats began waking, emerging from the house and various hidey holes onto the porch. Inigo, Don Pedro and Carlotta began scolding Rita for sitting outside with Turtle instead of filling their bowls with food. Carlotta went so far as to slip between them where she began nudging Rita with her left paw, all the while continuing with a soft whine. Eventually, Rita told Turtle she had to go inside.

"Abuela shouldn't see you here," she said pulling away. "She'll be mad at me if she does."

"Meet me at The Lots later today," he said.

"I don't know if I can. I'm being punished for yesterday."

"Yeah, me too," he said with a sly grin. They were in it together. He fantasized it was the two of them against the world, like Bonnie and Clyde. The romantic thought made him feel even closer to her. "Try," he asked with urgency.

"Okay." She took his hands in hers, giving them a good squeeze. "Thank you for coming this morning. I really needed this." She kissed him gently on the lips. "Go," she said. As Turtle mounted Tyrone, she started into the house, stopped and turned around. "My friend's Kool," she called after him.

🐾 🐾 🐾

Ansley Meade decided to start his summer vacation early. Morning sun was peppering through the holes in the window shade. The room he shared with his two brothers was heating up—today was going to be a hot one—and yet he hadn't made any attempt to get out of bed.

Butch and Bubba were already off to school—*yeah, right!*—and Ansley had decided to sleep in, faking a stomach virus on the last day of school so he could lay there and bask in how well he'd ended the semester. His grades still sucked the big one—*the teachers are all out to get me*—yet he'd gone to sleep with a shit eatin' grin on his face, and it was still there when he awoke.

What a fuckin' moron, he thought, rolling onto his back and placing his hands behind his head. He stared at the ceiling. Actually, they were all morons—Lard Ass (although the lard was thinning), Rita, Mr. Monicker—and he'd proven it beyond the shadow of a doubt. He still couldn't get over how that that idiot, Jabba the Fat Fuckin' Turd, had backed him up. Just when things were starting to look shaky with Mr. M, Jabba backed him up.

114

Does he think I'm gonna be all grateful now and never whup his ass again? Think again, fat boy!

He laughed himself into a coughing jag over that one. He thought of how miserable Lardo looked when they hauled his sorry ass away. He'd gazed over at Ansley with a crybaby expression, and it took all of Ansley's willpower not to call out *Gotcha, sucker!*

That little romance is shot to shit now. He thought. *No way is Rita gonna spend another minute with that pathetic creep. Serves them both right. No one likes a show-off.* And that's exactly what they'd been doing with Lard Ass carrying her books everywhere as if he really was her *man,* and her shooting goo-goo eyes at his once-fat ass as if she actually cared. *Bet she cares now—cares about saving her own ass, that is.*

Ansley lay there, draped in a cocoon of self-pride. He always knew he was smart. Oh, they tried to make out he was a dumbass like Butch and Bubba, but he knew better. And now he'd proven it. He'd outsmarted all of them. And the beauty part, the part that would stick in everyone's craw, was they *all* knew he did it—his classmates, Mr. know-it-all Monicker, Principal Taft, *everyone.*

Proof, he thought. *The proof is in the pudding, or some bullshit like that.* He laughed again when he couldn't exactly remember the phrase he was searching for, or what it was supposed to mean. He was too wrapped up in himself to care.

Mr. Monicker was right: *the door **was** locked. I locked it myself right after I crushed his stupid hat and stuck it in Rita's cubby.*

"Fuck it!" Ansley murmured as another thought occurred to him. *I guess I have to go to school today after all. I'm going to be the talk of the entire campus. Can't miss out on that.*

Ansley rolled out of bed, pulled out one of his favorite *fuck you* tee shirts, the one with *If You're Happy And You Know It…* written across the front in bold in-your-face letters. He always wore this particular shirt the day after he'd dished out an ass whuppin', so his victim could see the grin on his face and know he was wearin' it just to fuck with him.

Perfect, he thought, as he slipped it over his head. The cool cotton felt good against skin tacky with dried night sweat. Ansley envisioned himself wearing his shit eatin' grin over the tee shirt all day. The teachers and principal would give him hard looks and roll their eyes, and he'd just grin back because there was NOTHING ANY OF THEM COULD DO ABOUT IT. They didn't have proof, and without proof he could rub their noses in his shit all he wanted. This was going to go down as the crime of the century, and he'd gotten away with it because he was smarter than them. Now *that* was truth.

Ansley Meade is about to make his debut as the most popular kid at school, he thought, mouthing cheers. Then he went into the kitchen and fixed himself a bowl of Cocoa Puffs. He had to moisten them with water. Butch and Bubba had finished the milk.

July 1982

When Lawrence was a little kid, the Barker family's yearly visits to Brigantine Castle were the highlight of his summer. Lawrence loved scary things, and Brigantine Castle's drafty towers, rat-infested dungeons (rubber rats, of course), and hidden corridors populated by ghosts and ghouls always scared the living crap out of him. But now that Lawrence Barker was thirteen, and a bona fide teenager, the yearly trips to the castle, also known as *Dark In The Park*, had become a lame joke perpetrated on Lawrence and his older brother Carl by parents who were too lazy to cut the umbilical cord.

As a kid, roaming the darkened corridors of the oversized, gothic Halloween haunted mansion was a scary thrill, but after four straight years, it had become a bore. Carl, who had just turned fifteen, had long ago been yammering he didn't want to go the castle anymore. But did their parents listen? Hell no! The castle by the sea and the amusement pier a short walk away, surrounded by ocean and green, green hills, were the only structures for miles. Their lazy parents had discovered a few years earlier that they could dump the boys off at the castle and pier and disappear to some other (more fun) part of the Jersey shore with their own friends without having to worry about Carl or Lawrence getting into anything. Lazy—that's what they were, too lazy to keep an eye on their own kids.

Lawrence knew Carl was up to something the minute he asked if Jack and Kirby could come along this summer. Carl was regaling the boys with tales of the bitchin (yes, he used that word) frights at the castle in front of his parents. It was as if he were describing a trip to Disney World instead of Lame Land. The boys *oohed* and *ahhed* in all the right places.

Horse puckey! Lawrence could smell it even if his too-dumb-for-their-own-good parents couldn't. There was something else he could smell, too—marijuana. Yeah, the clever boys stuffed towels around the cracks above and below Carl's bedroom door when they were in there smoking, and they were constantly burning incense, but Lawrence could still smell it.

Carl told his folks the incense was to kill the odor of his stinky sweat socks, and their mother was happy—yes, *happy*—that her son was finally

116

starting to care about such things. Lawrence knew if his parents weren't such party animals themselves they might have seen through the lie. I mean, come on! Does incense really mask the odor of pot? Of course not.

Lawrence approached Carl the Friday before the trip to Brigantine Castle.

"I want to get high with you guys tomorrow," he said, easing into Carl's bedroom and shutting the door behind himself.

Carl was lying on his bed watching TV. Actually, the TV was watching him. It was just past eleven in the morning, and yet Carl was already nodding off in a ganja haze.

"High? What're you talking about, dude?" he said, sounding like the stoner he had become.

"I'm thirteen now. I'm ready to hit a joint with you guys," Lawrence said and thumped his chest. Then he went over to Carl's dresser, pulled out the Thin Mint Girl Scout cookie box under the underwear in the top drawer, and dumped thirteen joints from the box onto the floor.

"Yo, yo, Dude! What the fuck? Suppose Mom or Dad walked in here right now?" Carl slurred. Then he slunk off the bed, got down on all fours and began sweeping the joints with his right hand into his left.

"They come in here, I'll tell them I want to be a pothead just like my big brother."

Carl began laughing the uncontrollable laughter of a pothead. "You got balls, kid," he said, choking on his stoner wit.

The next day, after their parents dropped them off, Carl promised that during the evening they'd meet up under the pier where he, Jack, and Kirby would indoctrinate Lawrence into the ways of the world. He said those exact words, as if he'd suddenly developed depth. Then he and his friends strolled down to the amusement pier in search of girls who might be looking for a good time.

Lawrence decided not to push it. It was early yet, and if he balked they might never let him hit a joint with them, and hitting a joint had become his greatest desire in life. For Lawrence, smoking reefer would be the true benchmark that he had entered his teenage years.

He decided to take a stroll through the castle and see if there were any good scares remaining. He preferred not to do it stone sober, but later that night, after he was *indoctrinated into the ways of the world,* he'd come back and experience Brigantine Castle in a whole new way.

Lawrence approached the castle gates. The entry area was crowded with a hodge-podge of entertainers there to lure in the suckers. There was a Hindu fire eater, a medieval juggler, and for the little kiddies, a life-size blue teddy bear. Lawrence remembered seeing the bear the previous summer. The little ones seemed to love the way the teddy bear danced, although Lawrence was too old for such nonsense.

Later, after a trip through the castle, Lawrence wandered down to the pier. The castle wasn't as lame as he thought it would be. The new chainsaw guy was pretty scary. The buzzing of his chainsaw chasing Lawrence through the darkness down a maze of corridors set his heart to thunka thunkin'. It was worth the price of admission. What a kick it would be to come back later and experience the chainsaw guy after he was toasted. He'd tell Carl, and Jack and Kirby about him, and maybe they'd come along. That'd be really neat, hanging with older teenagers.

The sun was beginning to set when Lawrence arrived at the pier. After he'd had his fill of hot dogs and salt water taffy, he felt it was time for another experience—getting high.

He looked around for Carl, Jack, and Kirby, and when he couldn't find them, he decided to go up on the Ferris wheel. The wheel almost always stopped when it was near the top, allowing riders a breath-taking view of the pier jutting out into the ocean. Lawrence would use the stop to gaze down at the pier from above where he was sure to spot his brother and friends.

Yet when the creaky old Ferris wheel paused at the top, Lawrence couldn't find the boys anywhere in the crowd. Surprisingly, what he did see was the giant blue teddy bear from outside the castle. It appeared as though the bear was gazing up at the riders on the Ferris wheel. From the way the bear was looking up, it actually appeared as though it was looking at him.

No little kids over here, teddy bear.

Once Lawrence realized he couldn't locate the boys down on the pier, he decided to sit back and enjoy the ride. Afterwards, he cruised the back alley where all the vendors parked their trucks and vans, searching for a cloud of smoke and a familiar fragrance. He was headed for the underside of the pier, although he was beginning to get the feeling he'd been sucker-punched by Carl. He was becoming more and more certain that by the time he found them, all the weed would be gone. *Damn!*

The alley smelled of old grease and stale sweat—nothing like the pungent sweetness of marijuana. Lawrence turned a corner, and something moved by the old Volkswagen bus up ahead. Leaning against the Volkswagen was the blue teddy bear. As soon as he saw Lawrence, he began to dance.

"Get outta here, bear. I'm not a little kid. I'm thirteen," Lawrence said as he barreled ahead. He was about to brush past the bear when the bear spoke to him.

"You're looking for the boys with the mara-g-juana, ain't you?"

Lawrence stopped short just in front of the bear. He was surprised at how clear the bear sounded, not muffled like a voice coming from inside a suit.

"How'd you do that? You got some kind of speaker in there?"

"I might," the bear said. He did a few more steps of his stupid dance.

"Fuck you, you stupid bear. I'm trying to find my brother," Lawrence said. He'd had enough of the dude in the bear suit. He figured if the bear had just seen them they were still in possession of their stash, on their way to the underside of the pier where he was supposed to meet up with them.

Lawrence started past the bear. As he moved past, he smelled a strange, acrid odor—like nail polish remover, but stronger.

He was moving away from the bear into the darkness when the bear said: "It's so sad when parents let children use such language."

Lawrence was turning back to tell the bear *fuck you* one more time. He didn't get around to it, though, because the bear's wooly arms swarmed around his neck, and something, a cloth, was in his face, and that smell of nail polish remover was stronger than ever. Not as strong as the bear, though. Lawrence tried to fight, but his brain was clouding over with confusion, and the fight was going out of him. He was starting to feel—high.

"That's it, don't fight," the bear said in a strangely soothing tone. Lawrence wanted to fight. He wanted to let the bear know he was no punk. He was thirteen, practically a man, but the words of the bear seemed to soothe him.

"Ookay," he mumbled through the rag over his nose and mouth.

Next thing he knew, he was slumping to the ground, and he realized how sleepy he was getting. He wasn't high, he was sleepy. It had been a long day.

"That's it," the bear cooed softly. "A few more moments and we'll get you away from those bad parents to a place where you can truly be happy."

✗ ✗ ✗

The Brigantine Castle was closed the next day as a countywide search for thirteen-year-old Lawrence Barker began. It was as if the boy had dropped off the face of the earth.

Local Sherriff Mark Fitzgibbons told the media there were several leads to follow up on as several park customers recalled seeing Lawrence throughout the day. He was certain the boy had wandered off to spend the night with some locals and would turn up soon. After all, things like kidnappings didn't happen in Brigantine, New Jersey.

Lawrence was last spotted around seven p.m. by Horace Carter, the twenty-two-year-old Ferris wheel jockey who said he remembered seeing Lawrence walking away after he'd ridden the Ferris wheel alone. He got the feeling Lawrence was looking for somebody.

While many visitors to the castle that day remembered seeing Lawrence, none of them mentioned a big blue teddy bear.

CHAPTER TWELVE

Bernie Pinkstring slipped away from the gathering, down the back staircase and into Miller's grocery. The air in the store was musty with the fragrance of overripe fruit. George Miller had given her permission to do a quick shop even though the store was closed.

Family and friends had all returned from a lovely service at Elysian Park and converged on the Miller's place for a repast. George had insisted on holding the repast in the little apartment above the store because it was Annabelle's favorite place in the whole wide world. Bernie knew that to be true. Annabelle Miller was a homebody who didn't care much for social gatherings. Her favorite thing was curling up on the couch for a night of TV, tasty snacks, and cocktails.

A little while ago, Bernie had commented—quite innocently, mind you—that she needed a pint of half-and-half for her coffee in the morning, and George told her to go downstairs and do a quick shop on him. The store would be closed for a few days of mourning, and he didn't want his special customers going without…or going over to the larger supermarket in the mall never to be heard from again. Bernie appreciated the kind gesture.

The store was exceptionally quiet when Bernie entered that afternoon, no bratty kids running up and down the aisles, no gossiping biddies hanging around the counter. She couldn't help but consider how nice it would be if she could do her shopping like this all the time. This was how celebrities did it—after hours, so they could stroll the aisles leisurely without having to deal with autograph seekers or the paparazzi.

She immediately felt the sure hand of guilt yank on her skirt the way Mother might have done when she got out of line as a young girl. This was a one-time thing. She should be grateful for it. She was only afforded the shopping privilege because one of her dearest friends had passed away. Thinking about herself at a time like this was just plain wrong, and God don't like ugly.

What a sweet, sweet man, Bernie thought, correcting her selfish and ungodlike thinking as she grabbed a hand-basket and started down aisle one toward the dairy case. That's when the thing hit her upside the head, a jolt of energy so powerful it sent her teetering like a rodeo clown who'd just received a double dose of hind leg from a Brahma bull. Bernie Pinkstring took two quick steps back, grabbed her head with one hand, and latched onto a shelf for support with the other.

"Oh my!" she exclaimed as she exhaled dizzily.

As her faculties began to return, Bernie realized she'd just received a jolt of psychic energy. This wasn't a nudge from some misguided spirit needing to get on over to the other side, either. This was the most powerful jolt of energy she'd received in her entire fifty-six years of existence. Her black Audrey Hepburn *Breakfast at Tiffany's* funeral hat was cocked drunkenly to the side as she caught hold of her breath. Her thoughts ricocheted wildly inside her head like a bullet in a stone quarry. *Who? Where? Why?*

Whoever the spirit was, he (yes, it was a young man, she was sure of that) was no longer present. That made the presence of psychic energy even more alarming. Usually when she got a powerful jolt, the spirit was nearby, but Bernie got no sense of him. This spirit was long gone, and yet a heavy measure of his psychic energy had been left behind. It was throughout the store, thick in the air, a whipped cream haze heavy with ill intention.

The most powerful vibrations were coming from aisle two. Bernie gathered herself, righted her hat, and moved toward the rear of the store to go around to aisle two and investigate. A part of her didn't want to investigate, wanted no part in whatever was going on in Miller's grocery. But Bernie knew it was her duty as a psychic and friend of the family to let George Miller know if something were amiss in his establishment.

The closer she got to the rear of the store, the harder it became to breathe. It was as if an invisible weight were pressing down on her. One thing for sure, the energy she was feeling was malignant energy, fraught with bad intention.

Despite her chest feeling as though an elephant were sitting on it, Bernie continued past the Miller Lite display and on around the corner at the rear of the store.

Even though it wasn't very warm, she saw that the soda case was fogged over, as if the refrigeration equipment had been working overtime to keep the sodas inside nice and cold. The glass was so covered with condensation, she couldn't see in. What Bernie did see was finger writing on the fog in the glass. The writing in the glass made her shallow breath hitch in the back of her throat. Her legs turned watery, and Bernie again reached for a shelf to hold herself up.

REDRUM

Bernie recognized the neatly written word in the glass from an old horror movie, *The Shining*. It was MURDER spelled backwards. The spirit had left this behind, she believed, as a sort of private joke. Bernie decided right then it was time to go.

She turned tail and, quickening her pace, moved away from the soda case, past the dairy case where, without stopping, she grabbed a half pint of half-and-half and continued on to the front of the store. She dropped her basket near the stack (George could sort it out later) and moved up the back stairs two at a time—something she hadn't done since she was in grade school.

Later that night, sitting at her dining table, pouring half-and-half into her coffee with a shaky hand (what she really needed was some brandy), Bernie allowed herself the luxury of thinking about what had occurred at Miller's Grocery earlier that day. Annabelle had been discovered, by her husband, lying on the floor of aisle two ten days ago, the same aisle that was now flooded over with malignant energy.

The coroner had ruled it a heart attack. Nobody thought anything of it, what with the way Annabelle scarfed potato chips, pork rinds, and other high cholesterol snacks. Everybody knew Annabelle's idea of a workout was sitting on her couch, exercising her jaws and eyeballs, reading, and watching hours of TV.

Yet as Bernie recalled the writing in the soda case glass, she knew Annabelle Miller did not die of a heart attack. She'd been murdered by a spirit. *Why?* Bernie didn't realize it was possible for a spirit to take a life. *If it was a spirit.* Whatever it was, it was something from the spirit world, an entity the likes of which Bernie had never come in contact with, and God willing, never would.

Bernie shivered as she wondered what the spirit thing might do to her if he found out she knew about his crime. She vowed never to tell a living soul what had happened that afternoon at Miller's Grocery, and decided it was high time she started shopping at the large supermarket in the mall.

❦ ❦ ❦

A.D. came back on Saturday, July ninth, 1988. Unlike the last time, Turtle didn't discover his brother sitting on his bedroom floor. Instead, Turtle came upon his brother at their favorite place in the world—The Lots.

It was a hazy afternoon, the sun playing hide-and-seek among the clouds, cooking up waves of oppressive humidity. The sweet fragrance of honeysuckle and butterfly weed, mixed with the garbage smell of the vacant lot, lay heavy in the air. The Lots had a fragrance all its own, neither good nor bad, fresh nor decaying. Years later, after Turtle was grown, he'd think of it as the smell of adventure.

A.D. was seated under a large maple tree, his back against the bristly trunk. A can of diet Dr. Pepper was turned up to his lips, his Adam's apple bobbing rapidly as he drank, making him appear as though he were starring in his very own TV soda commercial.

Turtle's punishment over the Kerwood Derby incident had come to an end, and Turtle had gone down to the deep part of the creek to fill his two super-soaker water rifles. He was returning up top with the loaded guns for a rendezvous with Rita. The summer had begun with miserable heat and stifling humidity, and Turtle thought it'd be a treat for them to have a soaking. That's what he and A.D. used to call it when they'd take their water rifles down to The Lots and spend all day hiding behind trees and in the tall grass, ambushing one another, putting down the Rebel Alliance, lasering water at each other until they were drenched from head to toe.

"This diet shit tastes awful," was the first thing A.D. said to him. Turtle had just come over the rise when he saw his brother sitting under the tree. A.D. wiped his mouth on the back of his hand. "You'd think if they were gonna make something new, they'd try to make it taste better. What's the point in making shitty-tasting soda?" He raised an eyebrow at his brother with a mischievous smile.

"Diet Dr. Pepper's not new," Turtle said. His voice came out huskily, as if he'd just awoken from a deep sleep.

"It's not?" A.D. peered at the can quizzically, turning it this way and that, just as a doctor might peer at a tumor on a patient's finger. "You can bet this is the last one I'll ever drink." He dumped the remaining contents into the dry earth beneath the tree, then tossed the can into the weeds. "Whatcha got there?" he said leaning forward.

From the moment Turtle had first seen his brother, his entire body had gone numb. His stomach began churning butter-like bile that flowed up the back of his throat like lava, lapping against his tongue with molten acidity before ebbing back down.

He gaped at his older brother, vomit rising into his mouth. He'd emerged over the rise carrying the super soakers along with the promise of a glorious day. That was no longer to be.

Over the past several weeks, as A.D.'s absence grew longer, Turtle had gotten used to the idea that A.D. wouldn't return. He'd very cleverly convinced himself A.D. had never returned in the first place. It had all been a dream, or a trick his mind had played on him. He'd had so much to deal with at the end of the school year, it was no wonder he'd been having such wild imaginings.

The trip to Miller's Grocery to steal the Tahitian Treat had been taken alone. Of course he'd been alone, which is why Mrs. Miller (rest in peace) didn't see anyone but him. He'd been acting out and using A.D. as his scapegoat. His parents were right; it *was* him who'd assembled the Millennium Falcon and left it on his brother's bedroom floor for them to find. He almost remembered doing so.

He'd been experiencing some form of temporary insanity. Nothing like Uncle Johnny, mind you, hence the word *temporary*. Now, with A.D. sitting right in front of him, Turtle had to revise his thoughts.

Crazy.

He at first tried to tell himself the temporary insanity must have returned. As difficult as that would be to accept, it was a lot easier than accepting the truth. He didn't want A.D. to come back. As much as he loved his brother, as much as he missed him, Turtle no longer wanted him back. With Rita in his life, A.D.'s presence felt like a complication.

A.D. saw his brother going pale and lurched forward, his face flooding with concern. "You all right, dude?"

Turtle lied. "Yeah. You were gone for so long, I didn't think you were coming back." A smile fissured onto his frozen lips. How he'd managed it, he didn't know.

A.D. relaxed a little and sat back. "Sorry about that, Mushmouse. It was unavoidable. You know I wouldn't leave you."

"I'm, uhh…glad….Welcome back." He could feel life slowly returning to his limbs. His smile broadened.

"Looks like you been working out, Rambo," A.D. said with a teasing grin.

"Let's get out of here," Turtle said abruptly.

"Why? We love it here. And it looks like you're planning a soaking. Who's the other gun for?"

"No one special." Something in Turtle's gut told him it wasn't time to tell A.D. about Rita, and maybe it never would be. "You," he said. He thrust the gun toward A.D.

125

"You don't wanna mess with me, dude. I'm the super soaking champeen of the world."

"Were," said Turtle. "There's a new sheriff in town, and his name's Turtle," he said, affecting his cowboy drawl.

A.D. grinned at his brother as he grabbed hold of the water rifle. He hefted it in his hands. It felt full. "You're diggin' yer own—" Before the last word was out a stream of water hit A.D. in the face.

"Talk's cheap, pardner," Turtle said with a grin, leaping out of range before A.D.'s return fire could strike him.

"May The Force be with you!" A.D. cried out, scrambling to his feet and firing away.

Turtle swerved away from the spray and into the brush. A.D. gave chase and waded into the tall grass, crouching low as he maneuvered himself deeper into The Lots.

"Use The Force, Luke," Turtle called, teasing A.D. with one of their favorite lines from *Star Wars*. He skidded down the embankment toward the creek.

"I'm gonna use it all right!" A.D. called back, giggling as he fired a shower in Turtle's direction.

Turtle began paralleling the creek bed. His maneuvering had purpose. He needed to get A.D. as far away from the area as possible. Rita would be arriving soon.

❧ ❧ ❧

That night they hung out in Turtle's room. They lay across his bed, comic books open on the floor beneath them, snacking from the stash box as they pored over X-Men adventures. During the day the old feelings had returned, the feelings of love and loss surrounding his brother. By the time they'd emptied their super-soakers for the last time, the setting sun was a golden haze in the horizon, and Turtle was conflicted.

Like it or not, he was bound to A.D., the bindings forged in the fires of years of constant companionship. He felt helplessly attached to him. It was as if he were a child with an old familiar teddy bear, one he'd had for as far back as he could remember. The stuffing was showing and an eyeball was hanging by a thread, yet no matter how ugly it had become, he couldn't let it go.

A.D. was a part of him. The past few weeks with Rita had been the most wonderful weeks of his life. Despite the Kerwood Derby incident—which might have crushed a different version of Turtle—the end of the school year had been a magical time. But Rita was his friend, and A.D. was his brother. His *brother*. Blood.

He suspected there was no way he could hang onto both of them. Telling Rita about his dead brother back from the grave was like saying Sayonara, senorita. He wasn't sure how A.D. might respond if he told him about Rita, either (Yes, *if*, not when), but he got an empty feeling in the pit of his stomach every time he thought about it. He tried telling himself he was waiting for the right moment to tell each of them about the other. But in his heart of hearts, he felt his wonderful new life was surrounded by the walls of Jericho, and that if the truth ever got out, the walls would come tumbling down.

He again thought of how things might have been if A.D. had never returned.

"You're getting' awful quiet over there, Mushmouse. You gettin' sleepy?" A.D.'s voice, gentle and soothing, pulled him from his thoughts.

"Nah. I was just thinking." His own voice seemed muted, even to himself.

"About what?"

"Umm, about us."

After a brief silence A.D. said, "Is this the part where we kiss?"

Turtle snorted out a laugh. Only A.D. could make him laugh so easily. "Pucker up, Buttercup," he said and reached for his brother.

A.D. rolled away from him, landing on his back. "Seriously. What's up?"

Turtle considered his brother, lying in the dark looking so very much alive. A.D. smiled at him. It was a coaxing smile. Since telling A.D. about Rita was off the table, Turtle's thoughts went careening around inside his head. His mind went into default mode, latching onto the kind of thing he would have told his protective brother two years earlier.

"Ansley Meade stole the Kerwood Derby," he said.

"Huh? What are you talking about?" A.D. was smiling at him. It was a playful smile as if Turtle were pulling his chain.

The story of the next to the last day of school began flowing from Turtle's lips. Even as he spoke, he felt the opening strains of hopelessness begin to play in the background. They played softly at first, a flicker in A.D.'s inquisitive eyes. The small voice inside should have told Turtle to stop talking, yet the words flowed, and as they did, A.D. rolled off of his back, first onto his side and then sitting up, listening intently, the familiar darkness building in his eyes.

A crescendo was brewing, like the end of a sad but brilliant overture, and Turtle got the sick feeling this song was going to end badly—a funeral dirge, but whose funeral?

Still, the words continued to flow. He couldn't stop himself. Whenever he was picked on in the past, or had a problem, he always brought it to A.D., and despite the sick feeling building inside, he couldn't help but repeat the familiar pattern.

A.D. was on his feet, pacing like a panther by the time Turtle had finished his tale. "Okay, come on," he said and began moving toward the door.

"Where?" Turtle's voice rose with panic.

A.D. turned to him, his face a mask of rage. "Where do you think?" he said, the rage spilling into his words.

"It's after ten o'clock." Turtle said, a near whine.

"Doesn't matter," A.D. replied. "Too much time has passed already."

"What are we going to do?" The words vibrated with fear.

"I don't know. I'll think of something on the way. Come on." A.D. looked at him pensively. "I'm sorry I wasn't here for you when this happened."

"That's okay," Turtle replied, wishing he could say more, wishing he could say this is my battle, not yours.

A.D. stomped across the room, placed his hand on the door knob.

"What are you?" The words slinked up Turtles throat and slid across his lips.

A.D. wheeled around, eyes incredulous. "What?"

"What are you?" he asked again. He was searching for anything that could keep them in the room.

"Not now, Mushmouse, okay? I'm your fucking brother. Okay?"

Turtle's head began to shake slowly. "Not okay. Before my brother died, he couldn't turn himself into smoke, crawl up my nose and shake loose long forgotten memories. No human being I know can do that. So forgive me for being so inquisitive, A.D., but WHAT THE FUCK ARE YOU?"

"I'M BACK!" A.D.'s words were a blast furnace of anger. "Let me ask you a question?" he said, taking a jab step toward Turtle. "What are *you*? What kind of man lets Ansley Meade get away with shit like that? You should be ashamed of yourself. You should've kicked his ass!"

"I can't beat Ansley."

"How do you know? Have you ever tried?"

"No," Turtle replied, and he could feel himself shrinking inside.

"I'm not gonna always be here to defend you, Turtle. But I'm here now. Let's go." He peered into Turtle's eyes, his own eyes blazing.

After a long moment, Turtle spoke. "Okay," he said, his voice a near whisper.

"Good," A.D. responded, releasing a tired sigh. "Good," he said again more softly as he turned and continued toward the door. After another moment, Turtle followed.

128

CHAPTER THIRTEEN

From the outside, the house on Brook Avenue revealed very little about the Meades who lived within. There was no way anyone could tell from the lawn going to seed that the Meades were a family consumed by unhappiness.

It was impossible to tell from the peeling paint on the sideboards that Allison Meade's bouts of sadness stemmed from her undiagnosed depression, or that she'd considered taking her own life and the lives of her three children several times.

The windows caked with grime also failed to reveal that right now Bert, Allison's husband, was snuggled in bed dreaming of hopping on one of the motorcycles he repaired during the day and riding off into the sunset, leaving the ten-ton burden of his family and his life behind. Nor did it say that this was a dream Bert had been having more and more lately, a dream he'd act on one day soon.

The welcome mat covered with mud did not disclose how hard it was for the Meades to welcome someone into the Meade home, a home where the occupants didn't feel welcome themselves. It was just a mat the Meades had set out years earlier, before their lives, like the lawn, had gone to seed.

"Down there," A.D. said. They'd stopped in front of the house for only a moment, A.D. quickly surveying the area. The rundown two-story clapboard was dark, and Turtle wondered if the Meades were even home. Wouldn't that be a stroke of luck if they weren't?

Turtle's heart had been racing the entire walk over. A.D. had been unnaturally quiet, and Turtle wondered what was he thinking, what was he planning. A.D. had left him alone at Miller's grocery to go in and steal the Tahitian Treat. Was A.D. now going to call out the Meade boys and disappear into the shadows while Turtle got the ass whuppin' Ansley had promised him?

A.D. started down the darkened driveway that led to the detached garage in the back, and Turtle followed. Their feet made a soft crunching sound on the sand and pebbles on the pavement, and Turtle was sure that at any moment a light would go on inside. They arrived at the rear of the house without incident.

Turtle stared up into the rear windows of the old house, fully expecting to see Ansley, or Bubba, or Butch peering out at them with angry eyes, but the house was silent, the window shades drawn against the darkness within.

"Come!" A.D. called in an urgent whisper.

The garage door at the end of the long driveway was open. The detached garage sat forty feet behind the house. Auto and motorcycle parts spilled out from within like fruit from a cornucopia. A late model Ford pickup sat ten feet from the garage door opening.

An old Mercedes 450 SL was stumped on cinder blocks off to the side. Bert had bought the heap at auction with dreams of restoring her to her old beauty. Those dreams had been dashed a long time ago. The Mercedes's dark colored paint job was completely weather-worn and had turned an angry shade of gray. The windshield, side, and back windows were covered with years of grime. There were cobwebs in the wheel wells.

The boys stopped beside the tail bed of the pickup and ducked down out of sight. "The tires," A.D. said in a loud whisper. "Slash them," he said, then slinked away into the shadows toward the garage.

"What?" Turtle squawked after him. "I don't have a knife."

"Oh," A.D. said, stopping for a moment to think. "Just let the air out then. You can do that, can't you?" he added with a note of sarcasm that wasn't wasted on Turtle. Without waiting for a response, he continued on and in moments was gobbled up by the darkness of the garage.

"Fuck you and the horse you rode in on," Turtle mumbled. It was a line they'd used on one another a thousand times, a harmless grenade lobbed at each other most times for a laugh. This time he meant it.

He could hear his brother rummaging around inside the garage. He again looked toward the house, his heart jitterbugging in his chest, expecting any moment for the back door to come swinging open and an angry Meade to come dashing out. After a short while, the noise in the garage stopped.

Turtle stared toward the silent darkness that was the garage for several moments, then sighed heavily. Resigned to his duty, he moved to the right rear wheel of the truck and unscrewed the valve stem. He mashed down on the pin inside and air began its whistling escape. It wasn't as loud as he imagined it would be. Looking up at the house, silent and dark, he told himself he might just get away with it.

130

He pressed down on the pin until his finger got tired; then he stopped and looked at the tire. Very little air had gone out. This was going to take a while. He again peered at the house. It remained dark and quiet. Grateful the Meades were sound sleepers, he went back to work.

A sloshing sound coming his way jarred Turtle from his thoughts. He looked up and saw A.D. grinning as he moved toward him through the darkness, hunched over like an old man. "Look what I found," he said, his voice trilling glee. He was holding a gas can. From the sound of the slosh it was near full. The fumes reached Turtle and stung his eyes. They began to water. "I think we done hit the motherlode, Festus," A.D. said in his playful western voice. There was nothing playful about the malevolence that gripped his expression.

"What the hell, A.D.?" Turtle clattered, either forgetting or no longer caring to keep his voice down. His heart was once again racing, thump-a-thumping in his chest as if it were about to knock a hole in it.

"That was taking too long," A.D. replied, pointing toward the tire.

"So now we're going to burn the house down?" Turtle's voice was shrill, like a mad person's.

"Course not. Just the truck. Move." A.D. flung the can out, splashing gasoline along the truck's left rear fender. Turtle didn't move in time and some of the gas landed on him. "Move!" A.D. commanded. He splashed again and the noxious liquid spurted from the can, running down the tires and onto the ground.

Turtle jumped back as the can flung out again. "All Ansley did was steal a hat." The gas fumes shot up his nose, stinging the membrane, making him feel as if he might sneeze.

"We gotta send a message, Mushmouse." A.D. headed back toward the front of the truck to the hood.

"All this time I thought you wanted me to fight him," Turtle called in a loud whisper.

"I did," A.D. called back as he continued pouring gas over the hood and fenders. From the sound, the gas can was almost empty. "You said you couldn't beat him. Right?" A.D. stopped and peered at his brother through the darkness.

"I know, but—" A.D. moved past Turtle, back to the rear of the truck. Turtle followed, the feeling of hopelessness trailing him like a pet dog. "But I don't want to destroy their property."

"He destroyed property, we destroy property. The X-Men would call this poetic justice." He poured the last of the gasoline over the tarp and motorcycle parts in the truck bed.

"But I could get in big trouble for this." He was sounding so pathetic, A.D. stopped pouring.

"No one's gonna get in any trouble, bro. They deserve this." He tossed the empty gas can into the shrubbery. An old style Zippo lighter appeared in his hand as if by magic. He flicked it open.

"Where'd you get that?" The panic in Turtle's voice had risen to a new degree of shrillness. He was more afraid in that moment than he'd ever been. This wasn't the boyhood fear of a monster or a ghost or an ass whuppin'. It was the fear he was about to participate in something horrible and life changing, something he could never take back.

"You know how resourceful I am, Punkinpuss," A.D. replied in a playful cartoon voice. There was nothing playful about the veil of evil strewn across his face. He scraped his thumb against the lighter wheel and the lighter flamed. It was a tiny flame, a mere flicker, and for a moment Turtle thought it was going to die.

"Whose out there?" a gravelly man's voice called from inside. A bulb above the back door came on casting an odd yellow glow over the area where the boys stood.

"Us!" A.D. called back. He tossed the lighter into the bed of the truck. The lighter landed on the tarp with a soft thud, and again Turtle thought it had died. Then the tarp ignited.

The Meades' back door banged open.

"RUN!" A.D. cried out, and he began sprinting past the open back door and up the darkened driveway, dissolving into the shadows.

"My fuckin' truck!" Bert Meade cried as he bolted onto the rear step of the house, wearing boxer shorts and what they once called a wife beater.

Turtle's eyes were still on the pickup. The fire began spreading along the truck bed and then *WHUMP*, a deep throated hum that seemed to suck all the oxygen out of the air erupted and the entire rear of the pickup truck ignited in golden flame. The flames shot up into the sky like a bottle rocket, illuminating Turtle's terrified face. He stood rooted to the spot, staring into the fire like a moth, hypnotized.

"My fuckin truck!" Bert Meade cried out louder this time, and began sprinting toward Turtle.

"Let's go, little bro," a voice called from the shadows.

Turtle turned to see Bert Meade barreling toward him, his face a mask of horror. "Aw, fuck," Turtle drawled. Bert Meade was on him, but instead of grabbing him, he brushed past, nearly knocking Turtle over.

"Bring the fire extinguishers!" he hollered over his shoulder. Turtle

132

turned back around, looking on as Bert Meade ran past the flaming truck and into the darkened garage.

A hand tugged at his shoulder. He turned, expecting to see Ansley Meade glaring at him in full ass whuppin' mode. Instead, he saw that A.D. had returned.

"We gotta get out of here, bro. We gotta get out of here *now*," he said, easy yet coaxing. He took Turtle by the hand and began yanking him up the driveway toward the street.

Turtle followed along like a zombie. One foot in front of the other was about all his brain could handle. It was as if the shock of the horror show he'd been witnessing had rendered him brain dead. Midway up, his senses (or survival instinct) finally kicked in, and he began running, slowly at first, like a locomotive pulling out of the station trying to get up a head of steam. Soon, he was running for his life.

The two boys bolted from the driveway and sprinted up the block. There was always a lot of running when they were younger, especially in the summer time. Running and laughter were Dawson summertime staples. No laughter this time, though. This time Turtle wasn't running from pirates or Federation storm troopers. There was nothing make-believe about the fear swimming in belly, bubbling up his throat so high he wondered if he'd have to stop along the side of the road and puke up his guts.

They were less than a block away when they heard the explosion. It rocked the neighborhood, sending a fireball into the sky over the Meade home, lighting up the heavens like the fourth of July. Turtle's legs buckled at the thought of Bert Meade going up in that explosion. He slumped to his knees, his legs feeling like they were made of some gelatinous substance that was impossible to hold him up. This time he did throw up all over his imitation Dr. J's.

A.D., who was running several feet ahead, stopped and came back. He helped his slumping brother to his feet as the foreboding sound of fire engines began playing on the night air, adding their own jaunty tune to the late night horror show.

"We can't run anymore, Turtle. If we run, we'll look guilty. Walk easy," he said.

As A.D. helped Turtle to his feet, Turtle thought: *we are guilty*. He refused to consider what he might be guilty of. Murder? Definitely mayhem. Whatever his guilt, it was too much to think about now. So Turtle walked alongside his dead brother, walking easy, keeping his mind as far as possible from what was going on at the Meade home; instead, he wondered what Rita might be doing on such a lovely night.

On the way home, they passed several thrill seekers drawn out into the night by the sound of fire engines and the yellow glow lighting up the sky. The thrill seekers scurried toward the fire, excitement in their eyes, just like the wise men following the star of Bethlehem on Christmas Eve. No one cast a second glance at the two boys walking in the opposite direction.

Not a word was shared between the boys during the walk home. For Turtle, it was as if he were walking home alone. Never before had he felt so isolated in the presence of his brother.

"What the fuck, man?" he finally managed. They'd moved up the walk-way to the Dawson house and had stepped off, disappearing into the shadows around to the far side.

"I...I didn't think it would blow up."

"What *did* you think?" Turtle inquired in a loud whisper. The boys had stopped just under Turtle's bedroom window. He faced his brother. The shock of what had occurred was wearing off, and Turtle's mind was filled with rage.

"I thought we'd get revenge," A.D. said, now sounding defensive.

"On *who*? Help me up," Turtle said, pointing to the open bedroom window just above them. A.D. cradled his hands. Turtle stepped into the cradle and was boosted up to the window ledge. He pulled himself up and in, then reached out to pull his brother up to the windowsill. They'd done this before.

Once the boys were inside he spoke again. "I forgot about you. When you were dead all I remembered was the good times. I'd forgotten about the other stuff."

"I'm sorry, Mush—" A.D. started a pained apology.

"Don't call me that!" The words fired from Turtle's lips. "I'm not your Mushmouse, or your Punkinpuss," he said. He kept his voice low, controlled, so his parents wouldn't hear, yet there was no hiding the rage that infused his words.

A.D.'s eyes sprung open in surprise, the white parts shining in the darkness. "You're...just upset," he said, back-pedaling.

"I'm *just* upset?" Turtle continued to rage, his voice growing thicker, like angry molasses. "He saw me, A.D. Ansley's father looked right at me."

"Does he know you?" Turtle couldn't tell if his brother was genuinely concerned or faking, but there was a noticeable shift in his tone.

"There aren't a lot of overweight, African American, thirteen-year-olds in Foster City, bro. If he doesn't remember me, I'm sure Ansley will be happy to point him in the right direction. The only way Mr. Meade doesn't turn me in to the cops is if he didn't live."

The brothers sat in brooding silence, Turtle listening for the sound of sirens moving in their direction. He was hoping for the sound. As frightening as it would be for the sirens to stop at their door, and for the police to come in and arrest him, it would be less than the horror of living with the consequences if there were no sirens. If there were no sirens it would mean that Ansley's father didn't live long enough to report what he'd seen.

Murderer. The word floated into his consciousness like a weightless egg. He'd used the word a thousand times before. Murder. Kill. Die. These were all fun words for an imaginative boy on a *Goonies* adventure. Yet today, the word shed the cloak of adventure, taking on its true horrific meaning, for Turtle knew with real murder came real consequences.

"What happened to you? I used to look up to you," he said.

"I died! That's what happened to me," A.D. replied, and Turtle could hear that he, too, was overcome with emotion. "I died," he repeated more softly. It was as if he were a sailboat, and the wind had gone out of his sails. "It's different, Turtle. You wouldn't understand, but being dead…it changes you. But I'm still A.D., still your big brother, still best friends, right?" This last part came as a whispered plea. "Right?"

"Why do you keep asking me to do horrible things?" Turtle asked.

After a moment's silence, A.D. replied: "I don't know. I guess I wanted to test your loyalty."

Every part of Turtle's body stiffened. "What? What did you say? My *loyalty*? Fuck you!" Turtle catapulted up off the bed.

"Hear me out, little brother. I need you to do something for me. That's why I'm back. It's something big. It's the type of thing you can't ask just anyone to do." He looked into Turtle's eyes. "I can never cross-over, can never rest in peace unless this thing gets done, so I…tested you."

Turtle was taken aback. "And did I pass?"

A.D. nodded. His eyes were vacant. "I know you'd want that for me, Turtle, to be able to cross-over, to be able to rest in peace."

In that moment, Turtle had a selfish thought. He thought of Rita. If he helped his brother cross-over, he could see his way clear to her. "You know I'd do anything for you. At least…I would have." His voice dropped an octave.

"I'm not so sure you'd have done this thing for me, Mu…Turtle. This is big." There was something about A.D.'s tone that sent a chill slicing up Turtle's back, the iciness moving like a cobra, coiling its way up his spine.

"And you need me to do this thing so you can cross-over?" he asked. He'd turned breathless, his words coming in an airy whisper.

"Yes."

"You should have trusted me enough to tell me that in the first place, A.D. Instead of asking me to steal a freakin' Tahitian Treat. Real best friends trust each other." He shook his head and sighed, and with that sigh he could feel his love and trust for his brother returning, an old familiar friend. He was a homing pigeon who would always return home. "The things you were asking me to do scared the crap out of me, bro. You never used to ask me to do things that were risky like that before."

"I know. I'm sorry." More silence, and then: "This thing I need you to do…it's risky."

Turtle swallowed hard. "What is it?" He could feel the invisible bindings that tethered him to his brother stiffen. He would always be bound to A.D.. He knew this now. He wasn't doing this for Rita as he'd convinced himself. Whatever he was about to do for A.D. he was doing because he had to.

"I need you to kill the Teddy Bear."

Turtle snorted out a weak laugh, a trial balloon, floated in the hopes that A.D. had been teasing him all along.

"So I off a teddy bear, and you get to cross-over. Is that it?" He forced a smile, even as the chill that had worked its way up his back was now clamping down on his shoulders and neck.

"Not *a* teddy bear. *The* Teddy Bear. That's what he goes by. He's not a toy or a cartoon character, Turtle. I wish he was, but he's not." There was sadness in his tone. "He's real. He's a dude wears a blue teddy bear suit. I'm sure you've seen him before—in the park, or at street fairs, dancin' around. He seems harmless, but he's bad news, Turtle. He kills young boys, and if you fuck this up, he'll kill you."

"What are you saying?" Turtle asked. The chill had now penetrated his skull, catapulting his mind back into shock, first the Meade fire and explosion, and now this. *Too much, too much.*

"The Teddy Bear is real, bro," A.D. said, gently yet deliberately, the look in his eyes turning deadly. His hand clamped down on top of his brother's. The hand was cold. "And the only way my soul will ever find peace is if *somebody* seeks my revenge and kills him."

136

book two

book two

CHAPTER FOURTEEN

The Teddy Bear came in the spring.

He arrived in Foster City on a blustery day in 1982 driving the beat-up Volkswagen bus he'd purchased when he was in his early twenties. The VW bus was considered an icon of the hippy counter-culture movement of the late sixties. He knew very little about hippies. He'd seen photos of them and didn't like the way they looked—dirty. For him, the old bus didn't represent anything in particular. It was simply a damn good purchase, an inexpensive, unpretentious mode of transportation. It was loyal. The bus had never let him down.

He'd spent three years from the late seventies on into the early eighties living on the Jersey shore residing in the tiny town of Wildwood, New Jersey. Wildwood, like most of the shore cities, was a seasonal town, bustling until summer's end when the tourists departed back to their bloated cities. What remained to wait out the brutal coastal winters were the locals, who mostly kept to themselves. He liked people who kept to themselves.

The Jersey shore had been good to the Teddy Bear. He'd rescued three boys while living there, all visitors, all incredibly grateful. But the Teddy Bear had a rule—when people started talking, it was time to move on.

The talk began during the summer of '82 when a five-year-old local girl, Christine Horner, went missing. Everyone believed it was her father, Tim Horner, who'd abducted the child after losing a long and contentious custody battle to the girl's recovering alcoholic mother, Emma Charles.

Despite the common belief about the kidnapping, a few of the local coffee shop busy bodies began wondering out loud about the loner who entertained children on the boardwalk dressed as a blue teddy bear. The wonder turned into curiosity, and he soon noticed the police observing him as he left his home in the morning, or while he danced on the boardwalk.

Even though Christine was found living with her father in Fort Lauderdale less than a month after she'd gone missing, he knew it was time to move on.

His name was Aldous Criss. Criss had had a very difficult childhood. Gerta, Criss's mother, never wanted children. She was a party girl, and when the son she called *The Mistake* came along, cutting into her *me* time, she was far from happy. She passed this unhappiness along to her son every chance she got. She beat him with an ironing cord for the least little infraction. Once, when he was ten, she sent him to the store for a pack of Pall Malls. When the man refused to sell cigs to a child, she beat him for coming home empty-handed.

Criss was twenty-five when he realized his purpose in life was to rescue the unhappy children of America from childhoods like the one he'd endured, and to take them to a happier place.

The first Foster City boy Criss saved came as a total surprise—a shocker, really. He'd gone to the Bijou Theater on a Saturday morning to audition for an animal character part in a new local children's television show. Criss had never thought about show business before, not really, but his love of children enamored him of the ad in the local paper, seeking actors to play the roles of life-sized animals who sang and danced.

Criss had been living in the Foster City area for just a short time back then and, of course, he'd come to town with his very own animal character costume. The Teddy Bear uniform. It hadn't been used for anything like acting before. Yet he envisioned himself saving children in a whole new way. On television he could reach out to hundreds, even thousands, of unhappy little boys.

It was perfect. No one knew how to be a lovable, cuddly teddy bear better than him. He practically invented the role. That's when Criss decided to wear the Teddy Bear uniform to the audition. Things went south from there.

"Why are you dressed like that?" the man said as Criss walked onto the stage. The man's name was Doug. Doug was the creator of the show along with his wife, Emily. Doug and Emily were seated in the front row, clipboards in hand. Doug hadn't spoken harshly. He was smiling when he asked the question.

"I'm the Teddy Bear," Aldous Criss replied with a sense of pride. He was on stage under the house lights, ready for his new career.

Emily whispered to Doug: "His voice is so crisp."

"He must be talking through some kind of speaker device in the mouth of the suit," Doug whispered back. Criss could hear them. The tiny equity waver theater was vacant except for the three of them (there were a few more actors waiting backstage). Their voices carried in the stillness.

Criss smiled. He always received reactions of delightful surprise whenever the Teddy Bear spoke.

"It's creepy," whispered Emily.

Criss shuddered inside the Teddy Bear uniform. He'd added that particular feature ten years ago, and this was the first time anyone had ever responded negatively to it. His face stung with embarrassment that soon turned to anger. *How dare she?* He pretended he didn't hear the snide remark from the stupid woman.

"We didn't ask anyone to bring their own costume," said Doug. He was a hippy type, with dark, overgrown hair, horn-rimmed glasses, and pleasant enough features, although his eyes were set too close together.

"I know. But every child loves a teddy bear," Criss replied in a jovial tone to let them know that if he'd heard them, he hadn't been insulted.

Emily cringed when he spoke. How rude of her.

"Unfortunately, there are no teddy bears in this show," Doug said.

"I'm sure you can make room for one as sweet and cuddly and friendly as me." Criss chuckled and did a few steps of his Teddy Bear dance. It always made the children smile.

"No. We can't," scoffed Emily, Doug's hippy bitch. "We have an elephant, a mouse, and a wise old owl." She spoke quickly. She reminded Criss of his mother, Gerta—never a kind word, always filling the airwaves with criticism. "The notice clearly stated we wanted actors to read for *those* roles." She was clearly not suited to be working with children.

"Of course," Criss replied. She was young, late twenties, with stringy, mid-shoulder brown hair, an ill-fitting, ankle-length floral print dress, and sandals. She had ugly, piggy feet. Criss wondered if she had children of her own. Probably not; if she did, she'd know of their affection for teddy bears. Whenever she did have children, they would be destined for lives of unhappiness. He filed this away for future reference.

"I can remove the suit and come back later," he said, although he knew he'd never set foot in the Bijou Theater again. If these were the kind of people that were working there, he wanted no part of show business.

"Yes. That's a good idea. Come back," said Doug.

Criss thanked them for their time—*you catch more flies with sugar than you do with vinegar*—and the audition was over.

He was still feeling the sting of rage and embarrassment when he exited the stage door into the alley behind the theater. That's when his day came alive. That's when he realized his real purpose for being there.

Standing in the alley, not ten feet away, was a small boy in blue and white pajamas—Criss's favorite colors. He couldn't have been more than five or six years old. He seemed frightened.

Criss looked up and down the alley for the child's parent or guardian. There wasn't another person in sight.

What kind of horrible parent lets a child so young go outside all by himself? And in his pajamas, no less?

The boy smiled at him. Despite the smile, Criss could see how unhappy he was. That's when he knew it was the hand of God that had brought him to the Bijou Theater that morning. He wasn't there for an audition. He'd been summoned there by God to save this child.

Criss eased into his Teddy Bear dance, and as expected, the child smiled (*Take that, Emily, with your ridiculous owls and mice*). He'd never saved a child without scouting him for several weeks, months even. One child he'd scouted for over a year. That day, however, he knew he'd been summoned there to save this child. *Now.* He began dancing up the alley toward his purpose.

Turtle

"It's against God."

By the time A.D. had finished running down the Teddy Bear's morbid history, Turtle was up and pacing. He'd become agitated as his brother spoke, and with good reason. His brother was talking about killing someone. He moved back and forth in the darkened room like a zoo animal striding the length of his cage and back, looking for a way out.

"Letting the air out of tires and stealing a Tahitian Treat are wrong. But this...this is *so* wrong! It's murder, A.D.," Turtle said. Mottled moonlight speckled his face.

"Who was always there for you, Turtle? No matter what. Fighting all your battles because you were too chicken to fight them for yourself."

"You didn't have to kill anyone."

"You don't know what I had to do!" A.D. stormed. "I did what I had to because you were my little brother, and I always took care of you."

Turtle stopped pacing and gazed at his brother, still on the bed. A.D. was highlighted by a shaft of moonlight that lit half his face. He was half in darkness, half in light, seeming like the black-and-white character from an old *Star Trek* episode they'd seen on TV. A.D. stared back at his younger brother with dead eyes.

"This isn't beating some boys up for trying to crash my lemonade stand, A.D. It's *murder.*" The word scraped against his vocal cords.

142

"I know what it is. Need I remind you that you may have killed some-one already?" A.D. used his hands to gesture an explosion. "Poof—boom!" he said.

"No, no! I'm going to get blamed for that but I didn't do it, *you* did. I'm not a *murderer*." Turtle squawked and went back to pacing.

"Don't look at it as murder," A.D. said. His voice had become calm, relaxed, as if they were talking about something as casual as the weather.

"Oh? And how should I look at it?" Turtle wheeled back around to face his brother.

"No living person knows about him but you," A.D. said, speaking softly. He moved his head slightly and came fully into the light. "He's killed a lot of kids, and he's going to do it again unless *you* stop him. That's not *wrong*, it's justice—just like *The Brotherhood of Evil Mutants*."

"That's a comic book! This is real life," Turtle squawked.

A.D. began shaking his head as if Turtle were letting him down. "Tur-tle, Turtle, Turtle," he said heaving a sigh.

"We don't need to kill him, A.D. We just need to expose him." He moved through the darkness to the bed and sat down beside his brother. "We expose him, he goes to jail, and the killing ends. *That's* justice, too."

"You do want me to cross-over, don't you?" A.D. said, his voice stiffen-ing.

"What? Of course I do, man."

"Then this. Must. Get. Done."

"I'd do almost anything for you, A.D. I love you, man, but killing is wrong. I do this, I'll have two deaths on my head." Turtle's voice turned ragged. This was feeling exactly like when A.D. had pestered him about exploring the haunted apartment building on Union Avenue when they were kids.

"Three," A.D. said. There was a dark shift in his tone.

"What? No, *two*." Turtle's eyes sprang wide.

"What about *my* death? That's on your head, too."

"You got hit by a car. How come we're not going after *him*, the driver?" Turtle called out in an attempt to change the subject. He was beginning to feel a sense of dread.

"Because I DON'T KNOW WHO KILLED ME!" A.D. bellowed, his voice so loud and thunderous the house shook on its foundation, the win-dows rattled like chains, the pictures on the walls vibrated. "Aside from you," he added, lowering his voice. "You faked sick and let me go out there alone."

"Naw, that's not true. I *was* sick. Remember?"

A.D. slowly wagged his head back and forth. "Naw, bro. You were scared. We both knew why you didn't go to the hobby shop with me that day. You were scared shit."

Tears formed in Turtle's eyes and began streaming down his cheeks. "That's not true," he muttered. His words, drenched in shame, were nearly inaudible. "You know that's not true. Take it back!"

"We both know it *is* true, Turtle. And I can prove it."

Turtle peered at his brother through tear-fogged eyes. "Huh?"

"Close your eyes. Close your eyes, and don't open them."

"But—"

"Close them!" A.D. commanded.

Turtle did as he was told. "What are you going to do?" he asked, sounding like a child. Even as he spoke the temperature in the room began plunging. In moments the air around him had turned thick and frosty. A foreboding overtook him.

"Don't open your eyes," A.D.'s voice called, swimming up from the cold.

"I won't," Turtle blubbered. He had a sense of what was coming.

A chilling vapor began moving up his left nostril, and then his right. He breathed it in deeply and the membrane in the back of his nasal passage burned as if it had been set on fire, yet he held his eyes shut tightly.

A distant memory drifted up from the sediment of memories long forgotten. It came as a ghost, shadowy and indistinct, yet in moments the vision cleared, and Turtle was transported back to the day before his brother died.

❦ ❦ ❦

Fourteen-year-old A.D. and eleven-year-old Turtle were standing outside the hobby shop on Prospect Avenue, staring in the large plate glass window with beggar's eyes. A large model of the Millennium Falcon hung front and center, suspended in air by invisible monofilament. A banner behind it read: An Exact Replica of The Space Craft Seen in *Star Wars*. Lower down in the window, amid the models of knights and soldiers and missiles and race cars, sat a smaller model of the falcon, the one they'd be purchasing.

"I betcha it shoots lasers," Turtle said, his voice vibrating with excitement, his gaze cast upward on the larger Millennium Falcon floating in the window above them.

"Naw, Mushmouse. It shoots photon torpedoes, just like in the movies," A.D. said knowingly.

"Right," Turtle said, his eyes never leaving the Millennium Falcon, his imagination running wild.

"Well, lookie, lookie, a couple of Wookiees," a teasing voice called from behind.

The boys turned, and before them stood Butch and Bubba Meade, although at that time, Turtle didn't know who they were. The Meade boys were laughing. There was orneriness in their eyes. Both boys had hit their growth spurt and were taller and bigger than A.D..

A.D. stepped forward in front of Turtle in big-brother protective mode. "Hi," he said. His voice was flat.

"Hi," the youngest of the Meade boys mimicked, his voice going high and whiny. This set off another wave of derisive laughter.

A.D. said nothing. He stood silently staring at the boys, his expression blank. Turtle knew the blank expression all too well. His knees began to rattle.

"What are you boys lookin' at?" the oldest Meade boy asked.

Turtle glanced over at A.D. who continued staring at the boys silently.

"Whazamatter? Cat got yer tongue?" the oldest Meade boy said.

"What if it does?" A.D. replied. The response was soft yet seething with open contempt.

Turtle had seen his brother in action before. A.D. was never afraid of a fight. In fact, most days he was itching for one. Turtle yanked on the back belt loop of A.D's jeans. There were two boys in front of them, and Turtle was sure as eggs he couldn't take either.

"What did you say?" the oldest boy said. He stepped up to A.D.. He was nearly a head taller.

"Whazamatter? Cat got yer *ears*?" A.D. said in the same mimicking tone the boy had used. He looked up at the boy. The darkness that often swirled in his eyes was there now, and he was smiling. It was the kind of smile you'd expect to find on rattlesnake before it struck its unsuspecting prey.

Turtle's entire body started quaking. He yanked harder on the belt loop.

The Meade boy took a step back. He wasn't sure how to handle this, the fearlessness, the anger, the danger in A.D.'s eyes. "This is our territory now. We don't want to see you two around here anymore, or there will be pain. Got it?

Turtle began nodding like a bobble head. *Please, A.D.. Please, please, please, let's get out of here!*

"Got it," A.D. replied. He turned to his younger brother. "You okay, Turtle?"

"Yep," he replied, his eyes pleading.

"Then let's blow this popsicle stand," A.D. said. He was trying to be smooth, sounding like an old movie hero. He turned and sashayed away, just like Han Solo might have walked away from some toughs at the Pirate City bar. Turtle smiled, letting out a relieved sigh, grateful he wasn't going to get his ass whupped. He followed. He did not sashay.

Later that evening, as they lay on A.D.s bed dreaming up adventures, A.D. informed him they had enough money to purchase the Millennium Falcon.

"Bull ticky," Turtle called out.

"No, seriously. We got it with the dollar I cadged last night. Tomorrow the Millennium Falcon will be ours."

Turtle should have been elated, yet an unease rose in his belly. He was getting the feeling there was something more to going to the hobby shop the next day, that A.D. was dying to run into the bullies again, dying to test their mettle.

He couldn't sleep. His fear had overtaken him, and all night he trembled at the idea of being forced to fight one of the bullies and getting his ass whupped. The next morning he announced he was coming down with something.

"You look fine to me," A.D. said. "And you'll feel a whole lot better after we get the Millennium Falcon in our hands." He smiled.

"Maybe we should do it another day."

A.D's eyes became darkening skies. He goaded Turtle to return to the hobby shop and pick up the model they'd been waiting a year for.

"I really want to go with you, but I think I got the flu. I feel like I'm gonna throw up. We can go another day."

"No!" A.D. said, the darkness swirling. "We waited a whole year for this."

"But I'm really, really sick, man—like dying. People die of the flu if they go out too soon."

A.D. took a deep breath and smiled. The clouds that had darkened his eyes parted. "No problem, Punkinpuss. I'll go. You stay here and rest. I'm sure puttin' it together will make you feel a whole lot better."

"I bet it will, too," Turtle said, casting a smile flooded with relief.

After counting out the crumpled-up one dollar bills three times, making sure they had enough money including the tax, A.D. patted his brother on the head and left his bedroom for the last time. "Rest here, in my room," he said.

"May the Force be with you," Turtle called after him.

"I'll be back before you know it, oh, Obi-Wan Kenobi," A.D. called back, and he was gone. Forever.

"Noooooo!" Turtle emerged from the memory screaming. He was lying in bed, tears of disgrace cascading from his eyes. His pillow was drenched in them. He bolted upright and gazed around the room. A chill still gripped the air. Turtle peered through the darkness, his eyes searching, though he knew he wouldn't see A.D. again for several days.

"I'm sorry," he called out, his voice echoing, drowning out the inner cry of *coward*. "I was scared," he muttered, whimpering.

He sat still as a painting for several moments engulfed in a cloak of shame. When no response to his apology came, he called out again. "I'll do it!" This was an anguished cry, ripping into the darkness. "I'll do it," he repeated more softly. Then he lay back, resting his head against his tear-soaked pillow, his eyes lost in the highways on the ceiling, as he listened for sirens. Only the sound of sirens could offer him any relief.

Ansley

Ansley Meade peeked through a hole in the shade of the bedroom he shared with his brothers, and looked down into the back to see what the hell his father was yammering about. He was always yammering about something.

His eyes widened, cartoon-style. "Holy shit! Dad's truck's on fire," he called to Butch and Bubba. Neither boy stirred.

As Ansley looked on, he saw his father running toward the garage to get a fire extinguisher. He brushed past a boy.

"What the..." Ansley said, his eyes growing even wider. The glow from the surging fire illuminated the boy standing on the concrete slab behind their house. It was Lard Ass Dawson. Lard Ass Dawson had set his father's pickup on fire.

Another boy reached from the shadows and pulled Dawson away. Ansley didn't get a good look at the second boy, who was back in the shadows too quickly. It didn't matter who Dawson's accomplice was anyway; nobody fucked with the Meade family, especially a Lard Ass. Ansley's skin began to prickle with indignation.

"Butch! Bubba! Lard Ass set Dad's truck on fire," Ansley called out loudly enough, yet both boys began snoring. He knew they'd heard him. Seems they didn't care if their father's truck was set on fire by one of his classmates, but Ansley did. "You guys suck, you know that?" The snoring increased in intensity, a loud and rumbling *fuck you!*

Ansley realized he had to take matters into his own hands. He hustled into a pair of shorts and the *If You're Happy And You Know It…*tee shirt he'd worn to school earlier. He ran from the room, doubled-timed it down the termite damaged staircase and out the front door.

When he hit the street, the two boys were still in sight, less than a block away, lit by the glimmer of a silvery moon. *Good. Fuckers.* Ansley took off on a run after them.

He couldn't believe the nerve of Lard Ass Dawson seeking revenge on him by burning up his father's truck. *What a moron.* Dawson was now in more trouble than he'd ever been in in his entire goody-two-shoes life. The fucker would probably go to jail for this.

Poor Rita, he thought. *She's gonna need some consoling.* He chuckled even as he got a hard-on at the thought that he'd be the first in line to console the Latin beauty. Another thought fired in his mind: *I like her.* He'd always liked her, which was strange considering he always thought he hated her.

The two boys turned the corner up ahead.

Ansley sped up, sprinting around the corner. He didn't see the boys when he'd made the turn, but he knew they were up ahead in the dark. He decided to stop for a moment and catch his breath. He'd catch up to them soon enough, and maybe hand Lard Ass the ass whuppin' he so richly deserved—if the other boy wasn't too big. If the other boy was big, he'd just threaten them until both boys peed their pants. Then he'd turn them in to the cops.

The side street he was on was silent, each of the row houses, lined up like wooden soldiers, was locked up tight for the night. The street was bathed in moonlight, pockmarked by the shadows of parked cars. Ansley began walking briskly up the street in the direction of the fleeing boys when somebody stepped from the shadow of the Volkswagen bus parked at the curb several feet ahead of him. No, not somebody, some*thing*—a big blue teddy bear.

"Hi there, Ansley Meade," the teddy bear said as if he was oh, so happy to see him.

Ansley had seen the bear entertaining little children around town over the years. He was a Foster City fixture, but he'd never heard the bear speak before. He was quite surprised the bear knew his name. He was also surprised at how clearly the bear's voice came through the costume, like a cartoon voice on TV. *He must have some kind of a speaker in the mouth part because his voice isn't muffled.*

The teddy bear started toward him.

"Not now, teddy bear. I got shit ta do," Ansley growled. He continued

148

moving up the street, his mind set on the two fleeing boys. As he drew nearer, the teddy bear stepped into his path and started to dance. "Get the fuck out my way, ya dumb bear!" Ansley said and shoved the bear. The blue teddy bear playfully staggered backwards in an over-exaggerated clown-type stagger.

"I will not tolerate such language," he heard the bear say as he was moving past. It was then he smelled the nail polish remover.

Turtle

Sleep was a foreigner in the Dawson home that night. Stan and Mabry had both been awakened by what they thought was an earthquake but soon realized was their son throwing a tantrum of some sort in his room. Stan wanted to go in and check on him, but he was too embarrassed after their last encounter. He and Mabry lay awake the rest of the night, listening to see if things got worse. Mabry again pressed the notion of military school to *fix* the boy.

For Turtle's part, when daylight began showing through his window and no knock came at their front door, he allowed himself to spiral into a fitful sleep in which he dreamed he was in prison. His jailer was a giant blue teddy bear who laughed at him and reminded him that fat boys never win.

He was asleep for all of twenty minutes, his eyes springing open when he thought he heard sirens. What he'd heard was his own snoring. He decided to get out of bed before the sun was fully up and fix himself a bowl of Froot Loops to calm his jangly nerves. He padded down to the kitchen. When he entered, he was surprised to find his father already seated at the kitchen table, lost in thought as he nursed a cup of black coffee.

Stan Dawson looked up at his son with a distant smile, forced and as artificial as the trees in the lobby of the local bank.

"Hey. You feel that earthquake last night?" he called.

"Umm, earthquake? No. I must have slept through it." Technically, it wasn't a lie since what they'd all experienced was not an earthquake.

"It was a doozie. Who knew we could have earthquakes on the East Coast." Stan took a sip of his coffee as Turtle removed the Froot Loops cereal box from the pantry. He shook it. Just enough left for one helping.

"Son, if you ever need any help…I'm here." Stan was staring at him with an expression Turtle didn't recognize. It made him uncomfortable.

"School's out, Dad. But, thanks," he replied.

"Not that kind of help," Stan muttered.

"Oh. Okay, thanks," Turtle said, not knowing how to respond. His father's demeanor was alarming to him. He wondered if he already knew about Bert Meade. But he couldn't. The phone hadn't rung all night. Turtle would've heard it. "Want some Froot Loops?" he asked.

It appeared as though his father's eyes were getting glassy.

"No thanks. Eat up." There was that smile again. Turtle moved to the refrigerator. "You know we, uhh…love you," his father said.

Turtle stopped, faced his father who suddenly looked tired and old. "Yeah. I know."

"Good."

A loud knock came at the front door. Turtle jumped at the sound. The container of milk slipped from his hands, dropping to the floor. Fortunately, it didn't explode all over the kitchen tiles. Turtle thought it was the only stroke of luck he'd had in days. His heart was palpitating.

Stan lurched up from the table. "Who in the world would come knocking this early in the morning?" he wondered out loud.

The police, maybe?

"I'll get it," Turtle called. He scooped the container of milk up from the floor, and without setting it down, exited for the front door. *Dead man walking.* He wondered if he asked the police to take him quietly and not say anything to his parents, would they oblige?

The knock came again, louder this time, and Turtle's heart rumbled. He arrived at the door, sucked in a deep breath, and pulled it open.

CHAPTER FIFTEEN

He was greeted by the most delightful green eyes.

"I'm sorry to come so early, but I knew you'd be worried," Rita said.

Seeing Rita standing outside his door when he was expecting to see the police was so out of context he didn't recognize her. He stood staring like a loon for several seconds, his mouth hanging open.

"Theo? Are you okay?"

"Rita," he finally gasped. "Come in." While she appeared worried, she looked amazing in a green-and-white top that made her eyes sparkle.

Her eyes moved from the startled look on his face to the container of milk in his hands. "I've come at a bad time," she said, embarrassment darkening her complexion. She took a step back.

"No, no. I was just having a bowl of Froot Loops. Come." He forced a smile, just like the one he'd seen on his father's face a short time earlier, grabbed her by the hand, and pulled her in.

He didn't know how he felt about her coming there and seeing him in the old gym shorts and Spiderman T-shirt he used as PJs. He didn't know why she'd come. He wondered if someone had told her about Bert Meade.

"It's just that, I knew you'd be worried," Rita said as he escorted her down the hall toward the kitchen.

"Worried about what?"

"About why I didn't show up at The Lots yesterday."

"Oh."

Rita heard the hitch in Turtle's voice and stopped in her tracks. "I guess I got it wrong." Her voice turned cold.

"No, Rita, it's not like that. I *was* worried about you…at least, I would have been worried. You need to hear me out." Life was suddenly coming at Turtle too quickly. He was a juggler who'd been tossed a few too many balls.

"Who's this?" Stan Dawson appeared in the kitchen doorway—another ball tossed in the mix.

"My friend from school, Rita. Rita, meet my Dad."

Stan fixed Rita with a fragile smile. "Pleased to meet you," he said, although his eyes told a different story.

"Nice to meet you, Mr. Dawson," she replied.

"We've, uhh, heard a lot about you," Stan said.

A look of surprise came upon Rita's face. Her eyes moved from Stan to Turtle as his eyes dove for his imitation Dr. J's. "Oh?"

"We'll be in my room," Turtle said quickly and began pulling Rita up the corridor.

"Nice meeting you," Stan called after them.

Turtle continued pulling her up the hall and into his room. Once inside, he closed the door.

"Theo, I think I made a mistake coming here this morning. And what did your father mean by—"

He kissed her. He placed his mouth on top of hers smothering her questions, just as a handy pot lid smothers a stovetop fire. Her breath caught—*hhh*—in the back of her throat as her mouth parted, and her tongue pushed forward, a sweet and delicious probe.

He kissed her because he knew he was losing her, and losing her would end his life. It was a life already waylaid by ruin, and if he lost her he may as well move on over to the other side. He kissed her because, even when all is lost, some things are worth fighting for. He kissed her because he loved her. He'd been wanting to kiss her like this—deeply, passionately—for a very long time but could never find the nerve. Now, with his life hanging in the balance, he threw caution to the wind and kissed her.

Rita swooned, leaning back against the door, her head knocking into the jacket that hung on the hook, her legs going wonky.

The kiss ended sweetly, and when it was done, Turtle lifted her hand to his lips and began kissing the tips of her fingers. His lips were trembling.

"I did a terrible thing," he said. He led her to sit on the edge of his bed, then began telling a tale that started when he discovered a boy wearing Spiderman PJs sitting on the floor surrounded by bits of unassembled Millennium Falcon, and ended in the Meade backyard with a deathly fire. It wouldn't be until much later that Turtle would discover why Rita never made it to The Lots the day before.

Rita

George Bailey was staring down Don Juan, who was seated in his favorite spot atop Abuela's lap. His back was arched as if he were ready for a tussle. Don Juan looked down at the scrawny cat from atop his comfy throne and yawned dismissively.

"Play nice," called Rita, observing the looming incident as she entered the room. "Don Juan, you spend all night with Abuela. It's someone else's turn to enjoy her." She moved to the couch and hefted the big orange cat from Abuela's lap. "All yours, George Bailey."

Don Juan didn't complain.

Rita was wearing shorts and a blue halter top with her two-piece swim suit underneath because, from what Turtle had told her, she was going to get soaked. She was looking forward to the soaking. As she started for the kitchen, Abuela glanced up from her reading.

"Is he coming to pick you up?" She said it innocently enough, yet Rita knew her abuela well enough to recognize a pin prick.

"No, Abuela. I'm meeting Theo at The Lots. It's not far. I'll be safe."

Abuela's eyes moved back into her book. "In my day, a gentleman always escorted his lady on a date," she said, pin-pricking her granddaughter again.

"It's not like that, Abuela," Rita said and began rushing for the kitchen before Abuela could poke more holes in her plans with tales of dating in the old days.

As she was feeding Don Juan his treat for relinquishing Abuela's lap (he purred her into giving him two), a knock came at the front door.

"You see," Abuela called as Rita moved through the living room for the door. "Your Theo turns out to be a gentleman after all, even if you don't want one."

Rita ignored her, although secretly she was pleased Theo had proven to be a gentleman. "Theo," she squealed with childlike delight as she pulled open the door. "This is a...surprise."

On the other side of the door stood her brother Sam, his wife, Elena, and her sister, Tora, who was holding baby Sam.

Elena

If there were a thousand and one places Elena could have chosen to spend a summer vacation, visiting Sam's abuela in Foster City would not

153

have been on the list. It wouldn't have made her second list, either. If there were a thousand and one lists, each containing a thousand and one places to spend summer vacation, God forsaken Foster City would not be on any of them. *This* trip to hell was all Rita's doing.

When Sam declared Rita had gotten in trouble at school, and that they needed to get to Foster City right away, Elena asked herself: *Did Rita plan this all along?* Rita was never a cut-up in school, always an A student, never into any kind of shenanigans whatsoever, so why now?

Why? Because it would be the perfect payback, forcing me to visit her there. That's why.

Rita was a cunning child; that was clear. Her battle to steal away Elena's family had not ended with her moving to Foster City as Elena had thought. It had merely shifted battlefields.

"Bring her back here," Elena had exclaimed when Sam said they should all go to Foster City. "We'll punish her by giving her extra chores all summer. That will teach her."

Sam was adamant. He insisted he had to see what was going on in Foster City for himself. He decided they should take the entire family on a little vacation. Baby Sam and Tora needed to get to know their abuela.

What comeback could she possibly have for a statement like that? If she complained, then *she'd* be the bad guy. *Very clever, Rita. Very clever.*

To top it all off, their arrival in Foster City contained one shock after another. First, there was the house. When Sam pulled up to the shanty on less-than-quaint Featherbed Lane, Elena asked him if he was sure he was in the right place. It looked to her like a flop house for homeless people. "It's been a long time since you've been here, sweetheart. You must have gotten it wrong."

When Sam assured her they were in the right place, Elena envisioned Rita, peering at them through her bedroom window, laughing hysterically.

The second shock was Rita herself. Elena didn't recognize her. She looked like a harlot when she answered the door. She was wearing shorts that went up to the top of her thighs, and a halter blouse that stopped just above her waist, revealing a hint of belly flesh. Her nails were painted more colors than an Easter egg hunt, and she was wearing lipstick. Elena would never have allowed Rita to get away with looking like a floozy when she lived with them. What was Abuela thinking allowing a thirteen-year-old to run around dressed like a whore?

The biggest shock of all was the cats. Their stench greeted her before the cats did. There must have been fifty or sixty of them. Sam said the smell wasn't so bad, just a faint odor. How kind. Abuela's house smelled like the city dump on delivery day.

It was clear that Sam's beloved abuela's Alzheimer's had gotten worse than anyone had expected. She'd become a crazy cat lady, and Rita, the little sneak, had been keeping it from them so she could run around like a floozie.

After observing the situation for all of one hour, Elena made a quick assessment. If Abuela were a horse, they would have put her out to pasture, but since she was Sam's beloved grandmother, the more delicate thing to do was to put her in a nursing home, the civilized version of pasture. However, if Abuela were committed to a nursing home, that would create another, even bigger problem. Elena would once again be faced with the question of what to do with Rita.

CHAPTER SIXTEEN

Rita was wearing a dour expression as she hung up the wall phone by the pantry. "He's not dead," she said. They were in the Dawson kitchen. "He was admitted to the hospital early this morning with minor burns but was released."

"Thanks for checking," said Turtle. He was seated at the kitchen table recently vacated by his father, who had disappeared back into his own bedroom. He blew out a sigh, yet he felt no relief. He sat, his head cradled in his hands, elbows propped on the table looking like a man whose worries had just begun.

"You didn't kill him," Rita said. A hopeful smile struggled to her lips.

"I know," he said without looking at her.

She gazed at him for a long moment. "Maybe he didn't see you."

"He looked right at me," said Turtle, wagging his head back and forth between his hands.

"Maybe he was looking through you to the fire. His truck was going up in flames. Sometimes people are so busy looking at something else they don't see what's right in front of them."

"He bumped into me, Rita. He nearly knocked me over." Turtle's voice was ragged and adamant.

"If he'd've told the police it was you, they'd be here by now." A pause. "Maybe he only saw your brother and didn't recognize him."

Turtle lifted his head. She was staring at him. There was a strangeness in the way she was staring. "He didn't see A.D.," he said flatly.

"How can you be so sure? Was A.D. invisible?"

"Of course not! I told you, he was in the shadows. Mr. Meade didn't see him, Rita. If anyone's going to get blamed for this it's me."

"Who else has seen your brother...besides you?"

It was the third question she'd asked about A.D.. Turtle narrowed his eyes at her, his face burning as he now understood the strangeness. She didn't believe him. To her, he was just like Uncle Johnny.

"You think *I* set the fire?"

"Not on purpose," she said almost apologetically. She became embarrassed to look at him.

"What do you mean 'not on purpose'?"

"I mean…maybe you weren't yourself when it happened. You've been under a lot of stress lately." She was staring at the Froot Loops box on the table.

"I'm not crazy," he said, daring her to meet his gaze. His face was burning.

"You're mad at me," she said, her eyes meeting his.

"No," he said, letting out a long, slow breath. "I thought you might not believe me, but I…hoped." His voice dropped an octave.

"You're hurt."

"I'm not crazy, Rita. I thought I was. I thought: 'this is impossible, I must be crazy.' And it *is* impossible, but I'm *not* crazy. He's real!"

"It's just that…"

"You have to believe me!" His voice became tortured. "I don't have anyone but you." His eyes became misty.

"I want to believe you. I really do," she said, her voice quavering. "It's just that…Can I meet him?"

"Of course you can meet him. But he's gone for a while." His voice was low and husky with emotion.

Doubt resurfaced in Rita's eyes. "Lying low until things blow over, huh?"

"It's not that. He—"

Turtle stopped abruptly as the voice in his mind intruded. *Slow down, Tonto. You've said too much already. You tell her about your role in A.D.'s death, or the promise you made to him, you may as well cry yourself a river 'cause your girlfriend will be gone for sure.*

"I don't want him to come back," Turtle said. "Things'll be much better if he doesn't come back."

"Then maybe he won't," Rita said, offering an encouraging smile "Maybe this scared him so much he'll stay away for good."

"You mean, maybe this scared the crazy out of me?" he said. His lips were tight.

"Don't put words in my mouth, Theo."

"I'm sorry." He gazed at her, his expression softening. She stared back with a look of open pity. "The fire didn't scare him off, Rita." He began shaking his head again. "You should have seen the look on his face when he was pouring the gasoline over the pickup truck. He was like a little kid at Christmas. Giggling and shit. He'll be back, and when he comes back, I'll introduce you to him." His voice had dropped to a near whisper.

He was thinking about murder again.

Elena

Elena was helping Sam sort through all of the unopened mail and stacks of bills when she found them—letters from the bank threatening foreclosure. There were three in all. Abuela had not been keeping up her payments to the bank. If they didn't make-up the back payments soon, the house would go into foreclosure.

Sam couldn't believe it when Elena showed him the letters. He was certain his abuelo, Tito, had paid off the home a long time ago. His grandfather was good with his money. "He would never have left Abuela with the house not paid for."

"He's from another generation," Elena said soothingly. "He probably didn't realize it had to be paid off."

"Of course he realized," Sam said. He was getting angry. "How could he not realize?"

"Well, don't take it out on me. I'm just the messenger," Elena said. They were sitting in Abuela's tiny kitchen, the only room in the house that didn't smell of cats. She came over and began massaging his shoulders.

"Sorry," he said. "I just can't get over the mess my grandfather left my grandmother."

"Let's look at this as a blessing in disguise. Abuela needs to be put into a nursing home. You know that. She's no longer capable of taking care of herself. And Rita. Well, you can see she's no help. Did you know she stole your old warmup jacket from high school? I found it in her closet." Sam flinched when she disparaged his beloved sister. She didn't care. She pushed on. "I say we sell the house before the bank comes and snatches it from us. The money from the sale can be used so that your sweet Abuela can live out the rest her life in style."

She felt the knots in Sam's shoulders begin to relax. "Yes. I like that idea."

"Good," Elena said and continued massaging. "I'm sure it won't be much, but it'll be enough."

She was smiling inwardly. Elena had no intention of using the proceeds from the sale of the house on a nursing home. Social Security could take care of that. Several years ago, Sam's grandparents had signed the house over to him. After they'd moved on, they wanted the proceeds from the sale of their home divided equally between their grandchildren. Sam was the executor of their estate. He was the eldest and the most responsible. So, technically, the house belonged to Sam.

Elena's plan was to eventually convince Sam to buy another home with the proceeds of the sale, one that would grow in value. *A much better legacy for your brothers and sisters.* The house would be in New Jersey, maybe not Hasbrouck Heights, but somewhere nice near where she grew up. They'd been wanting a home of their own for some time. Now, with the help of Sam's grandmother, they could finally afford the down payment.

She knew this would take some convincing, perhaps even the advent of a second child, but she was certain that in time she could convince Sam this is what was best for everyone.

"Let's keep this just between us for now. We'll scout around for a nice place near where we live for Abuela before we upset anyone" Elena said.

Sam agreed it was a good idea. She definitely had a way with him. She continued to massage his shoulders.

❧ ❧ ❧

As the days passed, Turtle got used to the idea that Bert Meade had not seen him behind his house that night. Bert was alive, and the police had not come knocking at his door. He was off the hook. He tried consoling himself with the idea that since Bert was alive, he hadn't taken part in a murder. Yet he almost wished he hadn't gotten away with it. His brother would be back soon, and when A.D. returned, Turtle would have to do as he'd promised. If only he'd been carted off to jail, he wouldn't be able keep his promise.

How did a summer filled with so much potential turn out so fucked up?

Turtle looked back with envy to when the stolen Kerwood Derby was his biggest problem. Oh, how he wished he could turn back the clocks to problems like that one, schoolboy problems, problems that didn't involve dead brothers back from the grave, pickup trucks going up in flames, and murder.

His relationship with Rita had been strained since he'd told her about A.D.. It was like a funeral whenever they were together. They pretended everything was fine, but whenever they spoke to one another, it was always using short sentences, neither of them ever saying what was really on their minds. They didn't touch nearly as much as they once did. And when they sat in their favorite spot in The Lots, staring into babbling Foster Creek, they no longer held hands, and they never laughed.

He told himself the change was because of Rita's own problem. At the end of the summer she'd be returning to live with her brother in New Jersey. He knew how much she hated living with her Aunt Elena, how much she loved living with her abuela Maritza in Foster City, and how much she loved him.

It's for the better, he thought. His life was over, anyway. Rita Calderon was the best thing that had ever happened to him, but he was not good for her. At least she could have a rich, full life. To do that, however, she needed to forget about him and get on with it.

He began making excuses as to why he couldn't hang with her: he had to run errands for his mother, or his father had given him his own summer reading list as punishment for the Kerwood Derby. She was busy anyway, always cleaning the house for her sister in-law, Elena, who never thought it was clean enough. He started spending more time alone in his room. Comic books and *Chocodiles* were once again his friends.

One afternoon, after returning from a walk over to Miller's Grocery to replenish his stash, he found his parents in the living room waiting for him. He knew something was up even before he saw the somber expressions on their faces. His father was home from work far too early.

"Turtle, we need to see you in here," his father called as he tried hurrying past.

The drapes were drawn when he entered. Scant light filtered in, creating deep shadows in the room, along with a sense of foreboding. They were seated side-by-side on the sofa. The TV was off.

"Did I do something wrong?" Turtle said as he entered. He was certain this could not be about Bert Meade, the Millennium Falcon, or the Kerwood Derby. Normally he'd be on edge walking in with his parents sitting in darkness, looking the way they did. Today, the edge wasn't there.

"No, you didn't do anything wrong, son," his father said, searching for a jovial tone. He smiled. Turtle's mother fidgeted. "We've been thinking about your brother."

Turtle stiffened. "What about him?"

"He's been gone for two years, and yet we all still feel him. You feel him, don't you?"

Turtle nodded. He realized he was dry-mouthed.

"Your mother and I would like to help you get past these feelings," his father said and smiled again. Turtle remembered seeing the strange smile

160

before, the morning after the fire when he'd found him in the kitchen drinking coffee.

"Dad, I'm not sure what you're talking about." He looked from his father to his mother, who was stone-faced. She seemed to be looking through him.

His father's smile faltered. "You know we love you. Remember how much you and your brother used to love to play with toy soldiers when you were kids?"

Love? Toy soldiers? He wasn't making any sense.

"We're sending you to military school," Mabry blurted. Her words seemed to come from out of a hole. She was expressionless when she spoke, her face remaining like stone, only her lips moved.

"What?" Turtle's eyes grew wide.

"Don't try to talk us out of it. It's already done," Mabry said. "When the school year begins in the fall, you will be heading off to Hargood Military Academy in Virginia."

Turtle looked from his father to his mother. His father was wearing a guilty expression. His mother was not. For some reason unbeknownst to him, he found it funny, not only the juxtaposition of their expressions, but the whole crazy thing. He began to laugh and, once he started, it was as if a flood valve had been opened. Laughter spilled out of him.

"You made a special trip home from work just to tell me I'm going to fuckin' military school?" he said between waves of laughter. He stood up and saluted his father. "You needn't have bothered, sir. You could've just left a note on my door." He saluted his mother. "Theodore Turtle Dawson present and accounted for…but not for long, right?" This seemed to be the funniest thing of all. It doubled him over with laughter.

He turned and started from the room. There was a time when news like this would have crushed him. *Unwanted.* Yet in light of all his *real* problems, military school was a joke.

"Turtle!" Stan called, his voice ringing with alarm. "What's gotten into you?"

"Nothing, General, Dad, sir. Nothing at all. As you were."

He exited laughing.

❧ ❧ ❧

He went to his room and broke out the *Chocodiles*. He wolfed down two of them, sputtering up globs of golden cake through explosive laughter.

He may have been laughing, but on the inside where things mattered most, his heart was being ripped to shreds. He knew where he stood with his parents, had known for a long time, so why was he feeling so horrible?

A lone tear listed down his cheek, and he willed it not to fall. It did not obey. Fat tears dripped onto the chocolate snack in his hand. The tears were falling because he was losing everything he cared for.

His brother, his protector, whom he'd been tethered to almost since birth, had put him in harm's way. He wanted to ask why, but he knew why. Because A.D. knew it had been *his* cowardice that had caused his death. Turtle wasn't driving the car that had run his brother down, but he may as well have been, and so shame-filled tears continued to fall. If only he hadn't been such a punk, his life would have been so, so different.

Rita deserves better.

More tears fell because he loved her, yet in loving her he knew he had to let her go. *Rita deserves so much better than me.* She was better off in New Jersey, believe it or not, better off with Elena. She didn't know it now, but in time she'd see.

She loved him as he loved her. He knew that, could see it in her eyes, feel it in her touch, hear it in the tinkling sound of her laughter. Puppy love—that's what adults would have called it. Yet the love of a young heart is as powerful as any. Young hearts beat the strongest. Young love is the fiercest love of all.

He knew their love, so strong, was like a raging forest fire that was gobbling up thousands of acres of forest as if they were kindling. The fire needed to be put out. It needed to be put out in stages. Moving back to New Jersey would be the start of it, at least for her. A new school, a new boyfriend would be stage two. Of course, he also knew as sure as the dawn, his fire was never going out. That's the price one pays for a mighty love.

Coward. She deserved better.

Liar. She deserved better.

Murderer. She deserved so much better than him.

His tears continued to fall, but not for himself; he'd not shed a single tear for himself. Rather, his tears fell for the loss of his youth, the loss of the faith he once had in his beloved brother, and for the loss of the love he and Rita had shared.

❧ ❧ ❧

It rained the next several days. It started the following morning, a torrential downpour that quickly filled the sewers, leaving several inches of water in the streets confounding the early morning commute. Later on, it settled into an oozing drizzle that lasted throughout the day.

It was a depressing day, perfect for how Turtle had been feeling. Once he realized the rain wasn't going to let up, keeping him inside, he hunkered down behind closed doors, settling in with a bag of Cheetos (newly added to his stash), and the newly published *King-Size Annual Avengers*. The shiny front cover featured an ad to win a ten-speed racer.

What I wouldn't give for a ten-speed, Turtle mused. Allowing his mind a temporary respite from depression, he imagined himself winging through the streets of Foster City on such a mean machine. He thumbed to the middle of the comic in search of the coupon he needed to fill out to enter the contest, but by the time he found it, his depression had resurfaced, coming on like a fog.

No sense entering this. I never win anything, he thought, and heaving a misery-filled sigh he went back to the beginning of the magazine.

He was reading it for the second time, this time admiring the artwork when a knock came at his door.

"What?" He screeched, in perfect adolescent disdain.

After a pause: "Your girlfriend's on the phone," called Mabry from the other side of the door.

"Who?"

"Rita," she said, the name a sour patch on her tongue.

✗ ✗ ✗

Despite his mother's protests, he rode Tyrone, braving the heavy drizzle and puddles the size of ponds to get to her: "I'm going AWOL, officer, Mom. Don't wait up for me."

He'd been surprised by the call. As delighted as he was to hear from her, at the same time he was troubled. He'd done a masterful job at distancing himself. But how could he ever refuse her if she called?

He'd heard tales of older boys at school who'd dumped girls as if they were throwing away old sweat socks. The story of one boy, he didn't remember his name, was legend. He'd gone over to his girlfriend's house for lunch. It wasn't anything special, but she'd prepared it herself. Her parents weren't home, and after lunch she gave him "dessert." It was shortly after she'd given herself to him that the boy dumped her. Legend has it he walked out of her house, leaving her in tears, eating an apple. He boasted the apple was far better than the dessert she'd given him.

Turtle wondered how a boy could treat a girl who cared so much for him so cruelly. While he knew he had to be tough with Rita if he was going to make the split-up stick, he also knew he could never be mean about it.

He hadn't been over to the house since her brother and his wife had arrived, and he wondered if they'd demanded to meet the boy who'd gotten her in trouble at school. He wasn't looking forward to that, but perhaps this would create the perfect opportunity for them to part company permanently.

They're forbidding me to see you, Theo.

Then you must obey.

The idea of never seeing her again was heartbreaking, and he had to remind himself it was for her own good.

By the time he arrived at the house on Featherbed Lane, his jacket and Baltimore Orioles baseball cap were drenched. Rita came to the door, a ray of sunshine in light blue shorts and a dark blue top that highlighted the green of her eyes. When she saw him standing there, a puddle of water pooling up around his sneaks, her arms went around him, pulling him in close. His heart thundered in his chest as he realized how much he'd missed her.

His wet clothing against her skin eventually made her pull away.

"You're dripping wet," she exclaimed. "You need to get out of those things right away or you'll catch a death of summer cold." With those words she pulled him into the house.

The first thing he noticed different was the odor of Pine Sol lingering in the air. It smelled as if the entire house had recently been sanitized. As Rita guided him toward the kitchen, he also noticed there were no cats circling their feet.

"Am I going to meet your brother and sister in-law?" he asked.

"They're gone. They left yesterday."

"Oh," he said, feeling a sense of relief. He wasn't going to be confronted by them. But that also meant he couldn't use them to let her down easy.

They arrived in the kitchen, and she pulled him out of his jacket. "You need to get out of that shirt as well," she said, draping the wet jacket over the back of a chair.

"Where are all the cats?"

She let out a long whistling sigh and shook her head in disgust. "Most of them are outside. It's raining so they're probably under the house. *She* made them sleep outside at night. Well, all except Don Juan. There was no deterring him from his husbandly duties no matter how she tried." She laughed lightly. His heart danced at the sound of it. It was the first laughter he'd heard in what seemed like forever. "After a few days of Elena, the others stopped coming inside all together. I feed them on the porch now. I'm sure they'll come around soon. They haven't realized she's gone yet."

"Elena sounds like a one-man wrecking crew."

"Worse," she said and tugged at his shirtsleeve. "You need to get out of this."

"I'm not taking my shirt off, Rita," he said firmly. It would be too embarrassing for her to see his belly protruding just over his waistband. "Why did you call me?" he asked, plowing past the embarrassing moment.

The pretext at happiness dissolved on her face like sugar in hot water. "I'm sorry. I didn't know who else to call." She sat down heavily on one of the kitchen chairs. "Thank you for coming." Her tone had shifted to one of desperation.

"What is it?" he asked.

She stood up again. She seemed older when she did, as if she'd aged twenty years in just a few seconds. "Come. I'll show you."

Abuela's bedroom was shrouded in a thick darkness. The drapes were drawn tight, and a sour odor hung in the air. Abuela was in bed lying on her back, her Einstein hair a tussle on the pillow. She seemed asleep although her eyes were open. Don Juan looked up from his spot at the foot of her bed when they entered, and yawned.

"Abuela? Look who came to see you—Theo. You remember Theo, don't you?" A tiny bit of light appeared in Abuela's eyes.

Rita nudged Turtle forward. "Say something."

"Hi Abuela. It's me. I'm uhh, back for some more molcajete." Rita smiled at the mention.

"Closer," Abuela called in a raspy tone. Her voice was a glimmer of what it once was. She crooked a finger signaling them over.

When they arrived bedside, Abuela looked up at Turtle and smiled. "Yes. I think I remember you. A nice young man. What's your name again?"

Turtle shot Rita a quick concerned glance. She wouldn't look at him, although from the mist in her eyes, he could tell her heart was breaking.

"Theo," he said. "Remember the night I came over and Rita hemmed the waist in my pants?"

"Rita?" she asked, her face twisting into a question mark.

Turtle shot Rita another concerned look. Her eyes were on Abuela. "Your granddaughter?"

"Ah, yes," Abuela said and smiled. "She's a very good girl. Rita."

Turtle got the sense she didn't know it was Rita who was standing right next to him. He again glanced over at Rita. Her lower lip was trembling.

"What happened to her?" he asked when they were seated back in the kitchen.

"I'm not sure. I don't know if it's her Alzheimer's or that she's given up because of the news. But once we got the news, her light started going out."

"What news?"

She sighed deeply. "I told you he was going to move us all back to New Jersey and put her in a nursing home. If that wasn't enough to break her heart, just before they were leaving, Elena came into the living room where we were sitting and told us they were selling the house."

"What?"

"Sam was outside with baby Sam and Tora loading the car, so he couldn't hear. She said Abuela hadn't been making payments on the house and that if they didn't sell it we'd lose it. Theo, she was smiling when she gave us this news."

"Whoa," said Turtle.

"I know this house seems small and insignificant, but she and my Abuelo always wanted to keep it in the family. This was very important to them, that they leave something behind for us."

"I'm so sorry."

"Then, Elena had the nerve to say 'Don't tell Sam I told you. He's under so much stress lately. I'm sure he couldn't handle the pressure of you pleading with him not to sell the house'." The tears began to fall. "*He's* under stress? After that, Abuela went to bed and never got up again."

They sat in silence for several minutes.

"Thank you for coming," Rita said after a while. His hands were on the table. She found one and began kneading it, as if keeping her hands busy was the remedy for keeping her misery at bay. Her nails were painted a deep maroon; the polish was scratched and chipped.

"I'm so sorry," he said again. He wished he had the magic pill that could make her feel better. He recalled the last time he tried and had failed miserably at it.

I want to be brave for her, he thought.

He realized then that he'd always wanted this. Boyfriends were supposed to protect their girlfriends. Their relationship was coming to an end, and he wished that just once he could do something extraordinary for her. He wanted to be her hero.

Rita spoke: "She said something just after she drifted off into this crazy fog. She said 'He wouldn't have lied.'" Rita was staring at him as if searching his face for answers.

"Who wouldn't have lied?"

"Who else? My abuelo, Tito. But you know who would have lied? My brother's wife, Elena." She practically spat the name into the air.

"You think Elena's lying about selling the house?"

"No. I think she lied to my brother to *get* him to sell the house. I don't believe my grandfather would have left Abuela with nothing. He prided himself that all of us would be taken care of."

"Ask her," Turtle said.

"I tried. I can't get through to her. Every time I bring up my abuelo, she starts talking about the old days when he was still alive."

They sat in silence for a while longer, Turtle feeling trapped under the net of helplessness as Rita continued massaging the back of his hand.

"Maybe I should try," he said after a while.

"You?" Rita was looking at him as if he were joking.

"Sure. Why not?"

It was his one last chance to be her hero.

They went back into the bedroom.

"Let some air in here," Turtle said.

"Yes, of course," Rita replied. She moved around the room, throwing open the drapes and opening the windows. Muted light from the gloomy day streamed in.

Turtle moved to the side of the bed. "Abuela, it's me again," he said softly.

"I know your face," she said, squinting at him.

"Theo. Rita's friend."

She smiled. "Yes. Rita's a good girl."

"Rita's worried about you."

"Me? Tell her not to worry."

Rita had again joined Turtle bedside. He could tell from the hitch in her breathing that Abuela's continued lack of recognition was hard on her.

"She's worried because this house that you love is going to be sold."

A sadness came over Abuela. "No," she said, and began wagging her head back and forth.

"It's true," said Turtle.

"Tito's a good man. He would not have lied. It's my house now," she said, continuing to shake her head.

"I believe you. But how can we prove it?" Turtle asked.

She mumbled something he didn't hear.

"What did you say?"

"Mickey Mouse," she said softly.

Turtle glanced at Rita. She shrugged.

"Abuela, what about Mickey Mouse?" she asked.

"Mickey Mouse will take care of us. Tito used to say 'Mickey Mouse will always take care of us.' He would not have lied."

"Abuela!" Rita suddenly screeched. "You have to come out of this!" she called, losing it. "Mickey Mouse is not real. Did abuelo, Tito, pay off the house or didn't he?"

"It's my house now," Abuela said again. "*Our* house!" She was becoming agitated. Her body began trembling as she wagged her head back and forth. "Our house, not theirs. Not *hers*."

Turtle shot a hopeless look at Rita and shrugged.

"It's okay. Thanks for trying," Rita told him. She moved closer to the bed.

"It's all right, Abuela. It's all a mistake. Nobody's selling your house." Abuela immediately calmed down, smiling like a child who'd just been given an all-day sucker.

"I told you." the old woman said with third-grader-like satisfaction. "Tito wants us to share our good fortune with the entire family."

Rita smiled back. "I'm going to fix your lunch now."

"All right. And who are you?"

"Rita."

Abuela's smile broadened. "Rita's a good girl."

❊ ❊ ❊

Turtle got what he would later call his bright idea while he was still at Rita's, although he didn't say anything about it to her at the time. He was sitting in the kitchen drinking tea and quizzing her about Mickey Mouse.

"Maybe your grandfather bought stock in The Disney Company. Walt Disney created Mickey Mouse," he said. The tea was something called Red Zinger. He didn't much care for it. He didn't like tea at all, but girls seemed to like it, and so when Rita offered, he accepted.

"My grandfather knew nothing about the stock market. He had his doubts about banks. There's no way he'd give his money to a stock broker."

"So what do you think?" he asked. He sipped his tea. It was tart, and he tried not to make a face.

"I think Abuela has lost touch with the real world."

The drizzle outside had softened into a fine mist, almost like fog. Three of the cats had found their way inside. George Bailey was seated on Rita's lap while Turtle wracked his brain for a more satisfying solution to the riddle. That's when he got his bright idea.

As Rita began to prepare Abuela's lunch, he made up an excuse to leave, claiming he had to bring a few things home from Miller's for his mother to start supper.

"Thank you for coming," she said as she walked him to the door.

"Yeah, sure. No problem. Sorry I couldn't help."

"You helped," she said and offered up a pained smile. "See you tomorrow?"

"Okay. Sure."

She moved in to hug him, and he stepped away as if he hadn't noticed. He moved out onto the porch. *Let her down easy.* He pulled on his still wet baseball cap and jacket, and maneuvered Tyrone off the porch and onto Featherbed Lane.

"The sky looks awfully mean," he said, figuring if he kept talking she wouldn't have a chance to call him back for a hug or a kiss. "Better get goin' before it starts stormin' again. See ya," he called over his shoulder as he pushed off. He didn't look back. He felt like the boy who walked out the door eating an apple.

✗   ✗   ✗

The rain-swelled sewers had washed out many of the roads, and he had to pick his way home, going down odd streets that took him a roundabout way. As he rode, he thought about the bright idea. If he could pull it off, it would be his one heroic deed before he became a murderer.

In his heart, Turtle didn't think he'd ever become a murderer. He would try because he owed it to A.D. He would try because this one act, one way or the other, would offer him relief from his parents' indifference, from bullies, from his own guilt, from the demands of love. Relief from all these, wrapped up in one tiny little pill. He'd do it because when he failed, it would be over.

He kills kids, and if you fuck this up, he'll kill you.

He'd go out like a movie hero, like one of *The Goonies* even. But he needed one big heroic act first. It was all up to A.D. If A.D. could go inside Abuela's head and find the memory that could turn things around, he could save the house and finally be Rita's hero.

He was fantasizing about the bright idea, about the look of gratitude that would be on Rita's face when he pulled it off. She'd throw her arms around him and he'd say, *It was nothin'.*

Turtle was well into the fantasy. The pickup truck coming toward him from the opposite direction was moving rapidly on the wet asphalt. Turtle maneuvered Tyrone as close to the flowing curb lane as possible to avoid being splattered by the truck's wake. As the pickup neared him it swerved into a large puddle in the center of the road. The truck's huge tires kicked up a beach-like wave, splashing water up over him.

The filthy street water flowed into his eyes and mouth. He was blinded by it, disgusted by the taste of old macadam. He skidded Tyrone to a stop, coughing and sputtering up gutter water. As his eyes cleared, he realized that the pickup had not continued on. The truck had u-turned and was now idling behind him. He turned, surprised to see Bert Meade climbing out of the cab. Bert's eyes were red dots of murderous intent.

"What the fuck did you do?" Bert roared as he stomped toward Turtle, his work boots kicking up a violent spray.

Turtle's heart began pounding like a pneumatic drill. He turned the bike around and tried pushing off, but Bert was on him, grabbing Tyrone's handlebars and shaking them, impeding his progress. Bert's right hand and forearm were swathed in bandages.

"I swear, if you hurt him, I'll kill you, you little pig fucker," Bert said, not letting go of the bike. He shook it again and again, bouncing the front tire—*boom, boom, boom.*

"I didn't do it," Turtle said reflexively. "It was my brother."

Bert released the handle bars and took a step back. His eyes went wide, and Turtle saw that the red in his eyes was because he'd been crying.

"Your brother?" he said, his voice sounding far away.

"Yes! I swear it. It wasn't me," Turtle said. He measured the distance between himself and Bert, gauging his chance at escape.

Bert Meade took a few more steps back, then plopped down right on his ass in the middle of the street. "You don't do something like that to people's kids. It's heartless. What happened to your brother was an accident," he said as the fight tumbled out of him.

It was the perfect opportunity for Turtle to push off, race home, and hide under his bed. He didn't, because what Bert had last said sent an odd prickling racing along the base of his skull.

"What was an accident?" Turtle asked.

CHAPTER SEVENTEEN

"Those boys are a pain in the fuckin' ass, I swear. But it don't mean I don't love em." Bert noticed the odd way Turtle was staring at him, as if he'd just stolen the Pope's crown. His voice hardened. "There are days when all parents feel their children are burdens, what with having to take them everywhere all the damn time: school, basketball practice, soccer practice, the doctor. Sometimes I think we aren't parents at all. We're nothin' but unpaid chauffeurs, but it don't mean we don't love em." A sadness came into his eyes. "You don't understand how it is having three kids and a ball-breakin' wife. You're just a kid yourself. I had a family to raise."

Turtle wasn't listening to any of Bert's gobbledygook. "What did you do to my brother?" he urged.

It was as if he'd punched the man in the mouth. Bert's eyes went hard. They narrowed on him. "Me? I did what I fuckin' had to, that's what. I was new in this town. No one was goin' to step in and make sure my family was cared for if I went to jail. It was an accident, an honest mistake. I did what I had to." Bitter tears sprang into the man's eyes.

"What did you have to do?" Turtle urged. The prickling had moved from the base of his skull and was now racing up and down his arms and legs. He moved in closer.

"Bring him back, you little pig fucker," Bert said. His voice was low and seething. "Bring him back safe and sound, and I won't tell a soul it was you." His voice went even lower. "I promise you, you'll be joining me in hell if you don't."

"What did you do to my brother?" Turtle raged. The words exploded up his throat. He was hovering over the man who began inching himself backwards, his butt sliding along the wet pavement.

"I ain't gotta answer to you. You are not my Lord and savior. I did what

I had to do. And I swear on my mother's grave, you don't bring my boy back, you'll have hell to pay."

Bert continued sliding backwards until he was at the truck. He heaved himself up against the fender. "There's a clock on you now, boy. Bring mine back or maybe…maybe you lose a family member, too."

"I already lost a family member," Turtle called out, his words a blast furnace of rage.

"Fuck you!" Bert called back. He climbed into the truck and began backing it away. It was then that Turtle noticed the black and brown burn marks scorching the pickup's paint job, saw the new black primed hood replacing the original that must have been mangled in the explosion. The pickup backed down the length of the street, turned at the corner and was gone.

Turtle stood in the fine mist staring until truck had been gone for several minutes, feeling as though his brain had just been scrambled like an egg. He believed he now understood why he hadn't heard sirens, why there'd never be any sirens. It was then he noticed the hand bills stapled on the trees that lined the street. Something told him to go over and have a look-see:

Missing
Ansley Meade Age 13. Last seen on the Night of July 9th leaving his home wearing shorts and a tee shirt.

A recent school photo of Ansley occupied the center of the leaflet.

❧ ❧ ❧

The boy had been complaining. Criss hadn't rescued a child in a while and had forgotten that they all complained at first. It wasn't that they longed for their old, miserable lives. Who would? But misery was all they knew, and so they complained.

The boy's complaining was loud and vulgar. His voice carried throughout the house shaking the old rafters. It agitated Brutus who barked *shut up!* into the night. The boy's snappish behavior along with the dog's barking those first few nights made him think he'd made a mistake until he recalled the familiar pattern.

They all complained, at first.

The unlikely timing of his most recent saving had been the hand of God, just as the saving of the six-year-old a few years back had been anointed. He'd been watching the house for several weeks, getting a sense of the family's schedule, but mostly making sure he'd chosen the right child.

It was late at night, and he was sitting in the bus strategically parked at the end of the street, observing, when two boys came running from behind the house, heading in the opposite direction. Criss's ire was immediately stoked as he watched the boys moving away.

What kind of reckless parent allows their children out so late at night?

He was thinking of following the boys. They seemed like perfect future candidates for the club, when his boy, the boy he'd been called to save, emerged from the house, following his friends down the street.

It took some fast thinking and the hand of God for Criss to accept that this was indeed the right child and the right moment. Circling around the block, he'd managed to get ahead of the boy and had situated the bus on the street the boy would be coming down. But Criss had a rule: he had to be in uniform when he picked up a child. That was a rule he'd never broken. Rules are what added order to the world. Without rules we'd be living in chaos.

The teddy bear uniform was in the back of the truck but no time to get into it. That's when the boy lingered at the corner for several minutes, allowing him the time. It had to be God. The boy had no reason to linger, his friends were getting away, and yet he stood there.

Thank you, Jesus, for helping me do your good work.

Now the boy was safe in his basement, complaining up a storm. Criss knew he was fortunate to have such a secluded home, on a quarter acre of land, with nothing but forestland around him. His closest neighbor was nearly a mile away. The boy could complain all he wanted. No one but he and Brutus would ever hear. However, he had to admit he hoped the complaining would end soon.

Criss had his mother to thank for the secluded home. He did so begrudgingly. After years of man-hopping the way puddle jumpers hop from island to island, Gerta had married a man who actually had some money. This on her third—or was it her fourth—try. She left Criss, her only heir, the money and the house.

He grinned when he thought of Gerta's last days. If she had known what was coming, she mightn't have left him anything.

During those last several months when she was bed-ridden, he moved in and began taking care of her. By then her brain had been cooked, what with all the drinking and partying she'd done over the years, and she was experiencing a high level of dementia. All she could do those last months was lay there and complain. He gave her lots to complain about.

Although her meals were prepared by Meals on Wheels, he started adding a little *spice* to her food via small amounts of arsenic. The arsenic worked just as well as his research said it would. The effect was immediate: headaches, confusion, cramping, hair loss, stomach pain. It was glorious watching her suffer as she faded away.

Her doctor told him it was the result of the cancer that was eating up her insides, but he knew better. The problem was, she didn't. She actually thought this suffering was caused by illness. So he told her.

"You're such a good son," she said to him one evening when he was spoon-feeding her stewed chicken, green beans, and mashed potatoes.

"No, I'm not," he said rather casually. "I put arsenic in these mashed potatoes I'm feeding you. Just a little. Just enough to make you suffer. I put it in everything you eat. I've been doing it ever since I got here."

Her eyes shifted, and he could see her calculating as best she could, trying to recall the beginning of when she started feeling so poorly.

"Don't make mean jokes," she said, trying to laugh it off.

"It's mean. But it's not a joke. Just as all the ways you made me suffer growing up were no joke."

There were days upon days when her dementia was at its worst. On those days she had no idea who he was and babbled on incoherently. There were other days when she knew exactly who he was, her tormentor, possibly, her killer. He saved his worse torments for her good days. No sense wasting a good *fuck you, Mom.*

When she was clear and lucid, he told her how much he hated her. He turned the heat up in her room when it was hot out, and down when it was biting cold. Good thing her will had been finalized months earlier. He might have been left with nothing.

She tried to tell her doctor on one of his visits. "He's killing me," she said during a lucid moment. "Don't leave me alone with him. He's a monster."

Later, outside her room, the doctor said: "It's her dementia talking. She's always been a cranky old broad. You've been so good to her. Hang in there, son."

Criss, the dutiful son, said that he would. After the doctor had departed he went in to feed his mother her lunch.

When she was nearly done with the meal he said, "Remember that old mongrel someone gave me when I was seven or eight, Queenie? Remember how angry you were when she had diarrhea in the house? It stained the new carpeting. You said it was because I fed her off my plate instead of the Puppy Chow you bought for her. Remember that?"

Gerta stared at him, her eyes filling with horror, not knowing what was coming, but knowing it was something bad.

"You made me clean up her runny poop with my hands to teach me a lesson. Remember *that?* Well, guess what? I've added an extra dose of arsenic to your lunch today, and that much arsenic is going to make you poop uncontrollably. Oops. I know you can't clean it up with your hands, so I guess you're going to have to lie in it until I decide to change you. I won't be doing that for several days. Enjoy."

When she finally kicked off, everyone said what a good son he was, but she knew. She knew he was as bad a son to her as she was a mother to him.

She was gone now. The bad was behind him. Love was in his future. He was certain he'd shown this new boy more love in the past few days than the child had received in his entire twelve or thirteen years of life. He also knew that the complaining would end once he and the others christened the boy into The Teddy Bear Club. The boy had no idea how much love and affection he was about to receive when he was surrounded by his peers. It brought a tear to Criss's eye when he thought of the moment when the boy would see the beautiful future he had in store. It was downright touching.

🐦 🐦 🐦

Turtle slept.

His mind had been on the ragged edge, teetering on the verge of insanity when he finally arrived home from Rita's. He went to his room, striding past the living room where the TV was blaring, pulled off his rain-soaked clothes, threw them in the corner and himself across the bed. He immediately fell into a deep sleep. Perhaps it wasn't sleep. His mind was on information overload, and perhaps it needed to shut down for a while.

If he dreamed, he didn't remember. When he awoke, his tongue tasted like concrete, and he ached all over as if he'd just emerged from a grueling sporting event or a fight.

He lay there wrestling with what he'd just learned. Bert Meade had killed A.D. He'd all but admitted it, and now Ansley was missing, and Bert Meade assumed that *he* had set the truck on fire and, while Bert was putting the fire out, kidnapped Ansley. What a crazy idea that was. He was just a kid. He could never pull off anything like that, and yet Bert was delusional enough to believe he could. Something stirred in Turtle, call it pride. If Bert Meade thought he was capable of so much more than he actually was, maybe others did, too. Maybe he was.

He wondered if A.D. had a hand in Ansley's disappearance. A.D. said he didn't know who killed him. Was he lying? And if so, why?

None of what was happening made any sense. It was all too grown up

175

for him, and his head was again overflowing with thoughts that had no place to go. He wanted to go back to sleep. He needed to go back to sleep, to allow his addled brain more time to decompress. He closed his eyes and tried to clear his head. They weren't closed long before he heard a soft knocking.

He sat up, realizing it must be dinner time. "What?" he screeched.

"Open up. It's me."

"A.D.?"

"Yeah. What are you doin' in there, jacking off? Can I come in?"

"Come," he called.

Upon hearing A.D.'s voice, he went numb, his entire body feeling as if it had just been flash frozen.

A.D. entered. "Kind of early for bed, dude," he said with a teasing grin. "You hiding a girl under those covers? What's her name, Hand-sel?" He laughed.

"Hansel's a boy's name."

"I *know*," A.D. said, sounding his fruitiest. He threw his head back and his shoulders heaved with laughter.

Turtle said: "You're back sooner than before."

"I know. I'm getting the hang of it." He came over and sat on the edge of Turtle's bed. "Seriously, what are you doing in bed? It's not even five o'clock."

It's not? Turtle glanced over at the clock radio on his desk, surprised to see it was just three-thirty. The afternoon was creeping along.

"I had a headache."

"Oh." A.D. got up and moved to the desk, where he picked up the snow globe paperweight. "So...I heard you when you said you'd do it. You mean it?" There was no denying the caution in A.D.'s voice. He was look-ing at the paperweight, flipping it over and watching the snowflakes dance.

"What do you remember about that last day?"

A.D. turned to him, eyes wary. "You're not gonna help me cross over, are you?"

"I didn't say that. I'm just curious is all."

"Why now?"

"I don't know. I'm about to help you cross over. I guess I'd like to know as much about that last day as possible."

They stared at each other in what seemed to be a standoff. Then, A.D. nodded, sighed.

"I got hit by a car, Mu...Dude."

"It's okay. You can call me that. I like when you call me those names. I was just mad that day is all."

A.D. grinned. "You sure were, Punkinpuss. You were pissed off to the highest level of pisstivity." He chuckled, his eyes crinkling at the corners. Turtle recognized he was trying to get him off subject and didn't crack even the tiniest of smiles.

"Tell me what you remember," he said, his voice firm.

"Okay!" A.D. sighed again, as if a teacher had asked him to repeat something he'd said a dozen times. "I was crossing the street in front of the hobby shop. I was thinking of stopping by Miller's and grabbing us a few *Milky Ways* before I came home. We could chow down on space candy while we put the Falcon together. I'd taken the box out of the bag to get a better look at it. I was admiring the picture on the box—man, it looked good in that picture—thinking about how cool it was gonna look on my desk, or maybe we'd get some fishing line and hang it up above my bed like the one in the window. I was crossing the street and not lookin' where I was goin' and...Boom—" He smacked his hand into the snow globe. "Game over."

"You see what kind of car it was?"

A.D.'s expression soured. "This is not helping, Mushmouse. Bringing up the past like this. It sucks."

"I'm just curious."

"You think I'm not curious? You think I don't wanna know more?"

"Sorry, man." A pause. "I'm sorry I let you down that day, too." Their eyes met.

"It's all right. You were always scared of something back then." A.D. sat down in the desk chair. "That's what I remember," he said.

He gave himself a twirl in the chair. When he came back around he was smiling again. "I have it all worked out," he said. "You're gonna poison him. He won't even know you're there." He spoke as if he was hatching one of their *Goonies* adventures, not contemplating a real murder.

Turtle was stunned at how quickly the conversation had turned. One moment he was the inquisitor, the next he was a hit man receiving his orders.

"Poison?"

"Antifreeze. He's got it in his garage, not far from the fridge where he keeps his ice cold Gatorade. He loves the stuff." A.D. mimed opening the antifreeze and pouring it in. "Plop, plop, fizz, fizz. You're in, you're out. He drinks the Gatorade, he dies, and I am free." He twirled himself again.

"Oh." Turtle had been picturing something more elaborate, more daring, like something James Bond might have done. *Shaken, not stirred.*

"What? You don't like it?" A.D. asked, sounding annoyed.

"It sounds too easy."

"I tried coming up with a plan that even *you* could do."

Turtle heard the ring of sarcasm but decided to let it go. "Thanks," he said, dry mouthed.

"So... Tomorrow then?" A.D. shot him a guarded smile.

"Maybe."

"What's that supposed to mean?" A.D.'s expression darkened. A storm was on the horizon. He slapped the snow globe down on the desk.

"Whoa, there, Tonto. Keep yer shirt on. I'm gonna do it. But I need you to do something for me first."

A.D.'s expression soured. "Bullshit. You're just trying to weasel out of it. I knew it!"

"No, I'm not. Tit for tat, brother rat," he said in his best A.D. imitation.

A.D.'s eyes narrowed. "Okay. Spill. What do you want me to do?"

Turtle stared into his brother's eyes. A.D.'s were blazing. He got the sense A.D. was trying to intimidate him, yet he held his gaze.

❧ ❧ ❧

The boy standing in a pool of bright sunlight on Rita's porch alongside Turtle looked fourteen or fifteen. He was brown and lean yet with an athletic build. He wore a pressed blue shirt and chinos. *School clothes*, she thought. On his feet were a nice pair of *Nike* tennis shoes with the stylish blue swoosh. He was very well put together. He resembled Turtle in some ways. Yet his eyes held none of the cheer she saw in Turtle's. He'd been introduced to her as Turtle's brother, Adrian—*but you can call me A.D., everybody does.*

"You're Theo's older brother?" she inquired, tight-lipped.

"In the flesh... Well, not exactly." He had an easy laugh, and when his face lit up she could better see the resemblance.

"We need to talk," she said, hard eyes on Turtle.

"Umm. Okay."

After two days of rain, the sun had finally made an appearance. As far as Rita was concerned, the sun wasn't shining on her.

"Alone!" she said with an acid glare.

"Oh." He turned to his brother. "Wait here a minute."

"Sure," A.D. replied, grinning at them. "I'll stay out here and soak up some of this sweet fresh air." He breathed in deeply. "You have a cat?"

Rita yanked Turtle into the house and slammed the door.

178

"Whoa! That was rude," he said.

They were standing in the entry, just on the other side of the door. If Rita were a furnace, flames would have been shooting out of her ears.

"Theo! What kind of game are you playing?"

Turtle's expression shifted to one of dismay. "What? I told you I'd introduce you to my brother."

"You told me you'd introduce me to your *dead* brother."

"Okay," he said, still not fully understanding.

"When did you guys cook this up? Am I your only victim? Theo!" she rasped. "I trusted you. I trusted you with *everything*."

"I know that. Rita, that's A.D. It's not a trick."

"It's impossible."

"I know that, too. I told you that. But it's real. He's back from the dead, Rita. You've gotta believe me."

She began shaking her head woefully. "You and your brother, if that's who he is, are sick. You expect me to believe that boy out there is your brother's ghost?"

"It's true."

"Not a ghost," A.D. called from the other side of the door.

Rita yanked the door open. "Finally! We're getting somewhere."

"I'm an entity. More flesh and blood than a ghost. I can do human things, too," A.D. said. A teasing grin was playing on his lips. "Wanna see?" He puckered up and closed his eyes.

"GET OUT!" Rita screamed. She shoved Turtle out the door.

"Rita, you've gotta believe me," he called as the door slammed in his face.

"Go away. I never want to see you again, Theodore Dawson," she called though the door. Her voice was cracking. "Go away, or I'll call the police. I swear I will."

"We tried," A.D. said. He was still grinning.

"Shut up!"

A.D. chuckled. "I can't help it if your girlfriend doesn't want to believe in me. You're better off with Hand-sel anyway."

Turtle shoved A.D., who tripped on the top step and fell off the porch. "Shut the fuck up!" Turtle called.

A.D. went sprawling on his butt to the ground below. He sat dusting himself off, all the while grinning as if he'd just won the big hand in a poker game. "We tried, Mushmouse. I did my part. Now you have to do yours."

Turtle saw the smirk on his brother's face, and anger rose from his belly into his brain like mercury in a thermometer on the desert floor. His thermometer burst, and he launched himself off the porch onto his brother. "You knew this would happen," he screamed as he began pummeling A.D.

"Stop it, Turtle," A.D. said, fending off his brother's punches as if swatting flies.

He was still smiling, and Turtle knew he just had to wipe that goofy, shit eaitn' grin off his dumb brother's face. "You planned this!" He threw a roundhouse left that A.D. didn't see coming. The punch connected with his jaw—*blam!*

The smile vanished. "Stop, you little shit, or I'll beat the livin' piss out of you!"

"Fuck you! Do it!"

A.D. flung Turtle off as if he were a child. Turtle went sprawling in the dirt onto his back. Before he could move, A.D. was on top, wailing on him.

★

Rita heard the commotion outside. When she yanked open the door, A.D. and Turtle were at the foot of the porch, rolling around in the dirt like little boys. A.D. landed on top and began wind-milling punches while spluttering curses at his younger brother.

Rita's heart lurched. She ran down the steps and tried pulling A.D. off, but he was too strong. She tried wedging herself between the boys, hoping to absorb some of the blows. "Stop it!" she called. "Stop it! You're killing him."

After several moments she got through to A.D., bringing him out of his fighting haze. He shook his head, blinking rapidly as if he'd been hypnotized.

"Talk to him!" A.D. stammered. "He'll listen to you. Tell him people gotta honor their word. No matter what, you gotta honor your word."

A.D. climbed off his brother and stomped up the road.

Rita watched him go, then looked down at Turtle. He was a mess, with bruises on both cheeks. His lip was fat and bloodied.

"What does he mean by that?" she asked sternly.

"You're still my hero," Turtle said, looking up at her and forcing a crooked smile.

She helped him to his feet. "What was that boy...your *brother*, talking about when he said honor your word?"

"I need a drink of water," Turtle said in response.

Rita escorted him into the house. She took him to the bathroom where she washed his wounds with warm water. She handled him tenderly. A few of the cats peeked in. After several moments, their curiosity had been satisfied and each wandered away.

180

Once his wounds were clean, she brought him back into the kitchen where she poured him a tall glass of cherry Kool Aid. As Turtle drank, one of the cats, Carlotta, the yellow and white Manx, brushed against his legs. While he nursed the Kool Aid, Rita prepared a makeshift ice pack by folding some ice cubes into a paper towel.

"Delicioso," Turtle said, setting the drained glass on the table. "Thanks."

Rita came over and handed him the icepack. "For your lip," she said and sat down across from him. "Now. I think you have some explaining to do."

Turtle nodded. He placed the icepack on his swollen lip. It felt good.

For the next five minutes he told her another impossible tale, about how A.D. was able to turn himself into mist and climb inside his head and shake loose memories long forgotten. He told her he'd been a coward and that it was his fault A.D. had died. He told her why he brought A.D. there that day. He finished by telling her about the Teddy Bear, and the promise he made to help his brother cross-over. He conveniently left out anything to do with the Meades.

She stared at him for several minutes after he stopped talking. "Theo," she said, her voice was sandpaper. "I want to believe this story you've told me. I really do. It's just that…" Her words trailed off. Her face was a mask of confusion.

"Let me prove it to you. All you have to do is let him do his thing with your grandmother. I believe he can jar the right memories. If he can't, then we'll both know how crazy I am."

She gaped at him for another long moment. "I want to believe you." Her voice was ragged.

He picked her hand up from the table and kissed it. "I'm not asking you to believe me right now," he said. "I hardly believe it myself. All I'm asking is you let A.D. sit with Abuela for a little while. I promise he won't hurt her. If I'm right, maybe we get to save the house. If I'm wrong…you humored the crazy thoughts of your former crazy boyfriend. I need this, Rita. I need to do something good for you. If you love me, you'll let me."

"I do love you," she blurted. "That's the problem."

"I know," he replied.

She peered at him across the table. She didn't speak for a long, long time.

He knew she was thinking. He understood this was a big decision for her. He wanted so badly to continue pleading his case, and yet a stillness deep inside allowed him to hold his tongue. Finally, after several minutes of silence, she spoke:

"Don't you *dare* hurt her."

181

CHAPTER EIGHTEEN

Abuela was lying in bed whispering to herself when Rita brought the boys in. She wore a fresh white dressing gown, and her hair had been plaited, revealing neat rows of bony white scalp. The drapes were drawn, the light in the room muted. When the three of them entered, Don Juan hopped down from the bed and headed quickly for the door. This was odd behavior for him, and Rita made note of it.

"What's she saying?" Turtle asked as they moved closer to the bed.

"I don't know. I can't make it out. She does this sometimes. I think she's talking to my abuelo, Tito." Rita moved bedside. "Hey, Abuela. Look who's back. Theo. And he brought a friend."

Turtle glanced over at A.D., who hadn't spoken since he'd been in the house. He was surprised to see lines of concern creasing A.D.'s brow. He sidled up next to him and whispered, "What are you thinking?"

"I'm thinking that's one scary looking old lady."

"Seriously, bro. You okay?"

"Uh-huh," A.D. replied. He didn't sound okay.

Rita turned from the bed. "She's not coming out of it. I think we need to call this off."

"No!" A.D. called out, raising his voice. "We're good. I don't need her focused to do what I need to do."

Rita shot Turtle a troubled glance.

"You sure?" Turtle asked, now having his own doubts.

"Uh-huh."

"What should we do now, then?" Rita asked.

"Leave," A.D. replied. "I got this." He stepped forward.

"No. No way. I'm not leaving you alone with my abuela. You do this with me here or it's off."

A.D. turned to Turtle with an exaggerated shrug of his shoulders. "Women!" he muttered.

Turtle laughed out loud. "Good one."

The two boys chuckled for a few moments. Rita found none of what was going on in her abuela's room funny. She still couldn't believe she'd allowed Turtle to talk her into letting this *boy* work some mystical mumbo-jumbo on her grandmother. The only reason she allowed it is she wanted to believe, not so much in magic, but that Turtle wasn't a liar, wasn't going insane.

"Get some chairs," A.D. said. "You're gonna be here a while."

Five minutes later, Rita and Turtle were seated bedside in chairs from the kitchen. A.D. stood near the bed eyeing Abuela with what looked like trepidation.

"She's gotta close her eyes," A.D. said. He was leaning over Abuela, who lay wide-eyed, chattering away like a chipmunk.

"I don't think that's gonna happen, bro," Turtle said.

"You're right." A.D. turned to Rita. "Then you guys have got to close *your* eyes."

"Why?" she barked.

"I'm embarrassed for you guys to see me like that."

Rita's lips tightened. Turtle squeezed her hand. "Hey, we're gonna be right here. Nothing's going to happen to her with us right here," he said soothingly.

Rita looked from Turtle to A.D. "All right. Eyes closed. But for how long?"

"I'll let you know when you can open them. Okay?"

"Okay," she said with a shade of reluctance.

A.D. moved away from the bed, closer to Turtle. "You know I'll be gone after this, but I know you'll keep your part of it. The next time you see me, it'll be on the other side." He leaned closer, and they embraced.

"You take care," Turtle said.

"You, too."

"You're the best big brother," he said. He meant it, yet in that moment it felt forced.

"You're the best little brother," A.D. replied. He stood and stretched, sighing deeply. "Okay, you two, eyes shut tight, nighty-nite."

❧ ❧ ❧

Moments after she closed her eyes, Rita noticed the temperature dropping rapidly. She reached over, found Turtle's hand and squeezed it.

183

"What's happening?" Her voice was trembling with concern.

Turtle squeezed back. "It's okay. Just don't open your eyes."

"I won't," she replied, sounding like a lost little girl.

The temperature in the room continued to decline. She released Turtle's hand, pulled her arms tightly around herself and began rubbing her shoulders. "Oh, my," she said softly and began to shiver.

"It's okay," Turtle replied. The sound of his voice was a comfort to her.

The temperature in the room continued plunging until the air became dense, as if the atmosphere around them had crystalized. Rita's eyes were closed. She couldn't see her breath, but she knew if they were open, she'd see ice crystals forming in the air.

She thought of all the truths she'd ever learned, all the things she'd been taught to believe and not believe. This was on the not-believe list. Hell, it was at the top of the not-believe list. If what A.D. was supposedly doing to her grandmother was real, it was so fucking impossible.

"Whooo-noooo!" Abuela cried out. "Duele! Duele!"

"She says he's hurting her." Rita's eyes jammed open, and what she saw was frightening. Two bone white streams of smoke-like mist were traveling up her grandmother's nose. Abuela shook her head rapidly back and forth, trying to get away from the mist, but the mist knew its purpose and continued on.

"Abuela," she cried out. She pitched forward and Turtle grabbed her, slamming her back into the chair.

"Don't!" he said. "He's going in."

"But...but...but...."

Turtle threw his arms around her and pulled her in, holding her close. She thrashed against him, like an asylum patient fighting against the restraints of a straightjacket.

"It's okay," he whispered in her ear, clinging to her. "Just keep telling yourself this is for Abuela. This is to save the house."

"But...but...but...." After a few moments, the thrashing stopped and abuela's body went slack. Her eyes rolled up into her head.

He continued rocking her until everything went black.

❧ ❧ ❧

When she came to, Rita found herself slumped in the chair. Turtle was standing over her, holding out a cup of something.

"Drink," he said. "It's tea," he added with a cautious smile. "Red Zinger."

184

"Abuela," Rita wheezed.

"She's fine."

Rita peered around him to find Abuela lying in bed resting peacefully. Her eyes were closed, and she was now lying on her side. The blanket was down just below her breasts. Her hands were clasped together against her face like a sleeping child in an old picture book. Rita blew out a long slow breath. The atmosphere in the room was normal again, although the air seemed fresher.

She took the cup from Turtle's hand and sipped. "What happened while I was out?"

"Nothing. He's in there stirring up memories. I'm sure he'll trigger something."

Her gaze moved back to Abuela as she swallowed tea. "He did this to you? Went inside?"

"Yeah."

"What did he trigger?"

Turtle sat back down beside her. His eyes grew wide. "I was so young in the first one he gave me. A baby. It's the type of thing no one could possibly remember, and yet I remembered it as if it was yesterday."

"What did you remember?"

"Moms," he replied, a smile ghosting onto his lips. "I remember her wrapping me up in blankets as an infant. I couldn't have been home from the hospital for more than a few days, but I remembered. She was looking at me with so much love in her eyes."

Something shifted in his expression, and Rita could tell a sadness was coming on.

"'Don't cry, little Mushmouse. Mama's got you.' That's what she said, and I knew that at one time she loved me." He stopped talking and stared into his hands.

"I'm sorry," Rita said softly. "And I'm so sorry I doubted you. It's just that—"

"It's okay," he interrupted. "For a while there, I doubted myself."

Rita nodded and sipped her tea. Her eyes moved to Abuela, who seemed at peace. She wanted to ask about the bad thing Turtle promised to do to help A.D. cross-over, but she knew by now he'd do anything to help his brother, even risk his fool neck. She was reminded of the bravery she believed was in him when they first met. She'd been right about that as well.

"It's good," she said, sipping the tea again.

"Not as good as cherry Kool Aid."

He grinned at her. She knew he was trying to lighten the mood. "Not even close," she agreed, and smiled.

An intimacy had developed between them. She hadn't felt it coming on, and yet there it was with all the suddenness of a light being turned on in a darkened room. Their relationship was clear to her now. In that moment, she saw their future together. It was a good future. She didn't know what was going to happen with Abuela and the house, but sitting with Turtle so close she could smell him, she felt assured that everything would be all right.

There was just one hurdle they needed to cross for their future together to be fated. She had to get him to see that the bad thing he promised to do was wrong. He had to renege on his word to A.D. If she couldn't get him to do that, all the good he was doing would be for naught.

❧ ❧ ❧

Mabry was in his room again.

She told herself she'd come to clean, but Mabry knew better. She'd cleaned just a few days ago. She was there to commune with A.D.

During the past few days of rain, a malaise had settled over her, clinging to her skin like the meshwork of a net. And she'd been feeling so good lately. After making the plans to send Turtle to military school, she'd become energized, felt like doing something outside, shopping, or maybe even going to the beach. Yet once the rains came, all the good feelings drained away. She could literally feel them draining out of her. Now the rain had stopped, and the sun was trying its best to get into the house, but she didn't let it in, keeping the drapes drawn. The one room where she enjoyed sunlight was A.D.'s.

The curtains were pulled back, and the sun was gushing in in buckets. She was seated on A.D.'s bed wearing a black and white evening dress and listening to the song—*I Say A Little Prayer*—playing on the Walkman.

"Hey, baby. It's Moms," she whispered. She caught herself smiling, the first smile in days. She liked the extra "s" the boys added when they referred to her. It made her feel special. She wasn't just any old mom. She was *Moms*.

When Dione Warwick got to the part where she was wondering what dress to wear, Mabry said out loud: "You remember this dress? I picked it out special. I bought it for that fancy dinner the firm gave your father for saving them all that money that year. I remember that night when I came out of the bedroom dressed to the nines. You boys were waiting in the living room with your father for the big unveiling. When you saw me coming down the hall your eyes sparkled so bright. And there was this look on your face." She chuckled. "I realized you boys had never seen me dressed up

186

before. You said 'You look nice, Moms.' It's the way you said *niiice*, like I was the queen or something. I'll never forget that."

She was sitting on the edge of the bed, looking nice, adrift in fond memories of that special night. Dionne sang the chorus for the third and final time, building to the finish, singing lines about it being heartbreak for her. At that moment, the cassette tape did something it had never done before. It skipped. Mabry was jolted from her reverie. She looked down at the Walkman next to her on the bed. The tape was skipping as if it were an old record.

Heartbreak for me...heartbreak for me...heartbreak for me.

"What the..." She picked it up, looked in the little window expecting to see tape piling up inside the case, but the tape seemed fine, spooling from one little wheel to the other. She tapped the Walkman gently against her hand, but that had no effect. *Heartbreak for me.*

Mabry's heart began palpitating. She gazed around the room as if it had just become possessed. "A.D.?" she called. "Baby, is that you?" There was no response, just the sound of the tape repeating *Heartbreak for me* again and again. "Damn thing's broken." She hit the off button stopping the tape. *Click.*

She sat back on the bed and sighed, trying to get her rate heart to slow down. "You losing it, girl," she said with a chuckle.

The tape started up again.

Even though she could see that the Walkman was off, the off button in the upright position, the tape went on playing. It had moved ahead in the song, closer to the end. When Dionne sang the final *why don't you answer my prayer*, the tape broke.

Flap-flap-flap-flap

Goose flesh rose on Mabry's arms. A chill raced from the bottom of her spine to the base of her skull. She shivered.

"It's you," she said, her eyes going all spooky. "You're here with me." She suddenly found herself beaming like a child on Christmas morning. "I knew it. I knew it, baby. Moms could always feel you in here."

The tape continued spinning wildly. She turned the Walkman over, opened the back door, and removed the batteries. As soon as they were out, the tape player stopped. She set the Walkman down on the bed.

"You said something about heartbreak. What did you mean by that? I hope there isn't more heartbreak ahead for me. Moms don't know if she could stand anymore of that, A.D. I hope you're talking about something else."

She sat in silence for several minutes, considering what A.D. might have

187

meant by the cryptic message and waiting for another sign. She decided she'd figure out how to splice the tape back together. If she got it back together and played it again maybe there'd be more communication through the song.

She picked up the Walkman and opened the door to get a look at the cassette tape. Something moved on the floor by her foot drawing her attention. Something quite small. She leaned over to get a better look. On the floor by her foot crawled a tiny pet shop turtle.

"A turtle?" she softly drawled. It was seaweed green, a baby, moving in a herky-jerky walk-run motion.

There was no way a pet shop turtle could have found its way into A.D.'s room. This was another sign. A delighted smile appeared on her face. She was making progress. She sat back on the bed to work through the puzzle of what the turtle had to do with the words in the song. She was thinking for mere seconds when the smile on her face vanished.

Turtle. Of course. Turtle was the cause of her heartbreak. Turtle was in the way. If she removed Turtle from the picture, she could have better communication with A.D.

As soon as the thought entered an emotion emerged—shame. Mabry was ashamed of herself for thinking such a thing about her own son. *Mothers are supposed to love their children. All of them!* She knew she loved Turtle, but the love had been lost amid the haze of other, more powerful emotions.

"He'll be gone soon enough," she muttered, despising herself for putting voice to such a hateful thought. Then she scooped up the tiny turtle, took it in the bathroom, and flushed it.

CHAPTER NINETEEN

They sat for hours.

As dark shadows leisurely stretched across the walls, charting the path of the setting of the sun, Turtle began feeling antsy. They'd been there most of the day, at times chatting, at times in silence, always with a watchful eye on Abuela.

Turtle fought the urge to fidget. He wanted to seem at ease—*for Rita*—so he sat unmoving, not allowing her to see the maelstrom that was raging inside. He couldn't help but wonder if something had gone wrong.

Rita didn't have the same compulsion to sit still. She squirmed in her seat constantly. After a while she got up and moved bedside. "I'm sure she's fine," Turtle called, although the tremor in his voice betrayed him.

"She's sweating," Rita said.

"It's warm in here," Turtle replied. He squirmed. *Stop it!*

"No, it isn't." She placed a hand on Abuela's forehead. "She's burning up with fever."

"I'm sure she's fine," Turtle repeated.

"Stop saying that!" Rita barked. "You don't know if she's fine, so stop saying she is."

"I'm...sorry," Turtle replied, suddenly feeling small. "You're right. I don't know."

"Did you break out in a fever?" Her eyes were on him, searing into his flesh, burning out the truth.

"Umm...what?" Turtle asked, feeling smaller. He had to look away.

"Don't play dumb, Theo. Did you break out in a fever when your brother went inside your brain, or didn't you?"

"I don't know."

189

"What do you mean you don't know? Were you sweating when you came out of it?" Her voice was rising.

"I don't think so."

"Theo!"

"Look. Why don't you go get a cold compress to place on her head and cool her down? I'm sure everything's going to be all right." He tried to smile, but knew he had failed—possibly, at everything.

Rita's expression softened. "I'm sorry. I didn't mean to go off on you like that. I know you're trying to help."

He didn't reply. He sat there with that sad excuse for a smile on his face.

"I'll go chill some towels. Call me if she wakes up."

"Of course."

As soon as Rita was out of the room, Turtle moved bedside.

"Hey, bro, what's happening in there? You're starting to freak me out. You okay?"

The old woman lay still. Her breathing was shallow but rhythmic. To anyone entering the room it would appear as though she were sleeping, resting peacefully.

He had wanted to do something for Rita, something she'd appreciate, something to show her his worth. He was trying to be the hero for once in his life. Yet he knew down deep he wasn't made of the stuff that heroes were made of. Courage. Grit. Fearlessness. These were traits he had always seen in A.D. *He* had inherited the coward gene. As he stared down at Abuela, he felt stupid. He was a fraud, and if Abuela didn't wake up, he'd be revealed, the white rabbit hiding under the magician's coat, and could never face Rita again.

He leaned further over and whispered in her ear. "Come on, bro. I need you to come out now. I need for you to come out, and I need for Abuela to wake up."

"Is she awake?"

Rita startled him as she reentered the room, and he jumped back. She was carrying a large damp terrycloth towel.

"No. I was just checking," he said and plopped back down in the chair.

"You were talking to her. What did you say?"

He felt trapped. He didn't realize she'd heard. "I was talking to my brother. I told him it was time to come on out," he said, and braced himself.

She eyed him for a moment. "That's a good idea," she replied.

Rita moved past him to the bedside where she folded the towel neatly and placed it across Abuela's brow.

They resumed their vigil with Rita changing Abuela's cold towel every five minutes. Turtle knew she didn't have to change them so frequently. It was something to do, a project to occupy her mind to keep her from thinking the worst. Turtle had been thinking the worst. He didn't have a project to occupy his mind.

"Her lips are moving," Rita said as she placed the fourth fresh towel on Abuela's forehead. "She's trying to say something."

Turtle's heart seemed squeezed as he lurched to his feet and joined Rita beside the bed. Together they stared down at Abuela, who was now bathed in evening shadow. Her complexion had gone stark white. There was a patina of perspiration covering her face that set her aglow in the darkness. Her lips were cracked and pale and moving ever so slightly. Turtle wondered if this was a dying woman's twitch or if she were actually speaking. The grip on his heart tightened as he leaned in closer.

"Yes. She's speaking. I think it's what she was whispering when we got here," Turtle said, his voice ringing with hope. "Maybe she's coming around."

"Yes," was all Rita said. Her eyes were transfixed on her grandmother.

"I think it's getting louder," Turtle said. He wasn't imagining it. Abuela's voice was growing stronger. The grip on his heart loosened. "She's going to be all right," he rasped.

Abuela's eyes were still closed, yet her voice had risen, was continuing to rise.

"Estoy llegando a mi amor… Estoy llegando a mi amor," she called in a slow building chant.

"What's she saying?" asked Turtle.

Rita didn't respond. She was staring at Abuela as if stricken. "Abuela, wake up. Wake up, Abuela. Ahora!"

The chanting grew faster, rose in intensity. "Estoy-llegando-a-mi-amor," the words began banging into one another. "Estoyllegandoami-amor."

"What's she saying?" Turtle asked, this time with urgency.

Again Rita didn't respond. Her worried eyes were on her grandmother. "Wake up, Abuela. I need you here, now," Rita called. She reached out with both hands and began shaking the old woman. "Wake up!" she cried, growing frantic. "Abuela, you have to wake up now."

"Don't!" Turtle threw his arms around her, yanking her away from the bed. "We have to let this play out, Rita. What is it? What's she saying?"

"She's talking to my abuelo. She's saying 'I'm coming my love. I'm coming.'" She gazed at Turtle with grief stricken eyes. "We're losing her."

Abuela's head began whipping back and forth, right-left, right-left, like a prize fighter on the wrong end of a beat down. The whipping picked up speed, moving faster, faster, more rapidly than humanly possible, so fast her head was no longer present. It had become a distorted, wavering blur. The chanting continued, taking on a staccato, pulsating rhythm.

Rita fought against Turtle's grasp. "Let me go, Theo. She needs me. Let me go."

Turtle clung to her, dragging her farther away from the bed. Clinging to Rita was clinging to the hope that everything would be all right. He was certain that if he let her go, all would be lost.

Then, the convulsions started.

When Abuela's body began convulsing, torqueing around on the bed like a bug in the throes of a violent death, Turtle's heart seemed to stop as he finally had to accept he'd killed her. The convulsing caused the bed to begin thumping. Like a jackhammer, it bumped and lurched across the floor.

"LET ME GO!" Rita screamed, and he did. Why hold onto hope. He'd killed her. All was lost.

Rita charged across the room to be with her dying grandmother, and as she moved everything stopped—the chanting, the head shaking, the convulsions. Everything. The end came so suddenly. Rita staggered to a halt. Abuela lay as still as the dead. The hand that had been on her chest now dangled over the side of the bed. The room was now cloaked in silence. The air around them was thick with the pungent odor of death.

Rita cast a sorrow-filled glance back at Turtle, afraid to utter the words *she's dead*. "She isn't breathing," she said instead.

"Look," Turtle called. His mouth was hanging open, and he was pointing.

Opalescent black particles were drifting from between Abuela's parched lips, a cloud of dark shimmering soot.

"He's coming out," Turtle said. He'd never seen A.D. emerge, didn't know if this was how it was supposed to go, but the dark mist gave him fresh hope.

They gaped at her, awestruck spectators at the carnival sideshow gaping at the sword swallower or the fire eater. The shimmering particles rose like steam into the air.

The young couple found one another's hands in the darkness and clung to each other as the shimmering particles rose high into the air, dancing along the ceiling before twinkling out. As the last of the particles blinked out, Rita gasped. It was a heavy, sorrowful sigh, as if when the light had gone out, a life had been lost.

Abuela's eyes blinked open. She sat up with a start, like a child waking from a dreadful nightmare. Slowly she took in her surroundings. Rita gasped again, this time with incredulity.

Abuela peered around the room, reacquainting herself with her surroundings. Eventually her eyes settled on Rita. There was wonder in them, surprise that Rita was standing there. "I must have been having a bad dream. Sorry I alarmed you, niña. I'm fine," she said, a reassuring smile appearing on her lips.

Rita burst into tears.

"Stop that! It was just a bad dream," Abuela scolded.

"I know," Rita replied, the tears continuing to fall.

Abuela's eyes moved on to Turtle. Her brow furrowed. "What's he doing in here?"

"I…umm, was visiting Rita. We both heard you cry out and came running."

"That is sweet of you," she said. Her firm gaze swung back to Rita. "You shouldn't bring your boyfriend in here, niña. You don't want him seeing me looking like this." Her gaze moved back to Turtle. A wry smile had taken over her face, brightening it like a beacon in the darkness. "He sees me like this he might get the impression that this is how *you're* going to look one day, and then, poof, no more boyfriend."

Rita burst into laughter. Her tears continued to fall.

"I'm famished," Abuela said. Suddenly self-conscious, she pulled the covers up around herself. "I just remembered the recipe for my banana pancakes. Strange, I haven't thought of that recipe in fifteen years. Anyone else have a taste for banana pancakes?"

Relief, like adrenaline, flooded Turtle's veins. He was suddenly a hundred pounds lighter. He was grinning like the cat who ate the canary. "I do," he said, realizing his stomach had been growling for quite some time.

"Me, too," said Rita.

"Then please, both of you get out of here and let me make myself decent. And forget what you saw. I'll deny it anyway."

They both laughed as they exited the room.

Later, the house filled with delicious aromas. Abuela seemed energized as she moved about the kitchen preparing the banana pancake supper with Rita as her helper, although it appeared Abuela didn't need any help. She remembered where everything was, and when she opened the refrigerator, not once did she stand there wondering what she'd opened it for. Her mind was sharp and clear.

Turtle inhaled the happy sounds of eggs cracking, the sizzle of butter in the pan, the cacophonous clinking of dishes. This kitchen symphony was a fond reminder of Saturday breakfasts in the Dawson household in what seemed like a lifetime ago. A.D. could demolish a dozen pancakes in one sitting. Turtle used to marvel at how someone so slight could eat so many when he was full after two or three.

Abuela sang as she cooked. It was the first time Turtle had seen her so animated, happy, and vocal. He cast a glance at Rita, who was mashing bananas to dump in the batter. They shared a private smile.

"She singing "Guantanamera." It's about a man who had a romantic relationship with a woman, and she left him," Rita said.

"It doesn't sound like a sad song," Turtle said. He was sitting at the table playing with two of the cats.

"It's not," Abuela said. "I remember dancing to this and many great songs at the dance clubs my girlfriends and I used to go to on Saturday nights. What minxes we were. This was long before Tito," she said and laughed.

"My Abuela was a player," Rita said, and catching Turtle's eye, they both erupted in laughter.

The joy brightening Rita's face caused Turtle's heart to swell with secret pride. He was the hero. For the first time in his life he had proven his worth. He loved her and loved that he was able to do this special thing for her. It made him feel powerful.

Yet as joyous and powerful as he felt, there was an undercurrent of melancholy swirling around inside, fueled by his promise to A.D. He tried stuffing the gloom back down. He told himself that tonight was for celebration, for feeling good about himself, and yet every few minutes the sadness would bubble up in his gut.

Rita hadn't yet asked Abuela about Mickey Mouse or what Tito had done with the money for the house. She needed to get the information from her as soon as possible. Turtle feared this clarity Abuela was experiencing was temporary. She had Alzheimer's disease, and after a while it would return.

He would remind Rita to talk to her. *After supper*, he thought as he watched Abuela playfully teasing her granddaughter about the fresh coat of paint she had applied to her fingernails—alternate nails painted with silver and black lacquer. They were enjoying each other now, and he didn't want to disrupt it. *After supper*.

He teased and laughed along with them throughout the meal, although the gloom inside had kicked up like a dust storm in his belly. He was sure the pancakes were delicious, yet they tasted like sand, and went down like cement into his swirling gut. *The Last Supper*, he thought, the final meal Jesus Christ had shared with his Apostles before going off to die.

This was *his* last supper.

After tonight his relationship with Rita would end, had to end. Tomorrow he'd be heading off to kill the Teddy Bear. Kill or be killed, it didn't matter which. Either way, the best thing in his life was coming to an end.

After supper, he and Rita stayed in the kitchen to do the dishes together while Abuela and her cats retired to the living room and a good book.

"I haven't had time to thank you," Rita said as she filled the sink with water. He was the designated dryer.

"You have to ask her about Mickey Mouse," Turtle said as she soaked the dishes.

"I know," she said, the joy on her face dissolving.

"It's why I asked A.D. to do it. You have to save the house."

"I know, Theo," she said with a hint of annoyance. "She'll be sleeping when we're done out here. We need to ask her in the morning. Tomorrow, okay?"

He eyed her suspiciously.

"I'm not trying to get out of it. I know I have to save the house from Elena. I was just thinking, you should come over in the morning and we'll talk to her together. Okay?"

Turtle thought of all the heroes in all the great old movies. They never stayed around for the end. The hero did his good deed and rode out of town before the end, before all the thank-yous, before the applause.

"Okay," he said and reached for a plate to dry. "We'll talk to her in the morning, together."

CHAPTER TWENTY

He made himself a peanut butter and jelly sandwich to eat along the way. He cut it in half on a diagonal the way Moms used to. He hadn't cut his sandwiches in a long time and couldn't explain why he did it.

When they were little, they didn't realize sandwiches could be cut other ways or not at all. Then A.D. started school and announced one morning when Moms was making his lunch: "Don't cut my sandwich like that. That's for babies."

"Me, either," said Turtle, and he smiled at his older brother. They were in this no-cutting thing together. Moms shot them a look Turtle would much later realize was loss. Her boys were growing up faster than she wanted them to.

He put the sandwich in a baggie, then poured himself a Mason jar of grape Kool Aid. The Kool Aid pitcher had lemon slices floating on top, just the way he liked it.

A.D. had told him the Teddy Bear's house was a mile outside of town in an area everyone called the boonies. It was just beyond the town line, bordered by a forest that began at the town line where The Lots ended, and spanned out for miles. He figured he could bike there in an hour, maybe a little longer. If he left by ten, even with stopping for lunch, he'd arrive at the Teddy Bear's by noon. A.D. had told him the Teddy Bear wouldn't arrive home from work until around six p.m. That gave him plenty of time to poison the Teddy Bear's Gatorade and get out.

He placed the baggied sandwich and the Mason jar in the backpack he hadn't used since the sixth grade. Then he wheeled Tyrone out onto the porch.

"You heading over to that girlfriend's?" Moms called.

That was a surprise. Was she now going to forbid him to see her?

"No. We broke up. I'm goin' to The Lots," he called back.

Mabry appeared in the doorway behind him. "Really? That's too bad."

There was a pleasantness coming from the voice behind that compelled him to turn around. Moms was in the doorway. The familiar scowl was gone. She was wearing a blue pantsuit, as if she were planning on going out.

"It's okay," he said.

"Did you like her a lot?" she asked.

He thought about this for a while. Not about if he liked her, he *loved* her. He thought about how to answer his mother, who had never questioned him about anything that mattered to him before—ever.

"Yes."

She nodded grimly. "It's tough losing those you care—"

"*I* broke up with *her*," he blurted. He said it to hurt her. He wanted her to know he wasn't the loser in the family, *she* was.

"Oh," she responded, seeming surprised. "It's still tough, though. Isn't it?"

"I gotta go, Moms," he said and turned to push off. "I'll be home late."

"You be careful," she called after him.

I'll be even more careful when I'm in military school, he wanted to call back but didn't. He set his mind on the task ahead and pedaled Tyrone up the street.

He's a bad person, he told himself. *He deserves to die.*

By the time Turtle had pedaled across Union Avenue, he was breathing extra heavy. It wasn't particularly hot out, and there was a nice breeze pushing up from the South, yet beads of salty sweat popped up on his forehead like kernels of freshly popped popcorn. When he reached Prospect, his legs began feeling weary. He shouldn't have been tired. This was an easy ride for him, a piece of cake.

It was the task that was slowing him down. The task was weighing on him like an anchor around his neck. His shoulders ached not from the heft of his backpack, which contained a sandwich and a jar of Kool Aid, but from the burden of what he'd set out to do.

He pulled over on Prospect Avenue near Crone Drugs to catch his breath. *He's a bad person. He deserves to die.* No, that was the wrong way of looking at it. Instead, he told himself he wasn't going there to kill the Teddy Bear. He was going there to do a number of small tasks. One: go into the garage; two: locate the antifreeze; three: take a bottle of Gatorade out of the fridge and drink half; four: refill the bottle with antifreeze, and five: leave. That was the list of tasks he had to accomplish. These were the *only* tasks that lay ahead of him, so he needed to get all that morbid stuff out of his head. He was task oriented, like *The Terminator*. Follow the steps and go home. That was it; end of story.

He opened the backpack, pulled out the Mason jar and took a few swallows of Kool Aid. It tasted so good. *As good as that stolen Tahitian Treat? Better.* Once his breathing slowed and his legs felt fresher, he put the Kool Aid away and rode off toward the boonies.

❧ ❧ ❧

The revelation hit Rita like one of Jersey Joe's haymakers. She'd been lying across her bed, painting her nails, when it became clear. He wasn't coming. It was half past eleven when she realized she was going to have to face the truth. He wasn't coming because he was on his way to kill the Teddy Bear.

She should have known. Turtle would do anything not to disappoint his brother. The thought of what he might be doing in that moment hit her hard, and a sudden dread constricted her throat making it nearly impossible to breathe. She rolled onto her side and opened her mouth wide, wrapped her hands around her neck massaging her throat, trying to coax open the passageway enough to fill her lungs with air.

Something horrible was under way. She knew it, could feel it in the beat of her heart, the pounding of her pulse. She had to do something. She had to keep this horrible thing from happening. But how?

Rita struggled to her feet. "Abuela!" she cried out, but her call came as a wispy rasp and died in the air in front of her. "Abuela!" Although she could hardly breathe, felt as though at any moment she would pass out, Rita was moving across the room. She flung open the door and staggered out into the hall.

"Abuela!"

While her call came as a sigh, as distant as a cry from a mountain top, the cats heard her. Carlotta and Dulcinea looked up from their play. Carlotta mewed loudly, and Dulcinea darted down the corridor. Rita followed, certain the black feline was leading her to her Abuela.

She stumbled after the cat into the living room. By now her eyes were bulging. Red veins road mapped across the whites, tributaries of doom.

"Rita!" Abuela appeared seemingly from out of nowhere, her voice filled with distress. She was dressed in gardening attire, dungaree overalls and a big, floppy hat, and holding Dulcinea in her arms. "Rita, what is it?"

At the sound of Abuela's voice, Rita's throat finally relaxed, and sweet fresh air came rushing in. "It's Theo. He's in trouble," she said in short gasping bursts.

"What kind of trouble?" Abuela was now by her side. The cat was out of her arms, and she cradled her granddaughter on the sofa.

Rita again tried to speak, but this time nothing came but sputters and gasps.

"Breath, niña, breathe," Abuela said softly. She stroked her granddaughter's hair.

The soothing sound of Abuela's voice invited Rita's mind to relax. She took in several deep breaths allowing her heart to slow down. "You have a friend who can talk to the dead," she said breathlessly.

"Bernadette Pinkstring? What's she got to do with Theo?"

"We need to go see her, Abuela. I can tell you why on the way, but we need to leave now. If we don't go now, I'm afraid of what might happen."

Abuela gazed at Rita, puzzled by this odd request, but she knew her granddaughter, knew she was not one for histrionics. "She lives about a block from here. Put on your shoes, and we will leave at once."

Turtle

The Teddy Bear house was at the end of a private road, up a steep slope that he couldn't see over. Turtle left his bike in the undergrowth at the foot of the slope and walked the rest of the way. As he neared the top, the house came into view. It was a large Gothic Victorian home with pitched roofs that reminded him of *The Munsters'* house, but larger and creepier. The rickety old home sat back at the end of a large clearing, fronted by a cinder-covered circular drive with a backdrop of maple and oak trees.

There was no garage. To his left there was a falling-down old wooden barn with double sliding doors, the left of which listed off the track. But there was no garage. The right sliding door was pushed midway open, an inviting gesture.

No garage, he thought as he stared at the barn. *No fucking garage. He must have meant the barn was used as a garage.* He wondered what else A.D. could have gotten wrong.

He looked up into the sky as he headed for the barn. He didn't have a watch and attempted to use the placement of the sun in the sky to tell time. A.D. used to do it when they spent all day at The Lots playing. A.D. said it was what Native Americans did back in the days of the old west. He would look at the sky and say: "It's nearly five. Time to head home, Mushmouse." They'd get home and Moms would be midway through making supper, the house smelling of pork chops or pepper steak, the kitchen clock reading five-fifteen or five-twenty. "I was just wondering about you boys," she'd say.

199

It was a neat trick, and A.D. had taught it to him. Now the sun was almost overhead. Noon. Despite the slow going and three separate stops along the way, he'd made it there on time.

Turtle stepped through the barn door and into near darkness and stood for several moments, allowing his eyes to adjust to the gloom. Stables lined the left wall of the barn from front to rear. He could tell they'd been unoccupied for quite some time. The faint fragrance of stale hay and old wood hung in the air, mixed with the noxious odor of gasoline.

A.D. came to mind, giddy as he splashed gasoline over Bert Meade's truck, the same Bert Meade who'd killed him. Turtle's mind wanted to stay and ponder this irony, but he needed to get back to why he was there. Time, she was a-ticking away.

There was a work table at the center with a few hand tools sitting on top, and to the right, a sitting area with a small sofa and a TV sitting atop a wooden TV table. A small refrigerator sat by the arm of the sofa.

Seeing the refrigerator, Turtle's skin began to tingle. He quickly ran the tasks through his mind. *One: go into the garage; two: locate the antifreeze.*

He moved to his left and began looking into the stalls. The first stall contained wooden children's desks of the kind that were desk and chair in one. The desks had been tossed in helter-skelter. The second stall contained a mountain of something—machinery, he thought—under a large black tarp. In the third was a stockpile of automotive supplies: tins of motor oil, STP, Gumout carburetor cleaner, several gas cans that reeked of gasoline, and three containers of antifreeze.

Three: take a bottle of Gatorade out of the fridge and drink half. He went into the stall, grabbed a container of the antifreeze and, like an automaton, moved without thinking out of the stall and to the small fridge. Inside, there was bottled water, the remains of a Big Mac, something that looked like a salad covered with mold, and a six pack of Gatorade. *Three: take a bottle of Gatorade out of the fridge and drink half; four: refill the bottle with antifreeze.* He pulled a bottle of Gatorade from the six pack, was about to twist-off the lid when he went off script.

Suppose I'm wrong, he thought. *No,* he told himself. *Don't think. You're the Terminator. His purpose had been to eliminate Sarah Conner; your purpose is to eliminate the Teddy Bear. Do your job and go home.* He twisted the cap and the seal broke. He stopped again as perspiration began sliding down his sides, pooling in the soft fold at his waist. *Suppose I'm wrong. Suppose I kill an innocent man. No. A.D. wouldn't do that to me. A.D. has always protected me.* He stood there in the gloom and realized he needed to be certain. He'd always trusted A.D., but now he wasn't so sure he should.

200

He again gazed around the barn, this time looking for a sign, anything that said *this is the garage of a man who violates and then kills little boys.* He returned the Gatorade to the fridge and moved back to the stalls.

The children's desks indicated that The Teddy Bear might be a school teacher. That would give him access to children, but did wooden desks indicate that he was a killer? Of course not. He moved into the second stall, pulled back the tarp and was surprised to find stacks of mannequins and not machinery underneath. That was strange, but perhaps he'd been wrong about the school teacher angle. Maybe the Teddy Bear worked in a department store. Maybe he was the window dresser and dressed these mannequins for all the holidays. Maybe he wasn't the Teddy Bear at all.

The third stall held the automotive supplies. A few of the other stalls held kindling piled high. The rest were empty. He moved around the barn, examining the contents of the work table, looking under the cushions of the sofa. He found nothing to indicate that a murderer resided there.

Armed with his doubt, he moved out of the barn, squinting as his eyes adjusted to the daylight. He gazed across the expanse at the creepy old house. He looked skyward, again checking the angle of the sun. It was maybe just before one. He shot another worried look at the house and then, making his decision, started moving across the expanse. He needed to find his way inside. He needed to find something inside, anything, to indicate the man who lived there needed to die. If he found something, he'd have plenty of time to spike the Gatorade. If he didn't, he'd leave.

R i t a

Bernadette Pinkstring appeared anxious. They were seated in the room she called her parlor but was actually a tiny dinette. She was wearing her conjuring clothes, a bright-colored shawl she'd gotten from Stinson's department store over a plain, dark colored dress. Her vintage wide-brimmed hat with the gardenia hatband was on her head.

They were seated around a small table featuring the most gorgeous antique tea service. The teapot and cups were white china with rings of country red roses. Pinkstring had insisted on serving them tea even though Rita said the matter was urgent.

"All the more reason to have tea," Bernie Pinkstring said with a knowing smile. "I need to hear a little something about the person you wish to contact today, and what better way to get to know someone than over a cup of tea?" She had a confident self-assured way about her. At least she did until Rita began talking about A.D. When she told Bernie about the boy who said his brother was back from the dead, and that the dead boy said he was-n't a ghost, but an entity, the anxiousness began.

"I think these boys were just having their way with you," Bernadette said and winked at Abuela. "You know how high-spirited teenage boys can be," she added with a laugh.

Rita felt there was something not right about the dismissal. Bernie Pinkstring may have been smiling, but her hands had begun to tremor ever so slightly. Her tea cup rattled in the antique saucer, and she set them back down on the table.

"No," Rita said, annoyed. "Theo most definitely was *not* having his way with me. His brother is a spirit; don't ask me how I know but I know, and I need you to contact him. Now."

"My, oh, my. I admire your granddaughter's spunk, Marizza," Pinkstring said, mispronouncing Abuela's name. "But I'm afraid I can't just go bounc-ing around on the astral plane looking for the boy who claims to be an entity. Now, can I?"

She laughed and reached for her tea. Her hand knocked into the cup, splashing tea onto the table. "I'm just as clumsy as a mule," she said and began blotting up the tea with her napkin.

"You already know about him, don't you?" Rita said.

Bernadette Pinkstring stopped blotting and looked up, a deer in head-lights. "I know what you told me," she replied digging in with her heels. It was her eyes that betrayed her. They were twitchy, and she wouldn't fix on either of the women.

"Bernadette, my dear, I'm getting the feeling there is more here than meets the eye," said Abuela, holding the woman in her gaze.

Pinkstring composed herself. "All right. I may have come in contact with energy that fits that description."

"Then, help me," Rita pleaded. "We need to find out what's going on up there."

"I'm afraid it's not that easy."

Rita turned to her grandmother. "She's a fake. She can't help us. Let's go. We have to find someone who can, and quickly." Rita stood.

"You granddaughter needs to learn some manners, Marizza."

"It's Maritza!" Rita barked. "And you need to learn to be truthful. Which do you think is more important?" She pushed away from the table and started from the room.

"Wait, niña," Abuela called. Rita wheeled around, surprised to find that Abuela hadn't moved.

"Abuela, time is running out. If we don't find someone who can help

202

us, Theo is going to kill this man, or get killed trying." There was anguish in her voice.

Abuela looked to Bernadette, who had risen as well, all puffed up in hands-on-hips defiance. "My granddaughter is in love with this boy. Rita is not one to give her heart away easily. This boy she loves is in danger, and she's looking to you for answers. Bernadette, can you help her?"

Bernadette peered into Abuela's green eyes, and her own eyes turned heavy and sorrowful. Her hands fell from her hips to her sides. "He's dangerous," she whispered. "This spirit you want me to conjure has killed before."

"Oh, my God! Can you reach him?" asked Rita, stepping forward.

"I can try. But he will know that we know he's a murderer. I'm powerless if he tries to harm us."

"I'm willing to take that chance," said Rita.

Bernie again peered into Abuela's eyes. "All right." She released a weighty sigh. "I guess I am, too."

"Thank you, Bernadette," said Abuela.

Bernadette smiled at her and nodded. It was the smile of a man going to war believing he wouldn't be coming back alive.

"Your name isn't Marizza? Well, I'll be."

Turtle

The front door was unlocked.

Turtle pushed it open and peered into the anteroom. He was immediately greeted by mustiness in the air, with a chlorine-heavy undertow, like bleach. It stopped him. Instinct told him this was an unfriendly odor. He felt as though a thick chunk of ice was suddenly lodged in his belly. He shivered.

"No one's home," he mumbled. The words did nothing to diminish his concerns.

There was a side table just inside the doorway with stacks of old, dusty mail. An umbrella rack and a hatless hat stand stood near the door. The anteroom emptied into a corridor that was right off the living room. There was a staircase leading to the second floor.

Stop being a wussy, he told himself and stepped inside. He left the door open. The house was creepy, and he'd feel trapped if he closed it. He picked up a stack of mail from the table. A cloud of dust swept into the air. Some of the mail was so old and yellowed it could have been sitting for years. The name Gerta Criss was on many of the old circulars and junk mail. A few of the more recent pieces belonged to an A. Criss.

Two people live here, Turtle thought. Something else A.D. had been wrong about or neglected to mention.

Despite the ice cube melting in his belly, Turtle ventured further into the house. He walked lightly, and several times he looked back to make sure the door was still open and that, if he needed to, he could get out quickly.

He peered around the bend into the large but cramped living room. The room was stuffed with dark, oversized furniture. Every available surface was cluttered with newspapers, magazines, and more unopened mail. The clutter in the room made him feel even more claustrophobic. He glanced back toward the open door, now several feet away. Bright sunlight invited him to leave.

He swallowed. It went down hard as if his throat were constricting on him. He entered the living room. None of the grimy windows had any window coverings on them, leaving the clutter washed over with a yellowish hue, like an old photograph.

He moved across the room quickly, rifled through the papers on the claw foot coffee table. Nothing there cried out murderer. It was the everyday clutter of a hoarder.

Turtle had first heard of hoarding when the family went over to clean out Uncle Johnny's place after he'd gone away. What they found was a house that hadn't been cleaned since Aunt Jenny had left. Newspapers, magazines, empty cans were everywhere.

Turtle gazed around the room full of clutter, getting the feeling he wasn't going to find anything downstairs that would convince him a murderer lived here. He had to venture upstairs to the bedrooms where he could look through A. Criss's or Gerta Criss's personal things. His gaze moved to the staircase and he shuddered.

What am I doing here?

He was Turtle Dawson, Mr. I'm-afraid-of-everything. The same Turtle Dawson who still covered his eyes during the scary parts of scary movies, the same Turtle Dawson who avoided conflict at all costs, the same Turtle Dawson who called on his big brother whenever the going got rough. *What am I doing here?*

He was afraid to go upstairs. He had told himself he was doing this for Rita, then he had told himself it was a promise he'd made to his brother, yet as he stood there, the fear settling over him like a chilling net, he knew these were all lies. *I'm doing this for me.* The surprising thought came to him clear as day. He was doing this to prove he no longer needed to be taken care of. He was doing this so when he looked in the mirror, he no longer saw a coward looking back.

Turtle sighed deeply and headed for the staircase. As he climbed the stairs, he took a longing glance back at the open door. His legs were suddenly heavier, as if with each step the gravity that binds us all to this earth was doubling and tripling. His calf and thigh muscles quivered, but he didn't stop, couldn't stop, because he knew if he did, he'd run back downstairs, from the house, and down the hill.

Heavy-legged, he exited the stairs and stepped into a small corridor off of which there were five bedrooms. Four of the doors were ajar, more bright yet eerie light spilling from within. Turtle headed for the closed door. Behind the closed door is where the secrets are kept. Every TV detective knew that. He dragged over to the door and tried it. Locked. For the second time that day his skin began to tingle. He'd been right about the door. The Crisses lived alone at least a mile from their nearest neighbor. This door wasn't locked to keep one of the Crisses out, it was locked to keep everyone else out.

Turtle needed a key, but if he went looking for a key, it might take too long. He still had plenty of time to poison the Gatorade and get out, but he could see the sun slowly creeping into the Western part of the sky. Locating a key was out of the question.

I have to break in, he told himself, and with fear doused in adrenaline flooding his veins, he took two steps back and fired forward, launching his shoulder into the door.

Thud! "Aahhh!" he cried out as pain rocketed into his shoulder, the sound of his cry echoing throughout the house, yet the door was still in tact. A new thought came as he massaged his aching shoulder: *If I break down the door the Teddy Bear will see it, will know someone's been in his house and perhaps not drink the poisoned Gatorade.*

He decided to deal with that later. Right now he needed to know what was in the room, and to find out he needed to break in. If he didn't find what he was looking for behind the locked door, the Crisses would come home and report a burglary where nothing was taken. *No harm, no foul.*

This time he backed up as far as he could, braced himself and lumbered forward toward the door, hitting it with his full one hundred and seventy pounds.

BOOM! CRASH! Surprisingly, the lock shattered from the blunt force, and Turtle went careening into the room. The pain in his shoulder was immediate and explosive. His entire arm went numb and his vision was clouded by the pain. He actually saw stars.

When the fog in his head cleared, Turtle found himself doubled-over in pain three feet inside a small bedroom. There was no furniture in the room, save for a wooden chair in the center of the floor facing the rear wall.

"Holy shit," Turtle mumbled as for the third time that day his skin began to tingle.

The wall the chair was facing held a solid mass of photographs, many of them of young boys. Some of the photos were quite old. All the boys were in various stages of undress, all of their eyes leaking terror. Surrounding these photos were photographs of a large blue amusement-park type character—The Teddy Bear. Turtle began trembling upon seeing him for the first time. There were photos of the Teddy Bear dancing. There were what appeared to be press photos of him surrounded by children, and others of him shaking hands with men and women who must have been important people. It made him sick to look at them.

The adjacent wall held newspaper clippings and circulars featuring the faces of missing children—children Turtle knew had gone missing at the hands of the Teddy Bear. One wall was not covered with photographs or clippings. This wall was bare except for the large portrait of a well-dressed woman, *in her thirties*, he thought. The woman's face held a bright smile, but there was something off about the eyes. Turtle moved in closer for a better look and discovered the eyes in the portrait had been scratched out.

There was something else in the room Turtle had missed at first glance. Beneath the chair there was what appeared to be a photo album. He now moved to the chair with urgency, and with shaky hands opened the album. To Turtle's horror, he discovered a scrap book containing more photos and clippings, along with souvenirs of the Teddy Bear's murders. On the cover of the book was a red dymo label with the words: The Teddy Bear Club.

He opened to the first page, and there he saw an oath:

The Teddy Bear Club Oath
I will be a squareshooter, in my home, at school and at play.
I will be truthful, honest, and strive always to make myself
a better citizen.
I will always look out for children smaller than myself.

The oath went on for a full page. *The crazy bastard thinks he's starting a club,* Turtle thought in disgust.

As he thumbed through the book, he began feeling dizzy, his legs going wobbly. This book featured eight-by-twelve photos of the boys he'd seen on the wall in better days. These photos were most likely collected from the missing child circulars the families had circulated. Alongside each was a photo of a boy mannequin neatly dressed in school clothes seated at a desk, each mannequin a representation of the boy in the adjacent photo. Turtle recognized the desks and mannequins from the barn.

The book provided the proof that the Teddy Bear was a perverted serial killer. Turtle's belly churned, and as he thumbed through he realized he had to close the book or he was going to be sick all over it.

A.D. was right. The man—or monster—had been going about the business of kidnapping and killing boys undetected for years. Someone needed to put a stop to this horror. The Teddy Bear deserved to die.

ﹿ   ﹿ   ﹿ

He was back on task and the task was simple: *Three: take the Gatorade out of the fridge and drink half; four: refill the bottle with antifreeze.*

Any fear Turtle had been feeling was replaced by outrage. He took his time repositioning the door in the frame. At a glance, a person couldn't tell the lock had been broken. Hopefully the Teddy Bear would drink the Gatorade before he went into the room of his perverted pleasure.

Turtle bounded down the stairs, his battered shoulder throbbing with each bounce, toward the still-open door and daylight. Then, it was off to the barn to complete his list of tasks. He arrived at the door and gave the house one last, quick glance. That's when he noticed another door, a basement door just off the kitchen. The basement door was half open, and a soft yellow glow was coming from within.

At that moment he thought of Ansley. He couldn't explain why the thought had popped into his head, but Ansley had gone missing the night A.D. had set fire to his father's truck. Ansley was thirteen years old. Turtle didn't think this was a coincidence. *He could be down there*, he thought. Ansley's photo was not on the wall. *He could be down there and still alive.*

He stood in the doorway for several minutes, thinking. Ansley and his brothers had been nothing but mean to him from the moment they'd arrived in town. Ansley's father had killed his brother. So what if he was down there and still alive? *Tit for tat, brother rat.*

This'll just take a minute, he thought. He again checked the angle of the sun—two o'clock at the latest. He had lots of time—and headed for the basement.

CHAPTER TWENTY-ONE

Rita

The table had been cleared, the drapes drawn, and the lights dimmed.

Bernadette Pinkstring explained that she would try and reach out to the spirit of the boy, but if he knew they were aware of his crime, he may not want to talk to them.

"I understand," Rita said. Her heart was strumming like a banjo. She needed to make contact. She needed A.D. to tell her the location of the Teddy Bear house so she could go there and stop Turtle from committing a crime he'd regret the rest of his life.

"Let's hold hands," Pinkstring announced, stretching out her arms and wriggling her fingers. "Do not interrupt me once I begin. Strange things may occur while the boy and I are talking. Do not get up, do not run, do not let go of my hand. Do I have your assurances, ladies?"

Rita glanced at Abuela, who seemed to have no problem with the request. She thought of séances she'd seen in movies and on TV shows. Most of them were bogus, done by fakes who used tricks. The ones that weren't were in horror movies, and those always ended badly.

"Yes," Rita replied.

Abuela nodded, her expression turning grim.

Bernadette reached out and they all locked hands, forming a connective ring around the table. She lowered her head and began to whisper. Rita again glanced over at Abuela, who shot her a hopeful smile.

After just a few minutes, the whispering stopped. They sat in silence for several minutes more, Bernadette silent and unmoving with her eyes closed and her head bowed. The room had become so quiet, Rita could hear her own pulse pounding in her ears. Then, Bernadette's head rose and her eyes opened.

"I don't feel him," she said, letting out a long breath. "These spirits are usually quite talkative when they find someone who can hear them. Normally, I don't even have to go looking for them. Not only is your young fellow not talking, but I don't feel his energy. He's gone. I'm sorry." She released their hands.

"So, that's it?" squawked Rita.

"Think of me as being like a telephone. I'm calling, but no one's home. I'm sorry, baby."

"I have to find him, Abuela. We're running out of time."

"What can we do, niña? Bernadette is the only woman I know who has conversations with the dead."

"I don't know," Rita replied sniffling. "Thanks for trying, Miss Pinkstring." Her words were so filled with anguish they touched the hearts of both the older women.

"I'm truly sorry," Bernadette said to Abuela. "If I—" Her eyes shot open wide. She suddenly looked like one of those cartoon characters who'd stuck a finger in a wall socket. Her pupils had vanished. Just the whites of her eyes were showing. "I-I-I-I," she repeated the monosyllabic word in a stuttering staccato.

"It's her blood pressure," Abuela cried out. "I think she's having a stroke. We have to find her medication."

Rita was up and starting from the room. "I'll look in the bedroom."

"Don't!" Bernadette rasped.

Rita stopped short, turned back, and saw foam drizzling from the old woman's lips. Bernadette peered at Rita with her pupil-less eyes. "He fooled me!" she cried out.

Rita cast a troubled look at Abuela. "Should I look for her meds?"

"No," Abuela said. "I believe the boy is making contact."

Bernadette sat back down, wiped her mouth with her sleeve. "He's going to wake up soon," she said, now sounding like a child. "And when he does, he's going to be mad, but I don't care."

"Who's going to be mad, the Teddy Bear?" Rita asked, moving back to the table.

Bernadette cocked her head to one side, like a dog. "Who are you?"

"I'm Rita. Don't you remember me?"

"No. Did he tell you there was going to be others, too? He told me there was going to be others, but he lied."

209

"Who lied?" Rita asked.

"Him!" she said, as if Rita were an idiot for asking. "I don't care. I'm sick of it."

Rita again glanced at Abuela. This wasn't making any sense. She gazed back at pupil-less Bernadette Pinkstring. "What's your name?" she asked.

A wary expression appeared on the woman's face. "Why do you want to know?"

"I'll tell you mine, and you can tell me yours, okay? I'm Rita." She smiled at the woman seated across the table.

Bernadette cocked her head to the other side. "You already told me your name." Then: "Mine's Marty."

"Marty. That's a nice name. Where's A.D., Marty?"

"He's sleeping now, but when he wakes up he's going to be mad, real mad, but I don't care. He promised there'd be more kids to play with, but he's only bringing one more back for *him* to play with. So, poot on him!" A pout appeared on Bernadette's face.

"Calm down, Marty. I need you to listen to me, all right?" Bernadette nodded and sniffed back a tear. "Can you tell me who he's bringing back?"

"His brother," Bernadette whined. "I don't want him to come. If he comes, A.D. will have him to play with, and I'll have *nobody*." Bernadette Pinkstring began bawling like a six year-old. "I tried to tell his mother, but she wouldn't listen to me," she said.

Rita turned to Abuela with turmoil in her eyes. "A.D. didn't send Turtle there to kill the Teddy Bear. He sent him there to die."

❧ ❧ ❧

Turtle moved to the basement door and pulled it wide. The glow was emanating from downstairs. He stood in the doorway thinking of the three things he was most afraid of, had always been afraid of: ghosts, monsters, and darkened basements. *Fuuck!* he thought. He was now dealing with all three. He'd hit the scary trifecta—the pinnacle of his fears.

He stepped across the threshold. The smell of bleach was stronger here, mixed with something else. The odor was coming from downstairs. Fear bubbled up in his belly like lava in a volcano. It radiated out, attacking his arms and legs. He became tired—so, so tired. This was the time to run. This was the time to get the hell out of the house, run down the slope, mount Tyrone and ride away to tell the authorities what he'd discovered.

But he felt something else as well. At first he thought it was courage, but it wasn't courage, it was more a sense of duty. He'd always had it. He'd been duty bound to A.D. as now he was duty bound to do the right thing. The right thing was to not leave an innocent boy there to die if he could help it.

He started down the stairs and a part of his brain called out: *If there is a kid down there, once the Teddy Bear drinks the Gatorade and dies, he'll be free to go. No sense risking your neck for him. Just stick to the plan.* He paused. That made sense. Then another part of his brain spoke up: *If he's tied up—and he probably is—he won't be discovered for days. He'll die down there.*

He started down again. The stairs made scary movie creaks under his feet: *So what if he dies? Your life has been nearly erased because of Ansley Meade and his family. Let him die.*

"I can't," Turtle said out loud. "I really don't want to go down into this basement, but I can't let someone die who I could have saved. I just can't."

Perhaps it was courage. Perhaps it was a lack of good common sense, he'd never know. He continued downstairs. The voices in his head became quiet.

He reached the bottom. The odor was stronger down here, the heavy stink of chlorine making him feel a bit lightheaded. He gazed around, forcing his eyes to focus. It was a large basement filled with even more clutter. Toward the rear he saw the source of the glow, a single bulb hanging down over a cot. Ansley was on the cot. He wore a white hospital gown and was sprawled awkwardly—half on his side, half on his back. His neck was contorted to the side in an unnatural position.

The flesh of his arms and legs was a ghastly shade of yellowish white, the color of the chickens hanging in the case at Schultz's poultry market, but it was his face that was the scariest. It was pure white, snow white, sheet white, bloodless white, scary as fuck white!

Turtle's breath caught in the back of his throat. "I'm too late," he muttered.

Just then, Ansley's head moved. His neck adjusted and he moaned something. Turtle's eyes widened as his heart thumped. Ansley Meade was not dead. Not dead! Knowing the Teddy Bear's intentions for the boy it seemed impossible.

"Ansley!" he whispered loudly. "Ansley, it's me."

Ansley stirred, as if coming out of a dream. His eyes opened and he squinted at Turtle standing in the shadows. He moaned again, and Turtle realized his mouth was taped shut.

"It's me," Turtle said and stepped forward into the light. Upon seeing him Ansley's face registered shock and then disbelief.

Turtle moved to the cot. Sat down beside him and gingerly peeled back the tape. Ansley's eyes widened as he gulped in air, the way a man stranded on the desert might take in water—hungrily, greedily.

"You," he said, his voice low and scratchy. "You're with him?"

"No. It's a long story, but I came here to kill him. But I have to rescue you first."

"You?" Ansley uttered in disbelief.

His hands and right foot were bound to the cot with the kind of heavy plastic zip-tie handcuffs used by police. Turtle began trying to undo the ties, but it wasn't possible. They were too secure.

"You have to get out of here," Ansley said, his voice coming stronger now. "I don't know what you're thinking, but just go get the cops."

"No time," said Turtle. "I need to get a knife or something to cut your bindings with." He got up and began picking through the clutter, searching for a sharp object.

"You can't help me," Ansley cried out in a loud rage-filled whisper. "Go get someone who can! An adult for chrissakes!"

"No time," Turtle repeated.

"I want to live!" Ansley cried out. It was the terrible wail of an abused dog that stopped Turtle in his tracks. "Lard Ass, I want to fuckin' live!"

He turned. Ansley stared back, his face ravaged by terror fused with despair. This was an expression Turtle had never seen before but recognized instantly. Ansley had been brought back from the brink of sure death to the brink of freedom, and he felt—no, knew—Turtle was not his savior, could not be his savior. Turtle may have lost some weight, but he was still Lard Ass, and everyone knew Lard Ass was a loser.

That old, familiar funk, *unwanted*, flooded into his belly, and for one interminable moment he was Lard Ass once again, the same Lard Ass who scarfed *Chocodiles* at the first signs of trouble, the same Lard Ass who allowed himself to be bullied by anyone who cared to bully, the same Lard Ass who turned ostrich when things got scary. Yet as he stood there, he knew he couldn't be Lard Ass, not anymore, because Lard Ass *was* a loser, and he was not, he was Theo Turtle Dawson. He wasn't sure what that meant, but it sure as hell didn't stand for loser. He tamped the funk back down, and this time the funk responded like a campfire that had been properly doused with water, and was put out for good.

"Don't call me that ever again," Turtle said, his voice low, firm and steady. "I'm going upstairs to get a knife. I'm going to come back down here and free you. We're leaving here together."

"No! Get the cops!" Ansley cried out, eyes bulging.

"I'm going upstairs to get a knife," Turtle repeated then, he turned and headed for the staircase, leaving Ansley, a whimpering mess, behind.

212

"Don't leave me, Theodore... Theo, please!"

"I'm going upstairs to get a knife," he said once again without turning around. "I'll be right back."

☙ ❧ ☙

The kitchen was a mess, counter tops covered with the clutter of half eaten meals. The stench of rotten cold cuts and spoiled fruit funked up the air as fat, lazy flies circled half eaten sandwiches. Turtle got the feeling the Teddy Bear had created this mess on purpose. The locked room was neatly organized, even the barn was fairly organized, and yet everything outside the room and barn were a mess. He was abusing the house, as he abused others—on purpose.

The kitchen featured a big bay window that looked out onto the circular drive and the barn. The window was covered with grime, yet through it Turtle noticed that the sun hadn't moved much. It was two-fifteen, maybe two-twenty. He headed over to the butcher block that had been used as a makeshift dining table. Empty aluminum cans that once held beans, chili and ravioli were scattered over the top of the block.

There was a slotted knife rack on the counter beside the block. The stocks of three knives were visible. He pulled the first, a butcher's knife. It was a formidable weapon, but he needed something for cutting, not chopping. The second was a carving knife, but the third was smaller, a knife with a serrated blade. He tested the edge on his hand. The blade nipped through the hard flesh of his palm. This would do. He'd cut the ties with this knife and free Ansley. Ansley could then join him in the barn to poison the Gatorade or he could leave. It didn't matter. Despite all that was going on with him, one thing did matter—that he would no longer be Lard Ass. That if he were lucky enough to make it back, people would look at him differently.

He was starting from the room when he heard a noise from outside, a truck engine approaching. For a fleeting moment, Turtle thought that help had arrived—a gardener or perhaps the mailman. An adult, as Ansley had wanted. Yet as the sound grew nearer he knew it was him. It was *him!* The Teddy Bear. It wasn't close to six o'clock, yet A.D. had been wrong about so many things. Why should this surprise him?

He moved back into the kitchen, ducked down, and peered out the window, his mind racing. Escape was now impossible. In seconds, the truck would appear over the rise. He'd have to remain in the house, possibly all night or at least until the Teddy Bear went to sleep. He could then sneak out under the cloak of darkness—that is, if he wasn't discovered before then.

213

Outside, the chugging of the truck's engine grew louder. It was almost to the top of the rise. As the nose of the white and orange Volkswagen came into view, Turtle remembered the front door.

The front door was wide open.

He'd left it open because it gave him a sense of well-being. If the Teddy Bear saw that the door was open he'd know *he* didn't leave it open. He'd come in and investigate, and when he discovered that the locked bedroom had been broken into he'd know someone had been in his house, was possibly still in his house, and the search would be on.

"Aw, fuck!"

Turtle raced down the corridor, a mad man's dash, for the front door. Outside, he could see the nose of the VW bus about to settle, and when it did the windshield would have a clear view of the front door, a clear view of him. He went into a slide. A.D. had taught him the best way to attack home plate was to slide and slide hard. Turtle did. He skidded across the dusty floor like a major leaguer sliding home, kicking up a sanding of fine powder. He hit the door with his foot and it slammed shut. *Safe!* Perhaps.

Scrambling to his feet, he dashed back to the kitchen to see if he'd been wrong, to find out if the Teddy Bear had seen the door close and was now coming for him.

He ducked down and crept up to the window just as the Volkswagen rolled to a stop in front of the barn. The engine died with a soft wheeze. A man climbed out, never once gazing at the house. He walked around and slid open the side door of the bus. A large German Shepherd bounded out of the bus and into the woods.

"Don't go too far, Brutus," the man called. He had a pleasant voice, a neat, casual way of dressing, chinos and a crisp shirt that reminded Turtle of a school teacher. *Maybe he is a school teacher.* He had sandy brown hair, conservatively cut. He wasn't a very large man.

Turtle again wondered if, in fact, this wasn't the Teddy Bear, but a neighbor stopping by whom he could cry out to for help. The man leaned into the back of Volkswagen and emerged holding a mannequin. Corralling it in his arms, he headed into the barn.

CHAPTER TWENTY-TWO

Maritza Sanchez hadn't driven in ten years. She never drove much before that, but ten years ago all driving for her stopped. Driving was the man's job, and she'd had Tito for that. Once Tito was gone, she should have resumed the task, but she couldn't. Getting behind the wheel would remind her why she was behind the wheel, and that was a memory she chose not to endure.

So the 1967 Buick Skylark sat in the garage for ten years. She started it at least once a month and kept the tires fully inflated so that it would be operable when any of the grandkids came to town and needed a car. The grandkids never needed a car when they came, at least they didn't need one bad enough to drive a canary yellow, '67 Buick Skylark with a black landau roof. The paint had aged over the years, and instead of looking like a canary, the car more resembled a giant Lemonhead.

When Abuela Maritza climbed behind the wheel of the old Buick she knew it could get her in a lot of trouble, but her granddaughter had been so uncontrollably inconsolable over the fate of the boy, she knew she had to do it. Rita was the person she loved most in the world, and as Rita had to take a risk, so did she. She had taught her children that you needed to take risks in life. "No risk, no reward," she'd say. She truly believed that.

So when Rita asked to be dropped near where Marty told them the house was, she didn't hesitate.

She was helping Rita to save her man from the evil plot of his evil brother. That he was a dead brother made the plot all the more sinister. She asked if she should wait and Rita said no. She'd come home with Theo. Rita neglected to say she was prepared to die with him as well.

215

When Turtle returned to the basement, Ansley was waiting for him with hungry eyes.

"You have the knife?" he asked.

"Yes. But I can't use it now. He's back."

Upon hearing the Teddy Bear had returned, Ansley's face fell to pieces. "Cut me out now!" he called in a shrieking whisper so filled with anxiety it caused Turtle to cringe.

Turtle came over and sat at the foot of the cot. "I can't. He'll know. I'll come back for you when he's asleep."

"No, no! Cut me out now." The horror of his time in captivity was shining in Ansley's eyes.

"If I free you now he'll know," Turtle said. "He's in the barn. I'll hide somewhere in the house or outside until tonight when he's asleep." He began smoothing the creases from the tape that had been over Ansley's mouth.

"What are you doing?"

"It has to look the same or he'll wonder how you got it off with no hands."

"Listen here, you mother fucker! I don't care if he knows. Do not...Mmph!"

Turtle replaced the tape over Ansley's mouth. The boy's eyes swelled with fury. He mumbled something that sounded very much like *mphfuck mphyou!*

"I'll come back for you," Turtle said. "Promise." He cast a last glance at Ansley, who continued writhing and protesting. He brought to mind a small animal's frenzied attempt to free himself from a trap.

Turtle moved across the basement and headed up the stairs. He was near the top step, seconds from opening the door when he heard them enter, the man and the dog. He held his breath as he heard the dog bounding toward him, his nails scratch dancing along the hard floor. The dog stopped outside the closed basement door. Turtle didn't know why he'd closed the door when he came back down—a reflex from home, where their drafty basement always sent cold air up into the house. Moms was forever reminding them to close the door behind themselves and not let the heat out when they went down. He was glad he finally got the message.

The dog started barking at the door.

Turtle took an unsure step back. His foot nearly missed the step below and he teetered before regaining his balance.

"Quiet, Brutus," the man called.

The dog had heard him, could smell him through the door even

216

though the man couldn't. Brutus snuffled anxiously at the door, and Turtle knew he was taking in the scent of a human intruder. He took two more steps back, this time looking where he was going. The dog launched himself into the door—*boom!*—and began a frenzied barking jag.

"What has gotten into you? Not now, Brutus! We'll visit our guest later," the man called. "Quiet!"

The dog quieted, although he stayed at the door, sniffing and whimpering.

Gingerly, Turtle retreated down the stairs back into the basement. He was now trapped down there. He needed to find a good hiding place.

"It's all right," he whispered to Ansley as he moved past. He headed to the rear of the basement, beyond Ansley and the cot, picking his way through stacks of old clothes and tall cardboard moving boxes that remained sealed. There was furniture behind these things, a large armoire that Turtle thought he might be able to fit in. He could hide in there until late at night or morning, whenever it was safe to venture out.

As he was working his way past an old hand power-mower, he bumped the handle with his hip, knocking it into a stack of boxes. The box at the top was filled with Christmas tree ornaments. The jarring toppled it over and the box fell, hitting the power mower handle on the way down, making the mower bounce. The box and mower banged into the floor with a crash and the tinkle of glass.

Turtle froze as the dog started barking again. This crash could surely be heard by the man. It would most definitely bring him down into the basement to investigate. Quickly, Turtle picked his way back through the debris to Ansley who was glaring at him. *Loser.* Arriving at the cot, he hefted it up with both hands and dumped Ansley onto the floor, with the cot on top of him. As Ansley and the cot hit the floor, the basement door opened.

Turtled ducked low, picking his way back through the boxes as quietly as possible. Hopefully the man would see Ansley lying on the floor and believe he was trying to escape, causing the crash. Turtle knew if his crazy idea didn't work, the man would find him in minutes.

The dog arrived in the basement first and headed straight for him. Turtle wedged himself between a tall box and an old sofa. As he sandwiched himself in, his shoulder began throbbing from the pressure. He crouched as low as possible, but he could still be seen in the darkened basement if someone bothered to look.

"Stop, Brutus. Yield," the man called in a commanding voice, just as Brutus was about to leap through the stacks of boxes that would lead him to Turtle. The dog immediately stopped. His eyes were on Turtle. He growled.

"Go back upstairs," the man called. The dog hesitated. "I see what the problem is here. You be a good boy and go back upstairs now." The dog cast a hungry eye at Turtle and whimpered. "Go!" the man cried out, and Brutus turned and ran across the basement and up the stairs.

The man's eyes were on Ansley and the overturned cot. He did not seem angry or upset. Turtle tried to crouch even lower, wishing he could make himself smaller. If the man looked in his direction, he would surely see him. He wanted to try and get farther behind the box where he could maybe be out of sight, but if he moved, he might make a sound, and that would be his undoing. He breathed only in shallow breaths as the man made his way to the cot.

"You've made a mess," the man said. "You know the rules. You have to behave yourself. A good teddy bear always does."

He reached down and with one hand yanked Ansley and the cot from the floor, righting the cot in the motion. He had inhuman strength. Ansley was now settled back on the cot, his knees clenched together. He was looking up at the man. Turtle couldn't see his eyes, but he was sure they were filled with terror.

"I put the tape over your mouth to remind you to behave," he said. "You know what happens to bad little boys, don't you?"

Ansley began complaining and motioning with his head. Turtle was certain he was trying to give him up.

"Now, now. Bad boys have to take their medicine. That's the only way bad boys can become good teddy bears. Right?"

The man's insanity was startling. He had convinced himself that these kidnapped children wanted to be a part of his Teddy Bear Club. He moved in closer and settled on the cot next to Ansley. He pulled up the hospital gown revealing Ansley's bare behind. Turtle stifled a gasp. Ansley's bottom was a mass of angry red and purple welts. The man began massaging Ansley's bottom tenderly. Ansley whimpered like a pup. The sight of it was sickening.

"Now, now," the man said again. His breath was coming in short gasping bursts, as if he was getting off on the massage. "Now, now," he whispered.

He rose and reached up into a crease in the low-beamed ceiling, pulling a short crop whip from behind one of the beams. "Shh," he said. "No noise this time. The more noise you make, the more medicine you take."

He drew back the whip, his arm arching high and powerfully and swinging down with ferocious force. *Crack!* The sound detonated in the silence of the basement, and a lengthy red whelt jumped onto Ansley's bottom. He cried out in muffled, searing pain, and the whip came down again, and again. With the second or third blow the whip began drawing blood.

Turtle's eyes fogged over as he watched the brutal assault. *I should have cut him loose,* he thought. *I should have cut him loose, and he could have defended himself against this maniac.* He had to look away for fear that he would cry out in sympathy. The beating was over in just a few minutes. It may have been short, but it was horrifically brutal.

Finished, the man placed the whip back in the slot in the ceiling behind the beam. "Rest," he said, catching his breath. "Despite your indiscretion, you have a big night ahead of you. We have decided that tonight is the night for you to be inducted into the Teddy Bear Club. Congratulations."

Ansley lay writhing on the cot.

The man moved across the room to a cabinet where he removed a small bottle and a cloth. When he opened the bottle, the air in the basement became saturated with the odor of bleach and something else. These were the unfriendly odors Turtle had detected when he first entered the house. The man soaked the cloth in liquid from the bottle, then returned to Ansley.

"Rest, my brave little teddy bear," the man said again. He held Ansley firmly with one hand and placed the rag over his nose. It was as if he were force-feeding an animal. In less than a minute the writhing stopped as Ansley passed out, his head falling back with a thump against the cot mattress. "Rest," the man whispered, rising. He strode back to the cabinet where he neatly replaced the bottle and cloth. Then, without casting another glance at the passed-out boy, he exited the basement.

You should have done something, Turtle thought, and he moaned. A feeling of helplessness swept through him. *You should have stopped him.* But Turtle knew he was no match for the man. He pulled the small knife with the serrated blade from his belt and stared at it. *No,* he thought. *I couldn't have beaten him with this.* While the man wasn't very large, he was quite strong. Turtle knew if he had shown himself, the man would have subdued him.

He slid the knife back into his waistband and climbed out from his hiding place. As he did, his shoulder again cried out. He realized his right arm was swollen and stiff.

As he moved past the cot, he stopped. Ansley appeared like a sleeping child, his head again at the odd angle, his dark, unruly hair falling into his eyes. He no longer looked like the kid who had terrorized Turtle at school. Seeing him lying there, Turtle realized he was nothing more than a scared little boy, had always been a scared little boy.

He moved to the cabinet and removed the small bottle and the rag. He thought if he could sneak up behind the man and drive the knife into his back, he might be able to jump on his shoulders and slow him with the knockout solution. Then, when the man was unconscious, he could finish him.

As he thought this, another, more powerful thought emerged. Could he actually drive a knife into the man's back with the intent to kill? He had come there to kill, but not face-to-face or hand-to-hand. He remembered whining to A.D. "I'm not a *murderer.*" Now he wanted to be a murderer. Now he wanted to kill the fucking maniac, but the question lingered—*can I?* His entire right arm was pulsating with pain—still he knew, if he had the chance to drive the knife into the man—*fuck the pain*—he would.

Slowly, he moved up the basement stairs, taking his time so that the creaks in the stairs were shorter, softer, more whispers than cries. As he neared the top, he saw that the door was ajar. The man was in the kitchen. It sounded as if he were eating something from a can—*beans or ravioli,* he thought.

The sound of the spoon hitting the can in quick, hungry motions sent a ripple of desire firing through Turtle's belly. He was hungry. The only thing he'd eaten all day was the peanut butter sandwich. Turtle was not one to miss a meal plus several snacks in between. Oh, what he wouldn't give for a *Chocodile* right then. Turtle forced the thoughts of food from his mind. *Concentrate,* he told himself. He would fill his belly with the deliciousness of murder, satiate himself with the joy of rescuing Ansley.

He didn't hear the dog. He supposed the dog had gotten used to his scent. He no longer smelled like an intruder.

The sound of the can falling over, joining the others on the butcher block signaled the end of supper. "Lotta work to get done before the christening," the man said.

The dog scampered to his feet, his nails skidding along the floor. Panic sluiced through Turtle's gut. If they were coming for Ansley, they'd hear him scrambling to get back downstairs. His only hope was to stand there and pray they were headed elsewhere.

He held still and stopped breathing, literally stopped breathing, listening as the man and dog's footsteps approached the door, then moved past. He saw the man's shadow for an instant and then he was gone. As they moved away, he inhaled deeply, relief coming on like a tidal wave. The man and dog moved down the hall. The front door opened, closed. He waited another minute to make sure they were gone.

When he felt it was safe, he opened the basement door and moved into the kitchen. Gazing out the bay window, it surprised him to see that the sun had nearly completed its trajectory into the western sky. *Have I been here that*

220

long? The man and dog came into view heading for the barn. Now was his chance. It would be dark soon, and he was certain the christening the man spoke of would signal the end of Ansley's life. He couldn't let that happen. He moved across the room and headed back downstairs.

❧ ❧ ❧

Rita arrived at the foot of a slope where a mailbox was hammered to a wooden post. The top of this slope is where the spirit of Marty told her she would find the Teddy Bear house. The day had passed quickly. It was nearly sundown, and she was just now arriving.

The dread she'd been feeling since she'd heard of A.D.'s plan quickly turned to despair. She'd come to rescue Turtle, yet secretly she hoped not to find him there. Surely the thing that Turtle came to do had been completed by then, if he'd come at all. Of course, if he hadn't succeeded, if the Teddy Bear was as bad as A.D. had said and had overpowered him, then he was probably dead.

Not dead, she thought. *Theo is smart, and brave, and resourceful.* She told herself this with certainty.

She was about to begin moving up the slope to the house when a glint in the nearby brush caught her eye. Had the sun not been at that particular angle, dipping into the west, she would not have seen the shiny object. She followed the glint into the undergrowth where she spotted a chrome and black bicycle. Her breath caught. With her heart pounding, she peeled back some of the foliage to get a better look, and her worst fears were realized. Lying in the undergrowth was Turtle's bike, Tyrone. *He's still up there,* she thought, the despair returning, and this time she could not hold it at bay. She stepped from the shrubbery, her mind a reeling mass of jumbled emotion and, without thought, sprinted up the slope.

❧ ❧ ❧

Back downstairs, Turtle began shaking Ansley. "Wake up," he said. "We have to go now."

He removed the tape from Ansley's lips, and the battered boy's eyes fluttered open. As Ansley gazed around with rheumy eyes, Turtle went to work on the ties.

"He's in the barn," Turtle said. "We can sneak out of the house and into the brush, work our way down to the bottom of the slope where my bike is waiting."

221

"My ass hurts so bad," Ansley whined, sounding like a raspy old man.

"I know," said Turtle.

"I told you not to leave me tied up. I told you to cut me loose."

"I'm sorry," Turtle said. "You can be mad at me later, but we have to go now." He said this in a commanding voice that must have surprised Ansley.

"Okay," Ansley replied with no further complaint.

Turtle finished slicing through the last tie, and Ansley flexed his arms for the first time in what had to be days.

"You're going to be all right, man," Turtle said. "Test your legs."

Ansley struggled to get up from the cot and tried to walk. He stumbled and Turtle caught him.

"It's that fuckin' chloroform. He makes it himself."

"How do you know that?"

"He told me one night when he was... He bragged about it. He makes it out of bleach and nail polish remover so no one will ever be able to trace a purchase of chloroform to him. He thinks he's so smart. The fucker."

He is smart, Turtle thought. The Teddy Bear had been flying under the radar for ten years or more. Very smart.

Turtle released Ansley who tried to walk alone, but his legs were still wobbly, and Turtle again caught him before he fell.

"We have to go now, Ansley. I'm going to take you upstairs into the kitchen. He's in the barn and you'll be able to see it from there. I'm going to leave you there to clear your head."

"Where are you going?" Ansley squawked.

"Up to one of the bedrooms. There's a book up there that will send him to jail for the rest of his life. I want to get it."

"No. That's a bad idea. Screw my legs. We go now, just like you said. We don't need a book. *I'm* the book."

"You can hardly move. Up in the kitchen, where the air is fresher you'll be able to clear your head, and while you're clearing it, I'll get the book and be back in no time. I'll leave you by the window where you can see if he's coming. If you see him, hide in the living room until he goes down to get you."

"This dumb plan is sounding worse and worse. We don't know if he's coming down here to get me. We're not mind readers." Ansley was getting agitated.

Turtle opened his mouth; then thinking better of his planned statement, he said: "You're right. Hide in the living room, anyway. When the coast is clear, I'll come and get you."

He spoke with a self-assurance that Ansley had never heard in him.

"Cool. I'm ready. Let's go," Ansley said.

Turtle helped Ansley over to the stairs. The pressure on his sore right arm was terrible. He wanted to cry out, but he knew his pain was nothing compared to what Ansley had been through. He bit down on his lower lip trying to will the pain away. He needed a distraction, something to get his mind off his throbbing arm.

"How'd you do it?" he asked. "How'd you get the Kerwood Derby out of one locked classroom and into another?"

Ansley smiled. It was a prideful smile. "Wasn't me. It was Rita."

They were making slow progress, had just reached the third step.

"Maybe I should leave you here," Turtle said and released Ansley, who slumped. He had to grab onto the bannister for support.

"Y...you wouldn't," he stammered.

"Tell me how you pulled it off," Turtle said, again with command in his voice. He stared at Ansley with a firm gaze.

Ansley lowered himself onto the step. "I had a key," he said after a while. "It's a skeleton key. The same key opens all the doors."

"How'd you get it?"

"I got it from Bubba. Would you believe when he was in middle school he was on the basketball team?" Ansley emitted a derisive chuckle. "Bubba sucked at basketball. But back then, he actually gave a shit and wanted to get better. Mr. Price, the janitor, made a deal with him. He'd leave him in the gym after hours to practice alone. He'd hand him the key and Bubba would give it back to him in the morning. Sometimes he'd bring me and Butch along to help him practice." He was getting a far-away look in his eye. "So I convinced Bubba that I wanted to go out for the team."

"Basketball season's been over for months."

"No one ever said Bubba was the brightest bulb in the pack."

Turtle recalled thinking something similar when the boys had ambushed him.

Ansley smiled as if recalling a fond memory. "I begged him to get me that key from his old pal, Mr. Price. *I gotta work on my jumpshot*. That's what I told him. I promised I'd give it back to him in the morning. To tell you the truth, I didn't think it was going to work. I didn't think I could ever get Bubba to ask for it. He never does shit for me if it doesn't involve fighting. And I didn't think if he asked that Mr. Price would give it to him. But Bubba did, and Mr. Price did." The reflective smile morphed into a smug one. "Betcha Miss Grant wouldn't think I was such a dumb shit if she heard that, would she? Help me up."

Turtle helped Ansley to his feet, and they continued up the stairs. His plan had worked. He could no longer feel the shoulder pain. Instead, he felt a numbness that threaded through every muscle in his body, fueled more by sadness than anger. He didn't know why. He wanted to be pissed off that Ansley had worked so hard to ruin two lives, but he wasn't. He was saddened by it.

"It was for your own good. Girls like her don't stay with guys like you. She dumped you, right?"

"Yeah," Turtle whispered. "She's moved on."

He remained quiet the rest of the way up, fighting to control his swirling emotions. By the time he deposited Ansley in front of the bay window, Ansley was walking better. His head seemed clearer now. Turtle's wasn't. He couldn't believe he'd risked so much for such a miserable person.

"If you see him come out, whistle before you hide so I'll know. I won't be up there long," he said.

Ansley simply nodded, and Turtle walked away, leaving a recovering Ansley by the window. Moving quickly, he headed upstairs to the second floor to retrieve the damning book.

𓆏   𓆏   𓆏

As Rita arrived at the top of the slope, the house and barn came into view. They were decrepit structures that brought to mind a bygone era. She cringed when she gazed at the large Gothic Victorian home. Sinister energy emanated from its pitched roofs and projecting bay windows. *Maleficio*, Abuela would have called it.

As she stood gazing at the old home, she heard glass shattering, *a window*, she thought. Then, she heard someone whistle loudly. The front door of the old house swung open, and a boy, *Turtle*, she thought, barefoot and in a short tunic, ran from the house. He wasn't moving very quickly. The shadowy figure jumped off the porch and fell down. Without hesitating, he got up and disappeared around the side of the house, heading toward the rear of the property.

"Theo," she said softly, her heart growing heavier. He'd been captured by the Teddy Bear and was trying to escape.

Her first thought was that she had to rescue him, no matter what. She was about to take off in pursuit, to find him and pull him to safety, when a dog charged from the barn, across the open expanse, in pursuit of the boy.

It was a big dog, a fast dog, and she was certain the dog would catch him. She needed to stop this horrible thing. She needed to stop the dog from hurting Theo, but if she were going to defeat the dog, she'd need a weapon.

Rita started moving toward the barn, moving not on thought but on the instinct that she had to protect her own. There had to be a shovel or a pitchfork inside. She would go in and find a weapon, any weapon. She would then use the weapon to fight the dog, the Teddy Bear, Satan himself, anyone or anything who threatened her man.

❧ ❧ ❧

Moments after Turtle had entered the room and retrieved the book, he was interrupted by the sound of shattering glass. Then, Ansley whistled. The whistle meant that the man was coming, yet the shattered glass came first. It sounded as if someone had thrown something through a window.

He needed to go now. The man and dog were on their way back. Hearing the broken glass, the man would surely do a thorough search of the house.

Turtle's mind was suddenly in turmoil as panic set in. Maybe he could hide in one of the other upstairs bedrooms. A closet, perhaps, and if he was lucky, he could avoid detection. As he was about to leave the room, something caught his eye. The bedroom window faced the stand of maple and oak trees that lined the rear of the property, a gateway to the sprawling forest. Ansley was running for the trees. Turtle did an old movie double-take. *What's he doing?* he thought. *I told him to hide in the living room.*

Then it came to him, clear as a crisp fall morning. Ansley was giving him up and saving his own hide. He'd broken the window to draw the man back to the house while he made his escape. For some unknown reason, a smile appeared on Turtle's lips. *Smart move, Ansley Meade.*

The basement had made the perfect hiding place earlier with all its boxes and clutter. He could once again hide among the furniture in the back and possibly go undetected. His chances were better there than upstairs.

Slipping the book in his backpack, he started moving again. By now the man and dog were nearing the house. He needed to make it back downstairs before they came in.

Turtle sprinted from the room and ran down the stairs. As he descended, his eyes were on the door. What would he do if it started to open? Fortunately, it didn't. He reached the bottom, made the hard turn and ran for the basement door. He shot a momentary glance into the kitchen and out the bay window to gauge how near they were. Then he stopped short and did his second double-take in just a few minutes. He'd gone through his entire life without ever doing a double-take except when he was goofing around with his friends. Now he'd done two in one day.

225

The big bay window had a hole in it from where Ansley had thrown something through, but that wasn't the reason for the double-take. From where he stood, it looked as though Rita had just entered the barn. But that was impossible, wasn't it?

❦ ❦ ❦

The barn was dark, and it took several moments for Rita's eyes to adjust, but she didn't stop moving. She couldn't. Right now the dog was probably reaching Turtle and tearing into him. She continued forward and, when her eyes adjusted, she saw that someone had stacked several children's school desks near the barn door. She spotted a work table at the center of the room and began moving toward it. There could be a knife there, or a hammer, or maybe even a gun. A weapon.

"Hello, little girl," a pleasant voice called from one of the stalls to her left.

She didn't look. Instead, she made a quick U-turn and started back for the door, picking up speed.

"Don't run," the voice said. There was a chilling threat riding through the words that stopped Rita in her tracks. It wasn't the words that stopped her, it was something more deadly. "It will only make things worse."

CHAPTER TWENTY-THREE

The sound of a vicious dog attack intruded on the silence in the house. Ferocious growls coming from the woods behind the house amidst high-pitched screams signaled that Brutus had caught up with Ansley, was perhaps killing him.

A spasm of guilt again rode through Turtle's belly. Ansley had been right. He didn't need the book to convince authorities about the Teddy Bear. One trip to the house would uncover enough evidence to put him away for life.

He should have listened, but he knew even if he had, even if they were lucky enough to poison the Gatorade—which was at best a longshot now—Ansley would have found a way to betray him. He knew this with certainty. That's the kind of kid Ansley was—a little shit.

But there was no time for guilt, not now. If Turtle's eyes weren't deceiving him, Rita was in the barn and needed his help. But they had to be deceiving him—right? Rita being there was nonsense. Heck, it was more than nonsense; it was impossible. She didn't know where the Teddy Bear lived, and even if she did, Rita was at home with Abuela. By now Abuela had told her what she needed to know to save the house, and they were celebrating. Yet, if it wasn't Rita, that meant another girl, an innocent girl who looked like Rita, was now in danger and needed his help.

Turtle's thoughts were interrupted when the man exited the barn dragging the girl along, his arm draped around her neck, dragging her as if she were a dummy. It *was* Rita. This was no trick of the eye—it was Rita. Turtle recognized the green and white top, the bounce in her curly brown hair. He couldn't see her fingernails, but knew if he did, he'd see black and silver lacquer glinting in the sun. Rita had somehow found her way to the Teddy Bear's house and had been captured. She wasn't putting up a fight, allowing herself to be dragged along.

227

He drugged her with the homemade chloroform. Bastard!

Without thinking, Turtle ran the length of the corridor, swung open the front door and stepped out onto the porch. He had to confront the man no matter the consequences. He pulled the knife from his belt and clutched it, held it ready to plunge into the man's chest as soon as he was close enough.

The man didn't see him. He continued dragging Rita past where Turtle stood, moving behind the house.

"Enough, Brutus!" the man cried out. The dog's attack on Ansley stopped almost immediately as the man spoke.

As the man continued past, Turtle realized he hadn't been thinking clearly when he'd exposed himself. There was no way he could have subdued the man from the front. If the man had seen him, he might have killed Rita before coming for him. *Bad plan.* If the man saw him, they'd both be as good as dead.

Turtle began taking in long cleansing breaths. He needed to clear his head. He couldn't act on impulse now as he'd done with the Kerwood Derby. That ended badly, and if this ended badly, Rita would wind up dead. He didn't place much value on his own life, but Rita's...Rita's...

Without completing the thought, he crouched low, moving from the porch into the nearby brush. He considered running for help. He could make it down the slope while the man was retrieving Ansley's body. With both Ansley and Rita to deal with, the man would be slowed. He could make it down the slope and ride back to town for help.

He dismissed the plan moments after he'd thought it. There was no way in hell he was leaving Rita up there alone. The Teddy Bear was a maniac, no telling what he might do. Rape her and then kill her. He couldn't risk the chance that the authorities would arrive too late and find her dead. As important as it was that the Teddy Bear be stopped, it was more important that Rita be saved.

She'd risked her life for him, somehow finding her way up there to save him. It was his turn now. The man didn't know he was there, didn't know he existed. He had the upper hand as long as he remained in the shadows. It would be dark soon. Under the cloak of darkness, he could hide in the brush observing the man, waiting until the time was right to attack. And when it was, he would attack ferociously and kill him. The doubts he'd once entertained about plunging the knife into the man's back had all been put to rest. Now he wanted to feel the blade thrusting into the man's back, pushing past cartilage and bone. As sure as the nose on his face, when he got the chance he would kill him.

❧ ❧ ❧

Music was playing, a scratchy old recording from generations gone by. A tinny man's voice was singing: *Happy trails to you, til we meet again.*

Rita's eyes opened. Her head hurt badly, blood pulsing into her ears with each beat of her heart. She'd been asleep. No, not asleep. The man had grabbed her as she tried to run, put something over her face, some awful smelling solvent that knocked her unconscious.

How long had she been out? Where had he taken her? What had he done with Turtle? She tried focusing her thoughts, but it hurt to think. When she moved her head, it felt as though her brain were sloshing to the side, and when it hit the side—pain.

She was outdoors, she knew that, could feel the evening air moving against her skin. *What time is it?* The sun was down. *Turtle*, she thought again, and this time the thought was more urgent. The dog had attacked him and hurt him badly.

She tried moving and noticed only then that her arms had been bound behind her. Her legs were restrained as well with heavy tape. She looked down at herself and saw that she'd been encased in tape and was taped to a desk and chair.

She looked to her right and then her left. More pain and dizziness. There was a row of desks and chairs neatly lined up in front of her, each desk containing a mannequin. The mannequins were dressed in various forms of school clothing. A few had on private school uniforms. The mannequins were seated facing forward.

> *Happy trails to you, until we meet again.*
> *Happy trails to you, keep smilin' until then.*

The song was coming through an old loud speaker.

As her vision cleared, Rita realized the area was lit by tiki torches spaced evenly in front of a small platform that had been set up in the circular drive. Several feet behind the platform, there stood a mountainous pyre of kindling.

What the hell is going on? The eerie lighting, the tinny song piped through a crappy speaker, the mannequins, the pyre, the whole thing was so incredibly weird. It reminded her of a horror version of summer camp.

> *Some trails are happy ones,*
> *Others are blue.*

229

It's the way you ride the trail that counts,
Here's a happy one for you.

The lyrics to the old song were the most disconcerting. It was sounding to her like a sendoff song. Without warning, her adrenaline started to flow. Her gut was telling her that the pyre was meant for a human sacrifice. Turtle.

"Hello," she called. More pain sliced through the back of her throat. It hurt to speak, but her head was clearing faster now. She wriggled in the chair, even though she was firmly bound to it.

That's when she heard the moaning.

A boy was seated in a small chair off to her left, closer the house. He was bathed in darkness, and she couldn't get a good look at him, but she knew who he was.

"Theo!" she cried out against the pain in back of her throat. The moaning continued. "I'm glad you didn't do it, Theo. No matter what happens to us, I'm glad you didn't."

The front door of the house opened and then closed. Someone was coming, moving from darkness to shadow and into the soft yellow tiki torch light. It was the Teddy Bear. He was big and blue and dancing as he moved. Rita cringed at the sight of him. She'd seen him before, entertaining children in the park. Back then, she didn't realize how sinister he looked. Today she did. Today she saw the Teddy Bear for what he was—a monster.

The Teddy Bear moved to the platform and faced his audience of mannequins.

"Welcome to the Teddy Bear Club," he announced in a voice that was sweet and childlike. It was crisp and clear as if coming through some form of speaker system in the bear's head. The sweetness of it, and the clarity, made Rita's skin crawl. "We have a special guest with us today. I know how we feel about girls in the club—" He stopped short, leaned in as if listening to one of the mannequins speak. "I know, Lawrence, they can be such *bitches*. No one knows that better than me. But let's watch our language, okay? She is a guest." He gazed at Rita. "Not to worry. She won't be staying long."

Rita noted she was again squirming in her chair and commanded herself to stop. She was not going to be a victim—not *his* victim, not today. There was no one there to help her, but her. If she were going to escape, she needed to take her time about it. *My hands*, she thought. *I need to first free my hands, one finger at a time.*

She tuned the Teddy Bear out as he continued his speech to the man-

230

nequins. It was important that she concentrate. Rita breathed in deeply and, letting the breath out slowly, she began flexing her right index finger. *One finger at a time.*

When the Teddy Bear completed his talk, he moved into the shadows and returned with two large red gas cans. He began dousing the wood of the pyre.

A wave of pure terror rode through Rita's gut as the smell of gasoline filled the air. *Don't think about him,* Rita told herself. *Just do what you have to do. One finger at a time.* Her index finger, once curled into a fist was now starting to move. *Rita Calderon is nobody's victim,* she announced to herself. She'd come there to fight for Turtle's life, now she was fighting for both of them.

The tape around her right index finger had loosened. The finger was creeping through an opening. Now, onto the next finger.

The Teddy Bear moved off into the shadows again and returned with two more gas cans. He danced a demented dance as he doused the kindling with more gasoline. Then he turned from the pyre to the mannequins seated before him. "Let the christening begin," he cried out.

Producing a box of kitchen matches, he scraped one long wooden stem along the rough edge, and the match flamed to life. He threw the ignited match onto the pyre. It caught instantly, the entire area in front of the house lighting up with dazzling firelight.

Rita again felt her concentration drawn, knowing it wouldn't be long before the Teddy Bear did something with the growing inferno, like maybe barbecue her boyfriend. She squeezed shut her eyes. *Don't look. If you don't look, you can concentrate better.*

Yet she couldn't help but look. The entire area was bright with dancing firelight; the heat from the inferno was warming her face. The music stopped, and then another song began to play. This one, a jaunty march:

Now it's time for our new friend
to join the family
the Teddy Bear Club, the Teddy Bear Club,
Tee-dee, tee-dee, tee-deee.

She recognized the singing voice to be that of the deranged costumed creature before her.

The Teddy Bear was leading Turtle toward the fire. She'd thought he was wearing a tunic, but in fact it was a hospital gown. The gown was smeared with blood, dirt and grass stains from the fight with the dog. Turtle dragged his right leg which seemed to be hanging on by mere sinew. She thought she saw muscle, tendons, blood—or was that a trick of the flickering light and shadow?

He was led along peaceably by the Teddy Bear, a lamb to slaughter. His moans had toned down to soft brays, and she knew he had accepted his fate. No arguing, no complaining, no fighting. He was going to die—was, in fact, welcoming death because death would end his misery.

As he came more into the light, Rita's heart thumped. It wasn't Turtle. This boy was shorter, white. She thought she recognized him but wasn't sure. Yet what she was sure of gave her hope. The boy being led to sacrifice wasn't Turtle.

While her heart cried bloody tears for the boy as he moved with slow, purposeful steps, his sad eyes focused on the pyre, another part of her heart sang out with both joy and relief. It wasn't Turtle. As Rita came to the realization that her Turtle was still alive, the question arose: *If that isn't Turtle, where is he?*

CHAPTER TWENTY-FOUR

Turtle

Turtle poured the last of the antifreeze into the Gatorade. He wasn't taking any chances. He'd poisoned the entire six pack. He realized he may not be alive when the man sat down to drink the Gatorade, but he was going to get the child molesting, murdering bastard. Dead or alive, he was going to get him.

He'd been lurking in the shadows for more than an hour, watching as the man bound Rita to the chair and then created his theater of horror. He'd snuck into the barn after the man had taken out the last of the kindling. He had a clear idea of what was coming next, the christening the man had spoken of.

From the darkened barn, he saw the Teddy Bear emerge from the house and realized Ansley's time on this earth was coming to an end. Despite Ansley's leaving him to be captured, he still wanted to save the boy. He felt confident he could save them all. Confidence for him had always been in short supply—but not tonight. He focused on knowing that now that the man was wearing the suit he could not move as quickly, could not sense someone sneaking up from behind.

He'd taken a ballpeen hammer from the workbench. With it, he could sneak up behind the man in the teddy bear suit with ease, bludgeon him several times before driving the knife into his back.

The sound of a roaring inferno outside drew his attention. The glow of fire invaded the darkness of the barn. It wouldn't be long now. He needed to get into place. As he headed for the barn door, planning to once again disappear into the shadows only to emerge behind the man in the teddy bear suit, the big dog, Brutus, appeared in the doorway before him. The dog was eyeing him with silent, murderous intent.

Stupid! He'd been so busy working out his plan to kill the man he'd forgotten about the dog.

Turtle now slowly backed back into the barn. Brutus moved in after him. His eyes, dark as oil and just as shiny, were glued to Turtle, gauging his every move.

"Good doggie," Turtle called softly. His reply was a growl, and bared fangs. "Go on! Get outta here," he called louder, shaking the hammer at the dog. Big mistake.

Brutus growled louder and attacked. He flung himself at Turtle, teeth first. Turtle swung the hammer. It missed, and the dog's jaw clamped down on his hand and wrist.

"Aiii!," he cried out, releasing the hammer.

Pain exploded in his head. It hurt so, so bad, the worst pain he'd ever felt in his entire life. He tried freeing his hand and realized, as he pulled back, that flesh was being ripped from bone, trapped in the big dog's jaws. Blood spurted from the back of his hand as if spewing from a blood squib in a horror flick. Rather than lose the limb, he allowed the dog to rip at his flesh, tear into his muscle, tendon, bone.

He drove his left hand into his right pocket, frantically clutched at the bottle of chloroform and cloth and tried pulling them out to no avail. At the same time, he kicked at Brutus with his right leg. The dog released his hand, instantly clamping down on his calf where the vicious attack continued.

As painful as it was, this attack was much less painful than the one on his hand. The calf attack was a stroke of luck. It allowed him the ability to shove his bloody right hand into his pocket. More pain exploded. As he pulled out the rag and chloroform, he knew some of his flesh had been left behind in the folds of his pants, a goody waiting to be discovered later.

While Brutus ravaged his leg, Turtle managed to steady himself. He didn't shut out the pain, he couldn't. Rather, he embraced the pain as it produced twinkly sprays of white light behind his eyelids. He drew strength from the pain and for a moment wondered if this was how A.D. was able to fight so fiercely, taking two and three blows to give one good one.

He worked the top off the bottle with his left hand, doused the rag with the noxious liquid. Then he reached out. The moment he shoved the now bloody chloroform rag at the dog's face, Brutus released his attack on Turtle's calf and dove for his throat.

C r i s s

It was glorious. It was beautiful. The flames shimmied up the boy's legs, danced over his torso. In moments he was engulfed by them, an angel, brimming with golden light. He opened his mouth to scream, but no screams came, instead Criss heard him say "Thank you," and he knew the boy was finally free from a life of pain. The fire was burning out all the bad.

"Welcome to The Teddy Bear Club," he said, his voice cracking with emotion. It was that beautiful.

The ceremony never got old for him. He so enjoyed his mission in life, freeing children from oppressive parents. This christening was just as moving as the first. He thought back to the years before he'd started making things so official. This, of course—the christening, the ceremony—was better for the boys. It united them in a way they hadn't been before the ceremonies began. It made each of them feel special, knowing they were among the few to be selected.

The next few hours would be quite busy for him, dressing the boy in clothing befitting a fine young man, photographing him and then introducing him the others. *Yes, yes, a busy night doing the Lord's good work.*

Clunk!

Pain surged in the back of Criss's head. That was strange. He'd never felt anything like that at a christening before. It came again, and then again. This wasn't part of the christening. Someone was bludgeoning him from behind.

Criss turned. There was a black boy with a hammer in his hand. He'd never seen the boy before. Had the boy come with the girl? The boy was dropping the hammer and pulling a knife from his waistband.

Criss knew if he had not been in uniform the blows to the back of his head might have done more damage, might have knocked him unconscious.

"What are you doing?" he asked.

"You fuckin' murderer."

He noticed the hand holding the knife was damaged and bloody. The boy lunged for him and he stepped to the side. "Such language, and on someone so young." He glanced over at the girl who was staring at them wild-eyed. Yes, she knew this boy, had probably put him up to this. Women had been the cause of all the troubles in his life, and now this girl had been the cause of this boy's trouble.

The boy lunged again. He caught him by the arm, twisted it back until the knife fell to the ground. "You've interrupted a very important ceremony. Did *she* put you up to this?" He yanked the boy around to face the girl, whose eyes were now filled with remorse. "Yes. She did, didn't she? And now she has the nerve to regret it."

"Nobody put me up to this. I'm going to kill you," the boy said.

"I'm sorry, son, but I'm afraid you've got that backwards."

CHAPTER TWENTY-FIVE

"Hi, there."

When Turtle awoke he was back in the barn, taped to one of the chairs. Rita was seated across from him. The glow from the tiki torches outside cast her in an odd horror movie light, all shadow and angles. When his eyes blinked open, she smiled.

"What happened?" he asked.

"He got you with that stuff."

Turtle nodded. His brain felt like mush. His right hand was on fire.

"He wasn't happy when he saw what you did to his dog," Rita said.

Brutus, still unconscious, lay on the ground nearby. His eyes were half open in a sleepy haze. His tongue rested on the hard earth of the barn floor.

"I'm not happy with what Brutus did to me."

"He was going to wrap your hands like mine, but he felt the tape would staunch the flow of blood. He wanted you to bleed. He thought you would suffer more."

"Feels like he might have been right." Turtle looked down at his hands in his lap secured and bound by a zip ties. The right hand was a swollen mass of purple and red, covered with dried blood. He thought he saw tendons or nerves protruding from the wound. While there was a pool of dried blood on the floor beneath him, the bleeding had reduced to a slow drip.

"Don't take this the wrong way, but what the hell are you doing here?" Turtle asked. "You're the last person I expected so see."

"When you told me what your brother had asked you to do, I couldn't let you go through with it."

"Yes! Yes, you could! I had it all figured out, Rita. I was going to ride off into the sunset like a movie hero, but nooo!" He hung his head. It hurt to hang it. He didn't care.

"I have no idea what you're talking about. All I know is I couldn't let you go through with it."

"Great! And look where that got us."

"Theo!"

"You're right. I'm sorry. Part of me is glad you're here. Not all of me, mind you, but part of me. Where is he now?" Turtle asked in a tired, raspy drawl.

"He said he had to finish the ceremony. He promised he'd be back."

"Ansley?"

She hesitated a moment. "So that's who that was. I thought I recognized him. The Teddy Bear set him on fire, Theo. He's…dead."

Turtle didn't respond. He bowed his head. His failure to rescue Ansley along with Rita's presence piled onto his shoulders like a weightlifter's bar that had been overloaded with weights.

"What was Ansley doing here?" Rita asked.

Turtle lifted his heavy head. "I fucked up is all you need to know. I fucked up and here we are," was his cryptic reply.

"Theo, this is not your fault."

"Of course it is. I pretty much knew I was going to fuck this up before I came here. I just didn't plan on you. I'm a coward, Rita. I've lived as a coward; I'm probably going to die crying like a baby."

"Your brother set you up," Rita said.

He gazed at her with heavy-lidded eyes. "Is this where I say 'Whatchoo talkin''bout, Willis?'"

"Theo, please, don't be dismissive of this. And stop feeling sorry for yourself. It won't get us out of here."

"Out of here? Right." He chuckled.

"Your brother never planned for you to leave here alive. He was lonely in that nether world between heaven and earth. He wanted you to join him."

"Where'd you hear a story like that?"

"I went to a lady who talks to the dead. I was hoping to get your brother to tell me where the Teddy Bear lived so I could stop you before you did something you'd regret."

He was silent for a moment, settling on the idea that she would risk her life to keep him from committing murder.

"My brother told you this?"

"No. Marty did. He's a child that's been trapped in limbo with A.D. Your brother promised him company, but the only companion he was going to bring was you."

"I don't know, Rita—"

"Theo, your brother is not a nice guy. He may have been at one time, but he isn't anymore." She didn't want to tell him that A.D.'s spirit had most likely killed someone.

"He needed me to do this so he could cross over," Turtle said somberly.

"Think about it, Theo. People who need something done to cross over have information they want to pass on to the living."

"That's how it is on television."

"And murder is what really helps them cross-over?"

Turtle was again reduced to silence. Murdering the Teddy Bear never made sense. "Why?" he said softly.

"He missed you."

"That doesn't change anything. I'm not brave, and now you're going to die because of me. I wished you hadn't come."

He looked into her eyes. She didn't seem sad, or remorseful or angry. She seemed at peace. He chuckled. It was a mirthless laugh. "You're the best thing that's ever happened to me."

"I was two fingers into my escape when you showed up with that hammer."

"What?"

She laughed. "Some stupid thing I was trying." Her tone shifted. "He told me he was going to kill you first so I could watch. As much as he wants you to suffer, he said he wants me to suffer more."

"So what do we do?"

"You're right. We're never going to get out of here. Let's enjoy our time together as best we can." She was silent for a beat. "My friend's Kool," she said.

"That line's so stupid. I can't believe we ever came up with that lame-ass joke." He looked over and saw her smiling at him through the darkness. She appeared as radiant as ever, her green eyes sparkling in the low light, softening his heart. "My friend *is* cool. You're my friend," he said, showing his teeth. "My best friend."

The music outside stopped. Turtle knew the man would probably next go upstairs to retrieve the scrap book. Once he discovered the book was missing, he'd come down and make Turtle suffer some more.

A breeze kicked up in the barn, swirling the dust on the floor into tiny twisters. The gust of air passed over Brutus rippling his fur. When the wind died down, Brutus moved.

At first it was just a twitch in his extremities, but then the big dog began clambering stiffly to his feet. His eyes were still near slits, his tongue still hanging from his mouth. He faced Turtle. A soft whistle, like air being squeezed from a hand pump shimmied up the dog's throat. He started for Turtle, moving in a stiff gaited zombielike shamble.

"What's going on?' Rita called.

"I don't know. He's got like rabies or somethin'."

The dog continued lumbering toward him.

"Shoo. Get out of here. Beat it!" Turtle called.

"Leave him alone," cried Rita. "He's taken enough punishment. Bite me. Bite me!"

Turtle was embarrassed by her outcry. Could he ever be that brave?

He didn't find it odd that as the dog approached not a sound beyond that shrill whistle had been emitted from his throat. Turtle's eyes were too busy gazing at the dog's incisors as his mouth opened wide. The large dog arrived in front of him and went for his hand.

"Aiii!" Turtle cried out.

"Leave him alone!" screamed Rita.

As the dog silently tore into him, Turtle realized he felt no additional pain. At first he thought he'd become numb to it, that his arm and hand were like fruit dying on the vine. But that wasn't it. He looked down at his hands lying in his lap and saw that the dog's teeth were glancing over his wounds, barely touching them. The dog's gnashing teeth were going to town on the plastic ties. He bit and ripped, gnashed and ripped at them with zombielike fervor.

He got the sense the dog wasn't trying to harm him.

"I don't know what he's doing, Rita. It seems as though he's biting through the ties." He knew he sounded incredulous and thought this was, perhaps, another peek at madness.

"Are you sure?"

"He's trying to free me, Rita. It's...it's A.D.," Turtle cried out, his voice ringing with fresh hope. "A.D. has taken over the dog's body. He's come to rescue me."

Rita peered through the darkness and glimpsed the miracle happening right before her eyes, eyes that were filling with tears. "No, Theo. Marty has."

CHAPTER TWENTY-SIX

The man was in the house. He'd be coming for them soon, sooner rather than later when he discovered the book was gone.

When Turtle's hands had been freed, he made quick work of the tape on his legs and feet as the dog went to work on Rita. Her bindings took quite a bit more time. She was mummified in tape.

Once Rita was free, the big dog lay back down, as if he were going to sleep.

"Thank you, Marty," Rita said to the big dog, once again lying unconscious on the barn floor

Turtle and Rita crept from the barn, crouching low and staying in the shadows as much as possible. Once over the hump of the short rise that led to the road below, they sprinted down the hill. With each jarring step, Turtle's shoulder throbbed. His hand felt as if it had been bathed in molten lead. His eyes watered. He again channeled the pain. They were away from the house but not out of trouble, not yet. He needed to stay focused.

He pulled the bike from the underbrush. It was black as pitch out, something he hadn't considered.

"You have to sit on the seat," Turtle said in an urgent whisper.

Rita peered at him and then the bike. They were lit only by the mottled light of a crescent moon coming through the trees. "What? What about you?"

"A.D. used to ride me like this all the time. It was how we could both enjoy one bike. You sit on the seat, let your legs dangle over the side. I get on in front of you and pedal."

"That sounds dangerous."

"Said the girl who risked her life to save me."

"Let's just run for it," she said.

241

"We can't run all the way to town, Rita. He'll catch us."

Rita again gave the bike a long, hard look. "On the seat?"

"Yes."

The sound of the VW bus starting up interrupted their conversation.

"He's coming," Turtle said with urgency. "Trust me. I got this."

"Okay," she said, still with a hint of doubt.

She climbed onto the seat. "Like this?"

"Yes," he said as the sound of the VW's tires crunching against the cinder drive drifted down to them. Turtle climbed on the pedals and pushed down hard. He hadn't done this in quite a while...actually, he'd never done it before. He'd always been the passenger.

It was slow going, the load heavy, the bike teetering precipitously from side-to-side as he gathered speed. Fortunately, the push off was down a small rise, and he was able to get the bike moving. Once the bike got up some speed he could hold it steadier, pedal faster.

As they swung around the first bend in the road, he lost control and nearly went skittering off the road and into the brush. Using all his strength, and against great pressure to his injured arm and hand, he steered the bike back to the center of the road. *Channel the pain.*

"Close call," he called over his shoulder. Rita didn't respond. She was clinging to his shoulders for dear life, adding extra pressure to the injured one.

The sound of the VW in the distance on the road behind pushed him to pedal harder, faster. They wound their way down slopes and up rises. At times he could barely see three feet in front of him, yet he didn't slow down.

He found himself wondering if what she said was actually true. Had A.D. betrayed him? He wasn't the same A.D. Turtle had grown up with, the boy who'd spent his entire summer teaching him to hit a baseball, who spent Turtle's entire time with the chicken pox reading to him so he wouldn't miss playing in The Lots. The truth was, A.D. had long ago stopped being that kid.

The glow of the VW's headlights found them, ensnared them. It was gaining on them. Once caught in the bus's beam it was easier for Turtle to see the road in front of him, but he was already pedaling as fast as he dared.

"He's going to catch us," Rita said.

"No," he answered back.

They'd somehow miraculously gotten away from this man, the Teddy Bear. The taste of ultimate freedom tickled Turtle's senses. So near, yet so far.

"Get down, Tyrone!" he cried out.

He swung the bike around a sharp curve in the road, knowing the VW would have to slow down or risk toppling over. With the VW so close, this was their chance to create some distance and disappear into the blackness.

❧ ❧ ❧

Criss's mind was a jumble of rage. How could this have happened? How could they have escaped? This had never happened to him before. But, then, he'd never had a girl attend a christening before, either.

Women were so unpredictable. He knew that. As a child, every time he thought his mother was turning over a new leaf, doing some kindness for him, he'd discover she was in fact screwing him over. It was always the old rug pull for young Aldous Criss, time after time. How many times had she gotten away with it?

"Bitch!"

Criss pounded the steering wheel as the bus rocketed into the night. *No good*, he thought. *All women, no matter their age, always proved to be no good. It was in their bones, their genetic makeup, their DNA.*

He steered the bus around a bend. He'd found it difficult driving in the uniform, but it was necessary. He'd had no time to remove it. If he'd taken the time the bad children would have surely gotten away. He did need to remove the head, though. He couldn't see well enough to drive while wearing it.

As Criss took a quick, warm glance over at the Teddy Bear head resting on the seat next to him, a bicycle appeared in his windshield up ahead. He mashed down on the accelerator.

He'd told the girl he was going to kill the boy first, but now he realized that was a mistake. He needed to kill her first. She was the puppet master. Once she was out of the way, the boy would probably thank him for his service.

Criss sighed heavily as he realized his words had been all bluster. *Big talk from a small man* is what his mother would have said. *Bitch!* Could he help it that he was a gentle man? Despite growing up in a home filled with meanness, he had turned out gentle. He'd never harmed anyone before. He had a hard time stepping on a cockroach. If he'd had murder in his heart, he would have ended Gerta when he was young instead of merely helping her along as he did in her old age and illness.

While there was no murder in Criss's heart, there was loyalty, and a tremendous amount of it. He was fiercely loyal to all the boys he'd freed. His teddy bears needed him to ensure their continued happiness. If something happened to him, what would become of them? He would not let the Teddy Bear Club down.

As he drew nearer, he saw the two of them on one bike. "God, why are you challenging me so? I have been your loyal servant," he called out in a loud anguished cry.

This new challenge reminded him of Job—not that he read the Bible. He'd never read the Bible, probably only cracked the good book once, and that was when his mother had insisted under threat of bodily harm. But he knew about Job from a class he'd taken, or something he'd watched on PBS, he wasn't sure. Job had been challenged by God just as he was being challenged now.

"I won't let you down, God. I won't let your teddy bears down."

The bike was clearly visible now, the boy pedaling madly, while the girl—*the bitch!*—rode on the seat behind him. Wasn't it just like a woman to let the man do all the work? The bike banked sharply around a steep curve in the road and he swung the VW right behind it. Normally he'd have slowed, but he wanted to prove to God he was worthy and up for the challenge.

The VW went heavy into the curve, the nose of the bus pitching to the left. Criss tried straightening and overcorrected. The bus swung back, lurched across the road, and launched sideways into the brush.

❧ ❧ ❧

"He crashed," Rita said moments after the sound of Criss's misguided attempt to stay on their tail reached their ears.

"Good," said Turtle.

When they'd swung around the curve, Turtle aimed the bike into the soft, overgrown weeds along the side of the road. They, too, had pitched off the road into the soft grass. They took a hard spill, heading over an unseen embankment. Turtle went head over heels over the handlebars, landing in brambles. His injured hand landed hard, and the pain that followed was practically unbearable.

The soft grass broke Rita's fall. "Oh, my God, Theo. Are you all right?" she'd called out, not seeing him in the darkness.

"I'm fine," he said. "I did it on purpose."

When they were reunited, he explained his plan was for the bus to stay on the road and continue past them. He'd recognized they were at the county line where they could take the shortcut through the woods.

"Theo, that's crazy!" Rita squealed upon hearing the plan.

"I didn't know he was going to crash. We still need to keep moving." He began pushing into the foliage.

"Wait. What are you doing?"

"We're going the rest of the way on foot. Tyrone served his purpose."

"In there?" Rita remarked, peering into nothing but darkness behind the curtain of leaves that Turtle had pushed aside.

"This is the edge of the woods. The Lots begin just up ahead. We'll get back a lot faster this way. I can't tell you how many times we hiked to the end of The Lots and beyond."

"There's no trail," Rita said, her eyes on the jungle of foliage before her.

"There is. We just need to get further off the road to see it. Come."

He held a leafy green Elephant ear aside with his good hand. Rita stared into the blackness ahead.

"It's dark in there."

"Don't worry. I know The Lots like the back of my hand. All we need to do is to get where we can hear the river. The river will lead us to Foster Creek."

They moved downhill, pushing aside thick growth for nearly five minutes, Rita yelping and swearing bugs were landing on her every step of the way. When they reached the bottom of the slope the terrain leveled off. A well-trodden pathway opened up before them. Dappled moonlight spilled through the trees overhead.

"Hear that?" Turtle said, stepping onto the path.

"No."

"It's the sound of the river. It's just off to our right."

Rita craned her neck. "I don't hear anything."

"Shh." He moved closer to her, cupped his good hand to her ear. "Listen," he whispered.

They stood in silence for several moments. He hadn't been this close to her in quite some time. It felt good.

"Yes. I hear it. Down there," Rita said pointing, sounding like a kid who'd just discovered the Chocolate Factory.

"As long as we're in earshot of that sound, we're fine. We'll be following the river upstream to the creek." He offered an encouraging smile. "Then through The Lots, and home."

He removed his hand from her face. At that moment, standing in the darkness under a canopy of trees, he wanted to kiss her. Despite their dire circumstance, he wanted to kiss her.

"Okay. Let's go," she said, stepping away.

He turned back toward the trail. He didn't want her reading anything into the way he was looking at her. He'd seem like an idiot if she knew he wanted to kiss her now when they were running for their lives.

245

"Crap, crap, crap, crap, crap!"

Criss hated to curse. He thought foul language was for foul people, but in light of the challenges God was throwing his way, he couldn't control himself.

He was seated in the VW now lying on its side in a patch of roadside shrubbery. He could see that the engine, in the rear, was smoking, but he was fine, not a scratch. Perhaps the uniform had cushioned the blow.

He needed to figure out next steps. By now the children were almost to town. Pretty soon they'd reach the authorities who wouldn't understand his mission. He had to get back to the house, pack a bag, and clear out. He didn't want to abandon his teddy bears, but what choice did he have?

He needed to maneuver himself over the seat and into the rear of the bus where he could reach the side door. The driver's door was on the ground. No help there.

It would be awkward and challenging, especially in the uniform. He'd have to fight against gravity to get himself into the back, but it was the only way out.

He pulled his legs up so that his feet were just in front of the seat. Then, using his arms, he pushed himself up. It was tough going, especially in the uniform, but he knew once his feet were firmly on the front seat, he could use his more powerful leg muscles to propel himself over and into the back.

After several minutes of struggle, he was able to plant his feet and shove himself over the seat and into the rear. He rested for a few moments, catching his breath. After that, it was easy. He slid open the side door that was now above him and climbed out.

Standing in the soft grass, he realized how fortunate he'd been. Another two feet and the bus would have gone over an embankment, and he would have plunged possibly to his death. He looked up to the blackened heavens.

"Sorry for the cuss words."

And then, the Lord answered a prayer he hadn't prayed. The sound of a car coming in his direction on the desolate road could suddenly be heard. A fast moving car, and it was getting nearer. He scrambled out of the brush and onto the road. The car was moving rapidly and would come upon him quickly as it rounded the bend. He needed to be in the center of the road waving his arms, or the car's headlights might miss him.

Being in the road was risky. The car could come around the curve too fast to stop and flatten him. It was a risk he had to take. The car was headed toward town. If he got it to stop, there was still time to overtake the children on the bicycle.

From the sound, the car was almost to the bend. Criss stepped out onto the road, going on faith. He backed up a few feet, giving the vehicle as much room as possible to stop after it saw him.

He heard the tires squealing into the curve and began waving his arms. In seconds he was bathed in bright light.

"Stop," he called. "I need help!"

The car was on him in no time. It came rapidly around the bend, a high performance vehicle of some sort, and swerved to the left as he came into view. It screamed past, tires screeching, barely missing him. The driver slammed on the brakes and the car went into a long fishtailing stop. It came to rest fifteen feet ahead of where he stood.

"Thank you, Lord," Criss mouthed softly, his heart rumbling in his chest. The car sat waiting. He began jogging forward, and as he neared, the brake lights went off. "No. No. Nooo!" He ran faster as the car swerved back out onto the road and took off at a high rate of speed. And then the car was out of sight, the road once again silent, the night sky black.

He knew it was the uniform that scared off the driver. He couldn't blame him. How could the driver know he was a God-fearing man, doing God's work? *You can't trust anyone these days,* he thought.

He was turning to head back up the road toward the overturned bus when God shined on him once again. As he swung around, he caught a glimpse of something in the tall grass on the opposite side of the road, glinting in the moonlight. As he moved in to investigate, his heart skipped a beat. It was a bicycle that had been cast off into the brush. No, not a bicycle— *the* bicycle. The kids had also crashed when they came around the bend, and from the look of things, they'd taken off on foot into the brush.

"Thank you," Criss mouthed yet again. He had a small scythe somewhere in the back of the bus. With the scythe, he could cut through the undergrowth like butter. The bad children had a head start, but if God was still on his side, and it seemed as though he was, he'd catch up to them.

CHAPTER TWENTY-SEVEN

Despite the darkness and the fatigue that gripped their legs, they moved together at a steady pace. As they walked, the terrain became familiar to Turtle. A clump of butterfly weed here, a tall flowering stand of goldenrod there, conjured up memories of boyhood adventure.

The dense vegetation thinned, eventually opening up into a vast field. An old discarded metal box spring lay several feet ahead of them, a rust-coated beacon in the thin moonlight. They were now in The Lots. The rapscallion scent of adventure was in the air, a pleasant greeting to their senses, a welcome home like the fragrance of mom's apple pie.

The river came into view. The rambling tributary off to their left was Foster Creek.

"It's so loud," Rita said.

"It's the rain," Turtle replied. "I've seen it like this before when we've had a bad storm. The rain makes the river a lot higher than normal. The creek will be higher, too."

"I recognize this place." Rita stopped for a moment and looked around. "We're almost home."

"Yes," Turtle said.

It was still hard for him to believe after all they'd been through that they'd actually made it. They started, heavy-legged, up the slope toward the familiar rise and the tree he discovered A.D. sitting under drinking a diet Dr. Pepper not too long ago. Pretty soon they'd be walking down Canal Street.

A curved blade swung out of the darkness and sliced across Rita's midsection. Her eyes swelled open in anime surprise. Blood spurted from a ragged gash beneath her green and white top.

"Bitch!" they heard a man's voice cry, and Aldous Criss, a man's head on the blue Teddy Bear's body, stepped from the shadows.

248

"Rita," Turtle gasped.

She swooned to her knees, eyes moving skyward. In that moment, she looked like a sweet young child about to say her bedtime prayers. "Run, Theo," she called weakly as blood spurted from the wound and flowed over her chest. Then, she lay down to die.

Aldous Criss moved in to finish the job. He raised the scythe in a long sweeping trajectory that caught in the moonlight. Droplets of Rita's blood spraying from its blade danced before Turtle's eyes.

"Get up, Rita! Get up!" Turtle called, but instead of rising, she lay there, her eyes blinking shut.

Turtle jumped onto Criss's back. As the scythe was starting its downward motion—the kill shot—both his hands clamped around Criss's wrist. Criss was a strong man, far stronger than Turtle, who was known for his weakness, yet Criss's arm stopped in mid-air.

"Get off!" Criss cried out and began bucking and shaking like a bronco attempting to unseat its rider.

"Rita, get up. Get the fuck up!" Turtle called. Criss dropped the scythe and was now using both hands to dislodge him.

With the use of both his hands, he was able to grab Turtle around the waist and slam him to the ground. Normally, typically, all the air would have rushed out of Turtle with the force of being thrown so hard, but on this night it didn't.

On this night, the instant Turtle hit the ground, he rolled over and picked up the discarded scythe.

"Give that to me!" Criss cried out.

"Don't you die on me, Rita. Don't you dare die on me. GET THE FUCK UP!" Turtle screamed, his voice searing with emotion. He got to his feet and swung the blade at Criss, who danced away.

Life twinkled in Rita's eyes. She sat up as if waking from a dream. Her torso was drenched in blood. "Theo?" she rasped.

"Get to the creek," Turtle called. "Run."

Criss turned toward Rita. She was sitting on the grass, bleeding out, her eyes looking toward the afterlife. He no longer needed the scythe. She was moments from death. He could finish her with his hands. He took a step toward her, and the blade came down across his shoulder slicing out a hunk of blue teddy bear fur.

Criss felt a sting. He looked at his shoulder and saw traces of blood trickling onto the uniform. He turned back to Turtle. There was wonder in his eyes. He was having a hard time believing the boy had gotten this far. "Listen to me, kid. Neither of you are going to live through this. You have

249

to know that by now. She," he said pointing "is the cause of all your troubles. If it weren't for her, you'd probably be at home in bed with sugar plums dancing in your head. Instead, you're here. I'm going to finish her now, for both of us, and when I'm done, I'm coming for you."

With this, Criss turned back. He was surprised to see that Rita had managed to get up, managed to begin walking crookedly down slope toward the creek. The blade came down on his shoulder again, and this time he felt pain, real pain, but hadn't his life always been pain? As long as Gerta Criss was alive, he'd always be in pain. He had to end the pain. It was no longer the girl he saw walking toward the creek, it was the person who had caused him a lifetime of anguish, his mother, Gerta Criss.

Criss started after Rita, and Turtle again launched himself onto the man's back, trying to buy time. Rita needed to get into the water, they both did. If he could get Criss into the swollen creek, he was sure he could take him no matter how strong he was. The water would saturate the teddy bear suit, making it difficult if not impossible for Criss to move.

"Run, Rita!"

Criss again grabbed hold of Turtle and flung him from his back with incredible force. Turtle slammed into the base of an oak tree. His right hand went out to break his fall, and when it hit there was an explosion behind his eyelids. It was very much like the climax of the Fourth of July fireworks over Foster Park—bursts of stars shooting across the sky. Then, the stars dissolved, and the world faded to black.

❊ ❊ ❊

Gerta wound her way down to the stream, stumbling along. Criss moved down the slope behind her, madness dancing in his eyes. He didn't hurry. The threat of her boyfriend had passed. He was lying under a tree, no longer moving.

Criss stood at the water's edge waiting for Gerta to wade into the stream as her lover had commanded. It would make it easier for him to drown her. Then he would move back up the slope, pick up his scythe and slit her lover's throat.

He found it intriguing how far a person could be pushed. Here he was, a peace loving man, about to commit murder. It was her own doing. All the years of insults and abuse at his mother's hand had finally pushed him over the edge. *Justifiable homicide,* that's what the authorities would call it. Once they heard about the years of abuse he'd endured at her hand, they'd let him off scot free. They'd probably commend him for his years of incredible restraint. *I'm surprised you didn't kill her sooner,* they'd say.

She more than deserves this, he thought. He waded in behind her. She didn't even know he was there. When the water was just below her waist, he moved in close. "Mother," he called. "I've got a surprise for you."

❊ ❊ ❊

Turtle staggered to his feet. "Rita," he called weakly. He looked down the slope to Foster Creek. "No!"

The Teddy Bear was standing behind Rita in swollen Foster Creek. The water in this part of the creek was typically ankle high. That night it rushed along just below Rita's waist. Turtle realized he'd been wrong about telling her to get into the water. All he managed to do was make it easier for Criss to drown her.

With the loss of blood she was experiencing and no way to get her to a hospital, Turtle figured she had ten, fifteen, twenty minutes to live if he didn't act fast.

"No, Rita. Get out of the creek," he called, but his voice was weak. He couldn't be heard over the rushing sound.

Criss placed his hands on Rita's shoulders and pushed her down. She went down easy.

"No," Turtle called again as he staggered forward. "Stop."

The sound was getting louder now. So loud. What was it? It sounded as though a fast moving train was approaching The Lots. The Teddy Bear heard it, too. He looked up just in time to see the ten-foot wave bearing down on him from down river.

BOOM!

The wall of water sounded like an explosion that rocked The Lots as it hit the man, sending him flying into the air. The wave had come from seemingly nowhere, from downstream rushing upstream—but of course, that was impossible—a tidal wave in tiny Foster Creek.

The water washed out over The Lots covering the land and sweeping up debris, scrub brush and refuse as it moved. The man in the water-soaked teddy bear suit went under. Rita was swept away in the rushing water.

"Rita!" Turtle called. Water was already at his ankles as he rushed forward.

The Lots had become a raging river. Then he saw a hand emerge over the roiling foam, silver and black nails glinting in the moonlight as the hand went spinning downstream with the receding tidal wave.

"Rita!" He ran, sloshing through the water, working his way downstream.

The hand went under, but came quickly up again, clinging to a large piece of debris—the old metal bedspring they'd seen as they entered The Lots. Rita was clinging to it. She pulled herself up onto the bedspring and her head bobbed to the surface. The spring had gotten lodged behind a tree and was the only thing keeping Rita from being swept back down stream in the fast moving current.

"Don't let go," Turtle cried out. The spring was ten, fifteen feet away. He waded toward the tree. He eased himself onto the bedspring, knees first, and as soon as he did, it began losing purchase, leaning heavier into the fast moving current.

Rita was losing purchase as well, slipping back into the raging water. "Don't let go," Turtle called as he eased farther out onto the bedspring.

"I can't hold on. I want too, but I'm too tired, baby."

Tears sprang into Turtle's eyes. "No, no. You have to. You don't have a choice in this."

Rita's chin slipped under as the current dragged against her. In moments her entire head was under; her left hand let go. The fingertips of Rita's right hand were now all that was keeping her from being pulled out into the water, and they were slipping fast.

As her fingers released the bedspring, Turtle leaped forward. If she was going downstream, he was going with her. His injured hand slapped the water and grabbed onto Rita's wrist. As much as it hurt, he held her wrist in his hand. There was no way he was letting go.

He was now lying prone on the bedspring, his nose pressed up against the rusting metal. The spring was inching more and more into the current. Rita's head was still under. If he didn't get her out soon, she'd drown. He shimmied himself forward so that he could get a better grip, and as he shimmied, the bedspring shimmied forward as well and pulled free of the tree that was precariously holding it in place. The bedspring began winding slowly into the current, yet from this new angle, Turtle was able to reach Rita, grab onto her shoulders, and with all his might he pulled her onto the moving bedspring.

He yanked her free of the water, rolled onto his back and cradled her in his arms. "Rita," he whispered as she lay on top of him.

The bedspring was now entering fast water. It was metal, and Turtle knew there was no way it would ever stay afloat. As they entered the fast water, Turtle saw him go by—the Teddy Bear, floating face down and not moving, the jetsam of life in his water-logged suit, as the fast water of Foster Creek flushed him down to the river.

Turtle gazed at Rita in his arms. "Teddy Bear's dead," he whispered. Her eyes didn't open. She looked so at peace lying in his arms as the sinking box spring rushed toward the river. *My girlfriend is lying my arms,* he thought. *The perfect end to the perfect movie.*

That's when Turtle realized he was exhausted, too. So, so tired. He decided he was going close his eyes and when he opened them, if he were lucky, they'd be together in heaven.

CHAPTER TWENTY-EIGHT

When Turtle awoke a day later, he wasn't in heaven. He was in a hospital room surrounded by beeping machines, scary monitors, and his parents. There was also a police detective in the room, Angela Boatright.

Boatright had been on the force for eight years. She'd been a detective for nearly three. She was a tough-looking woman, with large hands and brown inquisitive eyes.

"Just a few questions," Boatright said to Turtle's parents when she saw that his eyes were open. "I know he's been through a lot." Boatright had been assigned to the case because, despite her tough exterior, she had a way with young people. Boatright smiled as she came over to the bed.

Turtle may have been groggy during his interview with Angela Boatright, but he wasn't taken in by her smile. He knew he had to be cautious. How much could he tell her—*really*? He didn't want to sound like Uncle Johnny, that was for sure, so he made up parts of his story and left out huge chunks.

When Boatright told him his story didn't make any sense, he shrugged.

"He drugged me," Turtle said in his own defense. "My mind wasn't clear most of the time. Where's Rita?" That's what was pressing on his mind. That's what had dragged him up from his drug-induced sleep.

Boatright shot his parents an uneasy glance. "The girl they found with you?" she asked.

"Yes."

"Let's talk about her later. I'm still trying to make sense of why you went to that man's house in the first place."

"I don't know. I was just riding my bike and wound up there," he replied. He looked her in the eye when he lied to her.

"That's awfully far for a bike ride."

"Yup. It is."

Boatright flipped the page in her note pad. "Can you tell me anything about the boy who guided the authorities to you? Did he ride up to the house with you as well?"

Turtle tried to remain calm, but his mind began firing on all cylinders. *Is this a trick question?* "What boy?"

"The boy who saved your life. He flagged down a unit on Canal Street. Told them you were in trouble in the vacant lot and then disappeared. We'd like to have a talk with him."

"I don't know anything about him. Sorry," Turtle said. He lay back on the bed and began to wonder.

"He made sure they knew he was your friend," Boatright said, again referring to her notepad. "Said his name was Kool, with a K."

"Hmm," Turtle replied.

"Anything you care to tell me about your friend Kool?"

"He's no friend of mine. Can I talk to Rita now?"

From the look on Boatright's face, she knew Turtle was holding onto something. Guilt? Fear? She didn't push it and left. She told his parents she'd return in a few days when he was more clear-headed.

A few hours later, the doctor came in and informed Turtle and his parents that his hand had suffered severe nerve damage. He had a few more surgeries ahead of him, but they couldn't be sure if he'd ever gain the full spectrum of use. Physical therapy would determine that. Tears appeared in Mabry's eyes when she heard the news. The tears had no effect on Turtle.

He was surprised that both his parents were actually at the hospital, and that they'd alternated staying during the night. He was never alone. Whenever he asked about Rita, he got the brush off. No one would tell him anything—most times, people wouldn't look him in the eye. It was maddening. He wasn't a baby. He could handle it. *If she's dead, just tell me.*

❧ ❧ ❧

The serial-killer story was top of the local news for several days. The reported version went something like this: Foster City resident Aldous Criss was recently discovered to be a child-molesting serial killer. Criss, who danced in local parks and participated in parades dressed as a blue teddy bear, was known around Foster City as a kind and gentle man. A search of his residence proved otherwise. The search provided authorities information on the disappearance and murders of at least twenty-two children over a fifteen year period, making Criss one of the most prolific child serial killers in history.

Criss was found drowned Saturday night in Foster Creek, which had experienced a freak flash flood on the night of the drowning. It is believed he was pursuing two or three more victims at the time. Criss's drowning was ruled an accident.

Authorities also found on the Teddy Bear Killer's premises (that's what the authorities were calling him now) the remains of a recent ritualistic child murder. Details of the murder were left out, as were the names of the children involved, all of whom were minors.

A few days after the initial report, it was revealed that thirteen year-old Ansley Meade was the Teddy Bear Killer's latest and last victim.

❧ ❧ ❧

On his third night in the hospital, Turtle was startled awake out of a bad dream. In the dream he was at The Lots with Rita. It was a bright spring day, and they were in the midst of a picnic when a scythe appeared from out of nowhere, glinting in the sun. Turtle couldn't see who was holding the scythe, but it sliced a hole in Rita's chest and blood spurted out all over him.

He sat up with a start, a clammy sweat blanketing his back, Rita's name on his lips. He looked down at his hospital gown fully prepared to see it drenched in blood, and sighed heavily when he saw that it was blood free. He glanced over into the chair across the room where his parents had alternated spending the night. The chair was empty. The room was dark with just a nightlight burning. As he lay back down, he heard a familiar voice.

"Hey," the voice called.

He sat up again, squinted into the darkness. Seated in a chair not far from the bed, bathed in shadow, was A.D.

They stared at one another for several seconds, neither of them uttering a sound. A myriad of emotions flashed, a myriad of questions fired through Turtle's mind. After a while he settled on one, and spoke: "The Teddy Bear's dead. Shouldn't you be gone now? Crossed over."

"Yeah, well, I guess I wasn't being totally honest with you about that."

"No shit, Sherlock," Turtle said, glaring at his brother, waiting for him to say something more, an apology perhaps. When none came he said : "Kool with a K. How lame is that?"

"I know. But I had to come up with a signal so lame even *you'd* recognize it," A.D. replied. A small, hopeful smile was pushing onto his lips.

Turtle knew the gentle sarcasm was A.D.'s way of making nice, but he wasn't rising to the bait this time. "Did you set me up?" he asked.

The smile on A.D.'s lips vanished. He let out a long breathy sigh. "All

256

my life you've looked up to me. All my life you thought I was so brave, but I'm not. It's as simple as that."

"Oh? That simple, is it? Thanks," Turtle said piling on the sarcasm.

A.D. sighed again. "I'm not a hero, okay? I'm not worth looking up to. To be honest with you, it's too much pressure. Everybody's afraid of something, Mushmouse. If they tell you they aren't, they're lying. Me, I'm afraid of a lot of things. You think Han Solo wasn't afraid of the Rebel Alliance? It's not about being fearless. It's how you handle the fear." He looked into Turtle's eyes, and when it appeared that the anger was abating, he continued.

"I didn't send you up there because I hated you. I did it because I missed you. I was afraid to cross over alone," he said, his voice dropping an octave. "I didn't know what the hell would be waiting for me on the other side, bro, and I felt the only way I could face it was with you. The way you looked up to me, I knew you'd give me the strength I needed."

"You wanted us to be together," Turtle said softly.

"Yeah, I did. Together forever, just like some lame-ass love song. I know that makes me a wussy, but I'm already dead, so what the fuck."

Turtle smiled at that one. He didn't want to, but the bindings that tethered him to A.D. were unbreakable. "It's kinda sweet, bro. *And* kinda fucked up." Turtle's face clouded over. "You killed Mrs. Miller."

A.D. lowered his head. "That was an accident." His voice dropped an octave. "When she saw me she started having a heart attack"

"And?"

"I got scared," he said, his voice sounding far away.

Doubt clouded Turtle's face.

"I knew she was dying, and it was all my fault." He was sounding like the young A.D., the one who taught Turtle how to skip stones. "I stayed with her. I placed my hands on her face because I thought the cool would soothe her, comfort her, you know, before she moved on. I even welcomed her to the other side. It was all I could do."

The childlike tone of his brother's voice touched Turtle. "All right," he said, and lay back on the bed.

"Goin' there was stupid of me. I just don't like anyone messin' with you."

Turtle sat back up, peered into the shadows. "Those days of protecting me are over, A.D. I have to take care of myself now."

"I know."

A silence engulfed them as both boys felt the seismic shift in their relationship occur.

A.D. broke the silence. "There's one more thing I need to tell you, Mushmouse."

"What?" Turtle asked, his nerve endings beginning to tingle. *He's come to give me the bad news about Rita,* he thought, squinting into the shadows.

"It's bad."

"That's okay. Tell me."

"Remember when you asked me if I remembered that last day?"

"Uh-huh."

A.D. sighed. "I lied to you about that, too. I remembered the way it happened, but I needed you to feel guilty so I pretended I didn't. Lay back, little bro, and I'll tell you what really happened when I went out to buy the Millennium Falcon."

May 16th, 1986

A.D. exited the hobby shop with the Millennium Falcon in his hands. All afternoon there'd been a fire in his belly. He tried telling himself it was because he was finally getting the Falcon, something he'd been wanting for a long, long time. But when he exited the hobby shop and the fire was still riding high, he had to face the truth. It wasn't the thought of owning the Millennium Falcon that had fired him up. It was the thought of running into the bullies again. He wanted to kick both their sorry asses up and down Prospect Avenue.

He'd waited outside the hobby shop for twenty minutes before going in. He'd gazed up and down the street. *I thought this was their territory. Where are they? Punks. Wussies.*

After purchasing the Falcon, he decided to walk around the neighborhood to see if he could spot them terrorizing some other little kid. All his life he'd been a skinny kid, until the past few years. Being skinny made him a prime target to get picked on by the mean kids—that is, until word got out about him. Word on Adrian Dawson was that he was an ornery kid always itching for a fight. He never started one, but he seemed to wind up in more than his fair share.

As A.D. was passing Foster Park, he spotted a big blue teddy bear entertaining the younger children as they're delighted parents looked on. A.D. smiled when the teddy bear danced. *Turtle would love that goofy bear,* he thought. *He's such a baby.* The teddy bear looked up from his dance and waved over at him. A.D. waved back, then continued his search for the bullies.

He was cruising along Union Avenue, close to giving up and going home, when he saw the boys in front of a tiny tire shop. Union had been nearly deserted since the big apartment building on the corner had been condemned. Most of the block was purchased by a developer who was going to put up a big, modern apartment building. The tire shop was one of the remaining businesses still in operation on the street.

A man had just locked up the shop. The man and the boys who terrorized A.D. and Turtle the day before all piled into a pickup truck parked out front. It pulled away from the curb, was moving up the street when A.D. stepped in front.

Bert Meade—new in town, a garage mechanic who'd just landed a job paying him a tad over the minimum wage he got on his last job—was behind the wheel. It was a happy time in the Meade household, until that kid stepped in front of his pickup.

Bert slammed on the brake, hollered out the window. "Move, kid!"

The boy didn't move. He stood in front of the truck daring the driver to hit him. A.D. was hoping one of the bullies would get out to physically remove him, but they stayed in the truck, yelling to their dad: "Hit him! Hit him!"

"Move, kid, or I'm gonna run you down," Bert Meade called.

Instead of moving, A.D. removed the Millennium Falcon from the bag, deciding now was the perfect time to admire the picture on the box.

"Hit him!" the boys cried.

Bert Meade was a proud man. He didn't want his boys thinking their dad was a pushover, so he revved the truck, making a considerable amount of noise. The boy didn't budge.

He popped the clutch and the truck pitched forward leaving a patch of rubber on the asphalt. He slammed on the brake.

The boy looked up at the moving truck as it banged to a stop a few feet in front of him and smiled. It was a daring smile. It was a smile that said Bert Meade was nothing but a fuckin' pussy.

"Move, kid! This is your last warning."

"Hit him," Butch cried.

"Cream him," Bubba called out.

The boy went back to admiring the model in his hands.

Bert tried to go around him, several times, but the kid kept jumping in front of his truck.

"Move!"

"Send someone out here to move me!" the boy called back.

That's when something in Bert Meade snapped. This little nigger boy was daring him to run him down. *Fuck it!* Back in the day, in the place where Bert grew up, it wouldn't have been a crime. It would have been nothing more than business as usual. Of course those days were long gone, but the attitude on this kid brought the old days back, front and center, for just one interminable minute.

"MOVE!" he hollered. *Nigger*, he thought.

He revved the truck until the speedometer hit the red line. That's about where his blood pressure was, then he popped the clutch. He had every intention of going around the kid. He was just trying to scare the boy.

He pushed the gas pedal to the floor. The truck fired forward, swerved to the left to avoid hitting him, and the boy moved.

CHAPTER TWENTY-NINE

Turtle's parents didn't tell him about Rita because they didn't know. She hadn't been admitted to Foster City General. Since she hadn't been admitted, they assumed she hadn't made it and didn't want to tell Turtle the bad news. But she had made it.

Turtle didn't know it, but when A.D. stopped the police unit on Canal Street that night, it wasn't to save his life. It was to save Rita's. The scythe the Teddy Bear had swung had pierced Rita's ribcage, puncturing her aorta. Turtle was right; if the paramedics had not come along when they did, she would have bled out.

Rita was airlifted to Johns Hopkins in Maryland, where a doctor Feinberg performed emergency thoracic surgery. He said it was a miracle she survived with the amount of blood she'd lost. Rita remained in a coma for several days after the surgery.

When she awoke, her brother Sam was bedside. The first scratchy word out of Rita's mouth was "Abuela." The next was "Theo."

Tears of both joy and relief ran down Sam's cheeks when he heard his sister speak. He smiled and said they were both fine. He wanted to tell her that her abuela had remembered why the backyard had been left looking like ruins. Her abuelo, Tito, had buried something back there. Each of the fifty or so "gopher" holes was actually a marker. Beneath each of the markers Tito had buried a Mickey Mouse cookie jar.

Maritza had first purchased a Mikey Mouse cookie jar when the children were quite small. Back then, the jar had held all the baked goods Maritza baked on Sundays: oatmeal cookies, chocolate chip cookies, Churros, and almond cakes. As the children grew older, the jar became where they stashed their rainy day money, money for Sam's communion suit and

Maria's Quinceanera dress. Tito would say whenever the family needed a little financial assistance: "Let's check with Mickey Mouse."

It was only after the children were grown that Tito, who didn't trust banks, decided that Mickey Mouse would ensure the family's financial future. Over the years, he purchased fifty or so Mickey Mouse cookie jars and stuffed each with cash. If a burglar came to rob them, he would never think to look in the unsightly backyard pock marked with gopher holes.

The cookie jars contained more than enough to pay off the house and then some. The money had now been transferred from Mickey Mouse to a bank account with Sam's name on it. The money would never be entrusted to Elena, who Sam was beginning to think was a tad self-centered. The only other name on the account was Rita's.

Sam wanted to tell Rita this and so much more, but her eyes were already beginning to close, and rest was the most important thing right now. This, and whatever else he wanted to say could wait, and so it did.

❧ ❧ ❧

It was late when Mabry arrived home from the hospital. She was feeling about as low as she'd ever felt. She was such a bad mother, and she knew it. Each day she went to the hospital and the nights she stayed by Turtle's side she knew it, and she knew he knew it.

She didn't know what she'd do if she lost him, her only living son, but she also didn't know how to feel the pain. Truth is, she didn't feel anything. She was stuck.

Mabry was moving through the darkness, down the hall past A.D.'s room and on her way to her own, when she noticed his door was open. She couldn't help but peek in, hopeful, always hopeful that one day he'd be sitting there waiting for her to come in and say goodnight, or to tell her one of his awful jokes that made her laugh so hard.

This night when she peered in, someone was seated in A.D.'s desk chair facing the doorway. She should have been startled. She should have thought it was a burglar or an intruder, but she knew it was him.

"A.D.?" she said, her heart so suddenly filled with joy she thought it would burst.

"Hey, Moms."

Her knees buckled. She grabbed for the doorframe to hold herself up. "I'm...I'm imagining this, ain't I?"

"Yeah, Moms. You are. Before you come out of it, I need you to do something for me."

"Anything," she wheezed.

"Come on in and have a seat." She entered the room and reached for the light. She wanted to get a better look at him.

"No, no. No light," he said. "You can't really see me, anyway. I'm in your head, remember?" He gestured toward the bed, and she came over, sitting at the foot of the bed opposite him.

"I miss you so much," she said, peering at him through the darkness.

He didn't answer right away, but when he did, his voice was a near whisper. "I know you do. That's why I'm back."

"Thank you, Jesus," she said, folding her hands and entreating the heavens.

"Moms, this is the last time you're going to see me."

"No!" she gasped.

"I'm sorry, but I've got to move on, and all this," he gestured around the room, "is kinda keeping me here."

"Oh?" she replied, not knowing how to respond.

"You know, you got a great kid sleeps right across the hall."

"I know," she replied, her voice dropping ever so slightly, belying her shame.

"Good. Now, I need you to close your eyes. And once they're closed, I need you to keep them closed no matter what happens, and while they're closed, I need you to think only about the good times we all shared. Can you do that?" He smiled at her, and it was as if a bowl full of sugar had poured over her heart.

"Yes, yes. Of course."

Mabry closed her eyes, and as soon as she did the temperature in the room began to fall. "I love you," she said. Even with her eyes shut the tears found their way onto her cheeks.

"I love you, too," A.D. replied. "I love you all."

✼ ✼ ✼

A week later, when Turtle arrived home from the hospital, he discovered A.D.'s room was in the midst of being converted into a den. His parents told him it was the perfect place for a teenager to entertain his friends.

Turtle knew from the time he'd spent in the hospital that a change had come over them. It seemed the thought of losing him had jarred them to the realization that one son was better than no son at all.

He was happy to be home, happy to no longer be invisible, but mostly he was happy because now he could go see Rita. The day he discovered she hadn't died at The Lots was a day that would forever be burnished into his memory.

It was nurse Jean Harlowe who told him. Harlowe had been named for a famous movie star of the thirties that most of her patients had never heard of. She liked to say the only difference between her and a movie star was that her name had an e at the end. She was the only one who laughed when she told that joke.

She wasn't his regular day nurse. She was a visiting nurse who had come in to change his dressings. As she changed the bandage on his wounded hand, she said he was her first celebrity.

"Yeah, right."

"Seriously. You do know you're not only the talk of the hospital, you're the talk of Foster City—the boy who brought down the Teddy Bear Killer."

There was no TV in Turtle's room, so he had no idea what was going on in the outside world.

"Really?" He was more than surprised by the news.

"Yes. You didn't know? You and your friend Rita Calderon are a celebrity couple."

He gasped. "Rita? She's alive?"

"You didn't know?"

"No," he said, annoyed with his parents who had to have known. "Is she here in the hospital?"

"No. She's at John's Hopkins. A specialist saved her life. You're a lucky man," she said, rubbing his good arm.

Turtle didn't hear much more of nurse Jean Harlowe's prattling about being a celebrity. He was too busy figuring out how to get to Rita.

Three days after nurse Harlowe's visit, he was released from the hospital. The following Saturday, his father drove him to Maryland.

* * *

The day before Turtle was to be driven to Maryland, he received a call from a woman who said her name was Bernadette Pinkstring. Ms. Pinkstring called to tell him there were two young souls sitting in her living room needing to get on over to the others side, and that his presence had been requested to give the boys strength.

Turtle knew about the woman from Rita. He also knew the souls belonged to A.D. and the young boy, Marty.

He told Mabry he was going out to get some air. She was reluctant to let him go, but he insisted he'd been cooped up in the hospital for so many days, he needed some fresh air.

"Wait a minute. Let me put on something a bit more presentable, and I'll go with you," Mabry said.

"Thanks, Moms, but I'd just like to get outside and think. Just for a little while. Okay?"

"Okay," she said with a reluctant sigh. "But you make sure you don't go to The Lots and touch anything that could infect that hand, now."

He smiled when she mentioned taking care of his hand. "I won't."

Without the help of his trusty steed, Tyrone, it took him quite a while to make it to Pinkstring's home. When he arrived, she hustled him into the living room. "My stars, your brother's been about as antsy as a polecat in a hornet's nest. He didn't think you were going to come. I told him you were on your way."

Turtle entered the living room.

"All right, boys. He's here," Pinkstring announced.

"Where is he?" Turtle asked, looking around.

"Your brother and Marty are right there on the settee."

Turtle looked over to the little sofa. It appeared empty. "I can't see him."

"Your brother's in spirit form, Sugar. That's the only way he and Marty can cross over to the other side."

"Oh," Turtle said, nodding solemnly as he realized for the second time in his life, he was never going to see A.D. again. He felt a twinge of remorse. He couldn't see that his brother was smiling at him.

"He's glad you came," Bernadette said softly.

"Me, too," Turtle replied, choking on the words.

"All right, boys. It's time," Bernadette said to the boys on the settee.

A.D. and Marty stood. A.D. took hold of Marty's hand.

"We goin' now?" Marty asked.

"Yeah," A.D. replied, dry mouthed.

Marty gazed over at Turtle standing next to Bernadette near the doorway. "He's not comin' with us?"

"No," A.D. said and took in a great, sorrowful gasp of air. "He won't be comin' for quite a while," he added, letting the air out slowly.

"It's just you and me?" the six-year-old asked, his tone brightening.

"Just you and me," A.D. replied.

"Don't worry. I'll play with you," Marty said.

"Thanks," A.D. said, turning his smile onto Marty. It was just the way he used to smile down at his little brother. "What now?" he asked Pinkstring.

"Give it a minute. You gotta open yourselves up. You gotta look for the light."

The group stood in silence for several seconds. Bernadette glanced at Turtle. Her eyes were nervous. "He's still afraid. Say something to him."

Turtle looked toward the unoccupied settee, stepped forward. "Hey, A.D., It's me."

"I know it's you, doof. You're standing right there," A.D. replied.

"He's smiling," Bernadette said. "Tell him it's all right to move on."

"Hey bro, when you get to the other side, could you please teach Marty how to hit your knuckle ball? One of us needs to conquer that pitch."

"Yeah!" Marty cried out.

"Will do, Mushmouse." A.D. replied. "Sorry I tried to get you dead, man."

Pinkstring relayed the message. "He says he's sorry he tried to get you dead."

"That's all right. You more than made up for it, bro." Then: "Go on now, A.D., or I'm gonna start cryin', and you know how you hate to see me cry."

Turtle couldn't see it, but at that moment A.D.'s eyes turned glassy.

It was then that a bright shining light appeared at the center of the room. It was about the size of a man's fist but quickly began growing in size.

"It's happening," Pinkstring whispered.

As the light expanded outward, a sun-drenched field came into view within.

"I'm seeing a field with grass and trees and a babbling brook," Pinkstring said.

"The Lots," Turtle whispered.

The field inside the light came clearly into focus as what appeared to be a large portal now occupied the center of Bernadette Pinkstring's living room.

"Go on, now," Bernadette said gently.

A.D. looked down at Marty. "Ready?" he asked. Marty nodded and, hand-in-hand, the boys crossed through the portal and into the field where they, too, were drenched in sunlight. They began moving down the embankment toward the creek.

"Careful now," A.D. said, clutching Marty's hand tighter as the young one stumbled on a rock.

The boys reached the bottom of the embankment. There was a stepping stone at the center of the shallow creek. On the far bank there was a cloud-filled void.

"Step out on that rock and then jump across," A.D. said softly.

Marty hesitated. "I might fall."

"No, you won't. You're a big boy, and big boys don't fall. Besides, I'm right behind you. Go on, now." A.D. released Marty's hand.

"Okay," Marty said, not sure of himself.

"They've stopped at the edge of the creek," Pinkstring told Turtle, giving the play-by-play. "You brother's coaxing the young boy to use the stepping stone in the water to get on over to the other side."

Turtle smiled. He could almost hear his brother's voice urging him along when he was growing up.

Cautiously Marty stepped out onto the rock, teetered there for a moment, and then leaped into the nothingness that was the far bank. A.D. followed. Stepping out onto the large stone, he cast a glance back over his shoulder and, in true A.D. fashion, said: "Time to blow this popsicle stand," then he leaped forward, following Marty into the void.

CHAPTER THIRTY

Turtle's heart was in his mouth when he walked into the John's Hopkins hospital room, his blood pounding in his ears. He had no idea what to expect. It was a large, private room, with comfy chairs and floral arrangements everywhere. *Nice,* he thought.

Rita's family was gathered around the bed, so many of them, that at first, he couldn't see her. There was her brother Sam, his wife, Elena, her abuela, her mother, and an assortment of brothers, sisters, aunts and uncles.

When Turtle entered the room, all eyes moved to him, and then the strangest thing happened. The group parted. It brought to mind the parting of the Red Sea. Aunts, uncles, brothers, and sisters all stepped aside, creating a path that led directly to Rita.

Without a word shared with any of them, Turtle ventured forward. As he moved toward her he could see that Rita was asleep. He was surprised at how pale she appeared, how fragile she seemed. She'd lost weight, and yet, she was beautiful.

He continued silently across the room, arrived bedside, kneeled, his face inches from hers, and listened to her breathe. It may have seemed a strange thing to do, but the sound of her breathing was like a song to him, singing that life was just on the other side of those closed eyelids. He thought of how not too long ago, he'd wanted to let her go, allow her to escape back to New Jersey where he'd never see her again.

Unwanted. Unloved.

The words appeared in his mind, and he knew if he'd done that cowardly thing and vanished from her life, that's exactly how she'd have felt. Knowing those feelings all too well, he couldn't do that to her. He couldn't do it to himself.

He knew in that moment that he'd never let her go, that he was tethered to her just as he'd been tethered to A.D. He'd outgrown those childhood bindings, but these new tethers, forged from love and respect, were made of stuff that could last forever.

As he kneeled beside her, he realized all eyes in the room were on him. He knew he had to do something. He leaned forward and kissed her, a gentle peck against the scar on her upper lip, the handsome prince planting the awakening kiss on the lips of the beautiful princess. He kissed her, and when he pulled back, it was as if the fairytale had come to life, because her eyes blinked open.

"Theo. What kept you?" she asked, her voice sounding as if it were coming from a mountain top, and all the joy that had been in Turtle's heart flowed into her eyes.

"Sorry," he replied. "It's a long story. I got here as fast as I could."

"That's okay," she said, and a smile like the sunrise appeared on her lips. "Tell it to me. I got time." It was the kind of smile that threatened to grab hold of a young man's heart and never let go.

And for the third time since he'd known her, Turtle began a long tale, this the longest tale of all, beginning when a feisty, green-eyed girl said *get your hands off my boyfriend*, and ending when he arrived at her side.

THE END

If you enjoyed what you just read please go to Amazon and leave a review. For a humble typewriter-jockey like myself, getting reviews (especially on Amazon) means I can submit my books for advertising. Reviews also help you share your reading experience with new readers. So please leave a review—it's a win-win for everyone!   —E. Van Lowe

Acknowledgments

Writing a book is no easy feat without the assistance of many friends, family, and readers to help ensure the storytelling rings true. Thank you all. Thank you, too, to my alter ego, Sal Conte, a dark fellow.

About the Author

E. Van Lowe is an author, television writer, and producer who has worked on such TV shows as *The Cosby Show, Even Stevens*, and *Homeboys In Outer Space*. He has been nominated for both an Emmy and an Academy Award. His first YA Paranormal novel, *Never Slow Dance With A Zombie*, was a selection of The Scholastic Book Club, and a nominee for an American Library Association Award. Included in his many books are bestselling novels, *Boyfriend From Hell* and *Earth Angel*.

He is also horror novelist Sal Conte, author of the 80's horror classics *Child's Play* and *The Power*. Sal's short stories "The Toothache Man," and "Because We Told Her To," are available as eBooks only on Amazon.

E lives in Beverly Hills, California, with his spouse, a werewolf, several zombies and a fairy godmother who grants him wishes from time-to-time.

Visit E at his website *www.evanlowe.com*.

Visit the publisher at www.WhiteWhiskerBooks.com

CPSIA information can be obtained at www.ICGtesting.com
Printed in the USA
LVOW01s1251210915

455063LV00003B/541/P

9 780986 326516